deity

STEVEN DUNNE

headline

First published in 2012 by
HEADLINE PUBLISHING GROUP

First published in paperback in 2012 by
HEADLINE PUBLISHING GROUP

5

Cataloguing in Publication Data is available from the British Library

ISBN 978 0 7553 8368 9

Typeset in Hoefler by Avon DataSet Ltd,
Bidford-on-Avon, Warwickshire

Printed and bound in Great Britain by
Clays Ltd, St Ives plc

HEADLINE PUBLISHING GROUP
An Hachette UK Company
338 Euston Road
London NW1 3BH

www.headline.co.uk
www.hachette.co.uk

For Mum and Dad
Thanks for such a loving home

Acknowledgements

Much love and gratitude go to my lovely wife Carmel for her continuing support and encouragement and to the far flung McKenna and Dunne tribes who spread the word and keep me up to my work.

As well as providing regular practical support, Jeff Fountain supplies insightful editorial comment on the content and direction of my work. A true mate.

I'm thrilled to have been signed to Headline, doubly so after being given the opportunity to work with a quality team of experienced and enabling people. So thanks to Martin Fletcher, Emily Griffin and Samantha Eades for your help and guidance in getting the *Deity* project to this juncture.

Thanks to fellow Weekenders' cricketer Joseph McDonald for taking the trouble to produce thoughtful and expert input on police procedures.

A big thanks to Richard Gardner (richard-gardner.co.uk) for making me look vaguely presentable on the cover.

Also my continuing gratitude to Waterstone's in the East Midlands for putting up with me in-store on more than one occasion – particularly Sean Heavens and the team in Derby, Glenys Cooper in Burton-on-Trent and Dan in Nottingham. Without their support of local writers, I wouldn't be in this position today.

Finally thank you to David Grossman, my agent, for providing his expert guidance.

And, of course, hello to Jason Isaacs.

Steve Dunne

One

January – three years ago

'HOW FAR, IAN?' ASKED THE smaller boy as he swung the rucksack on to the grass, narrowly missing a clump of dried sheep muck.

'A few hundred yards. See that bend in the river?' Ian raised an arm to indicate the curve of the water. 'Just past there.' He rummaged in a pocket and took out a pack of cigarettes. 'Want one?' he asked as he lit the end of his and inhaled a huge belt of smoke. His friend shook his head. Ian then produced a half-bottle of cheap vodka from his back pocket and spun off the cap. He took a long gulp and grimaced as he swallowed then breathed hard through the fumes. He offered the bottle to his companion who hesitated for a second then took it from him.

'Why the hell not?' He took an even longer draught than Ian and pulled an equally pained expression at the taste before handing the bottle back. He felt carefully around the light stubble on his face. 'How do people drink that stuff? My face is numb.'

'That's why.' Ian grinned.

They walked on, one behind the other, treading carefully along the muddy rabbit path that hugged the river. The water was fast and fierce from winter rains and sounded like the blood in their eardrums. The ground was damp and slippery and the pair lapsed back into silence as they picked their way along.

At the bend, Ian struck away from the path towards a large sturdy tree. Once there, he took out his cigarettes and vodka and tossed them to the smaller boy. 'Help yourself,' he said. 'I won't be long.' With that he set about climbing the tree, keeping his own rucksack on his back while the smaller boy picked up the vodka and took another tentative swig.

A few minutes later, Ian jumped down beside his companion and hauled off his rucksack. 'All set.' He took out a camera and pointed it at his friend who posed with the vodka and took another pull. 'Perfect,' he said.

'You got enough pictures?'

'Plenty. They'll lap it up.'

The other boy smiled and nodded, then looked back down to the river. 'Nice day, this.'

'The best,' retorted Ian.

The small boy turned and began to climb while Ian lit a cigarette and adjusted the camera for the piercing winter light. He walked away from the tree then turned to wave at his friend, who was nearly in position.

When he was ready, the boy raised an arm to acknowledge. 'Ready?'

'Ready,' shouted Ian from the ground.

The boy steadied his footing on the branch and looked out over the countryside. He had a fantastic view down the river – he could see the bridge and, beyond that, the otter dam. He even fancied he could see the tower of the Town Hall clock. His eyes darted further round to a dog scrabbling at a mole hill on a bank on the other side of the water. It was a Springer Spaniel – lovely dogs. 'Nice day,' he repeated, smiling.

He closed his eyes and stepped off the branch, even remembering to have *I love you, Mum* in his thoughts as he hurtled towards the ground. As he fell, he was sure he could hear the whirring of the camera. Wait till his tormentors saw the pictures. Then they'd know.

A second later, the tree shuddered as the snap of his neck ended his fall.

The rope held. Ian was pleased. Everything had gone well. He put the camera to his eye to take the money shots. 'Everyone will know you, my friend. Everyone will envy you.'

Two

THE MAN PLACED THE FINAL cone across Station Road and propped up the *Road Closed* sign facing Borrowash to the north. No traffic would be crossing the bridges in this Derbyshire village for the next half-hour. At first he'd considered blocking the road a precaution too far on such a minor route, especially at three in the morning, but when disposing of the dead, nothing was too much trouble.

He walked calmly back to the vehicle, climbed in and, without turning on the engine, rolled back down the slope over the railway bridge. Having reversed into the drive of a lone farmhouse, barely visible through the trees, he turned the ignition and drove slowly back on to the second bridge, spanning the River Derwent, before coming to a halt.

He skipped out, leaving the engine running, opened the back doors and pulled out the trolley. The metal legs unfolded and the man pushed the trolley to the low bridge wall. He stepped down on the brake. The pale waxy body was a late-middle-aged male, naked apart from the loincloth covering his genitalia. The man bent his head over the corpse, sniffing along its length. He caressed the dead face with latex fingers

4

then rubbed them together, feeling the waxy film of make-up lubricate his gloves.

Finally he stood, a crooked smile on his face, and ran his fingers through the corpse's washed and trimmed hair.

'Good as new.' He checked the stitching on the man's flank then prepared to lift the body. The scars beneath the corpse's nose drew the man's eye and he frowned. 'Nobody's perfect.' He placed his hands under the body and rolled it off the trolley and over the bridge wall, sending it crashing into the swirling water below. A couple of horses, grazing in a dark field, lifted their heads towards the noise for a moment before resuming their meal.

He watched the body disappear and an inert arm seemed to wave a last lazy farewell as it sank.

'Travel safe through the dark waters of chaos, my friend.'

After a moment transfixed by the soothing rhythms of the water, he rolled the trolley back into the vehicle and closed the doors, then walked the 100 yards back to the railway bridge to stack the cones on to the pavement. He left the cones in a pile – they wouldn't be noticed – but carried the *Road Closed* sign over to his vehicle and shoved it into the back.

Driving half a mile south towards Elvaston Castle on the dark highway, the man drew to a halt at another line of cones blocking the road. Once again, he skipped out, this time stacking both the cones and the *Road Closed* sign neatly in the back of the vehicle then drove on into the night.

Three

JIM WATSON SAT MOTIONLESS IN the dark warmth of his living room, listening to his wife's rasping snore. The pulse of the TV flickered in the corner, providing the only light source in the room. The volume was barely audible.

Watson wasn't looking at the screen and he wasn't listening to the programme – but to turn off the set, or even mute the sound, might disturb the ether in which his wife was cocooned and he couldn't risk waking her.

He exhaled deeply and, without moving his head, flicked his eyes resentfully towards her sleeping form on the sofa. Her mouth hung open, allowing a glimpse of the yellowed teeth she normally kept hidden behind the tight-lipped grimace that deformed her face these days. A strand of lank greying hair, matted against her cheek, flirted with the notion of trailing into her mouth, and had it not been certain to rouse her, Watson would have derived a malicious pleasure from seeing her gag on it.

He glanced at the clock for the hundredth time then returned his sullen gaze to his wife. Well past midnight and still the cow waited him out, enveloped in her grey shroud of a dressing-gown.

Watson was caught between two stools. Should he wake her up and push her off to bed half-asleep or leave her be, and hope she'd sleep through? Through what? A half-smile of anticipation creased his mouth but died at once, as his wife turned slightly on the cushions. The grubby towelling robe she insisted on wearing of a night threatened to mimic her mouth by falling open at the breast to reveal the flesh that once had enflamed, but now so disgusted him.

James Henry Watson was forty years old and this was his life. He turned away, repulsed. His aging wife had let herself go so completely, so wilfully, that just to look at her sickened him. And yet his disgust at her couldn't hold a candle to the loathing he inflicted on himself for hitching his life to hers. His harridan of a wife was an old woman at thirty-eight, and to make matters worse, he was still hard and handsome. When he scrubbed up for a night on the town, he could feel female eyes on him, assessing him, suppressing their desire as well as their bewilderment at the shrivelled hag on his arm.

In his building clothes he looked even better. In his check shirt, arse-clenching, slashed-knee jeans and scuffed Timberland boots, slightly weathered like his rugged features, he was a sight for sore housewives. Well toned and tanned from outdoor work with just a slash of grey in his curly blond hair, he was the recipient of open flirting and innuendo over endless cups of tea, while his five-pound-an-hour labourers nodded and winked at him behind the women's backs.

Bored thirty-somethings with a bit of money were the most persistent. Often they were lonely and frustrated and aware of time slipping through their fingers, their allure dimming with

7

every passing month, and only so much shopping and daytime TV could defray the monotony of their lives.

Many a time, while demonstrating his mastery of the finer points of conservatory bases to their baffled but adoring faces, he could feel their eyes wandering over his hard body, wanting him, daring him to undo his shirt so they could pull their expensively manicured nails across his bare chest.

But did he stoop to such betrayal despite the temptation, despite the many offers, despite the provocations from his acidic wife? Never. Jim Watson swelled with righteous indignation. He had taken an oath before God that he would never stray from the path of unswerving loyalty to his wedding vows. And he never had. But that only made it all the more galling to endure the daily servings of spite and suspicion from his wife's poisonous lips.

I know what these rich bitches are like, sitting around the house all day, dolling themselves up and looking for a cheap thrill. Think I don't see the way they look at you. I better not catch you . . .

Watson drew in another deep breath. God knew how he suffered. God knew Jim Watson was owed.

Finally he heard the noise he'd been expecting outside the house but, instead of his daughter's footfall, Watson heard a car glide to a halt. The engine sounded powerful as it idled, as though it were trying not to be noticed. Watson waited, ears pricked. He eased himself from his armchair and tiptoed to the curtain to pull it aside, and caught a raised voice followed by muffled wailing. Then he saw his daughter slam the door of a sleek sports car before turning to run to the house, while the sports car – a Porsche – roared away with a squeal of burning tyres.

Watson crept to the door as quietly as he could manage, all the while eying the snoring harpy on the sofa. He snuck out of the living room and gently pulled the door closed behind him, waiting in the blackness at the foot of the stairs.

A key turned in the latch and Adele stepped through the door and, after closing it, leaned her slim languid body against it as though holding back intruders. She looked to the heavens and released an intense sigh. Watson fancied he saw a tear wiped as he watched from the shadows. Her breathing was harsh and snatched as she fought for control but, after a few moments of puffing and panting, equilibrium returned and finally she was able to pull her frame upright from the door.

Still Watson watched from the gloom of the hall as his daughter ran a hand to her forehead, pushing it through her soft dark hair and down past the perfect curve of her neck. She took a final deep breath and straightened herself as though a decision had been taken, a course of action defined.

'Goodbye,' she breathed.

'Was that him?' said Watson, emerging from the dark.

Adele Watson started when she heard him and fumbled for a switch. A striplight flickered into life, unforgiving in its illumination.

'Dad. What are you doing up this late?' Adele attempted a smile to imply normality, though she couldn't hold his eyes.

'I should say the same to you, love.' Watson stepped into the harsh kitchen glare and closed a second door on his wife. 'Was that him – your guilty secret?'

'Guilty? What do you mean?'

'Well, he's got a car, hasn't he? A Porsche, if I'm not mistaken. You didn't mention that before. He hasn't driven up to the house either or I'd have known it.' Adele looked away. 'What have you got to say for yourself, young lady?'

'I'm eighteen, Dad. It's none of your business.'

'You're in sixth form, girl – for a while yet. You live in my house and you have no income. That makes it my business.'

'I don't think so,' she retorted, with an attempt at haughtiness.

'Well, I do think so, and I'll thank you not to take that tone with me.'

Adele's expression betrayed the preparation of further defiance but she side-stepped it. 'This is silly,' she said and made for the door. Watson moved to block her way.

'Answer me.'

'Answer you what?'

'He's got an expensive car.'

'Is that a question?'

Watson sneered at his beautiful daughter. 'Don't take that high hand or you'll know my wrath. Who is he?'

'He's a friend,' she answered coyly, after a few seconds.

'A friend?' he snorted back. 'You have a *friend* who drives an expensive car and you haven't mentioned him to us.'

Adele sighed, her eyes searching for a way to the stairs. 'Dad, I'm tired.'

'With a car like that, he must be a lot older than you, Ade.'

'Dad . . .'

'And I know what that means. You think I don't? Men like him – I know what he wants. I know what he expects . . .' He tailed off, unable to say the words.

'And what's that?' Adele flashed back, her dark eyes now smouldering into his.

Watson flinched as the blackest thoughts in his mind sought the right words. Eventually, sanitised, they emerged.

'Older men with money want certain things from beautiful girls. Am I right?'

Adele hesitated. She knew the information he was seeking but also knew it was better to withhold it. 'He's not that much older,' she lied. She saw him take a crumb of comfort but was sickened by her own weakness. *Tell him you're in love. Tell him about the sex. Tell him you're no longer a virgin.* She looked hard at her father, almost enjoying his anguish suddenly. 'Besides, I'm a woman now. I can make my own choices.'

Watson clenched a fist as his face contorted and Adele took a step back. 'Tell me who he is,' he seethed, but still with the presence of mind to keep the volume down.

'No.' Adele made to move around him but he grabbed her shoulders and shook her.

'Tell me,' he repeated, this time with a half-turn to the door behind him to ensure continued privacy.

Adele looked angrily at her father. 'You're hurting me.'

'Tell me who he is.'

She wriggled from his grasp and backed away but Watson followed her and trapped her against the kitchen sink. 'Tell me,' he insisted, grabbing her wrists and looking down at her full figure pushing against the fabric of her low-cut T-shirt.

'Please, Dad.'

Watson moved his body against her and forced her back against the cold steel of the drainer. 'Then tell me. Who is he?'

'He's not you,' she hissed, her face contorted into the expression of contempt, well-grooved on teenage faces.

As though physically slapped, Watson's head flew back and his grip slackened. Adele was able to push him away. 'What does that mean, Ade? I'm your father. I love you. I only want the best for you.'

'The best? I've seen the way—' Adele broke off and trained her gaze to the linoleum to avoid further confrontation, then looked to the door to close the conversation. 'I'm tired,' she said again.

'You're tired?' Watson snapped back at her, laughing, ready to fling more vitriol. 'What right have *you* got to be tired? You've never done a day's work in your life. Sitting around in classrooms, writing poems – that's not work. I work all God's hours to provide for you and your mother and not a word of thanks. Money for your A-level books, money for your university courses next year, no doubt. More books, more expense.' Again he ran his eye over her well-endowed figure adorned by designer T-shirt and jeans, tan leather Chelsea boots on her feet. She blanched under his gaze. 'Even the clothes you wear belong to me and your mother, and don't you forget it.'

Adele's discomfort turned to sudden anger and her eyes started to water. 'You want them back? Here.' She began to pull the T-shirt over her head, exposing her bra.

'Stop that.' He grabbed her arm to prevent the T-shirt revealing more flesh. 'Have you no shame before God?'

'Shame?' She laughed bitterly in his face. 'Hell, yes, I've got plenty of that, Dad.'

Watson's face creased in pain and he couldn't look at her. 'Don't be like that, angel. I don't want the clothes off your back.'

'Then what *do* you want? Tell me what I owe you. Give me a bill. You'll get every penny back.'

Watson's voice softened and he held his arms wide. 'Baby, I didn't mean it like that. It's just, you're so young, so vulnerable and yet you're becoming . . . soon you're not gonna need your old dad any more. What'll I do then?'

'You'll still have Mum.'

'And don't I know it.' He smiled weakly at her. 'How about a hug for your old man?'

'I told you – I'm really tired, Dad. I've got college tomorrow.' A sliver of doubt crossed her features for a second. *Can I face it now?*

'What's one little hug between Daddy and daughter? We used to have plenty of hugs.' Adele looked away. 'Is your boyfriend the only one you can hug these days?' Watson sneered.

'He's not my boyfriend any more, Dad.' Adele looked at him through her tears. The tears turned to sobs, and as she stood shaking in the cruel light, Watson gathered her into his arms and pressed her head on to his shoulder.

'There, there,' he whispered, rubbing her back, unable to keep the smile from his lips. 'It's all right. That bastard's not fit to lick your boots. No one is. I'm here, baby.' He stroked her hair. 'Your dad understands. You stick with your old man. I'll always be here.' Watson put his hands on her shoulders and held her away from him to lock his eyes on to hers. 'We don't need anyone else, do we?'

'What time do you call this, young lady?' said a gravelled voice from the door.

Father and daughter were both startled and Adele stepped away from him. She tried to smile at her mother to mollify her, but it was a weak effort. Her father didn't turn to face his wife but merely straightened, tight-lipped, and lifted his eyes to the ceiling.

Roz Watson seemed even smaller and more withered standing in the doorway, wiping the sleep from her grey face. She glared at the back of her husband's head through piercing little eyes, despite directing the enquiry at her daughter.

'Well?'

'Sorry, Mum. I was just going up.' Adele made for the door but her mum caught her wrist.

'Have you been crying?' Adele nodded without reply. 'What have you done, Jim?' she flashed at her husband. Adele made to speak but was halted by her mother's raised hand.

Watson finally turned. 'Nothing.' He looked at her defiantly and for a moment their eyes met.

'Mum, it's nothing like that.'

'Nothing like what?' said her mum. Adele looked around the room seeking an answer but was cut off before she could summon it. 'Bed.'

Adele rushed gratefully to the stairs and Roz Watson darted a final look of disgust at her husband before turning to follow.

'She's broken up with her boyfriend,' said Watson, to her shrivelled back. 'That's why she was crying.'

'I'm going up,' she said, but making no move. Instead, she paused, turned from the door and walked up to him. She smiled up into his face and grabbed his crotch, kneading his manhood in her thin papyrus hand. 'How's my favourite soldier? Ready to leave the barracks?' She pulled her robe aside and pouted up at him. 'See anything you like, lover?'

Watson smiled weakly back, his lips not parting.

She laughed and scuttled through the door to the stairwell. 'Don't be long,' she breathed invitingly over her shoulder.

When she left, Watson trudged back to sit in front of the TV. No power in heaven or on earth could make him bring forward the horror of their Sunday dry hump to midweek.

Adele sat on her bed in the dark, her face framed against the reflected glow of her laptop. She loaded Facebook and clicked on her personal details. A tear rolled down her cheek as she amended her relationship status to single. She then clicked to see who of her friends was chatting live at that godless hour.

Becky and Fern were chatting but then they always were. They shared a love of the trivial into which Adele had never been able to tap. They didn't care about the homeless. They didn't care about the environment. They weren't even vegetarians. If she wanted to talk about boys or clothes, she knew where to turn. She'd known them both since primary school but had never felt able to call them close. Even now, at college together, they had little more in common than a couple of classes. And whatever friendship they had, it always took second place to Becky's countless boyfriends.

Boyfriends – the thought returned her to the end of her relationship. She looked at the time. Half past one. Less than an hour ago, she'd been happy. Less than an hour ago she'd been in love.

'Correction. I'm still in love,' she muttered. 'And it hurts.' Not two hours ago he'd made love to her on a blanket in a field. He said he didn't have enough petrol to drive all the way out to the cottage. She should have guessed then – he just wanted a final quickie. Then she'd asked him if he loved her. A pause while he pulled his trousers back up. *Of course I do.* That was her second clue. Then say it. *I love you but I think we've taken this as far as it can go, Ade. You're going off to university. You're young and beautiful. You'll meet somebody else.*

She roused herself to forget and returned her gaze to Facebook. She scrolled down the list of chatting friends. There were at least a dozen online at that moment. She scanned the names, poised to click. A few seconds later, her hand released the mouse. *Facebook friends.* With a sinking heart she realised that she barely knew any of them, not really, not enough to pour out her deepest fears and emotions. A bit of goss and the odd social engagement was all she could ever share with them. She sighed then wet a finger and rubbed it over the dry salt round her eyes and on her soft cheeks. She cast her eyes around for a pen. She could tell Di. Di would listen. Di was her best friend.

A floorboard creaked outside her bedroom and Adele glared at the door.

'Adele.' Her father's voice, hushed but urgent.

The girl didn't answer. She pulled down the lid of her computer to extinguish all light and fixed her gaze on the door handle. It began to turn. Adele held her breath as the handle finished its rotation and the door was pushed to open. It caught on the back of the chair propped under the handle and remained closed.

'Adele.' She picked up the rising tide of anger in her father's voice but knew better than to reply. From deep within the house, Adele heard her mother's voice, but too indistinct to decipher. The door snapped back on to the latch and the handle was still. Her father paused motionless on the landing then managed a cheery, 'Night, Ade,' before she heard him padding back to his own bed.

Adele let out a long breath and raised the lid of her laptop again. She was about to exit Facebook when she spotted a new name had joined the online list. She highlighted the name but hesitated over the mouse. It was a big step. A second later she clicked on the name and typed a smiley face in the dialogue box. It was time.

Four

Thursday, 19 May

ETECTIVE INSPECTOR DAMEN BROOK WOKE to the sound of a barn owl hooting nearby. He still had his recently acquired reading glasses perched on the end of his nose so he pulled them off and laid them next to the reading lamp, still burning beside his bed. He inhaled the soft summer air nuzzling at his curtains and dozed for another minute, listening to the breeze ruffle the trees in the churchyard. Nothing else in the village stirred.

Brook felt the weight on his stomach and lifted the upturned copy of *In Search of The Reaper* from the duvet. He bent down a page and closed it before tossing it on to the polished floorboards. Local journalist Brian Burton's book documenting Brook's failure to catch the notorious serial killer was a few years out of date and so completely off the track that Brook had only persisted with it from a sense of twisted amusement – and the added bonus that it put him to sleep quickly.

He dragged himself out of bed and padded down the rickety stairs of his cottage, wearing only T-shirt and underpants. He

17

flicked at the full kettle and sat at the kitchen table, his eyes wedged shut. As usual the cup and tea bag sat ready for this nightly ritual so Brook could postpone opening his eyes and engaging his brain. The fact that he'd learned to disengage his brain at all was a profound blessing and it was not to be curtailed until absolutely necessary.

For many years Brook had been rudely awoken, drenched in sweat, by visions of old cases, rotting corpses and mumbling half-forgotten names as he stirred. As the years passed, the dreams of ravenous rats devouring decaying flesh had faded as Brook had left his past in London behind. At the age of fifty he'd made some kind of peace with himself, and although his solitary life was no richer, he could at least wake up in dry sheets.

The kettle clicked off and Brook waved goodbye to semi-consciousness. He felt around in the dark for his cigarettes but realised with a sinking heart that, in the unlikely event that his resolve to quit smoking might weaken, he'd left his last pack in his station locker.

On his first sip of tea, the phone rang and Brook squinted at the kitchen clock as he picked it from its cradle. Nearly four o'clock in the morning.

'Brook.' He listened without enquiry to Detective Sergeant John Noble, looked sightlessly into the distance to get his bearings then rang off with, 'I'll be about an hour.'

Brook pulled his coat tighter and stared longingly at the welcoming disc of dawn creeping over the horizon, unseen birds heralding its arrival as nature began to shake a leg. He closed his eyes, blocking out the noise of activity behind him, and wondered how many millennia this little scene had been enacted. Man, vulnerable and reverent, mouth slackened by awe, gazing to the heavens to greet the sun's approach, inspired and soothed by its promise of light and comfort.

Too often Brook's insomnia ensured he was as familiar with this ancient ritual as the primitive cave dwellers of Stonehenge or Avebury, dancing, praying or sacrificing their way into the goodwill of the gods. But for once Brook wasn't sitting on the bench in his cottage garden, nursing a tea and a smoke. Dawn found him shivering in the dank, misty fields to the east of Derby, awaiting the recovery of a body from the River Derwent.

He hated this part of the job – the wasted hours kicking his heels just to sign off on a suicide or a lone fisherman who'd waded in too far and been surprised by a deceptive current. Or maybe it was a show-off kid, swinging into the murky waters from a Tarzan rope and unable to clamber back up the slippery bank. Then more wasted hours, informing disbelieving relatives and ploughing through the paperwork.

Brook turned grudgingly back to the darkness of the river bank, itself burnished by the flashing orange suns of the emergency vehicles. He glanced resentfully across at DS Noble pulling on a Marlboro Light. Part of Brook's own dawn ritual involved a cigarette but he'd made the mistake of giving up three weeks ago. Again.

He debated whether to cave in and ask his DS for a smoke. After all, it was his only vice. He wasn't a womaniser or a heavy drinker like many in the job. He lived a sober, monastic life and did his work without complaint. He deserved to cut himself a little slack.

'Christ,' he muttered through a half-laugh and a shake

of the head. The justifications for having a cigarette were kicking in early.

A shout from the river pierced the early morning mist and the two CID officers moved off the adjacent cycle path and closer to the water's edge. Despite protective overshoes, their socks and trousers were already sopping wet in the heavy dew. A figure wearing waders and a bright yellow safety bib emerged from the gloom and splashed across to Brook and Noble through the boggy earth.

He waved to the two ambulancemen sitting in the warmth of their cab and made the hand signal for the gurney. 'It's a body all right,' said the man. 'Male Caucasian, fifty to sixty years of age. Been in a couple of days, I'd guess. Got caught on a fallen tree. They've got the harness on. They'll have him out in a few minutes.'

'Okay. Thanks . . .' Brook hesitated, an expression of panic invading his tired features.

'Keith,' finished the man with a sharp look at first Noble, then back at Brook. 'Keith Pullin. We've met several times before at refuse collections.'

'Of course. Sorry, Keith. It's late.' Brook had been caught off-guard, forgetting to take Noble aside and ask for the names he never remembered. He smiled weakly at Pullin but the damage was done and he was already stomping back towards the river.

'Technically it's early,' grinned DS Noble, tossing his cigarette butt into a puddle and pulling out a fresh one.

Brook shrugged then caught the luxuriant scent of Noble, igniting another cigarette. Unable to stand it, he set off towards his car. 'Give me a shout when they get him out, John.'

*

Noble watched as Keith Pullin, the portly, forty-year-old Special Constable, walked back over to him, sneering all the while towards DI Brook's shabby BMW.

'How's it going, Tom?'

'Very funny,' spat Keith Pullin, without a trace of amusement. 'Seriously though, how can you stand working with that knob?'

Noble shrugged. 'He's not a morning person, Keith.'

'Fuck off – he's not an afternoon or an evening person either.'

'Okay. You got me there,' admitted Noble. 'Let's just say he's a little distracted.'

'Why do you always defend him?'

Noble looked unswervingly back at Pullin but said nothing. Failing to get his answer, Pullin grunted and trudged sullenly back to the water's edge, muttering obscenities all the way.

Noble pulled heavily on his cigarette and sighed. He was used to the barbs aimed at his DI and once he might have joined in, but the longer he'd worked with Brook, the more he felt the need to provide a little balance to offset the abuse that flowed his way.

This little rite was a common occurrence in the field. Brook's inability to bond with fellow officers and the emergency workers they encountered – some Brook had known for several years – was always a source of mild amusement. But to the dozens working in D Division who'd gone unrecognised by Brook down the years, it remained a cause for deep resentment.

Noble wasn't sure how much Brook's time in London had shaped his behaviour towards colleagues, but since his move to the Peak District, Brook's mind always seemed to be elsewhere

– and forgetting people's names was the most recurrent symptom. Twenty years had passed since Brook had started hunting The Reaper in London, as one of the rising stars of the Met. But according to all reports, the case had broken him, with years of failure taking their toll and finally forcing him from active duty.

His breakdown quickly became public knowledge when Brook transferred to Derby Division, eight years ago. Sergeant Harry Hendrickson, a curmudgeonly old desk jockey in uniform branch, had taken a peek at his file and gleefully reported the facts to anyone who'd listen. And when Noble had drawn the short straw and been assigned to work with Brook, everyone had sympathised with him.

But then The Reaper had struck in Derby, slaughtering two families in their own homes, and Noble had found himself in the eye of the hurricane. At close quarters, Noble was able to observe Brook's extraordinary skills as a detective, in addition to the toll such a high-profile investigation took on him – especially as The Reaper remained at large.

'Eight years,' mumbled Noble, thinking back over their shared history. 'I deserve a medal.' He smiled at a memory of his early years working with Brook and his fruitless attempts to get to know him. He'd found out pretty quickly that Brook didn't do small talk, on or off a case. Unlike most people, Brook never mentioned his past and never spoke about his private life. And just to maintain consistency, he'd never enquired about the lives of his new colleagues in return.

At first, Noble had felt awkward during the silences and would instigate conversation, mentioning something topical from the news or the TV. But he'd quickly learned to expect a blank expression from Brook and soon gave up trying, realising that many of the events that people used as common currency in conversation were completely unknown to Brook. He just wasn't interested and often didn't speak at all unless it was required. Even his daily greeting consisted of little more than a nod.

As a consequence, people thought Brook cold and distant, sometimes downright rude, especially those who rarely had a chance to work with him. It didn't help that Brook wouldn't attend official functions, didn't socialise or go to parties, didn't even go to pubs as far as Noble was aware – not with colleagues, at least – even after a big case had been cracked.

More often than not he'd turn up to work, do his job then just wander off after his shift to his little cottage in Hartington where he . . . well, Noble wasn't sure, even after eight years. He knew Brook liked to read, which probably accounted for his freakish intelligence. He also liked to hike, and Noble had discovered two or three years earlier that most of Brook's holidays were spent marching around the Peak National Park surrounding his village.

Other aspects of Brook's life were still as unknown as the day they'd first met. He didn't seem to have a sex life, certainly not one that involved relationships, though there were rumours he'd had a fling with a WPC a few years back. That, and the fact that Brook was divorced with a twenty-year-old daughter meant he probably wasn't gay – a conclusion his home furnishings would seem to support.

Not that Noble had ever been to Brook's cottage: he'd never been invited. But just before his move out to the Peak District, Brook had lived in a grubby rented flat off the Uttoxeter Road in central Derby, and Noble had been forced to call round when Brook had been suspended. To his astonishment, Noble had discovered that his DI was living in the sort of hovel normally associated with squatters or junkies. No garden, no oven, no computer, not even a TV.

And yet, despite an unpromising start to their working relationship, their partnership had begun to flourish and a mutual respect had developed. Unknown to most, Brook generously underplayed his own role in an enquiry, going out of his way to give credit to subordinates for breakthroughs. And, although some colleagues persisted in thinking Brook arrogant, Noble had found the opposite to be true. Brook seemed to have no ego at all. He made absolutely no effort to make himself more popular and didn't seem to care what people thought of him. Consequently, he was deeply disliked and even hated in some parts of the Division, the more so because he was such a damn good detective.

Further, Noble had discovered that Brook had a dark but undeniable sense of humour, dry and cutting and, what's more, would actively encourage Noble to make fun of superior officers.

Perhaps the only thing that everyone admired about Brook was the hard moral position he took about police work and how it should be conducted. And if anyone deviated from his position, even his superiors, Brook was quick to take them to task. He had got himself into trouble several times for criticising Chief Superintendent Charlton to his face for his failure to see the value of a line of enquiry or for putting budgetary constraints above the correct course of action on a case.

Noble took a last pull on his cigarette and threw it in the same puddle as the first.

*

Brook clambered into the driver's seat, pushing in the cigarette lighter out of habit. He closed his dry eyes to ease the sting of too little sleep and happily lost consciousness almost immediately.

He woke to the sound of Noble tapping on his window and stepped out of the car. Only ten minutes had passed yet he felt refreshed. The sun was higher now and Brook was able to walk across the drying ground, placing his damp feet with more confidence. They walked towards the still scowling Pullin and the other two Scientific Support Officers in their protective clothing, as they worked around the corpse, now laid out on a plastic sheet. Brook and Noble pulled on their protective gloves as they approached the pale cadaver, face up and completely naked.

'No clothing,' observed Brook.

'Unlikely to be an angler then,' retorted Noble with a wry grin.

'A missing angler would have been reported,' said Pullin, missing the joke. 'This bloke's been in the water a couple of days, I'd say. Any longer an' he'd have started to bloat from the body gases. Could be an accident, could be suicide.'

'Not usual for a suicide to undress,' answered Brook.

'Not unknown either,' snapped back Pullin, ready to take further offence.

'Anyone looking for clothes along the banks?'

'We've got a couple of people walking upriver. Nothing yet.'

'Where's he gone in?' asked Noble. 'The bridge?'

'That's favourite,' replied Brook.

'Any clothes on the bridge?'

'Not a stitch, Sergeant,' said Pullin. 'But if it was a couple of days ago, maybe someone moved them. Still, he must have gone in the water nearby. There's a weir a quarter mile up there.' He indicated west with a nod of his head. 'And the river's not swollen this spring, so he's not come downriver from the city centre or he'd have been caught on the barrier.'

'So he's definitely gone in between here and the weir,' nodded Noble, looking round at the bridge.

There was a crackle on Pullin's radio. He listened for a second then replied, 'Okay, work your way back. Keep looking.' He turned to Brook. 'My people are at the weir. No abandoned fishing gear. No sign of clothing.'

'He's not going to travel here naked,' said Brook. 'And if he's a suicide, in my experience, he wouldn't undress without leaving his clothes where they could be found, maybe with a note in the pocket . . .'

'Goodbye cruel world,' added Noble.

'Okay, so maybe not a suicide,' conceded Pullin.

'Could be a skinny-dipper,' offered one of the ambulance crew.

'A swimmer?' Brook looked down at the bleached corpse then bent to look at the deceased's hands. They were open and empty. 'No, he's not a swimmer or a suicide for that matter. His hands are wrong.' He looked back to the bridge.

'The hands?' asked Noble.

'I've seen a couple of drownings, John. Even suicides jumping into the water will try and grab hold of something when they go under. They can't help it. It's a reflex.'

'He's right,' Pullin said reluctantly. 'Their hands usually clench tight with the effort to hold on to something. Anyone drowning in a river will have stones or weeds locked in their fists.'

'And this guy's hands are open.' Noble nodded.

'Is this even a swimming spot?' asked Brook, darting a look at Pullin.

'Hell, no. Far too dangerous,' replied Pullin. 'The current's not slow and the bank's too steep to be sure of getting out. Even kids won't risk it.'

'Someone might if they were drunk,' added Noble.

'But they'd still be able to struggle and grab on to things in the water,' said Brook.

'Maybe he dived off the bridge for a swim and was knocked unconscious,' ventured Noble. 'He wouldn't be struggling then.'

Brook pointed to the cadaver's wasted left arm. 'He doesn't look like any kind of swimmer to me. Not with that physique.' The torso was almost skeletal and the muscle tone under-developed. 'And look at these needle-marks. This looks like a drug abuser to me. Probably a heavy drinker too.'

'Right. Face and hands,' agreed Noble, turning over a pale dead hand. The face was covered with blotches and cracked blood vessels. Several old cuts and abrasions on the hands and knees as well as the face, added to the impression that here was a man who injured himself regularly. They'd both seen the signs before. The extremities of the heavy drinker took the brunt of damage from falls and fights, befitting the lifestyle of those who derived nourishment from a bottle and a needle.

'Some of these injuries could have occurred in the water though,' said Noble, indicating other scrapes and grazes.

Brook examined two vertical cuts descending from each nostril of the man's swollen and bent nose, clearly broken in the past. 'These wounds below his nose look post mortem,

maybe from sharp stones or discarded metal in the river.'
Something caught Brook's eye. 'Look at these marks on his
neck.' He leaned in for a better look at two small puncture
wounds, one on each side of the windpipe.

'Maybe we're looking for a vampire.' Noble grinned.

Brook glanced up without amusement then turned his
attention to the corpse's various tattoos. They were of poor
quality and all in the same washed-out blue. '*Flower of Scotland*,'
Brook read from one.

'Guess he's from Scotland,' observed Noble, with a straight
face.

Brook must have been light-headed from lack of sleep
because now he smiled though he made sure Noble didn't see
it. 'Good spot, John,' he said drily. 'These tattoos don't look
professional to me.'

'Prison ink, I'd say,' replied Noble. 'Might give us a lead
with ID.'

Brook turned over the man's now bagged right hand
after a glance at one of the Support Officers for approval.
The knuckles had LOVE tattooed on them, one letter on each
knuckle. 'No doubt he's got HATE on the other hand.' He stood
off his haunches.

'Why not just tattoo CRIMINAL on their foreheads
and have done with it?' said Noble, to a few appreciative
chuckles.

Brook looked at Pullin. 'Couple of days, you say – Keith.'

Keith Pullin was a man who didn't give his opinion lightly;
he gazed at the corpse, rubbing his chin. 'I reckon,' he
answered finally. 'There's no rigor mortis though – which
muddies the waters a bit. It all depends whether he died
before he went in or not. Given the hands, I'm thinking

maybe he was dumped, already dead, in the water. There's no foam around the nostrils and mouth either, which you'd expect from a drowning.'

Brook knelt again to turn the icy palm back up. Even through the protective plastic, the bagged hand told a story. Like the back of his hand, there were many of the scars from battles with the hard walls and pavements of modern city life.

'Looks like we can still get prints,' observed Noble. 'He's likely to be in the system for something.'

Brook nodded absentmindedly. He ran his latex fingers through the man's hair and sniffed his own hand then stroked the cold face with the back of his hand and sniffed again.

'What is it?' asked Noble.

Brook touched his fingers on the man's smoothly shaved cheek. Then he rubbed them together and held them to his nose. 'I don't know. I think he's had something applied to his face.' He offered his hand to Noble. 'Can you smell that?'

Noble sniffed then shook his head. 'Can't smell a thing – I'm a smoker.'

'Lucky you.' Brook had one last sniff. 'Make-up? Maybe someone's tried to make our friend look a little more lifelike, cover all the blemishes and broken blood vessels, probably post mortem.' He dropped his hand and looked at the head of the corpse. 'And see the hair? Look how well groomed it is – as if it was cut recently.'

'And the face is shaved as well. Think he's been tarted up for the coffin?'

Brook glanced across at Noble. 'Let's hope it's that.' Noble returned a grim smile.

Brook stood up and looked again at the bridge 150 yards away. The road across headed north into Borrowash village. 'Let's have a look over the bridge, just to tick it off. Is the Police Surgeon on his way?'

Pullin nodded. 'Keep your eyes peeled for those clothes,' he added.

Noble looked up expectantly as Brook turned back to Pullin with the briefest tic of annoyance. But instead of thanking him for a lesson in basic detection, Brook managed to dredge up a strained smile.

'Good idea, Keith,' he said, catching Noble's approving glance. Clearly he was trying to mend fences. Pullin's demeanour, however, remained sullen. Either he was still annoyed with Brook or had succumbed to the solemnity of standing over a life ended.

'When we've seen the bridge, let's find a café, John. I'm gagging for a cup of tea.'

'Shouldn't we wait for the PS?'

'We'll be back.' Brook made to walk away but then turned back. 'What's that?' He knelt to point at something in the dead man's side. 'There.'

Everyone gathered to follow Brook's finger indicating an area almost hidden underneath the body.

'I don't know,' said Pullin, peering closely at it. 'Looks like a bit of thread or string. Give us a hand,' he said to a colleague, and they rolled the corpse on to its side. The thread was visible now, the end of half a dozen large overlapping stitches along a five- to six-inch wound. The assembled officers narrowed their eyes to examine them.

'That looks like a serious wound,' offered Noble. 'And very recent.'

'Have you ever seen a wound with stitches like that?' asked Brook. He looked around the assembled team, opening the question to all comers.

'Looks like something you might see on a blanket or a sail,' said one.

'Or a tent,' said Pullin. 'I've never seen anything that loose on a wound of that size. Unless it's a DIY – maybe he did it himself after a fight or something.'

'Maybe.' Brook moved closer to examine the wound. On an impulse he prodded the corpse on the chest. Next he felt along his stomach. 'Well, well. That should make the post mortem more interesting, though I'm guessing our friend here may be no stranger to the process.'

'What do you mean?' said Noble.

At that moment, the two men holding the corpse let it roll back into position and as it settled, watery red liquid, viscera and, strangest of all, what looked like a couple of small leaves gushed noisily from the wound, causing all but Brook to jump away in shock.

'Shit!' shouted Noble, forgetting one of only three rules Brook had laid down to him when they started working together. *Don't swear in my presence, John. It betrays a mind that's not under control. Speak proper English if you know any. Oh, and one more thing, don't ever call me Guv.*

Brook laid a hand on Noble's shoulder. 'Easy, John. We're not in the Met.'

'Sorry,' replied Noble. 'But you saw that?'

Brook looked at his DS. 'I saw. And this is no drowning.' He stood gazing at the bridge and began to walk down the path towards it.

'Why so sure?' asked Noble, moving to follow.

Brook turned and smiled back at his DS. 'Because he hasn't got any lungs.'

Brook stood on the bridge and looked over each wall in turn, down to the river bank on either side.

'What are we looking for?' Noble finally asked.

'I'm not sure.'

'But you're sure the body was dumped from here.'

'A man with no clothes and no lungs has to be dead before he hits the water. Someone's transported him to the river and this bridge has to be the easiest spot to dump the body.'

They looked down at the undergrowth on either side of the river for any sign of disturbance but could see nothing. Nor could they spot any clothing or bundles that might contain clothes. The two uniformed officers returning from the weir continued the search at ground level but Brook and Noble were unable to direct them to anything of interest.

Across the fields their colleagues were working around the pale carcass on the plastic sheet, scraping, photographing and bagging head and feet. Another officer was erecting a screen to shield their activities from the occasional early morning jogger and dog walker.

As time wore on, traffic began to increase and cars passed them in rotation on the single track road, depending on the traffic lights either side of the two bridges. On one rotation, Dr Higginbottom, the duty Police Surgeon, drove towards them and slowed down when he saw them. Noble indicated the dirt track which would take the doctor to the scene and he continued on with a wave.

'Busy road,' said Noble.

'During the day,' replied Brook.

'But even if it was the middle of the night, assuming our John Doe was dumped from this bridge, someone took a massive gamble on not being seen by a passing car – especially if they were actually parked up on the bridge. I mean, it's not wide.'

Brook nodded. 'You're right. I wouldn't take that chance but maybe they were desperate.'

'They?' enquired Noble.

'Or he or she. But even a body that light needs lifting.'

'It's a low wall,' observed Noble. 'One person could do it, I reckon.'

After a further few minutes of unproductive examination, the two detectives continued north towards the second bridge spanning the railway line. A dirt-track drive for a farmhouse set back out of sight from the road had a sign warning trespassers about CCTV cameras. Brook raised an eyebrow at Noble.

'We'll check it out.'

'It's probably for show, but . . .' Brook shrugged.

Crossing the railway bridge, the first houses of Station Road appeared. Jason Wallis, sole survivor of The Reaper's attack on the Wallis family several years before, had lived briefly with his aunt further up the road. Brook tried to remember which house.

'Didn't young Wallis live on here?' asked Noble.

'I believe he did,' Brook replied, but his mind had already moved on. He looked around, his gaze alighting on a stack of traffic cones on the pavement. 'You were right, John. It is just one person. And he or she wasn't desperate at all but very calm and rational.' Noble looked at Brook, wondering if he was going to explain his reasoning. Instead, Brook walked over to the cones, counted them then looked back down towards the river. 'This road goes south past Elvaston Castle, right?'

'Right.'

'And beyond?'

'Through Thulston, then on to Shardlow or the A50.'

'And beyond the A50, the M1,' Brook remembered. He returned his attention to the cones. 'Make a note to check with the Highways Agency when they last did any work here. It's possible that whoever dumped our friend, faked a road closure.'

'That's a lot of forethought,' said Noble.

'That's what worries me.'

'And he'd need more than cones. Maybe a *Diversion* sign or something.'

Brook nodded. 'Get DS Gadd and a couple of uniforms over here. We're going to need a canvass of all the nearby houses as soon as possible before memory fades. See if anyone noticed anything.'

'Not very likely if it was the middle of the night.'

'No – but hold that thought, John. It's time for a cup of tea. There was a café at the junction when I came past – might be open now.' Brook jerked a thumb at the cones and made to set off along Station Road. 'My treat as you're guarding the evidence.' Noble sagged on to a nearby fence and pulled out his cigarettes.

Brook removed the lid from his polystyrene cup and watched the ambulance depart. Dr Higginbottom squelched over from the river bank in his Wellingtons, fastening up his trademark leather bag. He removed his glasses when he stood beside Brook and Noble, and eyed their hot drinks.

'Well, you were right, Inspector. He doesn't appear to have any lungs, or indeed any internal organs. I didn't want to poke around inside or disturb the stitching in case this turns into a murder inquiry . . .'

'Why would there be any doubt, Doctor?' asked Noble.

Higginbottom smiled. 'There's always doubt, until there's certainty, Sergeant. Now, who said that? I can't remember. But suffice to say, without a detailed examination, all I can do here is assure you that the subject is deceased and that he died before he went into the river. Keith Pullin seems to be in the right area for how long the body's been in the water. Between one and three days, very roughly. The body has the right amount of *cutis anserina*.'

Like most of the medical experts Brook knew, Higginbottom liked to confuse his audience with a bit of Latin before explaining in layman's terms. It was all those years they were forced to study a dead language and it had to be justified with a certain level of showmanship.

'Which is?' asked Brook deferentially.

Noble smiled. He was pretty sure Brook already knew.

'Gooseflesh,' replied the doctor smugly. 'At a guess I'd say he died a couple of days before he went in the water, but don't hold me to it. Do you want that tea, Inspector? I didn't have time for a drink before I got the call.' Brook handed his cup to Higginbottom and watched dismayed as the PS removed the lid, drained the contents, then handed the cup back with a contented sigh. 'But as to murder, it's impossible to be definite about Cause of Death without an autopsy. It could even be natural causes. One thing, he didn't drown, even before his lungs were removed. There's no haemorrhaging of the middle ear and no sign of cadaveric spasm. That's when—'

'We know,' said Brook, dispensing with deference after the theft of his drink.

'Oh,' replied a miffed Higginbottom. 'And do we know the deceased yet?'

'Not yet,' said Brook.

'Well, it shouldn't be hard to find out,' continued the doctor. 'Prison looks likely – he's had a hard life. I suspect he'd be homeless and he's a part-time drug abuser – probably alcohol too. His teeth were very rotten, worn down by the acids in alcohol, and there's evidence of intermittent needle-marks. My guess, he took drugs when he could get them, but not as a matter of course, which probably means he couldn't afford to buy very often – hence homeless, indigent, delete as applicable.' He grinned. 'Contrary to popular opinion, most regular addicts hold down jobs. Thanks for the tea, Inspector. I'll let you have my report asap.'

Brook winced faintly at the assault on the English language as Higginbottom marched back to his car to remove his Wellingtons. His eyes followed the doctor, then moved to his empty cup, then settled on Noble's untouched drink. Taking the hint, Noble hastily drained his own cup before it could be sequestered.

Back in his car, Brook didn't turn towards Borrowash to follow Noble to the A52 and back to Derby. Instead he followed the road south towards open country and the parklands of Elvaston Castle. When the road turned sharply, Brook pulled his car to the kerb and hopped out. He did a quick search of the ground, both on the pavement and the road. In a patch of mud at the side of the road he saw a circular mark that might have been caused by a traffic cone being placed there.

He looked back up towards the river bridge but it had been obscured by the bend.

Brook took out his basic mobile phone and switched it on. As usual, there were no messages – only DS Noble had the number. He spent several minutes trying to work out how the phone's camera worked, then took a rather grainy picture of the mark in the road and, after storing it, turned the phone off again.

He jumped back in the BMW and drove on into the leafy hamlet of Thulston, looking all the while for a stack of road-traffic cones at the side of the road. There were none. Leaving Thulston, he arrived at a T-junction. He looked left then right.

'So which way did you go from here?' A car horn sounded behind him so Brook swung right to pick up the ring road back into town.

Five

A S THE MID-MORNING SUN STREAMED over his shoulder, Adam Rifkind pulled a hand through his tinted blond hair to move it away from his face and show his handsome features to best advantage. The thirty-five-year-old lecturer eyed the handful of bored-looking A-level students scattered around Derby College's Media Suite, slumping in their chairs, exhausted from having to drag themselves out of bed at eleven o'clock in the morning for a seminar.

Few returned eye-contact. Some stared glassy-eyed into space, while others nodded their heads to iPods and texted friends they would see in an hour – assuming they weren't already in the same room.

Though he prided himself on his youthful appearance and outlook, Rifkind experienced an unexpected stab of yearning for his own carefree youth. He knew most of his students would deny it, but they didn't have a care in the world. No work, no marriage, no mortgage and no self-loathing – the bright futures they imagined for themselves were not yet behind them.

Rifkind looked at his watch and stifled a yawn. It had been a tough academic year, and finding time for his novel was getting harder. Late nights didn't help. At least that was one problem he'd finally solved.

He surveyed the apathy before him – Derby's finest preparing themselves for the outside world with a gentle snooze in Media Studies, the course which always attracted the oddest blend of students. Half of the group were padding out a vocational timetable of bricklaying and construction with the easiest-sounding course they could find and, unfortunately, no matter how much the prospectus emphasised the opposite, Media Studies would always appeal to those who thought it consisted entirely of watching films and TV.

The bear-like Wilson Woodrow and his cronies were part of that crowd. Derby's future builders, bricklayers and jobbing gardeners sat together on a row, riffing about whose parents had splashed out the most money for their offspring's phone.

But it wasn't all doom and gloom. The brightest members of his English Literature set made up the numbers and raised the level of debate whenever the need arose to discuss or, God forbid, write about what they had discovered during a particular unit of study.

Russell Thomson – Rusty, for obvious reasons – was one. A bright boy, he sat alone and seemed in no need of the distractions of his peers as he looked saucer-eyed at the blank screen dominating a whole wall of the media suite. He was relatively new to the area and had moved with his mother from Wales, for what reason Rifkind didn't know – though he had heard a rumour about bullying at his previous college. He wasn't surprised. Rusty was a strange and introverted boy who seemed to have very few social skills and held the majority of his conversations with himself.

Tall for his age but thin and stooping, his eyes were either gazing off into space or fixed on the ground as though he'd lost something. Rusty rarely looked people in the eye and this social failing was reinforced by a more tangible barrier – the ever-present digital camcorder which was always strapped to his hand, and invariably raised in front of his face on the rare occasions he lifted his head.

Strangely, he seemed to possess the intellectual skills of a more mature person when producing written work, and had an encyclopaedic knowledge of films which he unveiled at the most inappropriate times. On a recent careers evening, he'd informed Rifkind that his ambition was to work in the cinema, and the lecturer had been unable to stifle the unworthy thought that Rusty would indeed make an ideal usher. Naturally Rifkind hadn't voiced this opinion. At least not in front of Rusty's gorgeous young single mum – a MILF indeed.

In front of Rusty now sat the strikingly pretty Becky Blake conversing with Fern Stretton, her best friend. The pair chatted as though alone in the universe, about everything from boys to their annual *X Factor* applications. Becky was fixated on fame and fortune and she certainly had the looks, though her in-your-face attractions had never been a draw for Rifkind. Until recently her superficial charms had been twinned with that air of unabashed expectation that clung to so many of her peers – a serenity derived from unbroken dreams.

But Rifkind had the sense that something had shifted within her. He often noticed it with students around this age. For a couple of years in their teens the most promising carried that galling conviction that they owned the world, believing their lives would proceed exactly as they wished. Then, one day, an unforeseen setback would rouse them from their slumber and they were forced to face a future of hard graft and disappointment.

Well, Rifkind was convinced that reality had sunk its teeth into Becky recently because she carried with her now that slight bruise of knowledge that her life would not be quite as predicted, as though something in her carefully gilded future had been stepped on.

Rifkind looked at his watch again and fired up his laptop to register those present. Jake McKenzie hadn't yet put in an appearance. McKenzie was a blue-eyed, dark-haired Adonis, as talented academically and athletically as he was handsome, and Rifkind had heard that every girl in the college had thrown herself at him at one time or another. And yet he seemed to be a thinker, rising above the petty obsessions of teenage life, absorbing himself in his studies and his sport, at which he excelled.

Rifkind didn't mark him absent yet. Jake was in such demand that he was often late from some practice or other.

Kyle Kennedy, the other boy from his Literature Group, couldn't have been more different from Jake. He was slim with delicate expressive hands, lightly built with feminine, stubble-free features, large doe eyes and long lashes. Despite being very shy he was a popular confidant of some of the girls and this, above all, made him the butt of most of the gay banter flying around. But academically, Kyle had a fierce and probing intelligence and was well on the way to an A* in Literature. Predictably, this only added to the resentment from the less talented.

Rifkind took a breath as Adele Watson walked through the double doors. He hadn't expected to see her and she hurried to a chair, steadfastly ignoring his gaze. She was a talented, if

Steven Dunne

naive writer and very beautiful. Next year she'd be studying English Literature at Cambridge – thanks in part to his own inspirational teachings.

He examined what he could see of her face. She'd been crying, he could tell, but the thought caused him no guilt. In fact, the idea that he could still arouse such feeling in the opposite sex was a rush. She'd get over it. At Cambridge, she'd blossom into a woman with many attentive admirers and she'd learn soon enough that he'd been right to end their relationship. They'd had fun. They'd had great, sometimes passionate sex – and what could be better than that? But now it was time to move on. She had her whole life in front of her. And Rifkind had bigger fish to fry.

'Well, folks,' opened Rifkind. 'Half-term is looming and next Thursday's Media Studies will be our last day.'

Russell Thomson looked up briefly. *Last Day. A quasi-religious ceremony from the film* Logan's Run, *starring Michael York and Jenny Agutter. On Last Day, inhabitants of this dystopian future world reached thirty years of age and were put to death . . .*

'The end of another unit of hard work,' continued Rifkind, 'at least for the staff.' He grinned at the dozing amphitheatre and permitted himself the merest glance at Adele's dark-eyed beauty. 'And, of course, Adele.' At the mention of her name, her dark sleep-deprived eyes locked on to Rifkind for a second and she blushed.

Next to her, Becky Blake turned to give her a significant stare – *you're in there, girl* – then pouted back at Rifkind to get some of that life-affirming attention for herself. Every man in Becky's presence noticed her, she knew that much. But it wasn't enough. Since her mother's death from cancer, Becky had been at the centre of her father's universe and had grown accustomed to total devotion; she demanded no less from all men. They had to be in orbit around her and she knew all the moves to make that happen. At school, she'd learned from a young age that she could separate any couple, with her shock of long blond hair, mouth-watering figure and the best clothes an indulgent parent could provide. And although Rifkind was a bit too smarmy for her, she saw no reason to change the habits of her short life and glowered suggestively at him.

But Adam Rifkind only had eyes for Adele so, with a disdainful sniff, Becky muttered under her breath, 'You know he's married, Ade.'

Adele, unable to look at her, reddened. 'You don't say.'

Becky missed the hushed sarcasm and expressed her surprise. 'Didn't you know, girlfriend? Yeah, he's a sly fucker though. He takes off his wedding ring; you can see the line round the finger. And Mrs Sly Fucker is not much older than us, apparently.' She rolled her eyes lasciviously at Adele then turned back to Rifkind to give him an appreciative onceover. 'I would though,' she grinned, and Fern on her other side broke into a fit of giggles. A moment later they returned their attention to their iPhones, not seeing Adele gulping back her emotions.

'I see a good portion of the group are already exhausted and have decided to skip the last two Thursdays,' said Rifkind. 'No matter.' At that moment the double doors swung open and Jake McKenzie strode into the suite. He looked around for an available chair.

'Ah, Jake. Decided to favour us with your presence today. Hurry up and sit, please; the group are ravenous for knowledge to start.'

Jake smiled and hesitated. There were no chairs left except the one next to Kyle Kennedy.

'There's a seat next to Gay Boy,' chuckled Wilson Woodrow, the overweight eighteen year old with the zigzag haircut and buzzing earphones. 'If you don't mind catching AIDS.'

'That's enough of that,' admonished Rifkind as mildly as he could. He prided himself on his good relationships with students and didn't like to play the authority figure.

To avoid Wilson's confrontational leer, Kyle stared down at the floor through his John Lennon spectacles and buried his long delicate hands between tightly crossed legs. He wore the blank expression of the diplomatically deaf.

Jake made for the seat next to Kyle and sat down. Kyle looked up at him in greeting and then just as quickly returned his gaze to the floor.

'Today and next week we're going to be watching and critiquing a film so this morning we can sit back and chillax.' Rifkind paused to make sure his comfort with the patois of youth had registered. 'Today's film . . .'

Wilson produced a DVD case from his baggy clothing and held it under Rifkind's nose without having the courtesy to look at him.

The lecturer stared at the top of the boy's head and ignored the offering. 'Today we are—'As Rifkind clearly hadn't noticed the DVD, Wilson waggled it in front of his face again.

In the end, the lecturer accepted it with a sigh. 'Thank you, Wilson.'

'Will,' replied the boy gruffly, again without looking up from his iPod.

'Oh, you managed to hear that over the Death Metal?

Funny how I have to repeat things three times when I want *your* attention.'

Wilson gazed up at Rifkind, a pearl of wisdom on the end of his tongue. 'My dad says sarcasm is the lowest form of something.'

'Ignorance perhaps,' replied Rifkind, looking at the cover of the DVD with a sinking heart.

'No, it's not that,' answered Wilson, thinking hard.

'*Saw 4* – interesting choice.'

'It's brilliant,' agreed Wilson, as though revealing a great secret to which only he was privy.

'Is it as brilliant as *Saws 1, 2* and *3*, dare I ask?'

'*Saw 2* is my best film ever. But *Saw 4* is even better.'

Rifkind looked around the room to garner support for his upcoming putdown, but only Kyle Kennedy's brow furrowed in amusement so he thought better of it.

'Thank you, Wilson.'

'Will!' the teenager retorted, with a touch more aggression.

'I'm afraid we won't be watching *Saw 4, Will*. Rusty has—'

'What? Why not?'

Rifkind made sure to speak slowly because he didn't want to repeat it. 'Because, as you'll remember, at the start of the academic year, we agreed to have a rota for people to choose the end-of-term film, and I'm afraid you've had your turn.'

'Yeah, my turn is the *Saw* films. You have to see them all for it to make sense. They're a series.'

'I don't care if it's a series, Wilson,' he said, taking pleasure in repeating the boy's hated name.

'It's Will!' shouted Wilson, this time. 'And we're watching *Saw 4*.' He turned round to the gathering. 'Everybody else wants to watch it, don't you?' Wilson eyeballed the group. Only Jake and Becky returned eye-contact.

'It doesn't matter what everybody wants.'

'That's not very democratic.'

Rifkind smiled at him, beginning to enjoy the little power he had over the boy. 'Nor is bullying people into doing what you want.'

'I'm not bullying anyone. You want to watch *Saw 4*, don't you, Kylie?' he said to Kyle Kennedy, who bridled at the sudden attention. 'I'm talking to you, Faggot.'

'That's *enough* of that language,' said Rifkind.

'What language? English?' Wilson sneered. 'It's a crime to speak your own language now, is it? I was just asking Faggot—'

'I said that's enough,' countered Rifkind, attempting a show of strength that he knew he couldn't back up. 'We're wasting time. Rusty has chosen today's film. End of.'

'Geek Boy wasn't even here at the start of the year, so how can he be on the rota?' snarled Wilson.

'Give it a rest, Will,' said Becky. 'I couldn't be arsed. He's taking my slot.'

Rifkind grinned at Woodrow's tubby face. 'Happy now that democracy has been served?'

Wilson stared angrily at the carpet, urgently searching for another compelling reason to have his way.

'Rusty?' Rifkind looked expectantly at Russell's pale face as he handed over a DVD case.

'*Picnic at Hanging Rock*,' said Rifkind. He beamed approvingly. 'Interesting choice.'

'Who's in it?' growled Wilson.

Rusty cleared his throat and in a timid voice said, 'Nobody

famous, but it was Peter Weir's breakthrough film, made in 1975. Weir, you may remember, directed *Gallipoli* and *Witness*, starring Harrison Ford.'

There was silence as everyone stared at him. In the six months since he'd been enrolled at Derby College, he'd barely spoken to anyone and certainly hadn't dared to speak in front of classmates. He seemed to spend most of his time sitting in the refectory drinking Coca Cola and pointing his camcorder at everyone who passed.

'Nineteen seventy-five?' howled Wilson. 'Is it in colour?'

'Beautiful colour, Will,' nodded Rusty, warming to his theme. 'The cameraman was Russell Boyd and his use of vibrant—'

'Sounds shit. What's it about?'

'It's about an Australian girls' school in 1900,' interjected Rifkind, in case Rusty began to buckle under Wilson's interrogation.

'You're shittin' me. I'm not watching that shit. It sounds shit.'

'That is your democratic choice, *Will*,' replied Rifkind, hopeful that the bully might be about to leave. But instead he waggled his own DVD in Rifkind's face again.

'Here. We're watching *Saw 4*. Rusty don't mind.' Wilson grinned over at him. 'Don't worry, Geek Boy. You're not going to get battered. Your mum's a MILF,' he hissed at him with a leer.

Rifkind shook his head. 'Well, I mind. We're watching *Picnic at Hanging Rock*. In Media Studies, Wilson, we have to open ourselves up to a variety of genres, aimed at different audiences...'

'My name is WILL!'

There was silence for a moment but Rifkind refused to be fazed. He was smarter than Wilson and wasn't about to back off until he'd proved it. He sniffed coldly. 'You should enjoy this film, Will. If you'd been born two hundred years ago, Australia is where you would have ended up.'

'What does that mean?' A smattering of the students sniggered their understanding and Wilson rounded on them angrily. 'What the fuck are you laughing at?' His eye caught Kyle Kennedy smiling and he stood to confront him. 'Something funny, Gay Boy?'

Kyle's smile disappeared. 'I . . . no, I mean—'

'Wilson. Either sit down or get out!' shouted Rifkind, finally losing his temper.

'Gay boys don't laugh at me,' bellowed Wilson, wading through chairs towards Kyle.

Jake McKenzie jumped hurriedly between the two. 'Back off, Wilson,' he said calmly. He held a hand up to Wilson's chest, keeping him at bay with ease. 'You've had your say. Sit down or fuck off.' He flexed his neck. Jake was not just sporty but also a fitness fanatic and built like a middleweight. And as the object of lust for female students, he was naturally well respected by the male students.

Wilson looked him in the eye. A second later the pressure on Jake's hand eased. Wilson smiled and put his hands peacefully in the air. 'Sure, Jakey. Whatever you say,' he said softly. He turned back towards Kyle. 'We'll talk later, Faggot,' he added menacingly.

'No, you won't,' said Jake. 'You won't go near him.'

'Why are you defending the little bumder?' Wilson leered towards Jake, a further insult bubbling to the surface. 'Are you his *boyfriend*, Jake? You potting the brown with that little—'

Jake threw a hand to Wilson's throat and gripped it hard. 'What did you say to me, Fatso?' Wilson was choking and pawing at Jake's hand as he was pushed back over his chair. 'What did you say?'

'Get him off me,' gasped Wilson, trying to loosen Jake's grip but to no avail. Rifkind, Kyle, Becky and a few others grabbed Jake's shoulders and tried to pull him away.

'He's not worth it, Jake,' shouted Kyle, forcing himself into eye-contact. 'Jake, he's not worth it.'

Jake glared at Kyle then relaxed his grip on Wilson. He turned away to confirm his pacification and Wilson got to his feet, rubbing his throat.

'That's assault, that is!' Wilson screamed at Rifkind. 'And you let it happen.'

'You provoked that situation, Mr Woodrow, despite my asking you repeatedly to avoid confrontation. Now sit down.'

Presented with a direct instruction, Wilson said the only thing he could to regain face. 'No.'

Rifkind tried not to smile. The teenage God of *No*. He knew the script from here and Wilson was too stupid to resist.

'Wilson, I order you to sit down because there's no way you're leaving.'

Wilson looked back triumphantly, seeing his path to victory. 'You wanna bet? Just watch me.' He turned to leave, throwing an angry look at Kyle, whose eyes were now glued to the floor.

'You can't leave and you'd better attend next week or else,' shouted Rifkind, at the retreating Wilson, laying down his final ace.

'Or else what? You won't see me for shit.'

Rifkind faked a look of annoyance but broke into a big grin

as Wilson turned and snatched up his *Saw* DVD, storming towards the doors.

Wilson looked over at Kyle. 'Oi, Faggot.' He stuck his tongue out and pulled a finger across his throat.

Kyle looked up from the floor, gathering his courage. His look of terror gave way to a mocking smile and he blew Wilson a big kiss. The assembled students laughed and jeered as the fuming Wilson kicked open the double doors and stalked away, a couple of sympathetic friends trailing in his wake.

'Respeck, Kylie,' said Becky, holding her hand up for Kyle to high five. 'That asshole butt-munch got well and truly parred and merked.'

Kyle basked in a couple of backslaps until the worry reinfected his face. *I shouldn't have done that*. He looked gratefully up at his saviour but Jake looked away at once.

'Why do those with the fewest brain cells always have the loudest voices?' said Adele Watson to no one in particular.

Becky turned and poured her body back into her chair, looking over at Russell who had his camcorder in front of his face. 'Look at Steven Spielberg here. I hope that's going on YouTube, Geek Boy,' she said, striking a pose for him.

'Maybe.' Thomson pointed his camcorder in her direction. He lowered the camera and smiled at her briefly but her stony expression killed his pleasure and he blushed.

'Just start the film, Geek,' ordered Becky.

Nearly two hours later, the credits rolled in the darkness. Rifkind and most of the other students had gone to lunch an hour ago but Adele, Becky, Fern, Kyle and Russell had continued watching through the bulk of the lunchbreak and even sat in silence as the cast of characters scrolled down the screen.

'Wow,' said Kyle, standing and stretching his slender frame in the gloom. 'Sick film.'

'Hard to believe a film about a girls' school could be that good,' agreed Becky.

When the inert screen ensured total blackness, Becky edged towards the large curtain and pulled it aside. Bright sunshine streamed through the floor-to-ceiling windows of the Media Suite and she and Fern immediately bent to check their phones. Adele remained seated, unable to move. She stared straight ahead. There were tears on her cheeks.

Back in his office at St Mary's Wharf, Brook got his mouth around his second cup of tea and closed his eyes to savour its soothing heat while his computer loaded. He logged on then registered his dismay at the volume of internal emails in his inbox.

'Thirty-six emails – in one day,' he sighed. 'The tyranny of faceless communication.' Brook scrolled down the list checking for his personal buzzwords. Any email containing the words *Committee*, *Budget*, *Target* or *Liaison* in the subject line was deleted without being opened. Happily this was most of them and Brook was left with five relevant messages about open cases and upcoming trials.

After dealing with them, he rifled through the drawers of his desk for an *A–Z* he knew he had somewhere. He was both pleased and appalled to find his desk bereft of cigarettes. He remembered wistfully the pack in his locker given to Noble earlier that morning, as a demonstration of his willpower.

Brook flicked through the pages of the *A-Z* and stared at the sparse countryside to the south and east of Borrowash, taking in the minor roads accessing Elvaston Castle and Thulston. He didn't know the area well but it seemed very flat and he knew from his trips along the A50 to the M1 or East Midlands Airport, that the land on either side of the carriageway was prone to flooding. Indeed, even without flooding there was sufficient water around the confluence of the Rivers Trent and Derwent to merit a marina at Shardlow for the nautically minded.

Brook pulled the *Yellow Pages* from another drawer. His eye glimpsed a mangled, half-smoked cigarette butt behind some old papers, covered in dust and fluff. After a moment's hesitation, he picked it out of the drawer and brushed it clean like an old soldier polishing his campaign medals. He stared lovingly at the butt for longer than necessary then threw it resolutely in the bin, chuckling noiselessly at the absurd sense of achievement that followed.

Noble walked in, holding papers. 'We've got more uniform searching up and down the river, just to be thorough. Nothing yet. On the plus side, DS Gadd's organised a door-to-door on Station Road and, apparently, someone leaving early for London on Tuesday did see the road was closed. Every other resident says the road was open later that morning so it looks like you were right. Our perpetrator faked the closure while he dumped the body.'

'When was this?'

'Two days ago.' Noble consulted a scribbled note. 'A Mr Hargreaves left his house at three thirty in the morning to drive to London. He couldn't cross the bridges and had to take the A52 instead.'

'Three thirty,' Brook said thoughtfully. 'So we're unlikely to get witnesses walking the dog.'

'What about anglers? They get up at all hours to bag the best spots.'

'Get uniform to speak to every angler on that stretch. And maybe run off some notices to post near the bridges. Any chance of decent forensics?' ventured Brook, though he already knew the answer.

Noble shook his head. 'SOCO weren't confident, not at the scene anyway.'

Brook nodded. 'Water washes away many sins, John – though I prefer malt.'

'They did find a large piece of cloth in the river nearby. They've bagged it for tests but we don't even know if it connects with our John Doe.'

'What about the bridge?'

'Nothing.'

'Let's hope the body gives us an ID. What's that?' asked Brook, looking at the sheaf of papers.

'Statement taken from the lads who spotted the victim in the river.' Noble handed the report to Brook, who skimmed it briefly.

'Let's call him the deceased until we're told it's murder, John.' Brook yawned heavily and tossed the papers on to the desk. 'Decent lads?'

'Solid kids from good families. No juvey—juvenile cautions,' Noble corrected himself before Brook caught his eye. 'And those CCTV cameras near the bridge were dummies.'

'Any other cameras locally?' asked Brook.

'In Borrowash? Hardly. The only excitement round there seems to be the odd broken wing mirror.'

Brook put his head in his hands and rubbed his eyes. 'All this careful planning suggests our man's a murderer.'

'Man? So you've definitely ruled out multiple suspects.'

'I think so. Statistically we're looking for a male, especially as our John Doe may have needed lifting. And, whether he has accomplices or not, he was on his own when he dumped the body.'

'How do you know?'

'The traffic cones,' replied Brook, looking up at Noble to see if he wanted to take the reins.

Noble lifted his shoulders in a gesture of defeat. 'What about them?'

'He couldn't carry the cones as well as a *Road Closed* sign. Two people could have done it. After he dumps the body, he's in a hurry so he picks up his sign . . .'

'. . . and leaves the cones stacked on the pavement thinking no one would notice,' finished Noble. 'Presumably he blocked off the road from the other side as well – somewhere out of sight of the bridges.'

'I think so.'

'We should—'

'I already looked, John. There's nothing to see though I've got a picture of an impression in the road that could have been from a line of cones – all fairly pointless.'

'We might get a fingerprint from the cones he left behind.'

Brook wrinkled up his nose. 'Doubtful.'

'At least we know he must have driven off south, towards Elvaston Castle, because if he parked on the river bridge to dump the body, he must have run the hundred yards back up to Station Road for his sign.' Noble looked at the ceiling, thinking it through. 'But when he drove away, he pulled up to his other road-block so it was easier to put the sign *and* the cones in his car.'

Brook smiled approvingly at his DS. 'There you go. Though if he's transporting a body, some kind of van is more likely.' He pushed the *A–Z* towards Noble. 'All of which gets us to here, the junction of the B5010, where he turns right towards the A6 and A50, maybe heading for the M1 or back into Derby.'

'Or left towards Shardlow – assuming he's not from Thulston.'

Brook sighed. 'You're right. We're getting ahead of ourselves. Let's wait for Forensics and the post mortem to find out exactly what we're dealing with.'

The middle-aged man in a crumpled white chef's uniform stared in disbelief as Rusty spoke to him. He then turned and glared over at Kyle and the others, giving them a lingering look up and down. Finally he shrugged and a moment later followed Rusty to their table and set a tray of soft drinks down, before distributing them to the students. He wore an ID badge with the name *Lee* and the archaic title *Refectory Manager*.

Adele smiled for the first time that day. The uniform and the title seemed incongruous to her, since the pinnacle of culinary sophistication in the college café was cheese on toast. Nevertheless she added the word 'Refectory' to her mental list of arcane words for future use. Just in case.

Rusty smiled. 'Thanks,' he said, talking to the table.

'Aye. Well, don't get used to it,' said Lee. 'I'm not a fucking waiter.'

Rusty placed a pound coin on to the empty tray without looking up.

The Refectory Manager looked down at it in surprise, if not gratitude. 'Blimey. Think I'll have it framed.' He nodded his appreciation before trudging back to his till.

'Waiter service, eh?' teased Kyle.

'Hark at Simon Cowell over here,' added Becky.

Rusty was embarrassed. 'My mum was a waitress for a while, and they earn a pittance, so I try to leave a tip if I can.'

Adele beamed at him. He squirmed under her gaze. 'That's very thoughtful of you, Rusty.'

'Yeah, thanks for the drink, bruv,' said Kyle, taking a swig of Coke.

Rusty examined the camcorder strapped to his right wrist. 'No probs.'

'I can't imagine your mum as a waitress, Rusty,' said Adele. 'She's so pretty.'

'It wasn't for long. And there was nothing else she could get in Chester.'

'Don't they need models in Wales then?' asked Fern, turning to grin at Becky. To her surprise, Becky looked away, unsmiling.

'She must be raking it in now though, if you're such a moneybags,' said Kyle.

'Not really,' said Rusty. 'But it was my eighteenth last week so Mum's spoiling me.'

There was an uncomfortable silence round the table from all except Fern. 'Happy Birthday,' she said gaily, missing the sudden mood-change. 'Did you have a party?'

Becky and Adele rolled their eyes at Fern until she became vaguely aware she'd said the wrong thing.

Rusty smiled at the table, equally unaware of her faux pas. 'No. But my mum bought me this new camcorder.' He brandished it proudly. 'And a cake.'

'Your mum sounds nice,' said Kyle warmly. He nodded sadly at the others. Poor Rusty. Nobody knew. Eighteenth birthdays were a big deal in a life so short of landmarks. They were an excuse for wild partying and drunken revelry with friends, extravagant presents from parents and maybe even a cruise round Derby, hanging from a Stretch. Assuming you had friends, of course. He looked at Rusty and realised he knew very little about him.

Suddenly Rusty looked up into his eyes. 'What's a MILF?' The others darted their eyes around the table in panic. 'That is what Wilson called my mum, isn't it?'

It was difficult for the others to keep a straight face in the ensuing silence. Fortunately the writer among them came to the rescue. 'It stands for Mums I Like Fine,' said Adele, with a quick glance at Fern to discourage giggling.

'That's right,' agreed Becky. 'And Wilson's such a good judge of personality.' She stared at the top of Rusty's head, then open-mouthed at Fern and Adele. *Was this guy for real?* Social skills zero, street patter zero. She sneaked a glance at Fern, who was starting to snigger, and Adele who was mouthing at her to stop.

Rusty looked up again and smiled. 'Funny, I had Wilson down as a bit of a knobhead but he's right. Mum's the best. It's been very difficult for her, having to move again.' He looked away again, embarrassed, and no one pressed him to finish. They'd all heard the rumours of bullying.

'It's *my* eighteenth tomorrow,' said Kyle, changing the subject. He looked round at his fellow students with an apologetic smile. This time even Fern was on message and looked intently at her drink. 'Don't worry,' he continued. 'You don't need to waste your weekend on me. I'm not having a party either. Things are tight at the moment. There's just me and Mum. Daddy Warbucks offered to pay but Mum doesn't . . .' Kyle's voice became more halting and he began to wish he'd said nothing. 'Well,' he finished tamely.

'I couldn't come anyway,' said Fern, trying to hide her relief. 'My parents are taking me Bournemouth for the weekend. Lame or what?'

Adele laid a hand across Kyle's and fixed him in her gaze. 'You should celebrate.'

Kyle looked at her with his doleful eyes. 'Should I?' He emitted a half-laugh. 'I don't think so.'

'Well, I think so. You only get one eighteenth. And on a Friday too.' She smiled but felt a stab of pain. Friday was always her special night with Adam. The first time they'd made love was on a Friday, last summer at his cottage.

'He doesn't have to celebrate if he doesn't want to,' said Becky.

'Celebration implies happiness,' said Rusty almost to himself.

'Rusty's right. There'll be other times,' said Kyle. 'When I've . . .' He hesitated, then smiled sadly. 'But thanks, Ade.'

Adele's face hardened. 'Suit yourself,' she replied. 'You can sit in the corner fondling your Morrissey posters and feeling sorry for yourself. But I'm coming round at seven with your present and you damn well better be there, Faggot.'

Kyle's mouth fell open and there was shock and surprise around the table. Adele raised an eyebrow and glared at Kyle and he glared back. A second later Kyle's mouth curved into a huge grin as Adele started to chuckle. 'You saucy bitch,' he screamed at her in his campest voice. 'You're so un-PC, girlfriend.'

'That's a date then.' Adele laughed and everyone joined in. Even Rusty managed a thin smile.

Kyle looked around the table. 'And you guys are all invited.'

'Going Bournemouth,' repeated Fern.

Becky looked at her sternly. 'Yeah, leave me dangling, ho – that's dread.' She turned reluctantly to face Kyle. 'I normally wouldn't waste a Friday on you, Faggot, I want that understood, but if Fern's dumping me then I'm sure I can find an hour for you – as long as we're not listening to the fucking Smiths all night.'

Kyle smiled at her. 'Great. I'll lay on some booze. Uncle Len can afford it. What about you, Geek Boy? You gonna come?'

Rusty looked at him, puzzled. 'Me?'

'Yes, you.' Kyle nodded.

Rusty was still confused. 'You mean come to your party? As a guest?'

'No, as a waiter, you sherm. Yes, as a guest.'

It took him a little time for the penny to drop. Then his face lit up. 'I could film it for you,' he said. 'You'll be the stars. And I promise I won't get in the way.'

'We'll let you know if you do.'

'And I could bring another DVD,' he said excitedly. 'Have you seen *Badlands*?'

'Is it as good as *Picnic at Hanging Rock*?' asked Adele.

'You liked that?' asked Rusty.

'It was wicked,' said Kyle. 'Wondrous.'

'Pretty good,' conceded Becky.

Fern looked less certain but nodded in agreement. If Becks liked it, she liked it.

Rusty managed to lift his head towards Adele. Her eyes were still red from the tears. 'What about you? Ade?'

Adele stared off into the distance. 'Haunting,' she said finally.

Rusty smiled and looked briefly at each in turn, before returning his eyes to the floor.

Becky held her hands open. 'Just one thing, Geek Boy. What happened to the three girls in the film?'

'What do you mean?'

'Well, where did they go?'

'They disappeared. They walked up Hanging Rock and were never seen again.'

Becky pulled a face. 'I know that. But it's a film – what happened to them in real life?'

'You're missing the point, Becks,' said Kyle.

'*I'm* missing the point? Cheeky fucker.'

'But you are,' said Kyle. 'See, it doesn't matter what happened to them.'

'It matters to me.'

'Kyle's right,' said Adele. 'What matters is they left of their own accord, on their own terms.' She looked over at Kyle, who held her gaze for a second.

'Oh, is that what matters?' said Becky. 'Well, that's not what matters to me, Ade. I want to know if they really died. I mean, they must have found out what happened. Three girls can't just vanish like that, can they?'

'One of them was found a week later, remember,' said Rusty. 'But she had no memory of what had happened.'

'D'uh!' said Becky. 'I'm not a mong. I saw the film.'

'Yes, you did. And you should already know the most important thing,' said Kyle. 'They left their pain behind them for everyone else to bear.'

'Yeah, okay, they left their pain behind. Boo hoo! But what *actually* happened to them?' she insisted. 'I can't write a five-hundred-word review on just that. Three girls climb a rock and disappear. End of.'

'It's a mystery,' said Rusty, risking another smile.

'Stop grinning at me, Geek Boy, or you'll be wearing your teeth as a necklace.'

'He fancies you.' Fern laughed, leering at her friend. Rusty looked away, suddenly flushed.

Becky sidled round to him and put a hand up to stroke his cleanshaven cheek. 'Course he does. He's got eyes, hasn't he?' She remembered a line from the film. "Am I your Botticelli Angel?"' She giggled at Fern then turned back to Rusty and kissed him on the same cheek. 'Mmm, you've got quite the manly stubble, haven't you, Geek Boy?' She laughed.

'Don't be dread, Becks,' said Adele.

'What?' Becky held her hands open to underscore her innocence.

Rusty didn't move, a faint smile fixed on his face. He pulled the camcorder up to hide his reddening features and began filming her.

Becky's expression betrayed an objection but she didn't voice it. 'Stop hiding behind that thing, Geek Boy. Tell me.' Rusty kept filming so Becky gave in and pouted at the lens, fluffing up her curly blond hair with her hands and striking several poses. 'I mean, if it's based on a true story, where did they go?' she said as she looked at the camera with a startled expression.

'Here's a theory even somebody shallow and superficial can understand,' said Adele, an icy edge to her voice. Becky narrowed her eyes. 'Without doing a day's work in their lives, those girls became famous. They were frozen in beauty and time forever and here we are talking about them over a hundred years later. Jealous?'

Rusty put the camcorder down and smiled hesitantly at Adele. 'That's very clever, Ade.'

'Jealous? Me?' sneered Becky. 'You mental bitch.'

'When I go that's what I want,' said Fern. 'People everywhere talking about me, missing me. It'll be so sad. Like *Romeo + Juliet*.'

'Kylie's the jealous one,' continued Becky. 'He'd have loved going to a girls' school, wouldn't you, sweetie?' She directed her laughter towards Fern, who cackled her approval.

'All those gorgeous dresses to wear,' Fern answered.

Kyle managed a good-humoured middle finger.

'Never mind, Geek, I can guess what happened,' replied Becky, sitting back down. 'I'll bet those blokes raped and murdered them. Only sensible solution. Men are only interested in one thing. Isn't that right, Kyle?'

Kyle squirmed under her accusing gaze but this time didn't react. The limelight shifted quicker that way.

'No answer from Faggot.' Becky downed her drink and stood to leave. Fern followed suit. 'Well, I'll see you all at Sad Bastard Central tomorrow night. And you better not tell any cool people I'm coming to your party, Kylie.'

'I don't know any,' quipped Kyle.

Becky glared at him but decided not to challenge. She stalked away as if on a catwalk, Fern trailing in her wake.

Rusty stood to film them as they walked away. 'Poor Becky.'

'What do you mean?' asked Kyle.

Rusty stared at the table. 'To be so ugly inside.'

Adele gazed at him, a thin smile forming around her mouth. 'Maybe it's a cry for help, Rusty.'

Rusty turned the camera on Adele but lowered it when she became uneasy. He looked into her dark eyes briefly.

'Do they really not know what happened to those girls on the Hanging Rock?' asked Kyle.

'No, though there are lots of theories,' said Rusty, finishing his drink. 'The favourite is that they were buried under a rock fall somewhere near the summit. Me? I prefer not to know. That way they *do* live forever.'

'Live forever.' Adele nodded at him. 'Like angels.'

'Or gods,' chipped in Kyle.

'And poor Sara who flew to her death from the roof of the school – did she really kill herself? For real, I mean.'

'Sara?'

'The orphan – the girl who wasn't allowed to go on the picnic because her school fees hadn't been paid. She lost her best friend on Hanging Rock and later jumped off the roof of the school.'

Rusty shook his head. 'I don't really know. Most people concentrate on the girls who disappeared.' He looked at her, pleased, and then a moment later said, 'She had to content herself with being mortal.'

Adele nodded at him, her dark sad eyes mesmerising. 'And alone.'

At that moment Rifkind entered the refectory and glanced across at Adele. She darted a quick peek in his direction then looked away.

'You okay?' asked Kyle.

She raised her dark eyes to him and smiled. 'I will be.'

Six

BROOK DID A FEW HOURS' paperwork then set off home in the late afternoon as there was little more to be achieved after details of the incident had been entered on the PNC. It was a fine warm day though he was so tired he hardly noticed. The post mortem on the unknown corpse would take place in the morning, and without a cause of death and an ID, there was nothing left to do except pointless theorising.

Dr Higginbottom had already emailed a copy of his preliminary report. He couldn't speculate on COD but his initial inspection had shown that several, if not all, of the deceased's organs had been removed, so the corpse had clearly undergone a rudimentary post mortem.

One possibility mentioned by the doctor was that the body might have already been somewhere in the mortuary system but had been misplaced or misappropriated, so Brook had Noble contact the Coroner's Office to request a list of all recent post mortems performed on corpses fitting a broad description of their John Doe. Brook then compiled a list from *Yellow Pages* and the trade website for undertakers and funeral directors of all organisations who might employ a mortician.

He restricted the search to Derby and the surrounding area but even so there were still dozens. Death was a reliable employer.

One drawback to Higginbottom's theory was the unusual incision in the man's side. The doctor had never seen a corpse after a PM with such an aperture, and neither had Brook or Noble for that matter. More often than not, a British pathologist or mortician would cut a corpse down the middle of the chest from the neck to the pubis with a slight detour around the sinew of the belly button, because it was difficult to both cut and sew up afterwards. Brook had known pathologists who'd trained in the United States as Medical Examiners and used the Y-shaped incision often preferred over there. But no reputable pathologist would extract the organs of a cadaver from a six-inch opening on the flank. It just wasn't practical, according to Higginbottom.

Before heading for home, Brook and Noble searched the Missing Persons databases for both Nottinghamshire and Derbyshire and marked the files of the dozen men around the right age who were unaccounted for. Unfortunately, though some had seen the inside of a prison, none had been born in Scotland. The attached photo IDs for the subjects didn't look promising either, though some of the images were out of date, sometimes by many years, depending on the date of disappearance.

'Want me to start ringing round the funeral homes?' Noble had asked.

Brook picked up his car keys and shook his head. 'Let's have that conversation tomorrow when we have more information and maybe an ID.'

*

American Beauty *starring Kevin Spacey, directed by Sam Mendes in 1999 – an exploration of romantic and paternal love, sexuality, beauty, materialism, self-liberation and redemption.* According to Wiki at least. He could show them that film at the party. Adele would love it. Kyle too. Maybe Becky would be more cynical.

But the bonus was Ricky Fitts, one of the characters. He was young and cool and spent all his spare time filming on his camcorder. *Just like me.*

Rusty stopped at the side of the road and bent down to the pavement. Yeah, *American Beauty*. Life – a journey without meaning. This pigeon knew. You live, you get by, you die and everyone forgets you. He lifted his camcorder and zoomed into the pigeon lying on the ground, its neck slack, and its opaque sightless eyes half-open. Maggots were chewing through the bird's intestines.

A few seconds later he zoomed out and continued on his short journey across the Brisbane Estate, at the western edge of Derby. He replayed the short sequence as he walked through the cool night air then deleted it. His brand new Sanyo camcorder had great picture quality even at night. Just as well.

Becky Blake read the letter one more time, refolded it and slid it into the small gap between the carpet and the actor's make-up bureau which her dad had made especially for her. The light bulbs around the frame were to accustom his daughter to stardom.

She sat on the padded chair, cradling her old teddy bear and staring at her reflection in the illuminated mirror for what seemed hours. Finally, she sat up straight and Justin the bear fell to earth. She looked away from her reflection but there was no escape from her face – wherever her eyes wandered in her bedroom, her image glared sassily back at her. Sometimes writhing on a bearskin rug, sometimes peeping coquettishly over a bare shoulder, sometimes hands on hips in *Don't-fuck-with-me* mode. The confident, self-assured bitch snarled next to the vulnerable girl/woman, who jostled for wall space next to the siren looking for love. Her portfolio of portraits, professionally done and paid for by her father, filled the walls.

A tear fell as Becky turned to face herself on the wall. She couldn't meet her own eye and was tempted to trash the shrine, tear down every corrupting image and deconsecrate the pink room completely. Avoiding her own gaze, she looked instead at the few remaining posters fighting for space, posters that spoke of Becky's graduation from thirteen-year-old wannabe to the luminous cynicism of the eighteen year old. Thus the lacy chutzpah of Gwen Stefani was juxtaposed with the brassy sexuality of Christina Aguilera, the perky wholesomeness of Hannah Montana with the brooding promise of Rihanna.

With a sigh Becky stood in her silk slip as another tear fell. Calmly, methodically she toured the room taking down all the photographs her father had paid for then slid them under her bed. She flipped up the lid of her laptop and clicked off Facebook to load the document she'd written a couple of days previously. *Dear Becky, I am pleased* . . .

She finished reading and spotted the spelling mistake underlined in red but it was too late to correct – it was already two days in the post. As she closed the brief letter, a casual glance back at her mirror caught a movement outside in the darkness. A second later her eyes widened in disbelief at the sight of Rusty Thomson, Geek Boy, shinning his way along the branch of the large tree outside her window. Her initial impulse was to turn and vent her spleen, but to her astonishment she found herself watching him in the mirror, unable to move, as he slithered into position.

Instead of rushing to the window to scream abuse, Becky busied herself on her laptop keyboard, keeping her back to the window but her eye to the mirror to observe the gawky Thomson. A moment later Becky watched him lift his right hand. The faint dot of red light emanating from the object in his palm was confirmation of his intent. He was filming her. Geek Boy was filming her in her bedroom. *Cheeky fucker.*

She took several deep breaths then put her laptop aside on the bed and stepped over to her make-up bureau. She moved the chair so she could stand closer to the reflection and the lights. She stared at herself in the mirror again, this time with heightened interest. Her nipples had hardened under her slip and she brushed them with her forearms as she ran her hands through her hair.

Slowly, very slowly, she began to sway her hips from side to side, throwing back her head and opening her mouth invitingly. She cupped her breasts in her hands through the soft silk and massaged her nipples with fingers and thumbs. Then she crossed her arms over her chest and flicked the thin straps of her slip from her shoulders and down her bare arms.

Little by little she lowered the slip until, with a faint wobble, her breasts wrestled themselves free of the material and she pushed the garment to her waist. Swaying more urgently now, she eased her hands down her stomach before pushing the shiny slip to the floor, standing naked before the mirror. Finally she turned towards her bedroom window and stared intently at the red dot.

PICNIC AT HANGING ROCK – *A FILM BY PETER WEIR*

In the 1975 film Picnic at Hanging Rock, *set in Australia in 1900, a party of girls from a local college set out for a day at Hanging Rock, a local beauty spot. The film begins in Appleyard College and introduces us to the girls as they dress, wash their hair and press flowers. They are all very ladylike and it is clear that the college is private and parents have to pay to send their daughters there.*

Early on we meet the beautiful Miranda, who is compared to a Botticelli Angel by the French teacher from a book she's reading. Botticelli was a painter in the fifteenth century. We are also introduced to Marion and Irma who are also pretty, but it is Miranda who steals the film with her looks and also her sadness. She seems to know that she's not going to live very long because she tells her friend Sara, who idolises Miranda, that she must choose someone else to love because she herself is doomed.

Sara is appalled at this. She is an orphan who is picked on by the headmistress, Mrs Appleyard, because her foster-parent has not sent the money to pay for her lessons and so she is not allowed to go on the upcoming picnic. Irma compares Sara to a deer she found that died, fragile and pale and also doomed to die.

So things are all set up towards some kind of tragedy at Hanging Rock and every time we see a shot of the rock the music becomes creepy, as though some supernatural force is living there. Also, the girls spend a lot of time looking at the sky as though they are thinking about the afterlife and being angels.

At the picnic, the coach driver tells us his watch has stopped: another bad omen that the Hanging Rock is somehow not natural. Miranda asks a teacher if she, Irma and Marion can go and explore the rock. Another girl, Edith, nags them to come along too. She is not pretty but overweight and she always complains, in comparison to the calm beauty of the other three. As they disappear from view, Miranda turns with her long blond hair and waves at the teacher, almost as if she's saying goodbye.

On Hanging Rock the film becomes less natural. There is a lot of slow motion with weird sound effects and odd camera angles which imply that some unseen force is watching them. Also the girls seem very calm and resigned to their fate. At one point, Marion says, 'Surprising how many humans are without purpose,' which I take to mean that she sees no point in living. Also Miranda says, 'Everything begins and ends at exactly the right time and place,' as though she knows her time is up and she accepts it.

While Edith is whingeing again the three friends hold hands and set off further up the Rock. This is in slow motion and there is an unnatural rumbling as they leave. Edith seems to know something is wrong and begins screaming and runs off.

I found this film very moving. It was quite slow but I couldn't take my eyes off it. What I found most moving was the calmness with which the girls faced their death. They are the only ones in the film who don't seem to be suffering. They're leaving the world behind. Their pain is over and it is left to everyone remaining to suffer the torment of their disappearance and to wish they'd behaved differently towards them.

Back in the real world, Mrs Appleyard's school starts to go bust and she ends up drinking too much and then killing herself at Hanging Rock. Sara throws herself off the roof of the school because she misses Miranda so much and she can't bear the pain. The director is telling us that perfect love can't exist for very long and we have to settle for imperfect love or die.

Interestingly, one of the girls, Irma, is found but she can't remember anything and her life becomes really miserable again once she returns to normal life. The director might be suggesting she may have been better off dead because now she has to grow old and ugly and live with all her pain. He's also trying to tell us that a lot of the story may not be real and not to believe what happened because the first words spoken by Miranda are from a poem by Edgar Allan Poe which I found on the internet. 'What we see and what we seem is but a dream, a dream within a dream.' This tells us that reality and fantasy are being mixed up, like life may be a (bad) dream but there are different places where you can be happy, including when you go to the afterlife.

824 words
By Kyle Kennedy

Kyle checked through the text and saved it on to his pen drive. He lay back on his bed and flicked at a remote. He was bare-chested, his skinny frame glistening in the evening heat. Music drifted out of the speakers mounted at each corner of the room – The Smiths. He looked down at the pasty, almost white flesh on his puny torso and pulled on a T-shirt in disgust then gazed at the cloudless sky, the same sky the girls at Hanging Rock must have been looking at. He could hear the faint muffle of outdoor life continuing elsewhere even though his window was firmly closed against it.

His favourite song started to play – 'There Is A Light That Never Goes Out' – and he began to sing along. He nodded wistfully when Morrissey sang about the possibility of being run over by a ten-ton truck and that to die beside his lover in such a way would be a privilege. Kyle dug into his skintight jeans and pulled out a crumpled and dirty piece of paper. Unfolding it, he read the handwritten text.

Jake finished his hundredth sit-up and fell back on to the floor panting. He sat up and rolled over to do his press-ups when he noticed his mobile flashing. It was Kyle. Jake sat on his bed and looked at the sweat dotting his brow in the wardrobe mirror.

'Hello.'

'It's Kyle.'

'What do you want?'

'Jake. I'm outside.'

With phone in hand, Jake looked out into the dark sultry night. Kyle was at the front gate waving at him. 'It's late, Kyle.'

'I've got something for you. To thank you for this morning.'

'This morning?' asked Jake, though he knew very well what Kyle meant.

'When Wilson went for me at college. You stopped him hitting me.'

Jake smiled. 'Oh, that.'

'Can you come down? I'd knock on the door but I don't think your dad likes me much.'

'Wait there.' A minute later, Jake had slipped through the kitchen and out of the back door. He came round the corner of the house and walked towards Kyle, who pulled his hood down and watched Jake's panther-like steps.

Kyle grinned sheepishly. 'Hi, Jake.'

'Kyle.' Jake nodded back. There was a brief silence. 'Well?'

'Well, it's my eighteenth tomorrow.'

'Happy Birthday.'

'Thanks.' Kyle hesitated.

'Hope you're getting a new hoodie.'

'Sorry?'

Jake smiled to diminish any insult. 'That G-Star thing you're wearing. You ever take it off?'

'It depends,' said Kyle mysteriously.

Jake stiffened. 'Was there something else?'

'My mum's going away for the weekend with Daddy Warbucks – Uncle Len. He's kind of her boyfriend.'

'I know him,' said Jake. 'That old fart who dresses like Eminem.'

Kyle giggled and Jake reluctantly laughed with him. 'I know. A pensioner in a tracksuit. That's so not right on so many levels. Well, I'm having a few people round – not many, just a handful.' He grinned sheepishly. 'I don't have a block full of friends.' Jake's expression remained sombre so Kyle said his piece. 'About nine o'clock. Only if you want, of course. And no present, just presence.' Kyle laughed, embarrassed at his own pun.

Jake stared at him, making no attempt to reply. Finally he

squirrelled a glance at Kyle's hand. 'You said you had something for me.'

'Right.' Kyle handed over a pen drive, a CD case and a rolled-up poster. 'I've done that film review for Media Studies. I thought you might like to borrow it – you know, get some ideas for your own essay.' Jake kept his eyes on Kyle then unrolled the poster. 'It's Morrissey from The Smiths. Greatest Living Englishman,' Kyle looked around and laughed shyly, 'far as I'm concerned. And I burned you a Smiths CD – you know, just to thank you.' Kyle nervously rested one plimsolled foot on the other. He looked about twelve to Jake with his short crop and pale girlish features. Not even a suggestion of facial hair.

'You didn't have to. But thanks.'

Kyle took his hands out of his pockets and looked up into Jake's face but Jake had turned away.

'Was there anything else?' he said coldly.

Kyle looked at the ground. 'A ten-ton truck would be nice.' He pulled his hood back up and walked away into the night.

'What does that mean?' shouted Jake after him.

Kyle turned, a wistful smile on his face. 'When you listen to the CD you'll know. Track nine.'

Rusty walked slowly along the pavement, his eyes glued to the glow of his camcorder. What a result. Becky Blake dancing for him, stripping for him. *Forget* Animal House *starring John Belushi and directed by John Landis. This was no American frat-house comedy, this was . . . this was . . .* Body Double. *That's it. Brian de Palma's remake of* Vertigo *starring Melanie Griffith as the erotic dancer, performing her dance of death for the hapless Peeping Tom in a nearby apartment.*

Rusty grinned at the playback. Becky had seen him, he was sure. Cry for help? Goddamn right. He was so engrossed in the image of Becky's naked body that he didn't hear the noise from behind until it was too late. At the last minute the whirring of a bicycle registered and he turned in time to catch a flash of steel descending towards his neck. He screamed in shock and pain and fell to the ground, clutching at the wound.

As he hit the ground he tried to keep hold of the camcorder but it fell from his grasp and rolled along the pavement, coming to a stop with the lens facing him. As the blood trickled through Rusty's fingers, clamped to his neck, he tried to right himself but caught sight of the camcorder as he did so. The red light was on.

Ignoring his injury, he reached out a bloodied hand towards the lens just out of reach. A second later, he slumped down to the hard pavement with a rasping sigh, and lay motionless while the camcorder continued to store his image.

'What was that little pooftah doing outside?'

Jake turned at the foot of the stairs to face his father sprawled out on the living-room sofa, beer can perched on his belly. Jake wondered whether to pretend he hadn't heard and just bound up the stairs.

'I asked you a question,' growled his dad.

'His name is Kyle.'

'Yeah, that gay boy. Poor Steve Kennedy's lad,' retorted his father, unable to turn his face away from the TV. 'What did he want?'

'Leave him alone,' his mother said. 'They're friends. Kyle's a nice lad.'

'That right, Jake?' hollered his father, a mocking edge in his tone. 'Are you and that shirt-lifter friends?'

'Malcolm. I don't want to hear that sort of talk in my house.'

Jake turned away and shouted back from the bottom stair, 'He's in my Media Studies group. We sometimes swap essays.'

'Essays, my arse,' his father shouted back. 'Just mind you don't catch nothing.'

Jake started up the stairs. 'Why don't you have another beer, Dad? You still sound half-sober.'

'You cheeky little bastard,' bellowed his father, stirring himself.

'I wish,' Jake hollered back from his bedroom door.

'What the fuck does that mean?'

'That's enough, Malcolm. Sit back down. I'm trying to watch this.'

Malcolm McKenzie sank blearily back to the warmth of the sofa. 'Cheeky little fucker's cruising for a bruising,' he muttered under his beer breath.

Jake fed the CD into his music centre and pressed 9 on the remote. A grubby scrap of paper fell out of the blank case, which he stooped to pick up and unfold. It was a handwritten track list. Track 9 was called 'There Is A Light That Never Goes Out'. He turned the paper over. There were childlike drawings of unknown yellow flowers around the margins and a small poem in the middle which Jake read aloud.

> *Morrissey,*
> *you should have died when you was younger,*
> *For you then, we would have hungered,*

We would have seen some flowers then
And never seen your like again!!!!!

It was signed *KK aged 13*.

Jake listened carefully to the song until he heard the reference to a ten-ton truck. He skipped the song back to listen again.

Jake ejected the disc and sat in silence. The song was a love letter and Kyle Kennedy had given it to him. A moment later he carefully picked up the unfolded track list and tore it into tiny pieces. Then he picked up the CD and case and headed downstairs.

'Going out, Jake?' shouted his mother from the armchair. She was a small nervous woman with a birdlike way of moving her head. Jake's drink-befuddled father was on the sofa snoring and the TV was turned up to drown out the noise.

Jake smiled reassuringly at her as he zipped his tracksuit. 'I'm going for a run, Mum.'

'At this time? I was just going up.' *On my own* was left unsaid.

'I've got a lot of pent-up energy,' he explained. His mum nodded then looked at her husband without expression. Jake followed her gaze. He managed a watery smile. 'Anything good on?'

His mother looked at him for longer than felt comfortable. 'I've no idea.'

Jake turned away and opened the front door. 'I won't be long.' He jogged out into the warm night.

Jake turned left on to Western Road and continued to jog powerfully towards the new houses before turning on to

Brisbane Road. He kept his eyes peeled for Kyle. He knew roughly where he lived with his mother. Kyle's father had left them a few years ago because of the shame of having a gay son. Although Kyle's sexuality had only become blatant over the last couple of years in college, likely his parents would have known sooner. And Kyle's dad hadn't hung around to listen to behind-the-hand whispers.

After her husband's departure, Jake knew Kyle's mum had been forced to cope as a single parent, on a mixture of benefits and the bits of maintenance she could squeeze out of Kyle's dad, as well as the odd bit of cash-in-hand work serving at a stall in the Eagle Centre. The years of scrimping and saving had not been kind to Mrs Kennedy and she seemed old and worn out for her age, like his own mum. At least things were looking up for them moneywise. Leonard Poole, a pensioner with a big car, had been taking an interest in her for a year or so. There was a twenty-year age gap – Poole was about sixty – but he seemed to have plenty of money. 'Daddy Warbucks.' Jake laughed in spite of his mood. 'Good one.'

Ten minutes later, Jake slowed to a walk and put his hands on his hips, feeling the pleasant rush of adrenalin in his system. 'Maybe he's gone to a *gay* bar,' he panted, his eyes narrowing. Was there even such a thing in Derby? He'd heard rumours but he'd never seen any obvious faggots in the city. Just Kyle. Still, there had to be other faggots, didn't there? Because the secret existence of gayness dominated his and every other young male's life on the estate. Anything not quite right was gay. Anything morally dubious was gay. Bad situations were gay. If it rained in summer it was gay. Boring lessons were gay.

Even a slow computer was gay. Gay was a byword for everything that was wrong in the world.

Jake prepared to jog again as he turned down a sharp dip in the road. He stopped when he heard a noise, a shout from somewhere. He walked towards it. There was a gap in the houses and a path next to a stream cut through towards open ground where residents walked their dogs on nearby fields.

Another shout now, only louder, followed by a laugh. He reached the path and headed down through the trees into the darkness. In a patch of moonlit ground stood Kyle, his back against a large tree, held at the throat by the podgy hand of Wilson Woodrow. Three of Wilson's mates stood around laughing, smoking and filming on their camera phones.

Kyle saw Jake before the others did, his frightened eyes blinking in relief. He couldn't speak because Wilson's hand was squeezing his throat. A little blood seeped from his mouth. Wilson grinned at Kyle's terror then followed his tearful gaze of relief. He stopped grinning and let his hand fall when he saw Jake. The others turned too and mobile cameras were lowered.

'Hi, Jake,' said Wilson, holding up a placatory hand. 'We were just having a little fun with your girlfriend.' Jake stiffened. His eyes dwelled on the blood in Kyle's mouth. 'Oh, it's not what you think, Jake. That was an accident.' Wilson laughed and looked around at his amused crew. 'I was just looking at the cut, when you arrived. To see if I could fix it.'

Kyle, now freed, pushed past Wilson and stood before Jake, tears streaming down his face. 'Jake! I knew you'd come.'

Wilson and his friends stood ready to run despite their superior numbers.

Jake reached into his pocket and fished out The Smiths CD

given to him by Kyle. He tossed it on the ground. 'There's your CD, Faggot. Pick it up and get out of here while you still can.' He waited for Kyle to escape but instead of running, Kyle stood frozen. He glanced down at the CD case then up into Jake's eyes. The sobbing had stopped but the look of desolation on his face was far, far worse, as though someone had reached deep into his being and ripped out his heart and soul.

For what seemed an eternity, Kyle held Jake's gaze, then ignoring the CD on the ground, he turned to face Wilson, took a deep breath and walked back towards him.

Wilson grinned but confusion quickly flooded his face. *What was the faggot doing?* Kyle walked to within six inches of Wilson, smiled a bloody smile and touched his arm with a delicate hand. 'Hello, handsome.'

Wilson landed a haymaker on the left side of Kyle's head and he collapsed like a house of cards. 'Fucking queer.' His friends made to close in around the prostrate form but Wilson held up a hand to halt them. 'No. That's what he wants – the fucking perv likes it. I'm gettin' away from this freak.' Wilson stomped off, assuming the mantle of the injured party, his mute entourage trailing in his wake. 'All yours, McKenzie,' he hissed, making sure he gave Jake a wide berth. 'I'm going to get me some mature poontang,' he said, hitching at his crotch to make his meaning clear. 'Get the taste of gayness out of my mouth.' His friends sniggered their approval.

Jake watched them leave, laughing, shouting and texting others about their triumph. Then he turned back to Kyle. From a pocket, Jake pulled a small hand flannel which he used to wipe sweat from his face when he jogged. He ran down to the nearby stream and dunked the flannel into the cold water then ran back to Kyle, who was trying to sit up. Jake nursed his lolling head on to his knee and dabbed the blood from his mouth. He then wiped Kyle's brow, and the cold water revived him. 'Are you all right?'

Kyle's dark cow eyes opened and his long lashes fluttered as he focused. For a split second he made to smile then his face paled and he sat up. 'Get off me,' he muttered groggily.

'Kyle, you're—'

'Get off me.' Kyle squirmed unsteadily to his feet. 'Don't touch me.' He righted himself and managed to stand then staggered away towards the darkness of the fields, pushing past Jake's outstretched hands.

'Kyle!' shouted Jake after him.

Kyle lurched out of sight, sobbing. 'Leave me alone, you bastard. I hate you.'

Seven

B ROOK AND NOBLE ARRIVED AT the shiny new mortuary in the Royal Derby Hospital complex at nine the next morning and headed straight for the Post Mortem Suite. When they arrived, Dr Habib was already finishing work on the dead man and was preparing to remove his gown and mask while an assistant took the final photographs.

Habib was a short chubby Asian man with soft brown eyes blinking behind thick round glasses. His face was wrinkle-free, despite advanced age, his hair, sticking out from under his surgical cap, was reddish-brown save for a few strands of grey that hadn't seen sufficient henna.

After he stuffed mask and gown into a hazard bin, he muttered an instruction to his assistant who set down the camera and laid out the deceased's hands, palm up, and ready to roll on the fingerprint ink. When Brook and Noble entered the lab, fiddling with surgical masks, they ventured no further than the freezers.

Habib grinned when he spotted them. 'Inspector Brook. And Sergeant Noble also. Nice to see you. Just finishing up.'

'You got an early start,' said Brook.

'It's a lot quicker without clothes to bag and organs to remove,' said Habib. 'And we've got a backlog to work off.'

'What have you got for us?' interrupted Brook, fearing a lecture on excessive workload – Habib's favourite topic of conversation.

Habib paused, wondering whether Brook should be made aware of how much he had on his plate, then decided against it. 'More questions than answers at this stage, I fear. A tricky case – but very interesting.' He smiled warmly at his assistant who walked over to them, camera in hand. 'Gentlemen,' Habib gushed towards the detectives. 'Can I introduce Dr Ann Petty?'

'Detectives,' she said through her surgical mask. Brook caught a glimpse of her green eyes as she ran them briefly up and down, first Brook's then Noble's frame before returning to her work. The two detectives pretended not to notice. This wasn't a come-on but a reflex they'd noticed in every pathologist, undertaker or mortician they'd ever had dealings with. Without being aware of it, the technicians of death always ran an experienced eye over new acquaintances, to estimate their weight and assess how their corpses might present on a cold steel trolley. 'Slab happy' was the phrase Noble had coined to describe it.

'Does this mean you're no longer short-staffed, Dr Habib?' asked Noble. Brook darted a warning glance at him.

'For the moment,' replied Habib. 'For now, Dr Petty is under my supervision and will be replacing me when I retire next year, at which point *she* will be short-staffed.' Habib chortled at his joke and looked around the room for approval.

'Interesting case, you say,' said Noble.

Habib gestured them through to the office at the side of

the lab and removed his gloves while Dr Petty continued with the fingerprinting. 'And puzzling, though you'll be pleased when I tell you that we're reasonably sure the deceased wasn't murdered.'

'It was natural causes?'

'No, Inspector. But also yes. He died of alcohol poisoning. That's what I'll be telling the Coroner.'

'Is that a natural cause?' asked Noble.

'Not officially. But it is if you're a chronic abuser of alcohol and drugs. For this gentleman, ingesting large amounts of very strong spirits would be routine, judging from the condition of his brain. Also, needle-marks on his arms indicate occasional drug abuse. Probably heroin – we'll know for sure after more tests.'

'But he drank himself to death.'

'It looks like it. At first, Dr Petty and I thought alcohol levels were so high that maybe there might have been some element of coercion – nearly 500mg of alcohol per 100ml of blood. No normal person could be drinking at those levels without passing out. But there was no evidence of force in the usual places.'

'Usual places?'

'Specifically the arms and the mouth. If someone were wanting to force-feed alcohol to a person, normal practice would be to restrain their arms and head before forcing the bottle or glass into the mouth. It's very difficult to do and would require multiple assailants.'

'But—'

'But that usually results in cuts and bruising around the gums and mouth, sometimes chipped teeth. Obviously his mouth is not in tip-top shape but there's no sign of such trauma. Coercion would also present distinctive bruising on the arms and neck.'

'But there's none of that.'

'The body has the extensive bruising common to chronic alcoholics; some marks are old, some new – but nothing to indicate restraint.'

'Couldn't the alcohol have been injected?' asked Noble.

'Fresh needle-marks often take longer to present,' said Habib. 'We'll re-examine in a few days to be sure, but it's extremely unlikely because it's far too inefficient as a delivery system for that much alcohol.'

'Do we know what he was drinking?'

'Given the absence of the stomach, liver and kidneys it's difficult to be precise until we do more tests. We will need to slice and dice what's left of the brain for a more detailed analysis of toxins to be absolutely certain. The absence of blood . . .'

'Absence of blood,' repeated Noble.

'There's no clean blood. There was a little in the heart valves but that was clotted, and it would be contaminated. We've got enough for a blood group. And tissue samples should tell us . . .'

'What do you mean there's no clean blood?' asked Brook.

'Oh, forgive me, I thought you knew. This gentleman has undergone some form of post-mortem procedure and is in the first stages of being embalmed.' He walked them back to the body on its stainless-steel table. 'As well as removing all the organs, he was drained of blood. You see these two puncture wounds in the neck? They tapped into his major arteries. It's a common enough procedure for funeral homes. It stops discolouration of the flesh.'

'So we don't have a vampire at large,' quipped Noble.

Habib chortled. 'I'm afraid not.' The diminutive doctor placed a thumb and finger on either side of the cadaver's neck. 'These incisions have been made by a surgical instrument so tubes can be attached. Draining the body of blood would require time and patience and preferably a tank to store the blood.'

Brook nodded. 'So whoever did this might have access to specialist equipment.'

'Well, it's not essential, Inspector. Those preserving bodies in the Ancient World didn't have any. But these days, as well as a large tank to contain the blood, he might also use a pump to help the blood drain. Otherwise things could get a bit messy.'

'Not something that an amateur can do in his bedroom then,' muttered Noble.

'Absolutely not,' answered Habib. 'And strictly speaking he's not an amateur. Whoever performed this procedure possesses a fair amount of anatomical knowledge.' He indicated the large opening on the dead man's flank. The stitching had been removed and, without thinking, Habib pulled the wound open so they could see inside. Noble looked at the ceiling while Brook pursed his lips. 'This incision in his side was made to remove the internal organs and it's quite a skill.'

'Why remove the organs?' asked Noble.

'Well, unless he's making a large haggis,' sniggered Habib, releasing the flaps of flesh on either side of the wound, 'the usual reason is to hinder microbial growth and decomposition. And it is common practice in hospital mortuaries for examination purposes, unless there are religious objections.'

'Just hospitals?' asked Noble.

'There are scientific facilities that use cadavers, medical schools, that sort of thing – they have skilled technicians for such procedures. It's about preservation and, of course, reserving the organs for whatever procedures they might be undertaking.'

Dr Petty walked over to them, removing her face mask and cap. She had short blond hair with tinted highlights. Brook noticed Noble looking at her for longer than necessary.

'Speaking of undertaking . . .' she said to Habib.

'Yes. Undertakers and funeral directors would be more likely in this case.'

'Because it's not clinical,' said Brook, nodding. 'But cosmetic.'

Petty smiled at him. 'Right. Someone has very carefully, almost lovingly, begun the process of preserving his body. If he came to us as a suspicious or unexplained death,' she nodded towards the spread-eagled chest cavity, 'we observe the basics of our profession. We open them up completely for ease of access. It's not pretty but it gets the job done. Equally, if we need to see the brain, we use a skull key and a saw to take off the top of the head. The only reason to remove the organs through this small incision seems to be cosmetic.'

'To leave the torso unblemished.' Brook nodded.

'And this kind of cosmetic consideration is most likely to be found in the funeral service,' said Habib. 'Those gentlemen, and ladies perhaps,' he added with a simper at Dr Petty, 'are charged with bringing the dead back to life, at least while the coffin is open to relatives.'

'That would explain the haircut and shave,' said Brook.

'We noticed that,' said Dr Petty. 'And did you see the fingernails have been scraped and clipped too. Also the body was washed, with an antibacterial agent, possibly alcohol. It's difficult to tell after the body was in the water.'

'Maybe why he was dumped in the river,' observed Noble.

'More than likely.' Petty nodded.

'I hate to bring it up, but is there any sexual angle here?' asked Brook.

'There's no sign of any sexual activity, forced or otherwise,' answered Petty.

'And could the deceased have been through here already and been misplaced?' asked Noble.

'Indeed not,' said Habib sternly. 'We don't lose corpses – our procedures are too thorough. And if we had processed him he would have been cut open from the thorax, as you see.'

'What about the scientific organisations that use dead bodies?' asked Brook.

'I can't speak as to their procedures, Inspector,' replied Habib. 'But they'd only accept intact bodies. And they'd also open up the chest in the traditional manner.'

'So he hasn't been seen by any agency that does official autopsies or post mortems,' concluded Noble, scribbling in his notebook.

'We don't think so,' said Petty. 'Besides, any doctor attending this man could certify COD. But I'm guessing a doctor hasn't seen him or issued a Death Certificate. Being homeless, it's also unlikely the deceased has given informed consent for his body to be left to science.'

'And without consent, a medical school couldn't have his remains,' said Brook.

'Exactly. In the absence of next-of-kin, he would be routinely interred,' said Petty.

'So his death is completely off the books until now.'

'It would seem so.'

Brook rubbed his chin. 'So if the internal organs were removed . . .'

Habib nodded in encouragement. 'The intestines too.'

'. . . the intestines too,' echoed Brook. 'How did you manage to get blood from the heart?'

Habib grinned. 'The heart was put back.'

'Put back?'

'Exactly.'

'Why?'

'No idea.'

'You mean, whoever did this took out the organs and intestines but left the heart in,' suggested Noble.

'No,' said Dr Petty. 'The heart was severed from the arteries and removed with everything else, but some time later it was put back. There were even a couple of rough stitches attaching it to other tissue, presumably to ensure it didn't fall out of the cavity.'

Brook's brow furrowed. 'What condition was it in?'

'Very poor – the same as the brain. If he hadn't died of alcohol poisoning, I suspect his heart would have failed within the year,' said Habib.

'Could someone be farming these bodies for profit?' asked Noble.

'And put back the heart because it was diseased and unusable?' said Petty. 'No chance. Given the condition of both the heart and the brain, I'd say none of the other internal organs would have been suitable for transplant.'

'I see.' Brook prepared to leave.

'There's one more interesting thing, Inspector.' Habib walked over to a stainless-steel sink and picked up a small steel bowl to show Brook and Noble the two small pinkish-grey objects slithering inside. 'This is what's left of the brain. It's in two parts because it's going to be sectioned for analysis. As you can see, it's fatally compressed.'

'Unmistakable,' agreed Brook, glancing sideways at Noble – but for once his Sergeant didn't respond, preferring to stare steadfastly at the white wall behind Habib's head. Now Brook could detect the sheen of sweat on his brow and upper lip. Once, Brook would've felt the same. He looked at his watch. 'John, go and find us both a cup of tea and wait for me in the gallery,' he said nonchalantly. 'I'll finish up here.'

Without speaking, Noble darted a glance at Brook and hurried out of the suite.

Brook turned back to the two doctors, both oblivious to Noble's discomfort. 'Go on.'

'You'll observe the necrosis affecting the brain's tissue. Very damaged and typical of the alcoholic. But look at this.' Habib held the bowl out to Dr Petty and she picked up the two pieces of brain in both hands and turned them over. Habib indicated a series of cuts in the underside. 'If we examine the underside of the brain, we can see the membrane has been punctured several times. Indeed, there has been some slicing of the brain into smaller pieces, some of which are missing.'

'Missing!' exclaimed Brook.

'Now why this was done we can't be sure,' continued Habib.

Brook narrowed his eyes. 'Wait a minute. Pieces of the brain have been removed?'

'Yes.'

'But when we found the body, the skull was intact.'

'It was.'

'Then never mind why. *How* could someone do that to the brain with the skull intact?'

'Good question, Inspector.' Habib and Petty walked Brook back over to the ice-white corpse and pointed to the scarring below the deceased's nostrils. 'We're not sure but we think someone has fashioned a tool, a kind of thin sharp probe a bit like a scalpel only longer and more robust, possibly hooked at the end. When placed inside the nostril at the correct angle, it can be forced up into the brain to puncture the membrane and allow the CSF to drain away.'

'CSF?'

'Cerebrospinal fluid,' chipped in Petty, moving to the far side of the cadaver.

'Sounds painful.'

'Not if you're already dead,' she said, unsure if Brook was being serious. She pointed to the incisions on the upper lip. 'The tool was pushed into the nostrils, causing these cuts as well as invisible scarring inside the nostrils. It would've been pushed up the nose, and forced through the cartilage and finally into the brain propelled by a heavy object such as a hammer . . .'

Brook grimaced and looked around for Noble. He spotted him upstairs in the gallery holding two plastic cups and smoking a cigarette. Despite the reinforced glass screen between the gallery and the lab, Brook felt sure he could smell tobacco smoke.

'. . . and cut into the brain. Then the detached pieces must have been pulled back down through the nose – hence the hook.'

'Nice. And you don't know why, Doctors?'

Petty shrugged. 'If I were starting out in anatomy back in

the Dark Ages, I might puncture the brain like this to see what happened. Otherwise, your guess is as good as mine.'

'And when you say a tool was fashioned, does that mean that such a tool doesn't exist?' asked Brook.

'Why would it?' said Habib. 'We don't need to get to the brain through the nose these days.'

'These days? So such a tool may once have been used?'

Dr Petty nodded. 'Hundreds of years ago. Longer even. Ancient anatomy isn't my field. But if someone wanted to spend hours removing the brain without disturbing the skull, they'd certainly have to create one.' She paused then smiled at him. 'I'll be happy to look into it,' she added.

Brook nodded his thanks and left.

The front gate clattered outside and Becky jumped out of bed, pulling aside the shade on her bedroom window. The postman strode towards the house with a bundle of letters. This was it. She strained to listen and heard her father jump up to collect the mail. She held her breath and continued to listen for any reaction and heard first voices, then footsteps scuffling hurriedly up the stairs. She jumped back into bed. When the knock came on her bedroom door, she pulled the duvet back over her head. Another knock and a muffled conversation followed. Finally the handle turned and her father stuck his head into the gap.

'Becks,' he said softly.

Even without a word said, Becky knew her stepmother, Christy, was with him because the stench of stale tobacco hung in the still air – it followed her everywhere like her own toxic cloud.

Becky tried to affect the noise of sleep and her father made to close the door but his wife's voice stayed his hand. 'It's ten o'clock, for Christ's sake. Wake her up. It's important.' Her father must have hesitated. 'I'm telling you, Fred. She should have been up hours ago.'

'She's tired,' he whispered.

'From what?' replied Christy, raising her voice. 'Opening all the gifts you give her? You spoil that girl, Fred, now wake her up.'

'I'm awake,' said Becky from under the duvet. She sat up, flinging the duvet from her head and glaring at her stepmother with undisguised hatred. 'Happy now? Not that I could sleep with that stale fag ash polluting the air,' she added.

'Watch your tongue in my house, lady,' retorted Christy.

'*Your* house?' snarled Becky, an ugly frown distorting her doll-like features. 'Since when—'

'Stop it, you two.' Her father laughed in the light-hearted manner he affected to bridge the gulf between the two women in his life. He came and sat beside his daughter on the bed. He had an envelope in his hand. He placed it on the bed in front of her, looked expectantly into her eyes then lifted his hand to stroke her hair. 'Aren't you excited, darling? It's finally here.'

Becky flicked a glance towards her stepmother's sour gaze then smiled warmly at her father. She kissed his neck and played with the curl of hair around his ear to further stick it to Christy. 'Course I'm excited, Dad.'

'Open it then, princess. Put us out of our misery.'

Becky thumbed the envelope open and unfolded the letter. Without emotion she handed the letter to her father who read greedily. He stopped, took a deep breath and looked at his daughter.

'Are you going to read it, or what?' asked Christy.

Fred Blake smiled. *'Dear Becky, I am pleased to tell you that we are able to offer you a place at our modelling agency, and would be grateful if you could contact us to arrange a meeting as soon as possible.*

'You did it, princess!' he shouted. 'You did it!' He flung his arms around his daughter and she buried her head in his chest, unable to hold back a tear. 'You're going to be famous, Becks. Can you believe it? My daughter, a fashion model. Rebecca Blake, Supermodel,' he announced, with a portentous wave of the arm. 'You'll be on the telly, maybe in films. You'll meet famous people. You'll go to New York, Paris, Rome . . .'

'I'll be based in London, Dad,' Becky reminded him, grinning.

'Of course.' He laughed.

'But only after I pass my A-levels.'

He grinned again. 'Beautiful *and* smart. You'll knock 'em dead, honey.'

Becky held out her arms for another hug then sneered at her stepmother over his shoulder. The answering smile was sullen.

'Where are all your photos, love?' asked her dad, noticing the bare walls suddenly. 'All your portraits?'

'I thought I'd pack them away for the move to London,' Becky replied after a brief pause.

Her father hesitated then said excitedly, 'You're right. We'd better get organised; you're going to need a whole new wardrobe.'

'So I guess we can kiss goodbye to a holiday this year,' observed Christy, turning for the door.

'Book your holiday,' Becky spat at her. 'The big fashion houses throw clothes at young models for nothing. It's free advertising,' she explained to her father.

'Free advertising,' her father echoed for the benefit of his wife. 'Hear that, Christy?' He gazed back, damp-eyed, at the apple of his eye. 'Your mum would've been so proud.'

Becky returned her head to her father's neck but, unable to keep her eyes from the door, looked up in time to see her stepmother stalking away. She grinned maliciously towards her retreating back.

Brook tapped on the window of the small hatch with his warrant card. The orderly looked up from his tabloid and gave Brook and Noble a steely glare before reluctantly dragging himself to his feet. He was small but powerfully built, despite advanced middle age, and was dressed in white trousers and snug-fitting, white T-shirt which matched his cropped hair and showed off hard, gym-pumped biceps. He barely glanced at them as he slid open the small window.

'What can I do for you, Officers?'

Brook spotted the blue ink of prison on the orderly's gnarled forearms and neck. 'Detective Inspector Brook, Detective Sergeant Noble,' he said, enunciating their ranks a little more distinctly than usual. 'Is your supervisor in?' Brook peered down at his ID badge. 'Danny.'

'Just popped out,' grinned the orderly, exposing a rack of teeth like an elephant's ribcage. 'I'm in charge.'

Brook pulled out the SOCO photograph of the dead man and held it up to Danny's cold blue eyes. 'Do you recognise this man? Social Services think it's possible he stayed here recently.'

The orderly looked briefly before shaking his head. 'Can't say I recognise him.' He glanced back up at Brook. 'You've tried Social Services then.'

'And the Job Centre. Without a name they're completely in the dark. They suggested we try here and the outreach centres.'

Danny nodded, sifting the information. 'That's fine. But we have a policy at Millstone House Shelter. If someone asks for help, we try to give it. We don't ask questions about their background or whether they've been in prison. We don't even ask for a name if they don't want us to know. A hard bed and simple food is all we can give, but we give it willingly.'

'Very commendable,' replied Brook.

'Look, we're not doing the census, buddy,' cut in Noble. 'We just want to know if he stayed here in the last month.'

'And you don't have a name,' said Danny.

'Not yet,' said Brook. He stared back at Danny's lived-in features. 'I think we'd better have a look round. Maybe ask some of your residents.'

'They won't be here for a few hours yet,' said Danny, still pleased to be so obstructive. 'Come back around five when the soup's ready. Fine day like today, they'll all be down at the riverside gardens tucking into a few tinnies.'

'Five o'clock?'

'Sure, if you like wasting your time. Even if you find someone who wants to talk to you, you won't get much sense out of them. Not after tea-time beers. You're better off coming back in the morning.'

Brook nodded. 'You've seen a lot of dead men, have you?'

Danny's grin disappeared. 'Sorry?'

'You didn't turn a hair at the photograph,' chipped in Noble.

Danny looked evenly into Brook's eyes. 'I've seen a few. I used to be in the life. You break into enough derelict houses to doss down, you're gonna find bodies sooner or later – or what's left of 'em. The lost ones. And, natural enough, the wretched and the desperate that come here are sometimes taken unto God in the middle of the night. This isn't a health spa.'

'You're not in the life now,' said Brook.

'Not since Jesus found me in the depths of my depravity and held out His hand to me. Me! No matter what I'd become and what I'd done, He wanted me by His side.'

'And now you do *His* work,' said Brook, making some effort to keep the cynicism from his voice.

'With a song in my heart, Inspector,' replied Danny.

'Praise the Lord,' sneered Noble.

'Noticed anyone else taking an unusual interest in your residents? Besides staff, obviously.'

'In what way?'

'Asking about your guests, where they might go after they leave here, maybe even plying them with alcohol.'

'The only alcohol allowed in here, friend, is already in their bellies when they arrive. And no, no one has been taking an interest in the lost souls who end up here. Except the staff.'

'And Jesus,' said Brook. Danny answered with a fake smile. Brook turned and signalled to Noble to leave.

'I think his name was Tommy. He was here,' said Danny. 'About three, four weeks ago.'

'Tommy?' asked Noble.

Danny turned to leaf through a ledger. 'Tommy Mac, it says here. I assume that's short for something. He was a Scot.'

'Is there a date?' asked Noble.

'April twenty-fifth for two nights.'

'Anything unusual about his visit? Anything happen to him, like maybe he got into an argument with someone?'

Danny shook his head. 'He came. He left. Far as I remember.'

'No one here he managed to aggravate, someone who might bear a grudge?'

'There's always conflict, Inspector. Spend a couple of nights here and you'd be arguing over a discarded tab end with the guy in the next bed. But the one redeeming feature about the demon drink is they rarely remember anything the next day.'

'Do you have CCTV?'

'Some. Thefts and assaults are not unknown.'

'Would you have it for Tommy's visit?'

'Not after three weeks.'

'I'd like a photocopy of the names of all the men who stayed here during those two nights . . .'

'I told you . . .'

'. . . or whatever names they gave. I also want the names of staff on duty while Tommy was here.'

'The staff I can give you. You'll need the director's permission for a list of guests. Not that they left contact numbers. They leave here and they become invisible again, as soon as the door shuts behind them.'

Jake sat on his bed, naked but for a towel round his waist, chatting on MSN with some of his fellow college footballers. They had a big game against Trent Poly at the weekend and his teammates were not shy in telling all their contacts on Facebook how convincingly they were going to win. *Trent Poly r gay*.

'Trent Poly *is* gay,' he said, but declined to correct their grammar online. Jake didn't usually join in such meaningless banter. He didn't see the point. They'd know the result after the match and the endless speculative boasting seemed like a waste of effort – doubly so if they lost. Tonight, however, he was happy to kill time, to be distracted by trivia and he spent another vacant half-hour trying to respond to his teammates' incoherent ramblings.

Kyle's Smiths CD was playing. After fruitlessly searching for Kyle in the dark fields the night before, Jake had returned to pick it up and bring it home. Now he was going to his party. What would Kyle say to him when he opened the door? Track 9 began to play. *Take me out tonight.*

Jake glanced sideways at the DVD-shaped parcel on the bed. *Picnic at Hanging Rock – Special Edition.* He'd bought it earlier today and it was expensive. His mum had wrapped it for him though he wouldn't tell her who it was for in case she mentioned it to his dad. When she'd asked if it was for a girlfriend, he'd let her believe it.

With a heavy heart, he typed in a final inanity, being careful to misspell a couple of words, and logged out of MSN.

Becky's face fell as Kyle opened the door to her. 'Shit. What happened to you, Kylie?'

He smiled weakly at her despite the painful swelling around his face. 'You should see the other guy – not a scratch on him,' he joked.

'But what . . . ?'

'I had a disagreement with Wilson about my sexual orientation.'

'That fat tub of guts. At least you've got a sexual orientation.'

Kyle giggled then winced in pain. 'Don't make me laugh. It hurts.' He ushered her in. Becky couldn't hear music or even a

99

TV. Only Adele was there, sitting on a small sofa with a bottle of untouched WKD in her hand, staring into space. She glanced up at Becky and smiled when she saw the jeans, trainers and sweatshirt, the leather rucksack over her shoulder.

Becky nodded back at her and looked around. 'Geek Boy not here?'

Adele shook her head. 'Not yet. Do you want a drink?'

Becky prepared to refuse, citing her skin as the reason. A model must have beautiful skin. 'Don't see why not.'

Jake stood beneath the streetlight outside Kyle's house. He'd been there nearly five minutes, just watching, wondering what to do. He'd seen no one arrive and no signs of life. There wasn't even the barely muffled pulse of loud music that had greeted his arrival at every other teenage party he'd attended. Maybe Kyle hadn't come home after the previous night's beating. Maybe he was lying out in the fields injured or dead. For the first time in his life, Jake envied people who smoked.

With a deep breath, he approached the glass front door and raised a hand to knock. But instead of knocking, he waited. He couldn't hear anything; no music, no laughter and none of the usual loud screeching and shouting for attention that characterised every other conversation held at such gatherings. It was as quiet as the grave.

He stood frozen, his hand aloft, ready to pound on the door. Finally he lowered his arm and walked around the side of the house where there was a large floor-to-ceiling window. The curtains were drawn but Jake could see movement on the other side so he drew nearer and fixed his eye to a crack in the material. He pulled back and turned away, deep lines of confusion etched on his brow. A second later he walked back down the small drive and set off for home.

Becky stood at the sink in Kyle's kitchen and wiped the last of the talcum powder from her face. When she'd finished, she stared at her reflection in the window. The harsh strip-lighting left no hiding place for all the minor blemishes that others overlooked but she obsessed over. She looked away at once.

The noise of the TV increased as a door opened and Adele came over to put a hand on her shoulder. 'Okay, Becks?'

Becky smiled faintly. 'Always.' She laughed. 'Lamest party ever, right?' Adele smiled back. 'I should text Fern and tell her she got off lightly.' Adele raised an eyebrow but Becky had already realised. 'Right. No phones.'

'Come and watch *Badlands*. You'll like it.'

Eight

Saturday, 21 May

THE NEXT MORNING, BROOK JOGGED up the steps of the entrance to Division Headquarters in St Mary's Wharf, and waited for Noble to swipe his card against the sensor before following his subordinate through the smoked-glass door. Sergeant Harry Hendrickson was on the Duty Desk and spotted DI Brook hurrying by. Hendrickson was in his late fifties and had a face like Sid James on a bad day. He'd never got over being rejected by CID in his distant youth, and a detective as clever as Brook had become the natural focus for his resentment, the more so because Brook wasn't a local man.

Hendrickson sneered as sourly as he dared in Brook's direction, but the senior officer kept his eyes glued firmly to his feet. Noble in turn gave Hendrickson no more than a glance as the pair passed.

'Morning, Detective Sergeant,' bellowed the uniformed officer when Noble didn't acknowledge him.

For once Noble didn't answer or react to the fake bonhomie. Usually he nodded a greeting, played along to keep a foot in both camps as he had with Keith Pullin the other morning. But this was getting out of hand – too many people felt they could be openly hostile and Noble decided it was time to stonewall the backhanded insults aimed at his superior.

Brook pushed through the door that led to the lifts but he ignored them and made for the stairs. At the same moment a lift door opened and Chief Superintendent Mark Charlton stepped out. Brook saw him from the corner of an eye but pretended not to notice and bounded towards the first step.

'Morning, gentlemen,' called Charlton, raising an arm and halting Brook in mid-stride.

'Morning, sir,' said Noble. 'How are you?'

'I'm good.'

Brook turned to face the Chief Super with barely detectable scorn. Noble watched him, wincing in anticipation. *Good at what?* was Brook's usual retort to such a greeting. More often than not it was followed by *Are you American?* Noble saw Brook open his mouth to speak but fortunately the moment passed without comment.

'What news about that floater?' asked Charlton, looking beyond Brook to his destination. Close to regulation minimum height, Charlton was always uncomfortable standing beside two six-footers. 'I've had Brian Burton from the local rag on to me about it. Just an old tramp, I heard.'

Brook raised an eyebrow. 'Even tramps have mothers. Sir.' Charlton and Brook's eyes locked briefly before the Chief Superintendent looked away, tight-lipped.

'You know what I mean, Inspector. The type to get falling-down drunk and end up in the river – the type worth a four-line paragraph on page eleven of the *Derby Telegraph*.'

'There's a little more to it than that,' answered Brook.

'Oh? How so?'

'We're still assessing that, sir,' said Brook. 'It's not suicide and it could yet be murder.'

Noble looked sharply at Brook.

'I see,' said Charlton. He tried to sound authoritative. 'Well, get your paperwork on my desk today and don't waste any more time on it than necessary.'

Brook smiled his reply.

Charlton was on the verge of turning away before finding a riposte to Brook's earlier gibe. 'You know, you glamour boys in CID never really have day-to-day dealings with tramps or the homeless and alcoholic. It's us in uniform that have always had to clean up their mess. The nurse punched and kicked in Casualty. The primary-school kids on their way home lured into a derelict house and sexually assaulted. If you'd seen what I've seen out in the field, you wouldn't think some of these scumbags had mothers.' He glared at Brook only to see that he'd already gone and was sprinting up the stairs.

Back in his office, Brook sipped on the over-sweetened vending-machine tea, aware that Noble was waiting for something.

'Something you want to say, John?' Noble shrugged so Brook asked it for him. 'Why did I tell Charlton it might be murder?'

'That would cover it,' answered Noble.

Brook took a sip of tea. 'Are we certain there was no coercion?'

'Habib and Petty were. And they've seen a lot more of these . . .'

'Tramps?'

Noble shrugged. 'For want of a better word. And we know

the path our corpse was on. He only had another year, according to Habib.'

Brook looked away. 'You're right. But I don't like Brass pushing us to sign off on cases before they're done and dusted.'

'So we're not ready to pass this down the food chain?'

'Not a chance.'

'Because of the planning that went into disposal . . .'

'Not just the way the corpse was dumped, John. The way it was filleted, treated with such care then just discarded in the water seems perverse. Almost as though . . .'

'What?'

'I don't know,' Brook said. 'But I've never seen anything like this. We should give it another couple of days at least.'

'You don't think it's a mortuary mix-up then?'

'You heard Habib. The body wouldn't have been cut that way if it had been through the system.'

'I also heard him say it wasn't murder.' Noble smiled at Brook. 'But I suppose if the Chief Super thinks all bets are still on, we don't get reassigned.'

Brook grinned back guiltily. 'That never occurred to me.'

'Course not.'

'But you're right. Charlton will have us back on fake IDs or, God forbid, break-ins if we sit around twiddling our thumbs.'

'A valuable public service that,' Noble suggested.

'But not our skill-set, John – and the householders of Derby deserve better than to have their cases dumped into our inexperienced hands.'

Noble laughed then looked back at Brook.

'Something else?'

Noble hesitated then said, 'Never mind.'

'No, spit it out. We don't crack cases by suppressing ideas.'

'It's not about the case.'

Brook took a sip of his tea. 'What is it? Come on, let's hear it.'

Noble braced himself. 'Okay. How come you go out of your way to wind up the Chief Super yet put up with all that crap from a nobody like Hendrickson?'

'Hendrickson doesn't like me?' asked Brook innocently.

'You know he doesn't and he's not shy about showing it. And he's not the only one.'

Brook looked into his tea cup. 'Like . . .' He looked up to Noble for help.

'Keith Pullin.'

'To name but one.' Brook nodded.

'That'll be the day.'

Brook grunted in brief amusement. 'Some time ago, Charlton tried to get me to take early retirement and he wasn't subtle about it.'

'Well, you did undermine a case by going to the *Telegraph* behind his back.'

'Two innocent people were being railroaded, John. I couldn't let that happen.'

'And Charlton hasn't forgiven you.'

'I obviously told you all this.' And when Noble laughed without mirth: 'Something funny?'

'You could say,' replied Noble.

'Enlighten me. Come on, let me in on the joke.'

Noble took a sip of tea. 'How long is it since your transfer to Derby, sir?'

Brook looked briefly at the ceiling then back at Noble. 'Six years?'

Noble shook his head in disbelief. 'Eight – it's eight years since you moved up from the Met and eight years we've worked together.'

Brook shrugged. 'If you say so.'

'I do say so. And you ask me whether you told me about Charlton trying to get you off the payroll.'

'And did I?'

'No, you didn't. And if you had, it would have been the first time in those eight years that you told me anything that didn't relate to a case. Everything else, every bit of gossip, every personal detail, I have to drag out of you. Sir.'

There was silence for a moment before Brook cleared his throat. 'I'm sorry. What do you want to know?'

'We could begin with my question about Hendrickson.'

Brook sighed. 'What should I do? Tear a strip off him?'

'It's a start.'

'He never says anything that would look insubordinate on paper.' Brook rubbed a hand on his forehead. 'And frankly, I don't care enough about what he thinks. Or Charlton. Or Pullin. As long as *you're* okay with me, John, I can handle the rest. Or have I misread that situation too?'

'No, you haven't,' said Noble. 'It took a while, mind, and it's only because I work with you day in, day out. I thought the same as everyone else when you first arrived. Toffee-nosed Londoner – you know what, lording it over us yokels.'

'What changed your mind?'

Noble narrowed his eyes in thought. 'Seriously – you have no ego, no agenda. You don't care about the politics or furthering your career.'

'I must care about my career if I resisted early retirement,' reasoned Brook.

'Oh, you care that you have a job to keep you busy, and you

care that it's done properly. But you're not concerned about promotion or getting in the papers or a pat on the back from Brass. The only important thing to you is the case. That's your strength.'

Brook smiled sadly. 'I sense there's a *but* coming.'

'You sure you want to hear this?'

'I'm a big boy, John.'

'Okay. Your strength is also your weakness. You don't care, full stop. You understand the work, the hunt, the detection – but you don't care about the people you work with. That's a weakness in their eyes and it makes your job harder because nobody is willing to put themselves out for you. So you've only got yourself to blame for the contempt people like Hendrickson show you.'

Brook looked up at Noble as though about to object, but he remained silent. Then: 'That sounds like a terrible weakness,' he answered softly.

'It would be unforgivable except for one thing.'

'What's that?'

'The person you care about least is yourself.'

Brook nodded after a few moments of contemplation. 'Thank you for your honesty. I can't argue with any of that. You're right, I tolerate the contempt. It's the price I have to pay.'

'To pay for what?'

Again Brook paused. 'Keeping the blinkers on.'

'What does that mean?'

'You're not making this easy, are you?' Brook took another sip of tea. 'It means that I'm so clueless about all that stuff people do to maintain relationships that it's simpler just to opt out.'

'What stuff?'

'Small talk. Conversations about nothing, feigning an interest where there is none.'

'It's what normal people do to get by, sir.' Noble searched for the right words. 'Is this something to do with your . . . thing?'

'Mental breakdown, John. Never be afraid to use the correct vocabulary.'

'Is it?'

'It was a long time ago.' Brook stood and walked across the room to look out of the window. 'But, yes. Indirectly.'

'How?'

Brook turned to face Noble. 'Keeping control over the things that might threaten my state of mind means excluding distractions.'

'Like remembering people's names.'

'It's not deliberate, Jim.' Brook apologised with a raised hand. 'Not funny. Sorry. But – it's hard to explain. Some days it's like walking along a tiny ledge on a high cliff or across a tightrope strung between tall buildings. You need to concentrate. Always.'

'On what?'

Brook uttered a half-laugh. 'On not concentrating. On weeding out everything I don't need to know.'

Noble nodded thoughtfully. 'So you think if you have a conversation about the weather you might miss your next step on the ledge.'

Brook shrugged. 'Something like that.'

'Then why don't you explain that to—' Noble's mobile phone broke the mood.

'Saved by the Crazy Frog,' said Brook under his breath.

Noble listened intently. 'Where?' He rang off to fix his eyes on Brook. 'Shardlow Gravel Pit. We've got another body.'

'I assume these are manmade,' said Brook, gesturing at the flooded gravel pit.

'So Keith Pullin says.'

'How many are there?'

'A lot,' answered Noble. 'There's a labyrinth of other small roads criss-crossing the site under the A50. They dig out a pit, abandon it and then it floods.'

'CCTV?'

'Only at the main gate. Other access roads like the one behind us might have a barrier which is usually closed at night but they don't lose sleep over gravel thieves. Even locals can get lost in here.'

'Get what CCTV they have and a list of employees just the same. A body dump requires a vehicle.'

Noble nodded then pulled out his cigarettes and put one in his mouth. He held the packet out to Brook, who looked longingly at the contents.

'I've given up, John,' he said unconvincingly.

Noble held the pack steady. 'Help you concentrate. It's a long way down.'

'That it is,' Brook agreed. He took a cigarette and accepted the light from Noble's cupped hand. He coughed up the first life-affirming lungful of smoke with a roll of his eyes to the heavens, oblivious to the late afternoon traffic screaming past on the sunbaked A50 a dozen yards away, hurtling towards Stoke in the west or the M1 and East Midlands Airport to the east.

Brook was broken from his tobacco reverie by the noise of a diver splashing to the surface of the flooded pit some sixty yards away. The diver thrust up a thumb at his partner in the dinghy who turned to start the small winch at the rear of the boat. The thin steel line tightened under its load but gradually began to wind up while the diver in the water put his head under to check progress.

At the water's edge, Keith Pullin kept his eye on proceedings and Brook heard the indecipherable crackle of the radio attached to the breast pocket of his field vest. Pullin leaned into his shoulder to listen.

'Copy that,' said Pullin. For good measure, he raised an arm to his colleague in the boat before turning away from the opaque water to organise a body bag and PVC sheeting from the Support van. He squelched towards Brook and Noble, both standing on higher ground to keep their feet dry.

'Any idea if it's the same MO?' asked Brook, as Pullin passed. 'Keith.'

Pullin looked at Brook with restrained amusement. 'Hard to tell, Inspector. Bob reckons this one's been in a lot longer.'

'Then why isn't the body floating?' asked Noble.

'Maybe it's weighed down.'

'Or maybe it has no organs and intestines,' offered Brook.

'That would nullify a lot of the body gases, aye.' Pullin was impressed, in spite of himself. 'No flies on you, Inspector.'

'There might be when we get the remains ashore,' said Brook, taking another loving puff on his cigarette.

To Brook's surprise, Pullin laughed briefly. 'Good one.' He regained his taciturn expression a second later. 'Either way, we're going to need a butter dish so you'd better suit and boot if you want a peek.'

Brook nodded and took a last pull on his cigarette, ambling back to his car to discard the butt in the ashtray. No sense throwing his DNA to the floor of a potential crime scene.

Noble walked with him. 'This should be fun.' A butter dish was Scene of Crime speak for the heavy-duty body bag, meaning the flesh of the deceased would be yellow and putrid, the fats in the flesh turning to pulp, like rancid butter. In that condition, the skin would peel off easily and any hair could be pulled out with little effort. If the recovery team weren't very careful, vital pieces of evidence from the body could be lost.

Having donned protective coveralls and grim demeanours, Brook and Noble returned to the water's edge. The police diver was back in the boat and his colleague was manoeuvring the large body rescue bag underneath the pale mass held tight against the boat by the winch. They wouldn't risk manhandling the remains aboard if the body's integrity was suspect, especially as shore was only yards away.

'Who found him?' asked Noble.

Pullin jerked a thumb at a car on the access road. In the back seat sat a man, ashen-faced with eyes like dinner plates. 'Angler over there – Peter Fenton, lives in Ambaston. Says he hooked on to something big and when he pulled it up it was a body.'

'He must've thought he'd landed Jaws,' quipped Noble.

'Male or female?'

'He couldn't tell. Says the body was naked except for some kind of loincloth.'

'Loincloth?' said Brook.

'Like what Sumo wrestlers wear to cover their todgers.'

'I know what a loincloth is,' replied Brook, trying to keep the irritation out of his voice.

'Well, that's what the hook caught on,' explained Pullin.

'So that stray piece of material from the Derwent actually could be part of our first MO,' mused Brook.

'Sounds reasonable,' said Noble. 'Where's Fenton's rod and tackle?'

'He dropped it,' answered Pullin. 'Shock, I suppose. If it's not still attached to the cloth it'll be at the bottom of the pit.'

'And there are fish in there?' said Noble.

Pullin shrugged. 'I guess. Doesn't matter to fishermen. They're all nuts.'

The boat's engine noise deepened as the dinghy set off at a leisurely speed towards the bank. The sun was starting its descent towards the horizon and Brook looked at his watch and then at Noble. 'Better get a statement from Mr Fenton.'

Noble turned to Brook with a quizzical glance. 'Will you be okay?'

'I'll be fine,' said Brook with a tight smile. One of the Scene of Crime Officers tapped Brook on the arm and handed him a small tub of Mentholatum ointment. Brook stared at the jar then dipped a finger and smeared some below each nostril. 'Ask him for any names of other anglers he knows who like to fish here. Maybe someone saw the body being dumped or at least noticed someone suspicious who didn't belong. Then get on to the station and see if an ID for our Derwent body has come through; also tell Forensics to make the cloth we found in the river a priority. Unless it's a monogrammed towel, they probably won't get much from it, but at least we now know it could be significant.' Noble nodded and turned to leave. 'And John. Get on to DS Gadd, Morton and Cooper as well. Tell them to clear the decks. We meet in my office in two hours.'

Noble caught Brook's eye briefly. They exchanged a nod. He could see his DI had that feeling again. It was the dread he got when something big and nasty fell into their lap.

While he waited for Noble, Gadd and the others, Brook sat at his desk with his hands cupped under his chin. He stared at his monitor showing the Google map of the terrain east of Derby, the dumping ground of both corpses. He would have booked one of the smaller Incident Rooms for the briefing with its large, detailed map of Derby, but didn't want Chief Superintendent Charlton to get wind that he was scaling up an inquiry into a pair of deaths that hadn't yet been declared murders.

Noble entered the office and pinned a few grisly photographs to the display board before sitting down on the one available chair. Detective Sergeants Jane Gadd, Rob Morton and Detective Constable Dave Cooper followed, carrying their own chairs.

Brook looked at his watch and addressed his fellow officers. 'We're all here. Sorry we're briefing on a Saturday night, but there it is.' Gadd and Morton raised their eyebrows at Noble. Apologies from Brook were rare. Noble raised his eyebrows back at them as though it were the most natural thing in the world. 'I want this inquiry up and running first thing tomorrow morning as we may only have a couple of days on this.'

'Sunday morning!' exclaimed Gadd, before she could stop herself. 'No problem,' she added quickly.

'Good. John, how much does everyone know?'

'Only that we found a body in the Derwent. And now another in Shardlow.'

'They're connected?' said Rob Morton.

'They are,' Brook replied tersely. A vision flashed across his mind of soft wrinkled flesh parting like a dismembered jellyfish less than two hours ago. He would never forget the noise as the wound in the dead man's side had been pulled open and the heart, though roughly attached to tissue in the cavity, had rolled out on to the plastic sheet. 'It's the same MO.'

'So we have a serial killer on the loose,' said Cooper, trying not to sound pleased.

'Hold that thought, Constable,' retorted Brook, before gesturing to Noble, who produced his notebook to begin the briefing.

'We've got an ID on the first body, a vagrant found in the River Derwent on Thursday morning, east of the Borrowash Bridge.'

'That's a long way from spare change,' said Morton.

'He wasn't there by choice,' said Brook. 'He was already dead when he was dumped in the water, almost certainly from that same bridge in the early hours of Tuesday the seventeenth.'

'When the road was closed?' said Jane Gadd.

'Correct.' Noble pointed to the head shot of the deceased. 'Tommy McTiernan was from Aberdeen. He was fifty-five years old and had convictions for vagrancy, theft, aggravated assault, drunk and disorderly and a string of other offences which led to a grand total of nine years inside, served at various times and institutions. He has no family and no fixed abode.

'Why he was in Derby we don't know, but we do know he was in the city as recently as three weeks ago because he signed into Millstone House Hostel on the twenty-fifth of April and spent a couple of nights there. We checked with the director. He's sending us whatever information he's got on other residents staying on the same nights. There's no CCTV for the time Tommy was there but as far as we're aware, nothing untoward happened while he was at the Shelter. The few staff there are low paid but dedicated to their work. One of those, Daniel O'Shea, has convictions for affray and GBH, but that was twenty years ago – before he found Jesus,' he added.

'McTiernan's movements after leaving the Hostel are unknown until we found him in the Derwent. Fortunately the body was caught on a fallen tree or it would have been further downriver. Even so, it wasn't spotted for a couple of days until two lads saw it from the bridge and went to investigate. The body was naked although we now think McTiernan may originally have been wearing some kind of cloth to cover his genitalia, because a piece of material was recovered nearby and our second body found yesterday was similarly dressed.'

Noble looked up to shake out any questions then continued. 'You won't be surprised to hear that Forensics don't have a lot to go on after immersion. However, Tommy McTiernan's corpse had undergone an unusual . . .' He paused, looking for the right word before glancing at his superior for vocabulary.

'Procedure,' finished Brook.

'Procedure,' echoed Noble. 'McTiernan's body was drained of blood and his internal organs and intestines had been removed.'

'Not while he was alive?' asked Gadd.

'No. McTiernan was already dead. He died of alcohol poisoning.'

Gadd's face clouded over. 'Alcohol poisoning? That's usually self-inflicted.'

Noble looked at Brook then back at DS Gadd. 'Yes.'

'So he wasn't murdered?'

'Probably not,' replied Brook softly. He paused to look across at Jane Gadd, wondering if she was going to ask why five CID officers were about to spend their weekend on this. It was a legitimate question but she'd clearly decided against it.

Noble continued. 'Shortly after death, Tommy's organs were removed and, we assume, whoever removed them began the process of preparing his body for embalming. His hair was cut, he was shaved, his nails were clipped and the body was washed and treated with chemicals.'

'So if he wasn't murdered, McTiernan's disposal is what? A DIY burial gone wrong?' asked Morton. 'Or a funeral home mix-up, maybe.'

'It has been known, especially where there's no next-of-kin to claim the body, or kick up a fuss,' continued Noble. 'Given the nature of the procedure, we're fairly sure McTiernan hasn't been in the state system and hasn't had an official post mortem. But right now we don't know.'

'There was a case in Colchester five or six years ago,' said Cooper. 'A trainee undertaker sent the wrong number of corpses for cremation and before he knew it, he had a spare stiff on his hands. Rather than fess up to his boss and risk the can, he panicked and buried it in a field.'

Noble winced, awaiting the inevitable.

'Fess up?' queried Brook. 'Are you American, Detective Constable?'

'Sorry, sir,' replied Cooper with a sheepish grin. 'I pick up all sorts of slang from the kids.'

'Do you?' said Brook, unmoved. But a second later he smiled after a sudden inspiration. 'How *are* the kids?'

Cooper's mouth fell open. 'Erm, they're fine. Sir.'

'Good. Glad to hear it, er . . . Dave. You must bring in some pictures some time.' Brook caught the amused glance from Noble, who quickly returned his eyes to his notebook.

'The funeral home angle isn't a bad one,' continued Noble, 'because of the degree of cosmetic care. And we will look into the possibility of a mix-up tomorrow, but there are problems with that theory. Whoever dumped the body went to the trouble of stealing bollards and at least one *Road Closed* sign to block access to traffic either side of the bridge. Only when the road was closed did he tip the body in the water.'

'Pretty cool-headed,' agreed Cooper. 'Seems to point away from a random undertaker panicking.'

'And the fact that we now have a second body, as yet unidentified, but in similar condition, would seem to confirm that,' said Brook. 'So tomorrow we're going to get on the phone and talk to all the funeral directors in the surrounding area. We don't have time to visit face to face yet, and they may be closed on a Sunday, but if we ring them, they're likely to have an answering service to redirect calls or provide a contact number so they don't lose business. Speak to them at home if necessary and if you have a website, follow up with an email.'

'You're not expecting them to admit they've dumped bodies illegally.'

'Course not,' said Brook, 'but use your experience. Shortlist any firm that reacts badly to the question or rings any alarm bells with you at all. The other information we want is the name of any disgruntled employee, past or present, who has caused problems, particularly with regard to their attitude to the corpses.'

'Such as?'

'Whoever performed this procedure has specialist know-ledge and may have been in the industry. So we want names of anybody they consider took a morbid interest in the preparation of remains, that sort of thing,' explained Brook. 'Maybe someone's had to be sacked recently because they had some sick hang-up or acted inappropriately in some way. I'm sure I don't need to spell it out. Get names and addresses for follow-up on Monday. And the name of anyone who lives east of Derby, where the bodies were dumped, goes to the top of the list.'

Gadd, Morton and Cooper scribbled down their questions.

'Do we think there's a sexual motive?' asked Gadd.

'Not at this time,' said Noble.

'Anything else we need to know?' asked Rob Morton.

'Two things,' said Brook, looking at Noble. 'Although McTiernan's internal organs were removed, the heart was replaced and stitched back into the body cavity. Why, we don't know. Secondly, the brain had been attacked and cut up using a homemade tool which was inserted up the nose and into the cavity.' Brook watched his team cringe. 'Pieces of brain were then removed via the nostrils, we assume using some kind of sharp hook on the tool.'

'Jesus,' said Morton. 'Why?'

'We don't know, though removing the brain with all the other organs reduces decomposition and improves the embalmer's chances for successful preservation.'

'So if you do get a lead on a suspect ex-employee, find out what it was they did to the bodies, without revealing that MO,' said Noble. 'We keep that to ourselves to weed out the cranks.'

'The Embalmer,' nodded Cooper, pleased with himself. 'Catchy.'

*

Brook drove home late to Hartington and was tempted into the garden to drink in the early summer air and a small glass of Aberlour malt whisky. As he settled on to the bench, a jet-black cat dropped from the drystone wall on one side of his small sheltered garden. It bounded up to Brook and threw itself at his feet, wriggling around his ankles until Brook gave it the required attention. 'I've nothing for you, Basil, sorry,' he said, scratching the cat's neck. 'Or me,' he added, feeling his stomach rumble.

After ten minutes without provisions, Basil stalked away to resume his nightly rounds and Brook trudged indoors after he'd drained his drink. He yearned for a cigarette and resolved to buy some at the earliest opportunity. Noble was right. Cigarettes were Brook's only weakness and it was stupid, if not impossible, to impose rigid control over every aspect of his life. Without an Achilles heel, Brook wasn't human but a robot, unable to function, unable to do his work. Being a detective was not just a job to Brook, more a calling, a calling that required him to know about weakness – and if he tried to eradicate his own, how could he understand those of the murderers, armed robbers and rapists he was employed to catch?

Back in his kitchen, he opened the fridge. It was empty except for the half-eaten baked potato he'd picked at the previous night – and the night before that, he seemed to remember. It was going black. He tipped it into the bin and rummaged around the cupboards. He hadn't eaten for a day, by dint of neglect rather than choice, and he knew he needed fuel to keep going.

The cupboard was bare. Not even tins. But there was a

bottle of ketchup, a packet of tomato Cup-a-Soups and an egg carton with two eggs left. Brook fried the eggs and dabbed the yolks with ketchup then ate them mechanically before hauling himself up to his bedroom.

As he climbed into bed, he had a flashback of the pale yellow carcass from Shardlow Gravel Pit lying at his feet that same day. He shook the memory away. It wouldn't be wise to go to sleep with such an image seared into his consciousness.

He fell asleep but, as usual, he couldn't sleep past the early hours and after his first cup of tea, he dressed and drove back into the station as the sun was coming up.

Slumped at his desk just after seven, Brook found the list of funeral directors he'd compiled the other day. There were close to fifty. For something to do he began dividing the company names and phone numbers on to five separate pieces of paper.

Nine

Sunday, 22 May

A COUPLE OF HOURS LATER, Brook trudged out into the corridor and down to the ground floor to buy a vending-machine tea. After feeding coins into the machine, he plucked the too-thin cup from the service-hatch to the sound of raised voices. He wandered towards the duty desk for a better look.

Sergeant Gordon Grey, a close friend of Harry Hendrickson, with two years until retirement, was at the counter, trying to placate a nervous but not unattractive woman of about forty. She had clearly been crying, and was preparing to do so again. Behind her was a short overweight man, sporting a shock of combed-over grey hair and voluminous sideburns, which Brook assumed were a misguided attempt to hide his sagging jowls. He was at least fifteen years older than his female companion and, in addition to his dubious coiffeur, he'd made a pitiful attempt to dress young. The white training shoes and baggy blue tracksuit would have looked ridiculous on a man twenty years his junior.

'I've told you. His bed's not been slept in and Kyle would

never leave without telling me where he's gone,' pleaded the woman. 'You have to believe me.'

'Mrs . . .'

'. . . Kennedy.'

'Mrs Kennedy, it's Sunday morning and there'll be plenty of eighteen year olds waking up in strange beds or on friends' sofas. I'm sure your son Kyle will turn up soon enough – probably with a limp and a hangover, eh Len?' Sergeant Grey grinned knowingly at the man with the comb-over, who was affectionately rubbing Mrs Kennedy's upper arms.

'Steady on, Gordon,' said the man identified as Len.

Mrs Kennedy stared at Grey in confusion until the penny dropped. 'He doesn't behave like that,' she replied tersely. 'You have to do something.' She tilted her head towards her companion. 'We should never have gone away.'

The old man leaned into her for comfort. 'It's okay, Alice,' he said. 'There must be a simple explanation. We'll find him.'

'Of course you will,' said Grey soothingly. 'He'll turn up. Have you tried ringing him?'

The man gave Grey a patronising glare but declined to follow up with sarcasm.

'He hasn't got his phone with him,' said Mrs Kennedy. 'It's turned off and sitting on his bed. If you have kids, you must know how strange that is.'

'But if he's eighteen, he can look after himself.'

'No, he can't,' replied Mrs Kennedy, her face beginning to quiver. She pulled a tissue from her handbag.

'He's only just eighteen,' said Len. 'And he's . . . the sensitive type, if you know what I mean.'

'Len!' snapped the woman. She gathered herself together

and addressed the Sergeant. 'Are you going to take details or not?'

Sergeant Grey reluctantly picked up a pen. 'When did you last see him?'

'He was in his bedroom on Friday afternoon before we set off for Wales,' answered Mrs Kennedy. 'Later, he was having a few friends round for his birthday and—'

'Friday afternoon?' Sergeant Grey's manner took on a sterner hue.

'About three,' she confirmed, unaware of the change in Grey's demeanour.

Grey spoke slowly for emphasis. 'So his bed has not been slept in for two nights, after a party.' He put down the pen to address the man. 'Look, Len, you know the format. If I take details, they have to be entered on the National Computer and then eventually the National Missing Persons database. Then there's an automatic risk assessment. That will trigger man hours looking for a young man, *a student*, who's not slept in his bed for two nights after a party.'

Poole shrugged and gestured towards Alice behind her back. 'His mother is worried, Gordon. There must be something you can do.'

Grey sighed heavily. 'You're not making this very easy.' His face lit up for a second. 'Does he have any serious medical issues? That would justify a report.'

Mrs Kennedy shook her head. 'No.'

'Any sign of violence or a struggle at your home?'

'There's a sticking plaster in the bin with a little blood on.'

'How much blood?'

'About half an inch in the middle.'

Grey chuckled and threw his palms up. 'Then maybe he

grazed his knee. I'm sorry, but I'd have a job to classify Kyle as even low risk.' He gave the woman a pointed look to ensure she'd got the message. 'Look – go home. He's probably there waiting for you to feed him. I'll notify the local nick and have a word with the hospitals, unofficial like, to keep an eye out for him. If he's not back after the weekend, give us another ring and we'll start the process. Fair enough?'

Len nodded his understanding and guided the tight-lipped woman towards the entrance. She turned back suddenly and pulled something from her handbag, unfolded it and placed it on the counter. 'This was on his bed with his phone.'

Brook had heard enough and was preparing to return to his office when the grey-haired man looked up at him. To his surprise, the man nodded at him.

'Inspector,' he said stiffly.

Brook nodded back. 'Hello,' he replied, for once remembering to omit the pause for a name he didn't know. He looked again. He did vaguely recognise the man now but couldn't place him. After the couple left, Brook sauntered over to the counter.

Sergeant Grey stiffened in the effort to suppress his hostility. 'Inspector. Didn't see you there.'

'Who was that man, Sergeant?'

'Len Poole? He used to be the Chief Pathologist at the old Derby City Hospital. Before that Pa—' Grey pulled himself up quickly. 'Before that Asian guy took over.'

Brook looked into Grey's eyes and gave him a lingering stare. Finally he said softly, 'Dr Habib. And he's Indian.'

Grey pulled a face that said *what's the difference?* but managed to keep his reply neutral. 'That's him. Len married into decent money and retired early. His wife was a bit of a looker. No accounting for taste, I say. I heard she died a couple of years ago. He seems to have found a replacement though, eh?' Grey laughed suggestively but Brook didn't accept the invitation for man talk.

Instead he sipped his tea and raided his memory banks. Len Poole. He could place him now, though he hadn't known him well. They'd only worked a couple of cases together during Brook's first months in Derby and before Poole had left his job. He hadn't been invited to the retirement dinner.

He picked up the small leaflet left by Mrs Kennedy and absent-mindedly wandered off reading it. Grey smiled maliciously at Brook's back and picked up his pen.

Brook pulled the small A5 leaflet towards him and turned to his computer. It was very simple text on colour and could have been designed and produced on any PC. The few words were in red lettering on a black background.

DEITY

Take Control
Live Forever
Young
Beautiful
Immortal

At the bottom of the page was a website address. Brook typed in the address. The website was closed for refurbishment.

Several hours later Brook put down the phone and looked around the small Incident Room at his colleagues, either cradling phones under their ears or drawing lines through their list. He looked at his own defaced list. Not one disgruntled undertaker arousing suspicion or given the sack. It seemed staff turnover in the industry was very low because of the unique nature of the skills required for their work. Employees were invariably committed to the profession for life. Everyone in the funeral business knew everyone else, and no one Brook had spoken to had experienced the kind of difficulties which might sound alarm bells. From the looks on the faces of his team, they were encountering the same story.

He stepped past the bank of computers and checked there was water in the kettle that Rob Morton had had the foresight to bring in, as well as a jar of instant coffee and two pints of milk. He switched the kettle on and looked at his watch. It was nearly eleven on a bright warm Sunday morning.

Brook made coffee for everyone and walked over to look at the large map that nearly filled one wall. He stared at the bridge in Borrowash then at the approximate location of Shardlow gravel pit – approximate because many of the flooded pits were not on the map, having been dug out after the map was published.

The land between Derby and the M1 was flat and wet. Broken ground was home to two rivers as well as the many manmade lakes and waterways created by the extraction of building materials – an excellent place to hide the dead.

Brook took a sip of his coffee, again recalling the image of the body from the gravel pit – the swollen face, the pale buttery flesh. But even before the incision in the flank had been located, Brook had known this was the same MO. He knew enough forensics to realise that a body with organs intact should have been bloated from the decomposition gases but this . . . vacant vessel, this receptacle of some mother's hopes and dreams . . . had been exsanguinated and efficiently gutted like a pig at the abattoir.

'Penny for them,' said Noble, at Brook's shoulder.

'Stick it in your pension, John. I can't get a handle on this at all.'

'I know what you mean. Seems like we've only got half a crime here.'

'Exactly that. We've got one dumped body that hasn't been killed. And now a second that presents as the same MO. So what's the motive?'

'Maybe Habib and Petty got it wrong. Maybe McTiernan was forced to drink himself to death. That would make it murder.'

'It still doesn't get us a motive.'

'Some grudge against the less fortunate,' shrugged Noble. 'There could be a million reasons. Maybe one of Charlton's sexually assaulted schoolkids is finally getting even. Or maybe it's a necrophiliac with a thing for black-toothed vagrants.' He smiled. 'Motives aren't always obvious with a nut job.'

'Nut job,' repeated Brook with distaste.

'Or maybe Habib's right. Maybe someone's making haggis with human offal.'

'And black pudding with the blood,' added Brook. 'A psychotic butcher with a taste for human flesh – don't think I didn't consider it, John. But if someone has the privacy to do this, and the skills to process body parts so efficiently, they wouldn't need to risk dumping the bodies where they can be found.'

'So why dump the bodies at all, you mean?'

'More questions than answers at this stage.'

'Maybe our guy likes the adrenalin rush, people knowing what he's doing. That way he creates a climate of fear. He scares the public and feeds on that.'

Brook shook his head. 'Who's going to be scared? No one paid any attention to McTiernan. As Charlton said, this is page eleven stuff.'

'The second body might change things.'

'Not if it's another . . .' Brook cast around for a suitable word.

'Tramp,' offered Noble. 'Don't be afraid to use correct vocabulary. Sir.'

Brook smiled at being admonished by his own words. 'No one will worry about these *tramps* turning up dead. No one cared about the prostitutes the Yorkshire Ripper slaughtered until he killed that poor shop assistant.'

'So he's daring us to care.'

'Care? John, you're missing the point. If he didn't dump the remains we wouldn't even know they were missing.'

'So he's dumping the bodies to draw attention.'

'To find an audience, yes.'

'He's succeeding.'

'I know,' said Brook, rubbing his chin. 'But I don't think it's our attention he's after.'

'Why do you say that?'

'Because we don't understand what he's doing – but somebody out there does. And that's who he's doing this for.'

DS Gadd and DC Cooper walked over to join Brook and Noble. Cooper took a sip of his coffee and shook his head at Noble. 'Nada. I've spoken to Nottingham University Medical School. He's not theirs. And with a necrotic liver and chronic heart disease, Tommy McTiernan's physical condition put him near the bottom of every wish-list. There's very little demand for his body or his organs, even if they obtained consent – not for transplant, nor for research.'

'Same here,' said Gadd. 'Unwanted in life. Unwanted in death.'

'Somebody wanted him, Jane,' said Noble. 'And if we draw a blank on the phones it's looking more likely that McTiernan's body hasn't been stolen and hasn't been misplaced.' Noble's mobile phone began to croak and he moved away to answer it.

'Then how did our doer find Tommy?' asked Cooper.

'How do you find all the Tommys?' said Brook. 'You look on the streets.'

'You think someone's roaming the city looking for victims and just took him,' said Cooper.

'It's starting to look that way,' said Brook.

'Alive?'

'That would be easier than finding and transporting corpses,' replied Brook.

'Unless someone's tipping him off about fresh bodies. A doctor maybe,' said Cooper.

'What's in it for a doctor?' asked Gadd.

'All right, an ambulanceman then,' retorted Cooper.

'Same question.'

'I don't know, Jane. Money?'

'No chance,' replied Gadd. 'Besides, these tramps usually die in public, in a hostel, on the streets, in shop doorways, so we'd know about them first. Or they die in the back room of some squat and don't get found for weeks, maybe even months. The Embalmer's taking them alive. McTiernan was fresh.'

Cooper nodded. 'I suppose just picking them up and offering them a bed and a meal would be the easiest thing in the world.'

'And when he's got them where he wants them, he feeds them as much drink as they want and waits for the inevitable,' said Gadd.

'Patient man.'

'Maybe he's helping things along,' replied Brook. 'It's hard to say. But if he has all this privacy, once he's got them, he can do what he likes and he can take his time. Who would miss Tommy – a homeless man with no family? And even if McTiernan has friends on the street, his disappearance wouldn't be unusual. He's invisible, even to them.' Brook paused, deep in thought. 'That's the life.'

'He'd need an awful lot of privacy – and space.'

'Somewhere remote,' said Brook, moving back to the map.

'So how do we catch him, sir? And what do we charge him with? Littering?'

Brook smiled, then looked down at his misshapen sweater and shabby trousers. He turned to each member of his team in turn and looked at their smart casual clothes. 'Maybe we need a presence on the streets.'

Noble finished speaking on his mobile but continued writing in his notebook. 'That was Don Crump from the lab. The Forensics paperwork won't be done until tomorrow but he's given me the heads-up. The traffic cones are clean – no prints at all, not even legitimate workmen. Also, Tommy had been drinking whisky in industrial quantities.'

'Blended or malt?' asked Rob Morton.

'I didn't ask,' replied Noble.

At that moment, the door to the Incident Room opened and Chief Superintendent Charlton walked in holding a polystyrene coffee cup. He was dressed in a light grey suit with a white shirt and dark blue tie. There was silence. Charlton was rarely to be seen on a Sunday. Like a naughty schoolboy, Rob Morton removed a cigarette from behind his ear and put it in his pocket.

'Morning, everyone. Didn't mean to interrupt. I was on my way to church but as I didn't get my paperwork I thought I'd better come and see what was going on. Pretend I'm not here.' He shuffled towards the back of the room and on his way, the man who wasn't there caught Brook's eye for a few seconds. 'Carry on,' he beamed at Noble, sitting on a table to listen.

'Yes, sir. I was just going through some forensics about our floaters,' he explained to Charlton.

'I heard the second body wasn't exactly floating,' retorted Charlton without expression.

'No, sir.' Noble looked back at his notes. 'The cloth recovered from the Derwent looks like it was worn by McTiernan, probably as some kind of loincloth because the second body wore an identical piece of material. They're running tests on the Shardlow cloth now. The Derwent cloth is made of Egyptian cotton, nothing unusual about it though it did carry traces of the same make-up used on Tommy's face, as well as disinfectant, and we know the body was washed before being dumped. There were also minute traces of arsenic. No suggestion that McTiernan was poisoned though. It's probably from some cream applied to the . . . er, deceased.'

Noble looked at Brook then Charlton before continuing.

'The stitching in the wound was a shoelace. Also Egyptian cotton . . .'

'Maybe the killer works at Dunelm Mill,' said Charlton drily.

'Sir?' enquired Noble.

'It's a fabric warehouse,' muttered Gadd, tight-lipped, aware that Charlton's presence wasn't a good sign.

'Every time my wife goes to Dunelm she comes back with more cushions and another bloody duvet cover,' added Morton, smiling. Gadd elbowed him discreetly in the side.

'Any news on the murder weapon, Detective Sergeant?' asked Charlton. Noble didn't reply. Brook managed a private smile but also kept his eyes on the floor. 'Oh, hang on. There isn't one, is there? Because this isn't a murder inquiry.' Nobody spoke or looked in Charlton's direction and the Chief Superintendent let the silence fester for a few moments. 'Can you all leave the *Incident* Room for a moment, please? I'd like a word with DI Brook.'

Brook remained motionless as the rest of his team slowly gathered themselves and left in silence. Noble fired an enquiring glance at Brook as he closed the door, but Brook motioned him to leave.

'What are you doing, Brook?'

'Conducting an inquiry, sir.'

'I see. You've tied up five detectives on a Sunday just to investigate the death of an indigent who drank himself to death, according to Dr Habib.' Brook looked up at Charlton finally. 'Yes, that's right, Inspector – the post mortem results have come in. In fact, you knew the results when you spoke to me before.' Charlton glared at Brook, certain of his ground. 'Didn't you?'

'Yes, sir.'

'Did you see my email about the budget cuts?'

Brook paused. 'I saw it.'

'Then I'll ask you again. What are you doing committing so many resources to this? God alone knows what the overtime bill will be.'

Brook looked Charlton in the eye. *Why don't you ask Him when you get to church?* 'But now we have a second body, sir.'

'Murdered?' Brook said nothing. Charlton nodded. 'You don't know yet.' The Chief Superintendent paused, hoping to increase the pressure. 'I like to run a tight ship, Inspector, but with these swingeing cuts, I need people who are team players, people who play with a straight bat. What I don't need are cowboys.'

'You're right, sir,' said Brook quickly. 'I've been working too hard. It's affected my judgement. I'm sorry.'

Charlton was wrong-footed, the wind taken from his sails. His facial expression softened with vindication but inside, the disappointment of an opportunity lost was palpable. 'Well, I dare say you made the call as you saw fit.' His features darkened again. 'But I won't tolerate being lied to, especially in front of subordinates,' he continued, with a nod to Noble outside the door.

'Of course not,' said Brook, now the model of contrition. 'That was unforgivable.' Charlton examined Brook's face long and hard for any sign of insincerity. 'Perhaps I should take a few days off, sir. I've got plenty of leave owing.'

Charlton continued to stare Brook down, not wanting to be rushed. He couldn't escape the feeling that in some way he was being outflanked, but he didn't know how. Eventually he sat back and looked at the table. 'You don't like me very much, do you, Brook?'

Brook couldn't hide his surprise. 'Sir?'

'No, don't bother. I already know. I'm a bean counter, aren't I? And you're a force of pure detection, a seeker of justice.'

'Sir, I don't —'

Charlton held up a hand. 'It doesn't matter, Inspector. That's my job. I expect to be disliked. If I wasn't disliked, I wouldn't be doing my job properly. And if I wasn't doing it properly, you couldn't do yours. But you probably don't accept that, do you?'

Brook remained silent.

'And though we had a few problems a couple of years ago, I had hoped that we could have moved forward.'

Brook looked down into Charlton's face, this time with the feeling that *he* was being outflanked.

'You see, Brook, I'll be honest. I can't do what you do. I can't find the bad guy who doesn't want to be found. I don't have your skills. But by the same token, you can't do what I do. Clear the decks and sign the cheques, as my old Chief Constable used to say. Someone has to do it.' He paused. 'Look, you don't need to go on leave – and I no longer want you to resign. I made a mistake suggesting it. And one thing I learned from our . . . difference of opinion was – well, I know you have integrity. Briefing the press behind my back . . . you did the wrong thing but for reasons you believed were valid, and I should've acknowledged that.'

'Sir, I —'

'Forget it. Get your team back in here and finish the briefing. If you think this incident has mileage, I'll back you.

But I want to be kept in the loop. If you withhold information from me again, I'll bury you.'

Charlton stood with his untouched coffee and stalked away.

'Chief Superintendent.' Charlton turned at the door. 'Thank you,' said Brook. 'But I do have something I need to do. Three days' leave should cover it.'

Charlton nodded and walked out.

Ten

Wednesday 25 May

DI DAMEN BROOK STOOD IN the gutter looking up at the heavens. If he'd been at home, in his cottage garden, he could have picked out odd stars and constellations, but in the neon glare of the city his vision was impaired. He straightened his stiff neck with some discomfort and massaged it with his grubby hand. He'd never take his soft pillow for granted again.

Scratching at his three-day beard, he resumed his weary trudge through the centre of Derby, feeling the earlier rain still squelching in his shoes. As he shuffled through the darkened shopping precincts, he closed his eyes for long periods to relieve the sting of broken sleep on his pupils – broken by the cold, broken by the noise of others snoring or swearing or just gibbering senselessly, broken by a rat on that one occasion he'd tried to spend a night in a squat.

His mobile phone vibrated in a pocket and he fumbled through his different layers to open it, looking around furtively to see he wasn't being observed. Cheap though the phone was, a tramp talking on a mobile was an incongruous sight as well as an easy target for muggers.

Brook didn't look at the display. Only Noble had the number. 'You're up late. Where were you tonight? You missed our meeting and I missed my burger.'

'Sorry, sir. I've been busy on another case. I've also spoken to Dr Habib.'

'I'm listening.'

'We got prints from the second body and we've got a name. Barry Kirk – originally from Carlisle. He disappeared off the radar ten years ago when his business and marriage failed. There were all the signs that he was living rough since dropping out of sight – various minor convictions around the country, D and D, vagrancy, you know the routine.'

'And what about cause of death?'

'Same. Habib says alcohol poisoning but they'll need to run more tests. Parts of the brain were missing again as well as the organs.'

Brook saw a figure stir to look at him from a nearby doorway and moved further away.

'And there's been a development in another of your cases. I need to go over . . .'

Brook saw the man in the doorway looking at him and switched the phone to his other ear. 'John, I can't talk for long. But I'm not coming in for a few hours yet. I got a tip from a new face at Millstone House. Somebody at check-in this afternoon knew McTiernan and it seems Tommy was raving about some squat on Leopold Street.'

'Official?'

'No, it's just a derelict but this guy at the refuge, Mitch, says he can't wait to get back there tomorrow. It seems there's someone pretending to be from some agency calling round to drop off bottles of whisky.'

'Whisky? No agency does that.'

'Exactly. I'm going to check it out now.'

'Want some back-up?'

'That won't help. Speak soon. Wait, John. What did you have to eat tonight?'

'Er . . . Chicken Madras, why?'

Brook ran his lower lip under his teeth. 'Just wanted to know.'

He ended the call and put the phone on silent then squelched up St Peter's Street, past Waterstone's and the small clock-tower which showed two o'clock in the morning. The temperature had dropped and the cold hand of night was beginning to grip. Brook pulled his flimsy overcoat up round his neck, burrowed his hands deeper into his too-thin pockets then quickened his walk to get the blood moving. First order of business after he took a bath – get some decent boots, assuming his feet hadn't already rotted away to stumps. He pulled out a damp handkerchief and sneezed mightily into the cloth. An inquisitive dog popped its head out of a shapeless pile of blankets in a shop doorway and monitored Brook's laboured progress with a smooth turn of the head.

'Good dog,' breathed Brook as he walked on. The dog, placated, yawned and burrowed back down towards the heat of its owner.

Brook ran the back of his hand across his nose. All he needed – living rough with a cold. He came to a decision. He was exhausted. He couldn't take another night. This would be his last. The previous two had been fruitless – fruitless, that is, if you excluded the insights he'd gained into a life without a home. Three days and two nights on the streets, and so much about the behaviour and condition of the dispossessed had begun to make sense to Brook. The adoption of a flea-bitten abandoned dog, like the one he'd just seen, was more than a play for sympathy from punters with spare change. The animal offered warmth and the kind of unswerving love and loyalty that acted as antidote to the vitriol unleashed by the well-heeled walking by. He'd heard it all.

Get a job, you fucking tramp.

You stink.

Why don't you top yourself and do the world a favour?

And it wasn't just verbal. He'd seen people sleeping in doorways, urinated on by drunken teenagers, kicked awake by shopkeepers and threatened with worse if they came back. And despite being a DI, Brook had not intervened. He told himself it was because he didn't want to break cover, but a small part of him knew that it was more than that. In just three days of homelessness, Brook had become submissive and, in many ways, helpless. Now he actively avoided eye-contact with others, didn't want to be noticed, to be the target of abuse or engage with people whose first reaction towards him would be contempt. Brook had assumed the position.

For a second he paused and pulled off a damp glove to scratch his beard again – something had bitten him, he was sure. Living without the basic freedoms and comforts bestowed by an income had quickly reordered his priorities. Food, warm shelter and clean clothes were no longer taken for granted but had become the fundamental pillars of his existence. Brook had never been the sort of person to spend more time than necessary over basic functions, but after the first twelve hours padding around Derby, in the oldest clothes he could muster, he not only longed for a hot bath but had a hunger gnawing at his belly that he'd never experienced before.

After one full day, Brook stank to high heaven and had spent the emergency £20 note in his back pocket on the *Sub of the Day*, his first packet of cigarettes in a month and a small bottle of whisky, being careful to get the cheapest brands of both to allay suspicion amongst his new acquaintances.

He plodded on, taking the walk of the damned – head sagging forward, shoulders rounded, feet barely clearing the ground, like a prisoner in the Gulag. He reached the top of Osmaston Road and crossed the new link road, Lara Croft Way, which, like most road improvements in the city, had reduced traffic-flow to a virtual standstill during rush-hour. At two in the morning, however, it was deserted and Brook ambled across the four lanes, past the boarded-up bar, long since closed after a stabbing, and turned on to Leopold Street.

Just before reaching Normanton Road, Brook stopped and pulled out a grubby piece of paper given to him by Mitch, his new friend from the Millstone House Shelter. It didn't have an address on it; the homeless didn't use addresses – the consequence of being homeless, Brook supposed. Instead they preferred more traditional methods of navigation – a vague description of the location, the description of the house and how to get in.

Brook looked around and was held for a moment. On the other side of the road was a funeral parlour – Duxbury & Duxbury. He made a mental note to check they'd been contacted.

He turned back to the darkened, boarded house. He checked Mitch's note again and approached the steel security grille fastened over one of the windows. This was the place. He pulled aside the grille so he could see inside. It moved easily but it was far too dark to see anything. However, the smell of body odour hit his nostrils, as did a sickly-sweet smell which Brook associated with crack cocaine abuse. He listened for the scurrying of rats but heard nothing but the now familiar harsh rasp of sleeping vagrants mumbling and snoring in their fitful slumber.

Brook took a final breath of fresh air and lifted a leg through the window space, but his foot was suddenly held by a strong hand.

'Fuck a ye doin', pal?' said a voice of pure Scottish tar. Despite the many things Brook had learned about sleeping rough, one thing remained a mystery. Why so many vagrants seemed to be Scottish.

'Looking for Mitch and a place to kip,' Brook replied in as gruff a voice as he could manage. He hadn't yet slipped into the parlance as easily as he would've liked.

'We're full, pal. Fuck off.' The hand holding Brook's foot shoved it roughly back out of the window.

Brook didn't move away. He knew from his days on the street that the only way to get a result now was to fructify his vocabulary and employ an unfamiliar aggression. 'Who the fuck says?' he snarled back.

'You mouthin' off, Jimmy? Jock says, so fuck off afore ye get a busted mouth.'

Brook tried not to smile, his default reaction to any form of verbal threat. He was a Detective Inspector and had been threatened many times. Almost always such belligerence was for show, an attempt to gain control over a situation that was overwhelming the aggressor. And when a DI smiled back at hostility, the violent facade often crumbled and Brook knew *he* had control. But not this time. He needed an alternative strategy.

'I've got fags,' he said, producing a pack and holding them up to Jock's face.

Jock squinted at the pack and grinned. 'Giz un.' He reached for the pack but Brook lowered his hand.

'When you let me in.'

Jock eyed Brook then nodded. 'Aye. Well, one more won't di any harm, Jimmy.' He stood back from the window and Brook clambered in. 'What's yer name, Jimmy?'

'It's Jimmy,' said Brook, standing upright and surveying the room. He could see clearer now by the light of an old guttering lantern in the middle of the bare room. Half a dozen uninterested, glazed expressions fixed on him briefly then returned to gape at the floor.

'Straight up?' Jock coughed, laughing.

As soon as Brook was in, Jock went to Brook's hand and pulled the cigarettes from him. He yanked one out and held it to the barely alight lantern. He pulled the first drag deep into his lungs and coughed the smoke back up. 'Lovely. Here, Jimmy. Warm yer cockles.' Jock tossed a bottle towards him and gestured to the floor. 'Take a pew and join the party.'

Brook examined the bottle and pulled off the stopper, taking a sniff. 'What is it?'

Jock laughed and coughed at the same time. 'What is it?' he repeated, and looked round at the other bearded faces. 'We got a conn'sir with us, gents.' He cackled this time and took another huge pull on the cigarette.

A small man with a baseball cap flashed a gap-toothed smile back at Jock, and then narrowed his eyes at Brook. 'What does it matter, friend?' he said in a faint Yorkshire accent. 'It's barley wine, if you must know.'

'We finished all the whisky for breakfast.' Jock laughed again.

Baseball Cap continued to look at Brook as best he could. 'Have a sip,' he urged, looking over at Jock. 'Maybe you can tell us what year it is.' This time Baseball Cap laughed hard and wheezy and Jock joined in, shaking his head and muttering *What is it?* to remind himself why he was laughing so hard.

'Thanks.' Brook stuck his tongue in the neck and faked a swig, as was his custom all those years ago in the Met when his old boss Charlie Rowlands passed over his flask at eleven in the morning.

'Go on, finish it,' said Baseball Cap. 'Plenty more where that came from, Jimmy.'

Brook looked around at the floor and saw several empty whisky and barley wine bottles at the men's feet. 'You knock off an off-licence or something?'

Baseball Cap smiled thinly at him. He seemed to be the least inebriated of the group and Brook was becoming uncomfortable under his gaze. 'Let's just say we have a benefactor.' Baseball Cap grinned across at Jock but fortunately his head had slumped forward into unconsciousness. 'You know? A sugar daddy.'

'I know what a benefactor is,' said Brook. He scratched his itching beard again, eyes still locked on Baseball Cap. 'You sound like you've had a decent education.'

'Why shouldn't I?' Baseball Cap said. 'You think only stupid people end up on the skids?' He flashed a quick look round to check his roommates were too befuddled to follow. 'Education,' he hissed. 'That's where I know you from. Damen, isn't it?'

'The name's Jimmy,' said Brook softly.

'Fuck off, Damen. It's me. Phil.'

Brook didn't reply but squinted through the gloom at Baseball Cap. He obliged Brook by removing his cap and brushing the lank grey hair away from his face. From nowhere two jigsaw pieces of Brook's memory clicked together. 'Phil? Phil Ward? My God.'

The newly anointed Phil nodded. 'Cambridge Athletics. Alverstone's against the Centipedes, remember? We ran against each other in the five thousand metres.'

'Not for long,' recalled Brook. 'You were a lap in front of me at halfway, I remember.'

Phil looked away, pleasure tinged with sadness. He took a pull on his barley wine. 'I was quick back then. And I didn't smoke or . . .' He held up his bottle to save further explanation. 'I assume you're new to the life.'

'Why?'

'You look like you could interview after a wash and brush up.'

'You don't look so bad yourself,' Brook lied. Without his cap he could see the ravages of vagrancy on Phil's face – pockmarked ruddy cheeks which sank in towards his jaw, missing teeth, greasy thinning hair and the telltale jaundiced eyes which spoke of a liver failing under the assault of drink and drugs. 'What happened? You were going to be a dentist, I seem to remember.'

'Pharmacist,' Phil grinned. 'And I kinda still am.' The black grin faded. 'You haven't got any rock to spare, have you, buddy? I'll pay you back.'

'No,' answered Brook. 'Fresh out. And you haven't answered my question. What happened to you?'

Jock stirred at that moment and lifted his head at the same

Steven Dunne

time as the bottle went to his mouth. 'Nuttin' happened,' he mumbled after a long draught.

Phil's eyes flicked at the door and he disentangled himself from the scrum of semi-conscious men as delicately as possible. Brook followed him quietly out. Fortunately Jock's head had begun to loll again. Up the bare stairs and into a room that looked out over the heavily overgrown back yard. There was just a mattress in the room but the floorboards were scattered with drug paraphernalia – torn-up Rizla packets, scorched wire gauze, needles, blackened empty bottles for the crack smokers.

Brook turned back from the window as Phil closed the door behind him and stooped to pick up a needle. He held it like an axe above his head. 'What's happening, Brook? Is this a fucking raid? I know you're not in the life, man. You're fucking famous. You're The Reaper detective. I've read the newspapers. I've wiped my arse on you. You're still a copper, aren't you? 'Cos if you were on the street for real, you'd know the golden rule.'

'Golden rule?'

'What we did no longer exists. We don't have pasts any more. We don't have futures neither. We live in the present. The next score, the next high. That's all we think about in here. Dead men walking.' He moved towards Brook raising the needle higher. 'That answer your question, Detective Inspector?'

Brook tried not to look at the needle and held up his hands. 'This is not a raid, Phil. And that needle's empty.'

'Course it's empty, you sanctimonious cunt,' hissed Phil, now eyeball to eyeball with Brook. Brook could smell his breath, the sweat pouring off him, the stench of death. 'I emptied it into my veins. But what else is on there? AIDS? Hepatitis? You won't know until the first bout of flu, baby.'

Brook urgently tried to make eye-contact. 'Phil, you're not going to get busted. Listen to me, Phil. You're not in any trouble. I'm not here about the drugs. Put down the needle and let me help you.'

Phil couldn't hold the pose; tears filled his eyes and he crumpled to the ground, dropping the needle on to the mattress. 'I beat you by a lap and a half,' he wailed.

Brook stooped and picked him up by both arms and forced his way into his face. 'You probably still can, Phil. Why don't you let me help you? I could put in a word, get you on a programme.'

'I've been on programmes. They don't help.'

'So you just give up and stick a needle in your arm?'

'D'uh.'

The two men looked at each other in the gloom then simultaneously broke into silent laughter which lasted more than a minute.

Phil took a deep breath and wiped the tears away. ''The fuck are you doing here, Brook?'

'Looking for someone,' said Brook after a moment. 'I spoke to Mitch. He sent me. He was here last night.'

'I know Mitch. He went to Millstone for a bath and a bed.'

'He told me about Tommy McTiernan. He was here in this house.'

'Tiny Tom.' Phil nodded. 'He left a while ago.'

'When?'

Phil shrugged. 'A week? Two?'

'Left, how?'

'I don't understand.'

'Think. I need to find out where he went from here.'

'He left with Oz.'

'Who's Oz?'

'Ozzy looks after us, brings us gear.'

'He's your benefactor?' Phil nodded. 'Is he Australian?'

'No. English, I think.'

'Describe him.'

'I've only seen him clearly once and I was rammed.'

'Try and remember, Phil.'

Phil took a deep breath. 'He's younger than us. Forty, forty-five maybe. Short hair, well built, that's all I can remember. It's always at night see, after we've had a few.'

'How does he get here?'

'He has transport. A big van, I think.'

'A big van, are you sure?'

Phil fixed Brook with a glare. 'Damen, I can't be sure of anything. Maybe it was a car. All I think about is the . . .'

'. . . next fix. I get it,' said Brook, 'but did the next fix arrive at the same time as Tommy left?'

Phil thought for a minute then slowly nodded. 'You're right. Ozzy gave us a few bottles of whisky then Tommy left with him. Bath and bed, Tommy said.'

'And you don't know where.' Phil shook his head. 'Okay. Phil, promise me if he comes again, you won't go with him.'

'What?'

'Promise me, Phil.'

'Why? What's going on, Damen?'

'Tommy's dead. We found him in the river. We think another . . . vagrant has died as well. That we know about. Does the name Barry Kirk ring a bell?'

'Bazza? He was here. Is he dead too?'

Brook nodded in the dark. Phil's expression didn't waver. Instead he shrugged. 'Lucky him, I say. That's the life. We all know what's coming. If it ain't me, maybe I'll read about it in the crapper,' he sniggered.

'Phil, things were done to Tommy. His organs were removed.'

'Lot of use they'd be.' Phil sniggered again.

'Don't you get it yet, Phil? You're living in a body farm. Barry and Tommy were here, now they're dead. I think this guy Ozzy takes them somewhere and when they're dead he guts them like a fish.'

'So what? He brings us drink, sometimes some rock. Tommy wasn't my friend, Damen. We don't have friends in the life. Just rivals for the last smoke, the last drop. We're on borrowed time, man. Like I said. Lucky Tommy, lucky Bazza.' He grinned with pleasure. 'Now I've got a bottle of theirs with my name on it.'

Brook searched in his pockets and found a pencil. He wrote on the grubby wallpaper. 'I'm your friend, Phil. I can help you.'

'Is that right? Give me money then. I've got the rattles something rotten.'

Brook looked him in the eyes. 'I can help you if you'll let me. You're sick.'

'Don't fucking patronise me,' snarled Phil. 'I'm not sick. This isn't an illness. I'm weak, no moral fibre, no character. Geddit?'

'Okay, calm down.'

'I made my choices and I got it wrong. I fucked up so don't tell me I'm sick unless you're got a pill for failure.'

'You're right. I'm sorry.' Brook tore off the flap of wallpaper and scrunched it into Phil's top pocket. 'If this Ozzy comes back or if you want my help, money, a bed for the night, anything – that's my mobile number. Call me.'

'From a payphone? Just give me your mobile and I'll ring your landline, it'll be quicker.' Phil's face shone with sincerity.

'I'm a copper, remember. We both know you'll have sold the phone before I get to the end of the street. Just get to a payphone and use it.'

Phil grinned and Brook could see his rotting mouth. 'Is there a retainer for this service?' he asked sheepishly.

Brook fished around for the meagre change from his twenty pounds and poured it into Phil's hand. A noise caught his attention. 'Was that a car door?' He flung the flimsy door open and hurtled down the stairs to the main room in time to hear a vehicle pulling away. 'Out of the way,' Brook shouted at the throng of men swarming around the window, picking full bottles out of a crate. 'Move.'

By the time Brook had jostled his way past the sluggish scrum of men and vaulted out of the window, the lights had disappeared. He turned back to the silhouette of his fellow Oxbridge graduate, stooping to pluck his own precious bottle from the crate.

After a second, Phil came to the gaping window, spinning the top from his whisky and downing a huge swallow. Eventually he lowered the bottle and leaned on the sill. 'Where's Jock?' he asked.

Brook finally scuffed his feet across the forecourt of St Mary's Wharf station at a quarter to four in the morning having walked across the centre of town. He was annoyed that he'd surrendered all his change to Phil Ward, not that he could have enticed a taxi to pick him up at any time of day given the condition he was in. He'd tried phoning for a squad car but all units were tied up and even Noble had turned off his mobile.

He plodded wearily up the steps to the glass doors, dismayed to see Sergeant Hendrickson on duty at the front counter and wishing he hadn't left his smartcard in his desk. As he approached the intercom, Brook saw the uniformed officer muttering something under his breath which even a novice lipreader like Brook took to be, 'Look what the cat dragged in.'

Brook pressed the intercom, monitoring Hendrickson for further evidence of abuse. 'It's DI Brook. Let me in, Sergeant.'

Hendrickson unveiled his most obsequious smile and pressed his own button. *'DI Brook isn't on duty at this time, sir. Please call back later.'* He released the button and affected a return to pressing paperwork on his counter.

Brook's lips tightened and he pressed again. He did have his warrant card for emergencies so he pulled it from his shoe and, after brushing the condensation from it, forced it against the glass. He pressed the intercom button again. *'I'm* DI Brook. Open the door now.'

Hendrickson shielded his eyes from a non-existent glare and opened his mouth in fake recognition. He buzzed Brook into the station. 'I didn't recognise you in that get-up. Sir. Been to a fancy dress party, have we?' A PC whose name escaped Brook stood behind Hendrickson, smiling gleefully at the poorly disguised insubordination.

Brook made for the lifts. Hendrickson had never said anything to him that on paper would have been deemed inappropriate and Brook knew that to complain about a fellow officer's *attitude* would lead to further ridicule. However, on an impulse he stopped and turned to face him. 'I'm undercover, Sergeant – something you might have come across if you'd made the grade at CID.'

As Brook marched away, the expression on Hendrickson's face turned to hate. 'You fucking Southern cunt,' he spat when Brook was out of earshot. 'They should have left you in that loony bin and thrown away the key.'

Brook walked through the quiet station gratified to encounter nobody else capable of commenting on his appearance. In his office he changed into an old sweater and jeans and dumped his damp and dirty clothes in a bin bag for disposal. He'd only ever worn them on those rare occasions when he was forced to do a little garden maintenance but, after three days living rough, and with some of the substances now adhering to the fabric, they were better thrown away. He wouldn't be running short of scruffy clothes anytime soon.

Brook sat briefly at his desk and read various notes left for him by Jane Gadd about The Embalmer. The Millstone House enquiries had proved fruitless. Only three vagrants staying during Tommy McTiernan's visit had given full names, and none of them had been traced. Gadd had tried to find out whether Barry Kirk had visited the hostel but if he had, he'd done so under a false name.

Next Brook skimmed the forensic report on Kirk. His body had been in the water for eighteen to twenty days. But even with an approximate timeframe for the dumping of the body, they were struggling to identify any suspects at the site.

The few staff who worked at the sole security gate to the vast gravel pit road system had been interviewed. All were longtime employees and in the clear. Also, all the trucks and lorries captured on the only CCTV camera at the site over the last month had all been present on legitimate business, and although a couple of drivers had minor records, they too were beyond suspicion, according to their tachographs. The probe into ex-employees had also produced nothing thus far.

The list of anglers given to Noble by the man who reeled in Barry Kirk's remains had not rung any alarm bells either. All were solid citizens with nothing more than parking tickets to their names.

Brook sent a text to Noble about the possible abduction of another vagrant and asked him to hunt up any possible CCTV around the Leopold Street squat then walked wearily out to the car park, tossing the bin bag in his boot. He cranked the heating up high and sped back to Hartington through the deserted roads.

After a hot bath and shave he staggered up to his bedroom and collapsed on to the soft bed, for once sleeping through until noon without moving a muscle.

The man switched off the headlights long before reaching the turn on to the overgrown drive and a few moments later glided to a halt near the black outline of the furthest building on the complex. He killed the engine and clambered out to unload his supply of jars and tools from the passenger seat.

Looking about the pitch-black site as he walked silently but purposefully towards the heavy timbered doors at one end of the building, the man smiled in contentment. The gods favoured him. Nut, the Goddess of the Sky, had sent a canopy of clouds to cover his arrival. With the nearest artificial light a quarter of a mile away on the estate, no one would know he was there. Kids would sometimes roam by in daylight, but without windows to smash, they rarely lingered long enough to discover his lair. Besides, the building was on the edge of the countryside, with only a ploughed field between the derelict buildings and the river. The off-licences, pubs and shops that kids loved to hang around were in the opposite direction.

The man put down his load in front of the boarded doorway and felt behind one of the large shrubs growing out of control off to one side. He pulled out a small aluminium stepladder, with its camouflage of green radiator paint, set it against the right-hand doorjamb and climbed level to the swallow's nest wedged between the doorjamb and the wall. With a final look round, he put his hand inside an aperture behind the nest and pulled on a lever. A loud click sounded and the large timbered door on the right shifted slightly.

He jumped down from the ladder and returned to his vehicle to fetch his human cargo.

Eleven

BROOK REACHED HIS OFFICE JUST before two o'clock in the afternoon. With him he carried two bacon sandwiches and a polystyrene cup of tea. He finished the first sandwich while writing the report on his encounter with Phil Ward. He was unwrapping the second as Noble walked in.

'Welcome back to the land of the living. How was it?'

Brook smiled without humour. 'It was terrible. Don't ever let anyone tell you the homeless are having it easy. I'm not one for soft living, but after one night . . .' He shook his head. 'And if I ever suggest doing something similar in the future, John, I want you to have me sectioned.'

'What, again?'

Brook eyed him in mock censure and bit down on his sandwich. 'Forget I said anything. Where are we on McTiernan and Kirk?'

'It's going nowhere. Still no useful feedback from any funeral homes or medical schools. Same answer from local hospices. No missing bodies. No suspicious employees. Nothing.'

'What about Jock?'

Noble shrugged. 'I could put out an alert, but without a photo and even a real name . . .'

'Any film?'

'There are no CCTV cameras on Leopold Street. Jane's going to sift through any film for the Normanton area between two and three this morning.'

Brook took another bite. 'We might have to take the inquiry up a notch if we want to shake something out.'

'Charlton won't buy into that.'

'Probably not.'

'So the tip about the squat panned out.'

'I think so. The place is being used as a body farm, John. Tommy McTiernan and Barry Kirk were there. Somebody's supplying lots of drink to keep a stock of vagrants in one place. There was a case of whisky. Barley wine too. I just missed Jock's abduction.'

'You didn't actually see it happen then?'

Brook looked up. 'No.' Before Noble could comment, he held up a hand. 'I know, I know. He's a vagrant. He could've just wandered off. But somebody turned up to deliver alcohol in the early hours of the morning and I don't see an alcoholic tramp wandering away from that.'

'Maybe,' said Noble. 'You should brief Jane. She's working The Embalmer solo for now.'

Brook paused over his next bite. 'What does that mean?'

'It's your other case. It's pretty labour intensive. Me, Rob and Dave have been—'

'Other case? What are you talking about?'

'The missing students from Derby College,' explained Noble. Brook narrowed his eyes in confusion. 'I thought you knew.'

'I've been living rough for the best part of three days, John. How would I know?'

'Well, you're logged as the SIO.'

'I'm what!' exclaimed Brook.

'You were there at initial contact with the parent. You even took charge of a piece of evidence, so Sergeant Grey put you down as Senior Officer.'

Brook stared into the distance and closed his eyes. 'Deity.' He opened them again and pulled out the leaflet left by Alice Kennedy. He handed it to Noble. 'I just picked it up. I forgot all about it. Grey – that sneaky . . .' Brook omitted the noun he wanted to use. 'That's just great.'

Live Forever. Young. Beautiful. Immortal,' read Noble. 'Nice idea. This was at the parents' house, right?'

Brook nodded, suddenly feeling very tired. 'The mother . . .' He looked up to Noble for a prompt.

'Alice Kennedy.'

'She found it in her son's room – didn't she?'

'She did.'

'That'll teach me to take an interest.'

Noble typed the Deity web address into Brook's computer. 'Closed for refurbishment.'

'Same as last time.' Brooks sighed. 'So The Embalmer . . .'

'Sir, the Chief Super was very clear. As it's not a murder case, Jane's flying it solo at the moment.'

Brook shook his head in frustration. 'I read the Kirk Forensics note. No other developments?'

'That's it. It looks the same MO as McTiernan. There are traces of make-up on the loincloth. The fabric is Egyptian cotton – identical to the cloth we found in the Derwent.'

'Egyptian cotton,' repeated Brook.

'It's pretty common. You think it's significant?'

'Who knows? What else?'

'The rest you know. The heart was chronically diseased – it was removed then put back; the rest of the organs and the large intestine were gone and the blood drained. There was the same stitching on the gash in his side. His remaining hair looked like it had been cut – it's hard to tell. What fingernails Kirk had left were tidy and might have been clipped but they can't tell if the body was cleaned after so long in the water.' Noble shrugged.

'And still no COD?'

'The lab's working on it. It's tricky with an even longer immersion.'

'So it could still be murder.'

'Habib thinks not, but they're still doing tests.'

'What else?'

'The scars below the nostrils were also caused by some kind of sharp tool pushed into the nose to puncture the membrane on the brain and let the fluid drain away.'

'Same as McTiernan.'

'Right. One difference: Habib said Barry Kirk's brain was more cut up and the scarring was much deeper. The right upper lip was almost sliced through.'

'Did you run the MO through HOLMES and the PNC?'

'No hits on either database. Nothing even close to this MO came back.'

Brook fired up his computer and logged on to his internal email account. 'Ancient anatomy,' he muttered, narrowing his eyes.

'Sorry?'

'Something Dr Petty said. Is Egypt a member of Interpol?'

'I think so. I can check.'

Brook took a sip of his tea and ran his eye down the list of contacts. He clicked on Habib's email address and typed a few words and numbers, then sent it off to him marked for Dr Petty's attention. 'If they are, run the MO past the Interpol database.'

'You mean . . .'

'Yes, I mean ask Jane to do it,' replied Brook testily.

Noble raised an eyebrow. 'Because of the cotton?'

'No, because they have an ancient culture of embalming the dead.' Brook sighed. 'We have little enough to go on. The chances are the Egyptian police are still in disarray after the revolution, but it might be worth asking the question. Also . . .' Brook blinked and turned to him.

'What is it?' asked Noble.

'Kirk's upper lip was almost sliced through, you say.'

'Yes.'

'Worse than Tommy?'

'That's right.'

Brook pushed his chair back and stood. 'Kirk was dumped at least fifteen days before McTiernan.'

Noble's face wasn't registering enlightenment. 'Maybe longer.'

Brook smiled. 'My God, John. He's practising.'

'Practising?'

Brook nodded. 'Practising on the bodies.'

'For what?'

'When we know that, we'll know who we're looking for. He's removing all the organs, including the brain, and trying to leave the corpse cosmetically intact. But he's having the most trouble extracting the brain without leaving a mark, so he needs more bodies. With Kirk he was clumsy and almost sliced through his top lip but with Tommy, his technique had improved; the scarring wasn't as pronounced.'

'And you think Jock will turn up with less scarring than McTiernan under the nostrils because The Embalmer's improving his technique – interesting.'

'We should speak to Charlton.'

'We can't.'

'We must. Suppose the vagrants are just the first? Suppose he perfects what he does and gets ready to show us what he can really do.'

'Hasn't he already?'

'I don't think so. He's barely started. He's honing his skills, getting better, but he's still not good enough. Once he'd cut McTiernan's upper lip, he stopped hacking at the brain. He needs to leave the body without a blemish. That's why he didn't try to hack up his brain as much as Kirk. He'd already ruined him. We've got to convince Charlton to—'

'Sir, Charlton's not here. He's at a conference until next Monday.'

'A conference?' Brook was annoyed but then started to smile. 'A conference,' he said again. 'Okay.'

'Sir? I know that look . . .'

'We have no choice, John. This is urgent. The Embalmer needs more bodies to practise on. He got Jock last night in Leopold Street.'

'You're not certain of that.'

'As certain as I can be. He was grabbed before I could get to him.'

'And the missing students?'

'Students? You mean we're missing more than one?'

'As of yesterday evening we're missing three – two girls and the Kennedy boy, Kyle.'

'How do we know they're one case?'

'We don't, for sure. But apparently they were all at the same party last Friday night and no one's seen them since.'

Brook raised a sceptical eyebrow. 'A party? How old are they?'

'They're eighteen, all attending Derby College, all very bright –'

'– and all old enough to please themselves,' finished Brook. 'They've been to a rave, John, and got wrecked.'

'Or Ibiza. Or a festival,' Noble said. 'I know. Nevertheless, it's been reported and you're SIO, so until we find them . . .'

Brook sighed. 'Anything gone out to the press?'

'Not yet. There's no evidence of foul play or violence. Think we should?'

'For once, yes. They can do our job for us.' Then Brook changed his mind. 'But I suppose we can't let them run with it until we have a few facts.' He looked at his watch. 'Okay, John. For your sake, we'll do it by the book. Round everyone up, DS Gadd included. We'll have a joint briefing in two hours – both cases. Meanwhile, you can bring me up to speed on these students. I promise, tonight we'll talk to the parents.'

As Brook finished his account of the episode in the Leopold Street squat he looked round the Incident Room, hoping the rest of his detectives were feeling the same urgency. 'And the chances are we're not going to find Jock alive unless we can work out who's taken him. We don't have a picture, we don't have a surname and even "Jock" could be a nickname. On the other hand, we do have a name for whoever's dropping off the alcohol. His name is Oz or Ozzy. He's not Australian. He's early middle-aged and powerfully built.'

'Is that all there is to go on?' asked Cooper.

'You have to remember who's giving the description,' replied Brook.

'Ozzy. Do we know if *that's* a real name?' asked Gadd.

Brook shrugged. 'Unlikely. But even if it's an alias maybe it's a nickname he uses at work, maybe even at one of those funeral homes or hospices we spoke to on Sunday.' Brook looked around to see if the name rang any bells. 'No? Well, make a note of the name for any follow-up. We may have to do it all over again, this time face to face.' Brook tried to ignore the groans and turned to the large map of the Derby area.

'But for now, we concentrate on the house where Jock was abducted. It's our only active lead.' He pointed to Leopold Street. 'It's derelict, with no power, no heating, and it's home to about ten vagrants, though obviously that number is fluid. We're going to be doing surveillance ourselves, starting tonight.' More groans. Brook raised a hand. 'When Charlton gets back, I'll make sure we get more bodies on this, but until then it's down to us.

'Now, it's a tight road, so position your car with care. Our suspect has transport and we don't want to scare him off. You'll take two four-hour shifts. Rob and Dave, you'll take ten till two, so go home now and get some rest. John and Jane, you'll relieve at two tomorrow and stay until six. I've been out there three days so I'll take tonight off,' he added, unable to meet eyes. 'Remember, our guy's a night owl so he'll only come when the streets are deserted. This morning it was nearly three before he showed up.'

'You think he'll be back so soon?' asked DS Gadd.

'If he really has got Jock, probably not, but as it's our only solid lead, we can't take the risk.'

'And don't forget, if we're right, he has to keep the occupants happy or they might move on,' added Noble. 'So he might turn up just to deliver more booze.'

'Exactly. If he makes a delivery, try to follow him but it will be almost impossible for him to miss you at that hour. So if he's leading you round in circles, you'll have to bring him in and hope we can take it from there and get him to *fess up*.' Brook smiled and looked around the ring of four detectives who stared sombrely at the floor. He wished their expressions were an indication of the investigation's gravity, instead of regret at losing a night of TV and a warm bed. 'Finally, until Forensics puts us on the right track, we get stuck into the legwork. Jane, I want you to check out off-licences and bulk suppliers of alcohol tomorrow. You're looking for anyone buying large amounts of whisky and barley wine.'

'Barley wine they should remember.' She smiled. 'Nobody drinks that filth.'

Brook pulled a piece of paper from his jacket. 'Which reminds me. There's a funeral parlour opposite the house. Duxbury and Duxbury. Anyone remember who contacted them?'

'Me, I think,' said Morton.

'How did you leave it?'

'They were ringing me back.'

'Right. I'll follow them up.' Brook held out his arms. 'Any questions?'

'Do we drop the missing students?' asked Morton.

'You missed out the adjective.' Cooper laughed.

Everyone joined in; even Brook managed a thin smile. Normally he would have discouraged such levity about an active investigation but he felt the missing students were an unnecessary distraction.

'John and I will follow up on the students tonight. Anything else?'

'Any usable film?' said Cooper.

'Local CCTV is trained on the shops further up Normanton Road but Jane will be in the Viewing Room, checking the hour between two and three last night. We may get a shortlist of suspect vehicles, we may not.'

'What am I looking for?' asked Gadd.

'Vans, in particular. And get plates for follow-up if they look dubious.'

'But we're still not sure if this is a murder inquiry?'

'No,' said Brook. 'But when people who like to play with dead things are ready to escalate, it's the next logical step – especially if they run out of fresh corpses.'

'What I don't get, right, is – if this guy's going for cosmetic perfection, why cut open these bums?' asked Morton. 'Most of them are in a right state.'

'That's the point,' answered Brook. 'He's perfecting his technique on the most expendable members of society.' An image of Phil Ward sprinting away from him on the track made Brook pause. 'And let's not forget these *bums* may have families. Once they had what you have: lovers, jobs, a future. They've lost all of that. Miserable though it may seem to us, all they have left is life, and no one has the right to take it away.'

While Noble knocked on the door, Brook ran his eye over the small, well-maintained suburban garden basking in the golden glow of dusk. A *For Sale* sign nestled up against the garden wall. The house itself was neat, if nondescript, similar to every semi-detached they'd passed on the Brisbane Estate – a comfortable and characterless modern home for a small, hardworking family.

The compact driveway, its garage outgrown by modern vehicles, had two cars squeezed on to it – a sleek black Jaguar tight up against the rear bumper of a battered Nissan Micra. A good metaphor for Poole's relationship with Alice Kennedy, Brook decided. Poole had money from a generous pension and his former marriage and, even from the briefest encounter with the couple, Brook had gotten the impression that Poole's relationship with her wouldn't have existed without it.

'Come in.' Poole stood aside to usher Noble into the warmth of the house. 'Inspector Brook,' he nodded as Brook entered in turn.

'Hello, Len.'

'You remembered me then, Inspector.'

'I never forget a face.' Noble turned to raise an eyebrow but Brook ignored it. 'How's retirement treating you?'

'Mustn't grumble,' replied Poole. 'Still driving a Jag,' he added, as though it were relevant.

Brook followed Poole and Noble into a small, softly lit living room where Alice Kennedy sat on a sofa next to the uniformed Family Liaison Officer already there. The petite Asian officer held a cup and saucer and balanced an untouched plate of biscuits on her lap. Her hat was on the arm of the sofa and her thick black hair had been wound into a tight bun. She looked ill at ease for some reason.

'Constable.' Brook nodded at her. Unsurprisingly he had forgotten her name and gave Noble the usual blank stare to prompt his DS to identify their colleague at the earliest opportunity.

'Can I get you some tea, Detectives?' asked Alice Kennedy, her voice taut.

'No, thank you,' replied Noble. 'We have . . . other calls to make.'

'You mean the other parents, don't you?' She dabbed a handkerchief to an eye. 'I heard. Those poor people.'

'Has PC Patel brought you up to speed, Mrs Kennedy?' asked Noble.

'Yes. You've upgraded Kyle's disappearance to medium risk because it's been several days.'

'That's right. We're widening the inquiry. We'll be going to the college to ask questions, and we've circulated Kyle's details and the picture you gave us to the British Transport Police – all the ports and airports are on the lookout for him. We also think it's wise to email his details to Interpol as well.' Noble tried to smile reassuringly.

'Interpol?'

'It's an international Police Force, love,' said Poole.

'I know what it is,' she said crossly. 'But why?'

'In case he's jetted off to Ibiza or somewhere. They'll let us know if he's left Britain under the radar and slipped into Europe. Our border controls are not the best.'

'No, no, no. That's impossible,' said Alice.

'Why?'

'He doesn't even have a passport.'

Brook and Noble glanced at each other. 'So it would surprise you to learn that Kyle applied for a passport three months ago?' asked Noble.

Alice Kennedy looked genuinely stunned. 'Yes, it would, Sergeant. Are you sure?'

'According to the Passport Service.'

'It's something they check for missing persons over eighteen,' said Poole, with a pompous sniff. 'So they know the search parameters.'

'So he may have been planning a trip.' Alice's face brightened. 'I suppose that's a ray of hope.'

'We think it's significant,' said Noble.

'But why didn't he say anything to me?'

'As a parent, I have to say it's not unusual for teenagers to keep things from us.' A shard of personal anguish infected Brook's features for a moment but passed just as quickly. 'And when several young adults disappear together it can point to some kind of trip – sometimes to a festival, a booze cruise, even a holiday.'

'But it doesn't make sense. He's never been abroad before. We could never afford it after the separation.'

'I was thinking of treating him after his A-levels though,' interjected Poole. 'I was putting something aside for him. For a surprise.' He smiled across at Alice, hoping his assertion of economic well-being would bring comfort. She looked back at him without expression.

'Wait – wouldn't Kyle need his birth certificate for a passport?' asked Alice.

'Yours too, if it's his first,' answered Noble. 'Would Kyle know where they are?'

'Of course. I keep everything in the office in a folder. In case something happens to me.'

'Could you . . . ?' prompted Noble. She hurried upstairs to check.

Brook glanced across at Poole. When he thought nobody was watching, the former pathologist was staring at PC Patel. Noble had noticed it too. And without showing she was aware of it, Brook's uniformed colleague folded her arms across her chest.

'We wondered whether he'd asked you to endorse his passport photograph, Len?' enquired Brook.

Poole broke off his examination of Patel's body. 'Me?'

'Well, a family member or a parent isn't allowed to do it.'

Poole shook his head. 'He wouldn't ask me. He'd know I'd mention it to Alice.'

Alice returned to the sitting room deep in thought. 'They're there but I can tell they've been taken out of the wallet.'

'What about money? You told the other officer who called that Kyle had his own bank account,' said Noble.

'Yes. At Santander. It was a birthday present last year,' said Alice. 'I gave the officer the details.'

'We've got them. But there doesn't seem to be much money in there.'

'I put fifty pounds in a week ago, Sergeant, but he'll have spent most of it already,' said Poole, shrugging his shoulders. 'Kids, eh?'

'Is he expecting further funds?' asked Brook.

'His EMA was cut but we put in the equivalent every Friday,' said Alice. 'Thirty pounds pocket-money.'

'It's a direct debit, straight from my account,' announced Poole. Alice's face darkened. 'Should I cancel it?'

'No,' said Noble. 'If he's in the country, he may try to access the money. It would give us a lead.'

'What about transport?' asked Brook.

'Transport?'

'Does Kyle own a bicycle, for instance?'

'He does,' said Alice. 'It should be in the garage.'

'It's still in there, Sergeant.' Poole nodded. 'I had it out yesterday. Got to stay in trim at my age, you know.'

Brook answered his grin with a faint nod. 'What about any driving experience?' he said to Alice.

'Not even a lesson,' she replied.

'I was going to—' began Poole.

'Len!' snapped Alice, her hands splaying in exasperation. Len was puzzled by her outburst but remained silent.

'What about Kyle's mood?' enquired Noble, filling the awkward silence that followed. 'Maybe he was excited recently, buying new clothes, that sort of thing?'

'No, nothing like that,' said Alice. 'The only thing Kyle was thinking about was his exams. He's keen to do well. He wants to live in London eventually.'

'Could he have gone there?' asked PC Patel, in a high-pitched voice.

'He doesn't know anyone in London, so not without money, no.'

'You told us Kyle's on Facebook and we have his email account,' said Noble. 'Do you know if he's on any other social network?'

Alice shook her head. 'You mean Twitter? I wouldn't have thought so. He's just too shy.'

Brook nodded. 'Can we see his room?'

'Of course.'

'Perhaps he has luggage missing.'

'No, I told the other officer.' She buried her head in the handkerchief wrapped tightly around her bony fingers. 'It's no use – Kyle's dead. I can feel it.'

PC Patel put down her cup and placed her arms around the distraught woman. 'You mustn't think like that, Alice. We're doing all we can. You've got to stay positive for Kyle.'

Len Poole ranged up behind Alice to put a pudgy hand on her shoulder but she shook it off.

'Constable Patel's right,' said Noble. 'And you said yourself, the passport is good news. It means he was planning a trip. There's every chance he's fine. He's not in any of the local hospitals . . .'

'He wouldn't be if he was lying dead in a ditch.'

'After four or five days in a ditch the chances of finding Kyle's body would be high,' said Brook.

'But if he was alive he would have contacted me. I'm all he has; he wouldn't let me suffer like this.'

'But he left his phone, love,' said Poole. 'Maybe he can't contact you.'

'But why leave his phone? That's the point, isn't it?'

'What about his father in Stoke?' asked Noble. 'We've contacted him but he claims he's not seen or heard from Kyle.'

'That bastard,' she spat out with surprising venom. 'He hasn't seen Kyle for five years, or wanted to, and Kyle would never go near him, the way he rejected us.'

'But might he contact his father, let him know where he's going?'

'Before he spoke to me? No chance. But you're welcome to ask.'

'We will,' said Brook. 'I notice your house is for sale.'

'We're moving to Chester,' she said. 'We were there this weekend looking at houses. We're just waiting for Kyle to finish his exams.' Her lip began to wobble again.

'You say he left his phone behind. Have you checked his calls?' asked Brook.

'I couldn't. It's not working.'

'Mind if we try?'

She fished around in her handbag and pulled out her son's mobile. 'Here. And take his laptop from his room. If you can work out his passwords, maybe there's an email or—'

'We'll send someone to collect it.'

Noble produced an evidence bag even though prints were already compromised. Mrs Kennedy dropped the phone in and Noble tried to turn it on through the plastic.

'I'd give anything if Kyle was with his father, but he isn't,' said Alice. 'That scumbag dumped us both as soon as he found out . . .' She hesitated.

'. . . as soon as he found out Kyle was gay,' finished Brook.

Alice stared at Brook. 'Yes. How did you know?'

'Len told Sergeant Grey that Kyle was "sensitive". I assumed that was code.'

She nodded. 'Kyle is gay. Or he thinks he is. I was hoping it was just a phase.'

'But he's still a nice boy, Inspector,' chipped in Poole.

'And why wouldn't he be?' demanded Alice.

'I'm sorry, love, I only meant—'

'Does he have a boyfriend?' interrupted Brook.

'Don't be disgusting,' said Alice. 'He isn't like that. He isn't . . .'

'What? Active?'

'Not at all. I know Kyle.'

'You didn't know he applied for a passport,' pointed out Brook.

The tears appeared again and Brook gestured to PC Patel, who provided further comfort. Brook didn't enjoy this part of the job. Pushing and cajoling the vulnerable was distasteful but experience had taught him that such pressure ensured the best information.

When the tears subsided, Alice Kennedy tried again. 'You don't know him, Inspector. He's kind and gentle and shy. He wouldn't know how to approach . . . people . . . in that way.'

'So you think he's still a virgin?' Remembering the distressing circumstances of his own estranged daughter's loss of sexual innocence at fifteen, Brook made an effort to soften his tone.

Alice nodded. 'He would've told me. Not that he didn't fall in love.'

Brook smiled. 'But from a distance.'

'Exactly.'

'And had he fallen in love recently?'

She looked up at him. 'Yes, Inspector. I think he might have.'

'Any idea who?'

'He wouldn't tell me anything like that.'

'And might this person have been at Kyle's party on Friday?' asked Noble.

'It's possible, but I wasn't there. Besides, it wasn't a party, it was more of a gathering. He only had a handful of people he was friendly with. People like himself; shy, sensitive. He wasn't going to bother celebrating at all, but they persuaded him.'

'They, being?' Noble held his pen poised over his notebook.

'You've already got all the names I know. And there was only one other boy invited I knew about,' replied Alice. 'Russell Thomson. Rusty.' In spite of herself she giggled then looked round guiltily.

'What's funny?'

'You're going to ask if Russell could have been Kyle's . . .' She burst out laughing again. 'No. He is *not* Kyle's type,' she concluded. 'Rusty is even more shy and introverted than Kyle. He barely speaks when he meets you and when he does, he's too afraid to even lift his eyes off the ground. He makes Kyle look like Russell Brand, doesn't he, Len?'

'It's true,' conceded Poole, with a tight smile.

'And his mum is very pretty, isn't she, Len?'

'I haven't met her,' replied Poole. 'You saw her at a school social evening, remember. I wasn't there.'

'Russell Thomson?' Brook raised an eyebrow at Noble, who nodded. They had Thomson's address. Brook decided not to ask who Russell Brand was.

'And the two missing girls were also at the party?' asked Brook.

'As far as I know,' replied Alice. 'We were away. Kyle knows Adele Watson from classes and they sometimes study together. She's very smart but very serious. She's a writer – poetry, I think. Well, I'm not surprised. She has everything going for her. And she's really pretty. She gets on well with Kyle. Well, you know how it is with pretty girls and . . .' She tailed off, not wanting to hear the word again. When no one else filled the vacuum, she finally said, 'Gays.'

'What about Becky Blake?' said Noble.

'I didn't know her that well,' replied Alice. 'We've seen her around with that other friend of hers, Fern something. She's attractive in a cheap sort of way.'

'Bit full of herself,' agreed Len. 'Reckoned she was going to be a model.' The past tense prompted a discreet glance between the two detectives. 'Well, if her dad had the final say she'd be a shoo-in. Had the poor sod twisted round her little finger, she did. Nothing too much trouble for her – clothes, the latest phones.'

'Not the type to get on well with my Kyle,' added Alice. 'I'm surprised he invited her, but it takes all sorts. She may have been nicer than we thought.'

'What about alcohol and drugs?' asked Noble.

'I bought Kyle a dozen WKDs from Bargain Booze,' replied Poole. 'He could have asked for a lot more and I'd have given him the money, but he isn't much of a drinker.'

Brook eyed Mrs Kennedy for a reaction but she maintained the face of a stoic. Brook had been right about the basis for their relationship. Almost every time Len Poole opened his mouth it was to proclaim economic dominion over Alice. 'Mrs Kennedy?'

'Len's right,' she agreed, without looking up. 'Obviously he'd tried a few things. Don't they all? But drugs made him feel sick; tobacco too. He drank a lot for a year when he was sixteen and still working things out in his head. Nowadays children have to lay claim to adulthood before they're ready. It's so sad. Once he became more adult he had nothing to prove.'

'And when was the last time you saw Kyle?'

'I spoke to him on Friday afternoon before we left for Wales, through his bedroom door. I actually saw him last on the Thursday night. He went out with a CD and a poster. He said it was for a friend. Don't ask me who.'

'What time was that?'

'About nine.'

'What was his mood?'

'Excited, nervous. About the party, I assumed.'

'You didn't see him after that?'

'No. I heard him come in very late. He just ran up to his room and slammed the door.'

'So you wouldn't know what he was wearing last.'

'Not for sure, but he only ever wore jeans and a T-shirt,' replied Alice. 'And a blue G-STAR hoodie to go out in. That's missing.'

'What about next-door neighbours?' asked Brook.

'Neighbours?'

'They may have seen something the night of the party.'

'Well, there's Colin and Leanne, this way,' Alice said, pointing. 'They're away. And the Stevensons, the other side. They were here. They've got two young children.'

Alice Kennedy stood by the door as Brook and Noble searched the small bedroom. It was surprisingly tidy, even the bed was made. They found nothing of interest, with no sign of Kyle's secret passport, and left the laptop for the Scene of Crime Officers to dust for prints before possible removal. No kids used diaries in 2011. Kyle's entire life would be in his phone, his emails or on a social networking site like Facebook or Bebo.

'Is his room normally this tidy?' asked Brook. Mrs Kennedy shook her head. 'And you say you touched nothing except to pick up the mobile and the leaflet.'

'Correct.'

Noble produced the mobile, inside its clear bag. 'Where were they?'

'On the bed, the phone on top of the leaflet.'

Noble took the leaflet from Brook and arranged the two artefacts on the bed. 'Like so?'

Alice Kennedy nodded.

'What about the aftermath of the party?'

'Nothing out of place when we got home. No mess, no stains, no washing up in the sink, no empties. As if . . .' She bowed her head.

'As if he was getting his affairs in order,' said Brook.

'Only later did we realise it was odd,' she added. 'Oh, there was one thing. Blood.'

'Blood?' said Brook. 'Is this the sticking plaster?'

'Yes, it was in the rubbish. It was just a tiny bit, soaked into a small plaster. There was a bit of linen bandage as well. I assume one of them cut themselves.'

'Did the other officer take the plaster?' asked Brook, looking from Noble to Mrs Kennedy.

'No, I threw it out, though the bag should still be in the dustbin. They haven't collected yet.'

'Sergeant Noble will need to dig it out, with your permission.' Brook declined to look at his DS.

'Of course. It couldn't have been more than a graze,' she said, though her face now betrayed unease at Brook's interest.

Brook gestured around the room. 'Have you checked his wardrobe and drawers?'

'Yes.'

'Anything obviously missing?' asked Noble.

'He often went out with a small knapsack which he kept on the back of the kitchen door. It's gone. His MP3 would've been in there. Maybe some jeans and underwear, his G-Star hoodie. That's it.'

Brook was fairly certain that an MP3 was some type of modern Walkman. The detectives asked a few more questions then let Alice return to the lounge.

When she was out of earshot, Noble said, 'There's no SIM card in the phone.'

'That'll make things a bit harder. Kyle obviously doesn't want to be found.'

'You think that's what it is?'

'We'll see.' Brook stood in the middle of the room looking at the posters on the walls. 'Kyle had quite a thing for The Smiths – and Morrissey in particular. Nobody else gets a look-in.'

Noble turned to him with a mocking grin. 'That's groovy, daddio.'

'Yeah, all right John, I'm not dead yet. And it's not as though you're the right side of thirty. Besides, this is a lot nearer my youth than it is Kyle's or yours. You may not know it but Morrissey's a gay icon – tells us a bit more about Kyle.'

'That he likes gay icons,' chipped in Noble.

'That he thinks for himself and doesn't just follow the herd. He's different enough to choose what he likes rather than what's in vogue.' Brook sauntered to the window to look out over the road. He stopped and peered out into the gloom, his gaze held by a young man standing beneath a streetlight on the pavement outside. He was tall and powerfully built and wore a sweatshirt, baggy shorts down to his knees and chunky training shoes. Steam rose from him as he took an ostentatious breather, hands on knees. But in spite of this, Brook was convinced the young man was watching the house, looking directly up at him, framed in the light of Kyle's bedroom window. A moment later, the young man took a deep breath and turned to power away up the street.

Brook looked at his watch. 'Have we got DNA?'

'Toothbrush. The others too.'

'I've seen enough,' Brook decided. 'Get a copy of Kyle's passport application sent over. We ought to find out who endorsed his likeness on the photograph. Maybe we're looking for an older man.'

'A gay lover.' Noble nodded. 'But why hide it from his mum? It's not illegal.'

'Neither is masturbation but it's not something you would want your parents to know about, John. Especially if Alice knew who it was.'

'Somebody who'd groomed Kyle for a few years, you mean. A paedo neighbour maybe?'

Brook sighed but didn't rise to the bait. 'Possible. Check the SO Register tomorrow. See if it throws up a local name. Adele Watson and Becky Blake have passports, you said?'

'Their parents said so.'

'Check when they applied for them. If it was the same time as Kyle, we may be able to put this thing to bed.'

Brook gazed out into the blackness. The back of the Kennedy house overlooked fields attached to one of Derby College's small suburban sites. Like many such under-used facilities, part of the land had been sold to build new houses, and Brook could see the twinkling lights of new homes half a mile away. Another path passed the bottom of the garden and stretched out into the dark.

'Got it,' panted Noble, clutching a black bin bag.

'Where does that path behind the house go?'

'It leads up to the back of the college and then round to the new housing estate.'

'You've had uniform take a look, I assume?'

'Not the full monty, but yes. Why?'

'And the fields?'

'They're shared by Murray Park School and the college,' said Noble. 'It's a big area.'

'It's also dark and empty, John. They all lived close and walked to the party so, if Kyle and his friends wanted to disappear and no one saw them leave the house at the front, maybe they just walked away across the fields.'

'Charlton's going to love us finger-tipping that space,' said Noble, nodding at the darkness.

'We're not at that stage yet. We do the canvass, bins and grates, and see where we are.'

Twelve

'MR STEVENSON, I'M DI BROOK, this is DS Noble. We've come from next door.'

The man opened the door wider but turned round when he heard whispering behind him. 'Bed, you two,' he said firmly to the two curious infants poking their heads round the inner door. They scurried up the stairs, giggling.

Stevenson stepped outside and closed the front door behind him. 'How's Alice holding up? It must be awful. Any news?'

'We're still making enquiries and we were wondering if you noticed anything unusual last Friday night.'

'Honestly, no. Alice mentioned Kyle might be having a party but we forgot all about it, it was so quiet.'

'So you didn't see any guests arriving, for instance?' asked Noble.

'I saw one of the girls arrive. She had dark, mid-length hair and dark eyes. Very pretty. About half eight that would have been.'

'Walking?' Stevenson nodded. 'How was she dressed?'

'Jeans and a hoodie. Trainers, I think. Oh, and she had a small rucksack.'

'Not exactly party clothes,' observed Brook.

'I suppose not.'

Noble finished making a note. 'No one else?'

'No one.'

'What about leaving?'

'No. We'd be in bed by then, I guess, but we didn't hear a commotion or anything.'

'No cars or taxis idling outside the house?'

'Not that I heard.'

'No loud conversations?' Again Stevenson shook his head. Brook turned to leave. 'Thanks.'

Mr Stevenson raised a finger. 'There was one thing a bit odd. It may be nothing.'

'Go on.'

'It was around half nine. I thought I saw another of Kyle's friends arriving for the party, but I'm not sure – a young lad.'

'Can you describe him?'

'Tall, well-built and good-looking. I don't know him but I've seen him around.'

'You got a good look then.'

'Well, it was hard not to. He stood outside under the streetlamp for a good five minutes, maybe more.'

'Doing what?'

'Nothing,' said Mr Stevenson. 'I got the impression he was deciding.'

'Deciding what?'

'Whether to go into the party.'

'Did you see him go in?'

'Well no, that was the odd thing. I saw him disappear, presumably to go into the house. But a few minutes later, I saw him walking away.'

'Maybe he was just calling in?' said Brook.

'Maybe.' Stevenson shrugged. 'But the odd thing was, he had a present in his hand, wrapped up. I saw it quite clearly.'

'Not unusual for a birthday party,' observed Noble. 'He could've been dropping it off.'

'That's just it. He still had it when he was walking away.'

Brook and Noble stared down at the mattress. The pink mobile phone and the leaflet sat in the middle of the fluffy pink duvet. The phone was switched off.

'That's how it was,' said Mrs Blake from the bedroom doorway. 'We haven't touched a thing.'

Brook and Noble dropped the phone and the Deity leaflet into evidence bags and finished their cursory examination of the room.

'Did you check her calls?' asked Noble, brandishing the bag.

'We didn't touch the phone,' said Fred Blake, making the effort to speak.

'No point anyway. Madam wouldn't tell *us* the SIM code,' explained Mrs Blake with a hint of resentment.

'What about her laptop?'

'It's in the case at the side of the bureau.'

'Have you tried checking her emails?' Brook asked. 'Okay – you don't know the password.'

'Please take the laptop if it'll help,' Fred said.

'We will.'

Brook glanced at the make-up bureau with its halo of naked light bulbs. 'Any clothes or luggage missing?'

'I wouldn't know about that. It's hard to keep up with madam's wardrobe.' Mrs Blake looked to her stricken husband who simply stared, ashen-faced, into the distance. 'Fred? Anything missing?'

Fred Blake continued to stare until he became aware that his attention was needed, then he processed the question and looked up at Brook. 'She had a small leather Louis Vuitton rucksack that she took everywhere. There may be a couple of T-shirts missing from her drawers. Some underwear too.'

'What about her passport?'

'Her passport?'

'You told us before she had a passport,' said Noble.

Fred nodded. 'Becky wanted to go to Miami last year.'

'So that's where we went,' put in Mrs Blake. Her husband shot her a spiteful glance.

'So she'd had it a while,' Brook said.

'Over a year.'

'Is it still here?'

'She keeps it in there.' Fred pointed to a drawer of her make-up bureau which Noble searched. The passport was missing. Fred was suddenly excited. 'That's good, isn't it? She may have been planning to go abroad.'

'She might,' agreed Brook.

'When was the last time you both saw Becky?' asked Noble.

'Last Friday,' said Blake hesitantly. He looked at his wife who was putting a cigarette in her mouth. 'Christy?'

'Sounds about right,' she replied with a shrug, rummaging for a lighter. 'Before she went to the party at the gay boy's house.'

'His name's Kyle,' put in Blake, a pained expression on his face. 'He's a nice lad.'

'How did she seem?' asked Brook.

Fred Blake frowned at his wife as she lit up. 'You shouldn't smoke in here. You know how Becky hates it.' Fred looked away as Christy exhaled, long and slow, into the bedroom.

'Quiet, now you mention it,' she said. 'For her.'

'And did she say anything which struck you as odd?'

'Not to me'. Christy turned to Fred, who shook his head.

'What about money?' asked Brook. 'Did she have her own bank account?'

'No need,' said Christy.

'Chris-ty,' muttered Fred.

'She was strictly a cash only girl, and with an ATM for a father she always had more than she needed. Didn't she, darling?' Her husband narrowed his eyes at her.

'Did she ask for any money that Friday?'

'Ask and ye shall receive,' sneered Christy. 'Whatever she wanted.'

'For God's sake, woman!' spat Fred. 'Becky could be hurt or even . . .' His head disappeared into a massaging hand. 'She didn't ask for money on Friday. She had enough for a taxi home but it's not like she was going to a bar in town.'

'What was she wearing?' asked Brook.

'Yeah, that was a bit weird, come to think of it,' said Christy. 'She went out in jeans and a sweatshirt.'

'Colours?'

'Black jeans and purple sweatshirt,' said Fred.

'And why was that weird?' asked Brook.

'Most weekends she went out looking like a prostitute,' said Christy. Fred turned away, his fists and teeth clenching. 'Short skirt. Tits you could see from space.'

Fred Blake wheeled round, a sudden inspiration brightening his countenance. 'Maybe she was dressed practical. For a journey, like.'

Brook nodded. 'It's possible. Had she talked about wanting to get away?'

'No. Like we told the other officer, she was happy,' said Fred softly. 'She's never gone off before. Not without ringing us. Why would she leave her phone?'

'It's unusual,' agreed Brook.

'It's unheard of.' Christy laughed bitterly. 'The fuss she kicked up to get it.'

'Did she leave on foot?'

Fred nodded this time. 'She often walked. It was good for her muscle tone.'

'It's Wednesday now,' observed Brook. 'You last saw her on Friday, but only reported her missing yesterday morning.'

'When we found out Kyle Kennedy was missing. It was his party.'

'They were good friends?'

'I didn't think so,' said Fred. 'Kyle was . . .'

'A homo,' snorted Christy. 'But girls these days don't mind that, do they?' She smiled at Brook. 'They're not a threat.'

'I don't think she was looking forward to going,' continued Fred. 'But her mate Fern was away.'

'Mate, my arse.' Christy laughed. 'That dopey cow is just another one of her worshippers. Like you, fawning all over her night and day.'

Fred Blake spun round on his wife. 'Becky's missing, for God's sake, woman! Give it a rest.'

'Is she fuck. She's swanning off somewhere on our hard-earned cash.'

'*My* hard-earned cash.'

'Is that why you didn't report her missing until yesterday?' interrupted Brook.

The warring parents fell silent. Finally Fred said reluctantly, 'Christy may be right.'

'Halle-fucking-lujah.'

'We thought she might have gone away. She's eighteen, very mature, very certain of herself. She's got a key and comes and goes as she pleases.'

'So you thought she was staying with friends,' said Noble.

Fred shrugged. 'We'd still think that, if it wasn't for the phone. She was never off it. Texting every minute of the day.'

'To a boyfriend maybe?'

'Sometimes.'

'Anyone special?'

'No chance. She was the special one. They were queuing round the block for her. Not that my Becky is going to get bogged down with one of the local deadbeats and start churning out benefit bums. She has big plans.'

'Such as?'

'She's going to be famous.' He grinned suddenly, deflected from his loss. 'A Supermodel. That's why she didn't mess around with drink and drugs. It was bad for her skin. Always telling you off for smoking round the house, wasn't she?' he said to his wife, who deliberately blew cigarette smoke in his face.

'So she had nothing she needed to run away from.'

'Absolutely not.' Fred rummaged in his pocket and unfolded a piece of paper. 'Here. She got this letter last week from Models Select.'

'Haven't you framed it yet?' jeered Christy.

Brook took the letter and examined it. The heading was basic, the text brief and to the point.

Dear Becky,

I am pleased to tell you that we are able to offer you a place at our modelling agency, and would be grateful if you could contact us to arrange a meeting as soon as possible.

Yours sincerly

There was an illegible signature but no name typed. Brook looked at the top of the page. The address was 222 Kings Road, London. There was no email address, just a contact telephone number. Brook pulled out his mobile and keyed in the number before handing the letter to Noble.

'See? She's known since she was ten that she was special. And she was right. When she's got her A-levels, she's out of here and on her way to fame and fortune. She even took her portfolio off the walls to take to London.' He turned to Brook. 'Here, you think she might have already gone to London? Decided to pack in her studies?'

Brook glanced at his watch. 'We'll certainly check. If you could go downstairs and finish that list of contact numbers for her friends and sort out a recent photograph? We just need to finish off in here.'

To leave two men in their daughter's bedroom left the Blakes looking momentarily ill at ease, but eventually they padded off towards the stairs. As soon as they turned away, Brook flicked the call button on his phone.

'That letter's a fake,' said Noble. 'No proper address. No email.'

'And a spelling mistake,' agreed Brook, holding the phone to his ear. 'It looks more like amateur DTP than a company document.'

'How come her father didn't spot it?'

'Too much stardust in his eyes.' Brook rang off. 'The phone number doesn't exist.' He got to his knees and started searching under the mattress.

Noble started removing all the drawers from the cabinets, looking for documents taped to the underside. 'But his wife isn't so star-struck.'

'I'm guessing she's not even seen it. She's not interested.' Brook planted his face on the carpet and scanned the floor. He pulled a wad of glossy photographs from under the bed.

'Becky's portfolio is under here.' The photographs were in a heap and partially stuck together by the Blu-tack still adhering to the corners of the prints and the wall. Brook prised them apart and arranged them on the mattress. The teenager posed at them in a variety of moods and outfits.

'I wonder why she took them down?' asked Noble.

Brook knelt back down to be sure he'd missed nothing. He slipped a latex finger into the small gap between the make-up bureau and the carpet, and slid out a piece of folded paper. He opened it gingerly. This time the letterhead was a more professional affair, with all the usual contact information. Brook read the text quickly and passed it to Noble.

Dear Miss Blake,

Thank you for recently sending us your portfolio. It is with regret that I have to inform you that we don't feel you have the look that we are currently seeking. This is a subjective judgement and other modelling agencies may well feel differently . . .

'She wrote the other letter to herself after receiving this,' said Brook sombrely. 'So her parents wouldn't think she was a failure.' He smiled sadly down at the photographs. 'And then she couldn't face looking at herself.'

'And bolted because she couldn't handle it?'

'Could be – this is our second missing kid in personal turmoil.'

'It would only be temporary.'

'Sure, it's just a failed job application to us but it's a shattered dream to Becky Blake. This is probably the first time anyone's said no to her, John. When you glide through your youth without a care in the world, that first reality check is the hardest. And the bigger the dream, the bigger the shock finding out life isn't lived on your terms. Unhappiness is not a product they sell on TV. Some don't know how to cope with it.'

'You've got a TV now, have you?'

Brook smiled. 'It's just for research. I haven't joined the human race. Yet.' He selected one of the photographs of Becky for use in the inquiry. 'We'd better make a move.'

'*Live Forever*,' read Noble from the leaflet. '*Young, Beautiful, Immortal*. What the hell are they up to?'

'I'm not sure. But at least we now know they're acting in concert. This was planned. These kids weren't abducted. They left of their own volition.'

'Is that good?' asked Noble.

'For now.'

'You're sure the phone and the leaflet weren't on the bed?' said Noble, looking at the two artefacts on a chest of drawers beside the bed.

'I didn't find them,' replied Adele Watson's mother. She was a shrivelled, prune-faced woman with a leathery complexion and prematurely grey hair which she wore in long knotted strands. Despite the Family Liaison Officer informing her to expect a visit from CID, she was in her nightclothes and a large hooded dressing-gown that completely engulfed her. The contrast with the hard tanned body of her good-looking husband, a builder by trade, was stark.

'Mr Watson?' asked Noble.

Brook glanced up at James Watson from his examination of a large wardrobe. He seemed to be in a daydream, like Fred Blake, just staring, saucer-eyed, at the crumpled duvet of his daughter's bed. With a twenty-year-old daughter of his own, he wasn't surprised by Watson and Blake's reaction. Brook had given it a lot of thought – too much. Mothers were important to young girls, but fathers and daughters shared something unfathomable – a dark and mysterious bond that was always delicately balanced and easily contaminated.

'Jim,' prompted his wife.

Adele's father snapped out of his reverie and looked at Brook. 'That's how it was.'

'On the chest of drawers?'

'I just told you.'

'And the bed was dishevelled?'

'If that means was it a mess, yes,' replied Watson.

'On or off?'

'What?'

'The phone.'

'Off.'

'Did you check her calls?'

'I tried to.'

Brook looked up at him sharply. 'So you touched the phone.'

'Obviously. But I put it back exactly as it was.'

'You never told me that,' snapped Mrs Watson.

'That's because there was nothing to tell you, woman. I thought her last calls might show me where she'd gone, that's all,' he explained to Brook.

'And did they?'

Watson shook his head but didn't make eye-contact. 'The SIM card's gone. She must've taken it with her.'

Noble bagged the phone as well as the Deity leaflet, which was identical to the other two they'd collected. 'But if you tried to check her calls, you must have known your daughter's SIM Pin.'

'I told you. The SIM card's missing.'

'But you didn't know that when you tried to turn it on,' added Brook.

Watson nodded. 'One-one-nine-two.'

'My daughter would've died under torture before divulging that to me or her mum,' said Brook, playing Happy Parent for a moment.

'It's her date of birth,' snarled Watson.

'Did you also check her computer for emails?'

'Her laptop's gone.'

'Gone?' Brook glanced over at Noble then walked back to the wardrobe he'd looked in earlier. He plucked a laptop case from a hook on the back of the door. It was empty. 'Without this?'

Watson shrugged. 'She must have taken it in a rucksack instead.' Brook fixed his eyes on Adele's father. There was more than shock in his eyes. There was resentment. He understood it. It was part of the strange connection between fathers and daughters – the teenage girl pushing towards womanhood, the father, her jailer, imposing adolescence. Were Adele Watson and *her* father fighting this ancient battle? Brook recognised defeat in his face. What else would there be? Only one winner.

'Have you checked if Adele has her passport with her?' asked Noble.

'No,' replied Mrs Watson.

'Can you see if it's still in the house?'

'I'll go,' said Watson. 'It should still be with our passports. We went to Tenerife last summer.' He turned away.

'Go with him, Sergeant,' said Brook. Noble looked up at his DI. There was an edge to his voice that Noble had learned to detect. Something was wrong. He turned to follow Watson into another bedroom.

Brook smiled to reassure Mrs Watson, but she was oblivious to the sudden undercurrent. He ambled round the room and ran a finger across a shelf of books containing works by Toni Morrison, Virginia Woolf and Beryl Bainbridge as well as the anthologies of Ted Hughes and Sylvia Plath amongst others. He picked up the Plath book and opened it to the first page. In a beautiful hand Adele had written *I am, I am, I am*.

Brook returned it to its place and gestured at the almost bare desk. 'Is this where she kept her laptop?' he asked. Adele's mother nodded.

A lone book sat there instead. *The Collected Poems of Edgar Allan Poe.*

Brook smiled. 'That takes me back.'

'It's new,' said Adele's mother. 'She bought that last Friday.'

'The day of the party? She has her own money then.'

'Some. Though she isn't one to spend it on clothes and phones. Jim practically has to drag her out to buy her clothes.'

'Does he?' said Brook. 'I thought that might be more of a job for her mother.' Mrs Watson shrugged her disinterest. Brook opened the anthology to the bookmarked page. 'A Dream Within A Dream.' He closed his eyes, repeating the poem out loud from memory.

> *Take this kiss upon the brow!*
> *And, in parting from you now,*
> *This much let me avow –*
> *You are not wrong, who deem*
> *That my days have been a dream:'*

Brook hesitated and was forced to look at the text.

> *Yet if hope has flown away*
> *In a night, or in a day,*
> *In a vision, or in none,*
> *Is it therefore the less gone?*
> *All that we see or seem*
> *Is but a dream within a dream.'*

'Yeah,' Mrs Watson said dismissively. 'Her head was full of that sort of crap.'

Brook looked at the page. A single word had been written in the margin. *Miranda*. He closed the book and picked up a photograph in a cockleshell frame. A dark-eyed beauty glowered back at him through intense and mysterious brown eyes. He sensed a pent-up fury in her, an eagerness to be heard, noticed. He thought of his own daughter, Terri – oh, so impatient for the freedoms of adulthood. Adele and Terri weren't far apart in age or taste. Edgar Allan Poe for Adele Watson – with Terri it had been the poems of Robert Frost and the music of Radiohead, to confer the illusion of depth, suggest a worldliness that was yet to arrive.

Brook pulled open the drawers of the bureau and took out a purple box from one drawer. There were three fountain pens inside. 'Nice pens.'

'She loved writing – you know, the old fashioned way,' said Mrs Watson. 'Poems, essays. She was very bright. She had a place at Cambridge next year.'

Brook looked at her. Past tense again. 'Where?'

'Cambridge,' she repeated, louder and slower for Brook's benefit.

'No, where did she write? I don't see any papers or writing books here.'

'She had a notebook for ideas. If it's not there, she must have taken it with her.'

'What about a diary?'

'Not sure. But it's all online these days, isn't it?'

Jim Watson returned with Noble. 'It's gone. She must have taken it.'

'Well, that's good, isn't it?' said Mrs Watson. 'She's gone abroad somewhere.'

'It's a possibility,' said Noble.

'"Live Forever. Question Mark",' said Brook.

'Pardon?'

'Is that one of her poems?'

'How did you . . . ?'

'It's written on this blotter here,' said Brook, peering down at it. He gestured to Noble to add it to the Exhibits Officer's list then pulled off his latex gloves. 'Or maybe she copied it from the leaflet.' He smiled at the Watsons then looked casually at the walls.

'Jim Morrison, James Dean, River Phoenix,' he said, noting the posters dotted around Adele Watson's walls. 'Young, beautiful and immortal,' he added, suddenly thoughtful. 'Who's that?' he asked, nodding at a fourth poster.

The Watsons shook their heads.

'It's Kurt Cobain,' said Noble. 'He was lead singer with Nirvana.'

'Was?' enquired Brook.

'He shot himself.'

'And that?' Brook enquired, pointing to a poster of a young blond man over Adele's bed.

Watson scoffed loudly. 'That? That's a faggot.'

His wife frowned at him. 'That's Alexander Skarsgard. He's in *True Blood*.'

'What's that?' asked Brook.

'It's a show about vampires, if you can believe it?' spat Watson. 'And it's full of faggoty actors like him pretending to be men.'

'You're not a fan,' observed Brook patiently.

'Please,' he sneered. 'People will swallow anything.'

'I like it,' said his wife. 'The men are hot.'

'Jesus, Roz, give us a break.'

'Your husband's right, Mrs Watson,' Brook said gravely. 'All actors are gay.' Noble looked away, trying not to smile.

Watson became animated. 'Thank you, Inspector. But try telling that to my wife and daughter.'

'I mean, proper women are attracted to real men,' continued Brook. 'Firemen, soldiers . . .'

'Exactly,' Watson agreed.

'. . . builders,' Brook threw in.

Watson went back into his shell as his wife squinted suspiciously at him. 'I wouldn't know about that,' he muttered.

'So Adele is more interested in actors than builders,' said Brook.

'Well, her boyfriend isn't an actor,' said Mrs Watson.

'Boyfriend?' enquired Noble, looking at Brook. 'You didn't mention that before.'

'With a Porsche, as well,' said the shrivelled woman. 'You should speak to him.'

'What's his name?'

'She didn't tell me. Jim saw him though.'

'I never saw him,' blustered Watson. 'But he dropped her off last week and she was crying. She said he'd dumped her.' He smiled coldly at the detectives. 'So maybe that's who you should be out looking for.'

'And you don't know his name?'

'No,' said Watson.

'Perhaps Adele mentioned him in an email?' suggested Brook.

'No. Her laptop's gone – I told you.'

Brook held up a hand in apology. 'So you did.'

'And he drove a Porsche,' said Noble, making a note.

Watson hesitated now. 'Not definitely. But a sports car of some kind. Or maybe it was a saloon.'

'You told me it was a Porsche,' said Roz Watson.

'Either way, an older man,' prompted Brook, fixing his eye on Watson. 'With money.'

'I would think.'

Brook smiled warmly at the husband and wife. 'Well, if you could go downstairs and finish that list of contacts with PC . . .'

'. . . Crainey,' finished Noble.

'Right. And keep out of Adele's room in case Scientific Support Officers need to do any work.'

'There's something wrong there,' said Brook, when they were standing under the streetlight outside the front gate.

'I know. They seemed more angry than concerned.'

'And they didn't mention their daughter by name the entire time. At the Blake house it was Becky this and Becky that – same with Mrs Kennedy and Kyle.'

'Now you mention it,' said Noble, passing Brook a cigarette.

'Another odd thing – he seemed happy telling us his daughter had been dumped. That's not normal. Contrast that with a typical father like Fred Blake who thinks no one's fit to breathe the same air as his daughter. Anybody dumping Becky Blake would be bad-mouthed for the rest of his life.'

'Think Watson has an idea who the boyfriend is and plans to confront him?'

'That might explain his memory loss over the Porsche.' Brook took a deep lungful of smoke. 'But there's more to it than that. His daughter's missing but he hardly seems surprised or worried.'

'Like he knows where she's gone?'

'Or maybe *why* she might go.'

'Something to do with him, you think?'

Brook shrugged. 'Possible. We need to search the house.'

'Looking for what!' exclaimed Noble.

'The laptop, for one thing. And something containing Adele's writings.'

'You think Watson took Adele's laptop?'

'Maybe. Or maybe she hid it herself. Either way, Becky and Kyle both left their laptops behind. So where's Adele's?'

'Maybe they need one between the three of them so she took it.'

'And not even put it in its case?'

'It's odd. But why would Watson take it?'

'No idea. Perhaps he thinks there's something on it – a poem or a piece of writing or an email – he doesn't want anyone to see.'

'Containing what?'

'Who knows? It may be no more than father and daughter butting heads over her choice of boyfriend, but girls can be pretty vitriolic behind your back.'

'What about Mrs Watson? Do you think she's covering for her husband about something?'

'I'm not sure she knows there's anything amiss, not deep down.' Brook smiled sadly. 'Maybe even he doesn't.'

Noble nodded. 'So it may all be in his head.'

'Or Adele's. Teenage daughters are younger versions of our wives, John, so it's not a huge leap for that relationship to be corrupted. The boyfriend could have triggered something in him that caused conflict. Our daughters having sex with other men is the secret dread of all fathers, the first thing we picture when boys start looking their way. It's even worse when older men are looking.'

Noble kept silent, waiting for a corroborating anecdote from Brook's own past parenting. It didn't arrive. He threw his butt to the pavement. 'I'll put in a call to Social Services tomorrow. See what pops up on the Watsons. So where does this leave us?'

'With three unhappy kids looking to change their lives,' Brook said. 'Three abandoned mobile phones and three leaflets. This website . . .'

'Deity?'

'We need to find out who's behind it. Tell Cooper to start on it as soon as he gets in tomorrow. And get a warrant for the Watson house.' Brook looked at his watch then back to the front door as the uniformed FLO closed it behind him. Brook stepped to the rear of his car and opened the boot. He took out the small tightly packed bin bag retrieved from the Kennedy dustbin. 'It's gone eleven, John. Can you get a lift back with . . . ?'

'I can,' said Noble.

'Good, get some rest before your surveillance. Take this bin bag to the lab and give them the plaster. I'll call on this Russell Thomson on my way in tomorrow and then we'll see about going public.'

Thirteen

I T WAS CLOSE TO MIDNIGHT when Brook finally pulled up to his cottage in Hartington. To his annoyance, a lime-green VW Polo was parked outside his house so he had to leave his BMW in the cramped drive of Rose Cottage, the empty rental property next door.

He trudged wearily to his tiny porch carrying one of the Deity leaflets in a plastic wallet – something to think about in the lonely hours to keep his mind off the mortal remains of Barry Kirk.

He fumbled for his door key, trying to ignore his grumbling stomach. He hadn't eaten since his bacon sandwiches but hadn't had time to buy food again. Worse still, he hadn't bought cigarettes.

When Brook put his key in the lock and turned, nothing happened – the door was already unlocked. Had he forgotten to lock up this morning? It wouldn't be the first time he'd wandered out in an insomniac fug. Once he'd even forgotten to close the door.

He returned his key to his pocket, but instead of opening the door, he paused to listen. Something felt wrong. He knelt to lift the empty flower pot in the corner of the porch. The spare key was gone.

Again Brook racked his brains, trying to remember if he'd moved it to another hiding-place but his brain was too tired to cooperate. He came to a decision and pulled gently down on the handle and eased the front door open. It moved without a sound and he peered into the blackness of the kitchen beyond and listened. Without flicking on the light he couldn't be sure, but he sensed things were not how he'd left them earlier in the day. There were dark shapes on the kitchen table which he didn't recognise. He knew they couldn't be his. Brook didn't have clutter, knick-knacks, objets d'art nor any of the mementoes of a life lived. His development as a human being had been in suspended animation for years.

Brook took a tentative step into the shadows, then another. When he reached the foot of the tiny crooked staircase he gazed up to the trapdoor in the roofspace on the first floor. He had an unlicensed gun in the attic, a legacy of his entanglements with The Reaper. It didn't work but maybe that wouldn't matter, and he wished he'd hidden it in a more accessible place.

Brook remembered his training – Defensive not Offensive. He slid off his shoes and then his jacket, wrapping it around his leading arm. Burglars often carried large knives, not principally for protection but to sever the wiring of desirable electrical goods for ease of carriage. That didn't mean a surprised intruder wouldn't use it when cornered.

Suitably protected, Brook tiptoed into the small lounge, where a figure lay on the sofa, legs splayed across one of the arms, its breathing shallow. Brook leaned over to switch on a lamp.

He squinted at the face of the intruder then stood upright in bewilderment. 'Terri?'

The figure stirred and opened her eyes. 'Dad.'

'Terri.' Brook flung his jacket to the floor, sat on the sofa and hugged his daughter. 'It's really you. What are you doing here? Never mind. How long have you been here? Never mind.' He hugged her again, then held her by the shoulders in panic and searched in her eyes. 'What's wrong? Is your mother all right?'

Terri yawned and sat up. 'Dad, she's fine. Where've you been?'

'Work.'

She squinted at her watch. 'Nothing changes.'

'Why didn't you give me some notice?'

'I did. I emailed you, Dad. Two weeks ago. To tell you I wanted to come and visit. How often do you check your emails?' she said, swinging her feet to the floor.

Brook shrugged. 'Every couple of weeks. At least.'

She shook her head then smiled. 'You look well, Dad.'

Brook raised an eyebrow. He knew he was wasting away. 'For a workaholic who doesn't look after himself, you mean.' He held her tight again. '*You* look beautiful. You really do – just like your mum. Your hair suits you, short. I like it.' Brook stopped, looking sheepish. He wasn't usually the type to gush.

Terri smiled back. 'No flaws?'

He peered at her neck and examined her red-nailed hands. Her arms were covered. 'Still no tattoos?'

'Da-ad. I'm twenty years old.'

'So you've got one,' he probed.

'No, I haven't. But not because *all criminals have tattoos . . .*'

'I never said that.'

'Something very like it.' She laughed. 'Besides, I can't stand needles – remember?'

'Great. That rules out heroin as well.'

'You can smoke heroin, Dad.'

Brook did a double-take but laughed when she laughed. 'I can't believe you're here. I wish I'd known. I could've—'

'What, Dad? Emptied the fridge of sour milk and filled it with food? That'll be the day. After all these years, you're still all over the place. You and that bloody job. I don't know why you don't retire. Mum says you've got enough money.'

'I don't do it for the money, darling,' he said quietly. 'I do it because . . .' He hesitated, unsure how to explain.

'It's okay,' she said, putting a hand on his chest. 'Mum told me.'

Brook sighed. The elephant of his mental breakdown was still in the room but taking up a little less space. Unfortunately, that would leave more space for the second elephant – her stepfather.

'You must be starving,' he said to change the subject.

Terri bounced to her feet and led him to the kitchen. 'No, Dad. Far from it – I knew to come prepared. I brought wine and made spag bol. Would you like some?'

'Terri, I'd love some.'

So Brook sat down at the kitchen table while Terri busied herself at the tiny old-fashioned stove that had rarely warmed a pan. She poured him a glass of red wine and he nibbled on some French bread while he waited for his meal. He couldn't take his eyes from his daughter's back as she reheated the sauce and boiled more pasta. She was taller and seemed even more self-assured than he remembered. Her hair was shorter and her make-up a little subtler than that traumatic day on Brighton Pier, the last time he'd seen her. And, of course she was no longer wearing a school uniform. Now she wore figure-hugging jeans and a dark velvet v-neck top with long sleeves that nearly covered her hands.

Five years. His daughter was a stranger. Brook bit down on the melancholy. *She may be a stranger but she's here now.*

'So is that your car outside?'

'Yep. Mum bought it for getting round Manchester.'

'Does she know you're here?' Brook saw Terri's back stiffen as she paused to consider her reply.

'No.'

Brook nodded behind her back. Amy would never forgive him. Not content with destroying her first marriage through his obsessive hunt for The Reaper, Brook had done the same to her second, denouncing her new husband, the late Tony Harvey-Ellis, as a sexual abuser of their only daughter. 'Give her my . . . best wishes when you see her.' Terri turned round as though about to break some terrible news. He added gently, 'But only if you want to tell her you've seen me.' She smiled with relief and turned back to the stove. 'You're enjoying university?'

'Loving it, Dad.'

'And how do you like . . . ?'

'American Literature.'

'I know, I know,' protested Brook. 'All that Norman Mailer and Truman Capote.'

'Those old dinosaurs. It's all Jonathan Franzen and Amy Tan these days.'

'No place for the flawed old men, eh?' said Brook.

'I wouldn't say that, Dad.' Terri began to serve Brook's meal. 'I mean, Mailer's a pig, no question. But if you get past the misogyny and the drinking, there's a lot of elegiac, ravaged poetry in the man. Do you know what I mean?'

Brook smiled at her. He realised he hadn't stopped smiling since he'd seen her face. 'Yes, I do. This looks good.'

'I'm expecting you to eat it all.'

'Don't worry. This is likely to be the last home-cooked meal I'll get for a while.'

'Oh, no it's not. I'm staying for a couple of weeks. I mean if that's okay,' she added hastily.

'A couple of weeks? Does the university allow you time off?' said Brook, tucking in with gusto.

'I've got a dissertation to do so I need some peace and some space, Dad. Can I stay?'

'I'd love you to stay,' said Brook, before a frown invaded his features. 'I . . . er don't know how much time . . .'

'Dad. Don't worry. I'll be busy, and I'm sure you've got a hot case to crack.'

'Two,' replied Brook as he chewed.

'That's settled then. How's the Bolognese?'

Brook ladled another large spoonful into his mouth. 'It's the finest I've ever had, Terri.'

'That bad, eh?' she joked and plucked a second glass from a cardboard box of four then poured herself a large glass of wine.

'You brought wine glasses?'

'Housewarming present. I prefer not to drink out of jam jars.' She looked at him with a hint of a tease. 'I'll put them in the *glasses* cupboard later.'

He spoke ruefully back at her through a mouthful of pasta. 'You're not going to go easy on me, are you?'

'Dad, you've got a pint glass, a whisky tumbler and two jam jars to drink from. And one of them still has a label on. How easy should I make it?'

Brook laughed. 'In my defence, I've only been in the house

for four years and there haven't been many,' he looked away, 'well . . .'

'They're called women, Dad. I'm told they make good companions.' She fumbled in her handbag and pulled out a packet of cigarettes, unable to meet his eye.

Brook sensed she was ready for him so said nothing, but his face gave the game away.

'I'm twenty years old now. I can make my own mistakes.'

'I didn't say anything.'

'You didn't have to.'

'But you can't smoke in the house, Terri. That's a rule.' He finished his last forkful of pasta and gathered up his wine glass. 'Bring your glass and a coat. I'll show you why I bought this place.'

A minute later, father and daughter sat on the garden bench pulling lovingly on their cigarettes and looking up at the soft cottonwool of the Milky Way. For two people who hadn't conversed in five years, it was odd that no words were needed.

'It's great here, Dad,' she finally said, putting a hand on his arm. 'I wish I'd come sooner.'

Brook smiled in the darkness. 'You're here now. That's all that counts.' Then a thought occurred. 'You were a teenager.' Brook felt the rise in tension within her and realised she might be expecting a conversation about their last meeting. But it was worse than that. After missing her entire childhood and most of her teenage years, he was thinking about the case. He shook his head. What kind of father was he?

'Apparently,' she finally said.

Time to change the subject. 'Whose picture did you have on your wall?' he said before he could stop himself. He felt her looking at him. 'You know, actors, rock stars.'

'Why?'

Why – because you're interested in me, because you want to make up for lost time? 'Never mind.'

'No, tell me.'

Brook hesitated. 'A girl disappeared – two, actually. But I'm trying to get a feeling for this particular girl. Adele. She reminds me of you. Smart and beautiful.'

Brook heard the breath of her grin leave her mouth.

A moment's thought later. 'Leonardo Di Caprio. Brad Pitt. Johnny Depp.'

'Are any of those dead?'

'No, but I had a Jimi Hendrix poster. He OD-ed in 1970.'

'Twenty years before you were born.'

'Does that matter?'

'I don't know. I'm asking you.'

'Who was this girl into?'

'James Dean, Jim Morrison, Kurt Cobain.'

'Jim Morrison was a poet as well as a singer.'

'She writes poetry,' said Brook.

'What's that like?'

'We can't find any. We think she has it with her. But what does it mean, having all these dead guys on your wall?'

'Ah well,' said Terri. 'There's love and then there's perfect love.'

'Perfect love?'

'Sure. Perfect love is pure, immortal. It's wonderful – but to have it, one of you has to be dead.' The shadow of remembrance passed over her expression for a moment.

'Like Romeo and Juliet.'

'In a way, but they both died so it's different.'

'What does that mean?'

Terri took out two more cigarettes and passed one to her father. 'It means that girls of a certain age are inevitably attracted to bad boys because they represent danger and an escape from the humdrum reality of their lives. But with a dead guy you idolise from afar, you can form a perfect and pure relationship.'

'Go on,' said Brook.

'Well, the relationship is chaste for one thing. But that only increases the erotic possibilities – since they can never have bad sex. All the sex is idealised in the mind so it's always wonderful.'

'Interesting.'

'It is. And, of course, the dead guy is always yours. He can never get married or desert you – no other girl in the universe can claim him.'

Brook nodded. 'So she can never be rejected by her dead lover.'

'No. Hence their love is immortal. Nothing can get in the way,' she looked up at him, her smile tinged with sadness, 'until the girl is ready to move on. Didn't this Adele have any crushes on the living?'

'Some actor in something called *True* . . .'

'*True Blood*?'

'Right. Alexander . . .'

'Skarsgard,' Terri supplied.

Brook looked at the shadows of her face. 'Why do I get the impression you've studied this before?'

'Because I have. The *True Blood* series is a big deal in America.'

'It's about vampires. You're not telling me you study it as part of your literature degree.'

'Only insofar as it's a cultural event, Dad. It taps directly into what I said – the desire for perfect, immortal love.'

'So this actor's dead?'

'No, but he plays a vampire – so yes, he's dead but, more important, he's also immortal. That's why millions of teenage girls are besotted with the idea of hot vampires. You can have your beefcake and eat it.'

Brook smiled. 'How lucky am I to have a daughter so intelligent?' Terri didn't answer but Brook saw she was pleased. He yawned. 'You'll have to tell me more tomorrow. Right now I need to get some sleep. Listen, I'll have the sofabed . . .'

'No, you won't. This is your house. You get off to bed and get a good night's kip. I can sleep late.'

'Okay.' Brook stood and walked to the house. He turned to Terri as she sipped the last of her wine. 'Thanks, Terri.'

'For what?'

'Just thanks.' Brook put some blankets on the sofa and trudged off to bed. He looked out of his bedroom window, feeling well-fed and happy. Terri was stroking Basil on the garden bench. Even Bobby, Basil's painfully shy brother, had put in an appearance and was manoeuvring himself for some attention.

Brook glanced at the clock. It was a time at which he was more accustomed to being woken by insomnia. He lay back and was asleep in moments.

Diarmuid Strachan – Jock to his friends, enemies and anyone who might be likely to give him spare change – woke to the sight and sound of a rat nuzzling around at his feet, attracted by the putrid aroma of the fungus flourishing between his damp toes.

'Fuck off, ye bastard.' He kicked out a disintegrating leather boot at the beast, which skittered into the darkness. He sat up to scratch his whiskers, trying to focus on the small bar of light high in the vaulted roof. It was daylight. *Right nuff.* He pulled up his sleeve to reveal the half-dozen watches he wore to occasionally barter for enough coins to buy a drink. He peered myopically at each in turn, but each gave a different time. After working his way through three bottles of cheap whisky since Oz had picked him up, he'd forgotten that none of them worked. He only kept them because if he was begging anywhere near a clock large enough for him to see, he could sometimes set one to the right time and sell it to some unsuspecting Sassenach.

Just slow like me. S'good watch, pal.

He let his sleeve drop and tried to stand but fell back on to his hands, and although he banged his head hard on the wall, he felt nothing. Instead he took another groggy sweep around his gloomy accommodation. His new pal Oz had brought him here, picking him up in the middle of the night promising a bath and a bed. But he had no idea where he was or how long it had taken to get here. He knew there were white tiles on the wall and several hard cold slabs on which he'd banged his knees, but he hadn't yet been able to locate an exit. It was very dark but it was dry and warm and the bar never closed. Jock chuckled at his joke but stopped laughing when he realised he'd run out of whisky – the bar *was* now closed. *Right nuff.*

'S'why a cannae fuckin' see.' He heard a rasping cough far away, the echo sounding around the white-tiled walls. Jock strained towards the source of the noise. 'Zat you, pal?' He saw movement as someone carrying a torch entered and walked towards him, stopping at one of the slabs. He heard a clicking sound and saw it came from a battered old case being set down and unlocked. 'Who's there?'

'It's me,' said the voice he recognised from . . . before.

'Never thought I'd say this, pal, but you got anything ti' eat? You ken me?'

'You look well.' He sighed so even Jock could hear it. 'Despite all that whisky.' There was an unmistakable edge of disappointment in the man's voice. Jock mistook it for male bonding and began to wheeze with laughter as he tried to right himself once more.

'Whisky? I was drinking whisky out mi ma's teet.' He cackled asthmatically, and followed this up with a prolonged hacking cough.

The man chuckled back at him and looked in his case. He took out the pouch of surgical instruments and a bottle of methanol and looked regretfully at them. 'Well, I was saving these for a special occasion but as you're so set on an early death, I can hardly refuse a guest, can I?'

'Can yer fuck?' Jock scrambled to his feet like an Olympic athlete now and scuttled towards the man's voice, holding out a filthy hand to be guided on to the bottle.

The man unscrewed the lid, located Jock's hand around the neck and watched as he took a mansize slug. 'Drink hearty, my friend, and soon you can be reborn.'

Fourteen

BROOK CHECKED THE ADDRESS AGAINST Noble's scribble and stepped from the car. It was a bright morning with just a hint of a chilled breeze. Terri had been fast asleep when Brook crept out of the door at seven and, an hour later, he stood outside Russell Thomson's Brisbane Estate home – a small, dog-eared semi-detached with large wooden-framed windows that hadn't seen a lick of paint in a while.

Brook had very little information on Yvette Thomson. She was a single mum, according to Alice Kennedy, and had been in Derby for only a few months. Alice hadn't got to know her well and didn't know what she did for a living, but she had heard that her son Russell had had problems with bullying, hence the move to a new college in the middle of the academic year.

Brook knocked on the rickety glass door and stepped back to look for signs of life. All the curtains and blinds were drawn. He knocked again and this time fished in his jacket for his mobile. Noble would still be in bed, having left the surveillance on Leopold Street a couple of hours previously. Brook painstakingly tapped out a text for him to organise a briefing for four o'clock and a press conference for six. He made sure the punctuation was correct then sent it on his way with a hefty depression of the thumb.

The noise of a window opening lifted Brook's head.

'That better not be you, Wilson,' croaked a sleepy voice. 'I'm on evenings this week.'

'Mrs Thomson.' Brook shielded his eyes and followed the voice to the upstairs window. He could make out only the shock of black hair hanging down over a face.

'Oh, crap. Is this about the meter reading?'

Brook flashed his warrant card even though she wouldn't see it. 'Detective Inspector Brook,' he added for good measure. 'I'd like a word with your son.'

There was a shocked pause and some attempt to focus on Brook through the hair. 'Rusty? Oh God, is he okay?'

'It's nothing like that,' began Brook.

'What's he been doing?'

'He's not in trouble, Mrs Thomson. I just need to speak to him.'

She nodded. 'Okay. Catch.' She jerked her hand and a set of keys fell towards Brook, who caught them before they hit the drive. 'Let yourself in.' The black hair disappeared only to reappear immediately. 'And put the kettle on.'

Brook unlocked the front door which opened stiffly into a bare hall with a ubiquitous grey carpet that had seen better days. Unknown substances sucked at his shoes as he located and turned into the compact kitchen on the left and snapped on the kettle, which was full. A cafetière stood nearby. It already contained fresh coffee grounds and there was a small gift card still attached to the handle. It read, *Pour Eve. Merci, Phil.*

Brook located the coffee jar and added another spoonful, then unearthed another mug from a cupboard. It contained four cups in total – all from different sets. Brook smiled. There was even a jam jar.

When the kettle boiled, Brook filled the cafetière and opened the fridge. The only food was a half-full takeaway carton, a quarter of melon and a packet of butter. Brook plucked the milk from the door and made the coffee. He took a sip and opened another cupboard which was empty apart from three wine glasses.

'Do you have a search warrant, Inspector?'

Brook turned. Yvette Thomson stood at the door. She was about three inches shorter than his six feet, slender but with a full figure that strained against her snug white T-shirt. She was strikingly pretty and could've passed for late twenties but Brook knew, with an eighteen-year-old son, she had to be early thirties, at least.

She grinned suddenly at Brook's discomfort and her face lit up. 'Sorry.' She laughed. 'I've been watching too much *Law and Order*. Coffee! You angel.' She grabbed her mug, took a lingering mouthful and moaned with pleasure.

'Sorry to get you up this early, Mrs Thomson,' said Brook. 'I thought I'd catch you and Russell before you went to work.'

'It's Miss, though I'd prefer Yvette. And you could have given it another six hours.' She yawned. 'I'm working behind the bar at the Mermaid at the moment. It helps pay the rent while I study.'

She seemed in no hurry to enquire about his visit so Brook dredged up some more small talk. 'What are you studying?'

'I'm doing a course in Beauty Therapy at Derby College,' she replied.

'It seems to be working,' said Brook, for something to say.

She smiled at him and took another sip of coffee. 'I've missed a lot of the course actually – didn't start until November.'

'Must be tough moving during the academic year, especially for your son.'

Yvette considered Brook from behind her cup. 'What's all this about?'

'I need to ask Russell a few questions. Is he here?'

'Sorry. Rusty's hardly ever at home.'

'Pity. Who's Wilson?'

Yvette Thomson rolled her eyes. 'Oh my God – one of Rusty's mates at the college.' She looked away briefly. 'By mates, I mean fellow students. Rusty doesn't make friends easily.'

'And were you expecting him?'

'Wilson? No, but he keeps popping round, asking if I need any jobs doing. Well, it's a rented house so I'm not about to embark on home improvements, but that doesn't stop him asking. It was sweet at first,' she said, 'but it can get on your nerves. Apparently, he thinks I'm a MILF.'

Brook emitted a one-note laugh. 'I hate to say it, but I know what that is.'

'So do I,' she answered. 'A girl at college told Rusty it means Mums I Like Fine. Poor Rusty – so smart, yet so naive.'

'He's meeting girls at least.'

'Adele? She's *waa-aaa-ay* out of his league.'

'You're referring to Adele Watson, I assume,' said Brook. 'She was at a party with Russell at the weekend.'

Yvette gulped back her coffee and narrowed her eyes. 'Is that what this is about?' She put a hand to her brow. 'Shit, he's not been filming people without permission again, has he? I should never have bought him that bloody camcorder.'

Brook held up a hand. 'He's not in trouble. I just need to speak to him about who was at that party.'

'Did something happen?'

'He hasn't said anything?'

She looked at the floor, thinking. 'Come to think of it, I don't think I've seen him since.'

'You haven't seen him since?' repeated Brook. 'It's Thursday today. We're talking about last Friday.'

Yvette Thomson held her palms up. 'Inspector, I'm not a bad mother – but I work nights. Rusty's old enough. He has a key. He comes and goes. Have you got kids?'

'A daughter. She's twenty.'

'Then you'll know. If they want money or feeding, you see them. If they don't . . .'

Brook nodded, though he was in uncharted waters. 'Can I see his room?'

'Tell me what's wrong first. You're starting to worry me.'

'Kyle Kennedy was reported missing on Sunday. On Tuesday, Adele Watson and another girl, Becky Blake, were reported missing. No one's seen any of them since the party.'

'And you think . . .' She turned and ran up the stairs. Brook followed. On the dark landing she hesitated as though getting her bearings, then burst through a door and stood frozen against the sunburst from the window. Brook pushed past her. The single bed was unruffled. In the middle of the duvet a mobile phone rested on a glossy leaflet.

Yvette leaned over Brook's shoulder to read the only word she could make out. 'Deity.'

'Miss Thomson, you have to calm down.' Brook watched her rifle through a kitchen drawer.

'It's in here somewhere.'

'What is?'

She pulled out a sheet of paper and pored over it. 'This.' She looked at her watch and back at the paper. 'It's Rusty's timetable. He's got a Media Studies lecture in two hours. He never misses that; he's a big film buff.'

'But—'

'He'll be there, I'm telling you. He wouldn't leave me on my own.'

'Okay, okay. I'll come with you, just settle down. We need to inform the college officially anyway. In the meantime, we need a picture of him.'

Yvette shook her head. Tears were in her eyes. 'I haven't got one. We left a lot of stuff behind in the move.' She started to sob.

'All right. Before we go to the college, I want you to come back to Russell's room, if you can face it, and tell me if anything is missing . . .'

Yvette Thomson had finally calmed down enough for Brook to leave her on her own in the kitchen, writing out a list of contact numbers, as well as any places, apart from the college, Russell might hang out.

Brook returned to Russell's room to bag his mobile, as well as the leaflet. Russell's laptop was closed on a table but Brook didn't disturb it. He searched the bedroom quickly but found nothing of interest. There were only a handful of books, all connected to Russell's love of films: actors' biographies, memoirs and a book entitled *1000 Films to See Before You Die*. Despite his apparent love of film, there was only one DVD in the room – *Picnic at Hanging Rock*. He skimmed through the books quickly but found no sign of handwritten notes of the kind left by Adele Watson.

The walls though were covered with at least a dozen original movie posters, only some of which Brook had seen before. *Blade Runner*, *2001*, *Badlands*, *Belle de Jour*, *Vertigo*, *Psycho* and *The Godfather* were the films Brook knew. Others unknown to him included *Picnic at Hanging Rock* and *The Blair Witch Project*. Four dots of Blu-tack indicated a missing poster, but Yvette had struggled to remember what it was.

Brook looked around the room for something that might contain Russell's DNA. There were no combs or grooming products of any kind. Even a cursory glance at the bed didn't produce any strands of hair. Although shabby, the room appeared to be spotless.

Brook moved into the bathroom. There was only one toothbrush in a pot and it appeared to be brand new. He left it there. A canister of shaving foam raised Brook's hopes but there were no other shaving implements to accompany it.

'John. I'm outside Derby College – the Roundhouse site. You sound a bit groggy.' Brook looked at his watch. 'Four hours' sleep – that's plenty. Listen. We've got a fourth student missing: Russell Thomson – same MO as the others. I'm here with the mother. She's sure her son doesn't have a passport, but check it out. She also told me there's a course that Russell, Adele, Kyle and Becky take together – Media Studies. There's a lecture in fifteen minutes so I'm dropping in to see if this is a hoax.

'If they really are AWOL, I'll talk to the other students taking the course, see if they know anything. On that subject, get on to Charlton. If these four *are* missing, we're going to need a lot of bodies at the college tomorrow to interview as many people as we can – staff, students, lecturers, the works. It'll be a big operation but it has to be done tomorrow before the college breaks for half-term and memories fade.'

Brook listened for a moment. 'No, it's better if you talk to him. If he mentions budgets to me, well, I may not be diplomatic. Tell him I'll be holding a press conference tonight. That should get his attention. How did the surveillance go? Nothing. As expected.'

Brook rang off and walked back towards Yvette Thomson, standing outside the college's entrance. Her eyes were red-rimmed from tears, and despite the warmth of the day, she appeared to be shivering. Nevertheless she still managed to smile weakly at him.

As Brook crossed the car park towards her, he spotted a black Porsche parked in one of the reserved bays. He stopped briefly to jot down the licence-plate and bay number then continued on to the entrance.

'You look cold. You should've waited inside.'

'I'm all right,' she said. 'Besides, I forgot my accreditation.'

'I didn't,' replied Brook. Inside the entrance he flashed his warrant card at the attendant who buzzed them through the nearest turnstile.

'We've got ten minutes yet. Let's get you a hot drink.' Brook guided her towards the refectory and sat her down at one of the tables. He beckoned over a man in a chef's hat and ordered two cups of tea. 'Put lots of sugar in – it's good for shock.'

'Where are you going?'

'I won't be a minute, Miss Thomson. Just need to check something at the security desk.'

'Eve.'

'Pardon?'

She covered his hand briefly and Brook resisted the urge to pull it away. 'I hardly know you, Inspector, but you've been so kind. My name's Yvette but please call me Eve. That's what my special friends call me.'

Brook looked down into her eyes. 'Eve.' He smiled at her. 'That'll save a lot of breath.'

To Brook's surprise, she laughed, her distress forgotten for a moment.

Brook held the heavy wooden door for Yvette Thomson and followed her through into the Media Suite. A man in his early thirties with blond tinted hair, parted in the middle, was bent over a laptop, tapping attendance marks on to an online register. Meanwhile, half a dozen bored-looking teenagers stared vacantly or poked at their phones, their backs to Brook and Yvette. Only one student, a well-built and handsome young man feeding a DVD into a machine, stopped what he was doing and watched the pair walk to the front of the suite.

Brook returned the boy's unwavering gaze. It was the same young man who had stood under the streetlight looking up at Brook, as he and Noble had searched Kyle Kennedy's bedroom.

'Even for the day before half-term this is a poor turnout,' said the man to the laptop. 'Okay, start the film, Jake.' The boy appeared not to hear him and continued to stare at the detective.

'Adam Rifkind?'

The man looked up at Brook, startled. 'Can I help you?'

Brook ran a swift eye over the salon tan, the weak chin, the faint line of the missing wedding ring and the casual attire. 'I'm Detective Inspector Brook, Derby CID.'

'Eve,' purred Rifkind, suddenly seeing Brook's companion. He unveiled his most charming smile. 'I'm sorry, Rusty hasn't arrived yet.' His beam disappeared as Yvette Thomson hurried from the room, her hand over her face to suffocate the whimpering. 'Oh my God,' said Rifkind, 'so it's true.'

'True?' enquired Brook.

'These rumours circulating, that some of our students are missing.'

'Where did you hear that?' asked Brook.

'Other students.' He turned to a young blonde girl in the front row. 'Fern, did you tell me Becky was missing?'

The girl nodded. 'Sort of. I been calling Becks since I got back Sunday. She's my best mate,' she explained to Brook. 'Her stepmum told me she disappeared. Kyle too.'

'You don't sound too worried,' observed Brook.

The girl's expression turned to one of pity for someone as uninformed as Brook. 'Becks can look after herself. She's gone on holiday, her stepmum said. Her passport's gone – and Kyle's.' She leered. 'Reckon Becks is gonna shag him straight—'

'Yes, thank you, Fern,' interrupted Rifkind. 'Very colourful.'

'What about Russell Thomson?' asked Brook, addressing the room. 'Anyone know where he might have gone?' Brook's question was greeted by silence. 'Has anyone seen him or Kyle or Becky Blake since last Friday?' Again silence, accompanied by shaking of heads. Brook turned his gaze on to Rifkind. 'What about Adele Watson? Same questions.'

Rifkind's eyes widened and he appeared to catch at a

breath. 'Adele? She's missing too?' Brook could detect surprise in Rifkind's voice. It seemed genuine.

'None of them have been seen since Kyle Kennedy's eighteenth-birthday party, last Friday night.' Brook looked around the small gathering. 'Did anyone here attend the party?' All heads were shaking again. All except the boy identified as Jake. 'What about you, Jake?'

Jake looked down at the wrapping paper torn open on a nearby chair. Brook followed his gaze. 'I was invited. But I didn't go.'

'Why?'

Jake appeared unable to answer. When he did speak, it was with venom. 'Because Kyle's a faggot and I didn't want to catch AIDS.' While the other students laughed, Jake's face was like stone. Rifkind gave him a look of disgust but, to Brook's surprise, said nothing.

'It's a wonder you were invited at all,' replied Brook coldly. 'And even stranger that you should buy him a present.'

Jake looked at the DVD case and then at Brook. 'I told you, I didn't go.'

'No. But you must be very worried about your friend to stand outside Kyle's house, watching us conduct our inquiry.' Jake bowed his head without reply. 'Do you know who else was invited?' This time he simply shrugged. 'What's your surname, Jake?'

'McKenzie.'

Brook turned to the lecturer. 'Can I have a word in private, Mr Rifkind?'

After a brief hesitation, Rifkind nodded and indicated the door. 'Start watching the film, people. I won't be long.' He followed Brook to the door and turned off the lights as Brook held the door for him. In the darkness, a female voice boomed through the speakers.

> *'What we see and what we seem*
> *Is but a dream, a dream within a dream'*

Brook stopped in his tracks and turned back to the giant screen. A beautiful young girl with long blond hair was lying on a bed.

'We've seen this bit,' called one of the students. Whoever was in charge of the remote control returned the DVD to the main menu.

'*Picnic at Hanging Rock*,' said Brook under his breath before following Rifkind out of the suite.

'What can I do for you, Inspector?'

'You can tell me what it's like driving a Porsche,' Brook smiled. Rifkind narrowed his eyes at him. 'I saw it outside. The security desk told me it was yours.'

Still Rifkind eyed him, saying nothing. Finally he shrugged. 'It gets me from A to B,' he said, with a smugness that unexpectedly raised Brook's hackles. 'How can I help?'

'I'd like to hear about your relationship with Adele Watson.'

The double-edged nature of the request gave Rifkind pause but he sidestepped the trap without difficulty. 'Certainly. She's a very able girl, very bright – my star Literature student, in fact.' He looked coolly at Brook. 'She's going to Cambridge next year if she achieves her expected grades. And thanks to me, she will.'

Brook smiled politely to crank up Rifkind's discomfort. 'And she's a very pretty girl.'

'I wouldn't know about that, Inspector. I'm a happily married man.'

'Not according to her diary.' Brook paused. 'Unless Adele's having an affair with another Adam Rifkind who teaches here.'

Rifkind seemed suddenly out of breath. The walls finally crumbled and he looked around to be sure no one was watching his carefully constructed self-assurance being dismantled. He made to speak but stopped himself. At last he managed, 'She's eighteen. We . . . didn't do anything illegal.'

'That's reassuring,' answered Brook. 'But it may not tally with the Sexual Offences Act, Section 16, subsection (c) on Abuse of a Position of Trust.' He smiled again to quicken Rifkind's heart-rate. 'Where is she?'

Rifkind's head snapped back. 'I've no idea. You must believe me. I didn't even know she was missing until now.'

'You haven't tried to contact her?'

'No. We . . . broke it off.'

'When?'

'Over a week ago. And I haven't seen her since this time last Thursday.'

Brook nodded. 'So she dumped you.'

'No!' exclaimed Rifkind indignantly. 'I took the decision that we should . . .' He glared at Brook.

'Was she upset?' asked Brook.

'Why are you asking, if you know already?' Then Rifkind closed his eyes in self-reproach. 'You haven't read her diary, have you?' he added bitterly.

'I never said I had,' replied Brook, with an unnerving grin. Normally he disliked applying the thumb-screws, but he'd taken an instant dislike to Rifkind. He reminded Brook of Terri's stepfather, Tony Harvey-Ellis, the smooth-talking

Public Relations manager who had taken Terri's virginity when she was just fifteen.

'Listen, Inspector—'

'Mr Rifkind. I don't have any evidence of wrongdoing yet. Right now I'm only concerned with Adele's whereabouts.'

'I . . . I don't know.'

'Any friends or old boyfriends she might turn to for solace?'

'I don't think so. Adele is a one-off. She prefers her own company.' He smiled weakly. 'We writers usually do.'

'If she gets in touch . . .'

'I'll let you know immediately, I promise,' the man replied hurriedly.

Brook nodded. Rifkind was scared. That's where he wanted him. 'And your Porsche . . .'

'What about it?'

'It might be a good idea to leave it at home for a while.'

'Why?'

'Jim Watson saw his daughter getting out of a Porsche a couple of nights before she disappeared. If he turns up at college . . .'

Rifkind nodded. 'Ade was scared of her father.'

'Was she? Any idea why?'

'He could be very jealous of anyone seeing her. She never told him we were,' Rifkind assayed a vague hand gesture, 'you know.'

'Quite. Who's Miranda? A friend of Adele's?'

'Miranda? I don't know. I never heard her mention the name.'

'She wrote *Miranda* in a Poe anthology left in her room.'

'Oh, she's the main character in a film we started watching

last week. There's a version of a quote from Poe at the start. Typical of Adele to pick up on that.'

'*Picnic at Hanging Rock?*'

'Right. In fact, Adele and a few others were so taken with it they stayed through lunch to watch the rest.'

'Others?'

'Fern, Becky, Kyle and Rusty.' Rifkind's mouth fell open. 'Oh my God.'

'And what happens to Miranda – in the film?'

Rifkind was puzzled for a moment then said, 'She disappears.'

Brook nodded. 'Did Adele suggest watching it?'

'Er, no, it was Rusty, Russell Thomson. He's the film buff. Otherwise Wilson would've had us watching *Saw IV*.'

'Wilson Woodrow?'

'That's right.' Rifkind managed a smile at last. 'Not the sharpest knife in the box. There was a row about it and Wilson stormed out after having a go at Kyle.'

'Why did he have a go at Kyle?'

'Why do bullies have a go at anyone?' Rifkind shrugged. 'Anyway, it was Rusty's turn to choose so we watched *Picnic*.'

'I see. One final thing – which way to the Principal's office?' Rifkind's face fell. Brook smiled, but this time felt a twinge of guilt. 'I'll need to inform him or her about the inquiry.'

Brook dropped Yvette Thomson back at her house only when he was sure she was okay. She had no relatives and few acquaintances who could stay with her, and she spurned any attempt by Brook to get a FLO to stay with her. Instead, Brook took her phone number and promised to call round at the earliest opportunity.

He paused over the next question. 'Have you something with Russell's DNA on it? A comb maybe.'

She looked at the floor. 'In case you find . . .' Then: 'No, he doesn't use a comb.'

'It's just procedure,' said Brook hastily. 'Nothing to worry about, only I noticed there was only one toothbrush in the bathroom.'

She looked at him curiously for a second then bounded up the stairs. She returned empty-handed. 'It's my new one. Rusty's toothbrush has gone.'

'Maybe that's a good sign,' said Brook quietly.

Her face brightened. 'Yes.'

'Never mind. It's possible Forensics will find something in his room, if you could keep it locked . . .'

Brook pulled the BMW on to Leopold Street a little after midday and walked into the bare outer office of the funeral parlour. He pushed a button on the counter then turned to look at the derelict house across the road. Everything seemed quiet.

A tall, stooped man glided from beyond a curtain with a sympathetic smile already fixed on his face. He looked up and down Brook's physique in a flash. *Slab happy*.

'Welcome to Duxbury and Duxbury. I'm Lionel Duxbury. How may I be of service?' he asked in a voice of pure treacle.

Brook held his warrant card in front of the man's hooked nose. He gazed balefully at it.

'Inspector Brook. Why, yes, we currently offer a ten per cent discount for all members of the emergency services – even the ambulance crews and paramedics who attempt to whittle away at our profit margins.' He allowed himself a self-congratulatory simper. 'Your loved one would be in good hands for the final journey.'

'I'm only interested in the corpses you process.'

'I'm afraid we don't cater for such appetites.'

'Knock it off. You were contacted a few days ago by DS Morton, Derby CID, about recent employee turnover.'

Duxbury screwed his small eyes towards the ceiling. 'We were?'

'You were. We're looking for somebody who may have worked for a funeral parlour as an undertaker or mortician.'

'May have?' enquired Duxbury.

'Maybe he still does. His name might be Oz or Ozzy.'

Duxbury took a sharp intake of breath and tried to disguise it. Then he said weakly, 'Doesn't ring a bell.'

'Funny, if that bell in your head had rung much louder, I'd need ear plugs.'

Duxbury looked at Brook but said nothing. Brook just waited – it would come.

'Someone's complained?'

As no one had complained, Brook raised an eyebrow. *What do you think?*

'What's he done now?' asked Duxbury eventually.

'Just tell me who and where he is.'

'About a year ago Oz worked for us for two weeks as a hearse driver.'

'Not to work on the bodies?'

'No. We had an illness and were shorthanded so I reluctantly took him on.'

'But you let him go.'

'Two weeks later. We had to. He wouldn't give us a

National Insurance number, kept asking for cash in hand. Well, payroll were having none of that, obviously.'

'So you don't have an address?'

'No. He kept promising us his details but we never got them.'

'Full name?'

'Ozzy Reece.'

'Description?'

'Well-built, about forty, brown eyes, cropped hair.'

'Any tattoos, distinguishing marks?'

'I never saw anything.'

'Local accent?'

Duxbury nodded. 'I think so. But maybe from further north. He could be quite broad sometimes.'

'You said you didn't get an address.'

'No, but I think he lived near Shardlow.'

Brook looked up sharply from his notebook 'Why Shardlow?'

'He must have mentioned it once.'

'Did you take any pictures of him?' asked Brook.

'What on earth for?'

'ID badges, computerised records, that sort of thing.'

'I told you . . .'

'You don't have any records of him. I think I'm getting it.' Brook pointed at the derelict house across the road. 'Did he ever take an interest in that house?'

Duxbury looked at Brook as though he were a genius. 'Yes, he did,' he replied. 'Always going over to that window to look in, sometimes even talking to the tramps inside. Once I asked him why he was so interested.'

'What did he say?'

'He just laughed and said he was drumming up business.'

'Was he friendly with any of your other staff?'

'Not at all. He wasn't the type to fit in.'

'Did he have a locker or any place unique to him that might give us a DNA sample or a fingerprint?'

'No. There's the hearse, but he hasn't been with us for over a year, so . . .'

'And how did he turn up for work?'

'What do you mean?'

'Clothes? Transport?'

'We gave him the suit to take away with him. He turned up in that.'

'Where is it?'

'He never gave it back.'

'And how did he get to work?'

Duxbury shrugged. 'I assumed public transport. If he had a car, I never saw it.'

Brook snapped his notebook shut after tearing out a page to write his number on. 'Anything else you remember about him, call me. For now, I want a list of current and ex-employees who would've known him. Round your current staff up now, we're going to need to interview them all.'

Brook stared at Duxbury until he started looking for paper and pencil, before ringing Noble. 'John, we've got a lead on Ozzy Reece. Get DS Gadd and a couple of other officers over to Duxbury's Funeral Parlour on Leopold Street. And see if you can rustle up a composite artist to come with them. Yes, now.' He rang off and flipped round Duxbury's completed list. 'Only four people?'

'Yes. And they're all current. There's not a high turnover in our industry.' Duxbury coughed. 'I'm sure you understand.'

Brook nodded. 'So what did Ozzy do?'

'Do?'

'That might make people complain.'

Duxbury looked away. 'It's a bit . . . weird,' he finally said.

'I can handle it.'

'Well, I walked into the Slumber Room one morning and Oz was in there.' Duxbury hesitated.

'Yes?'

'He was interfering with a corpse.' He seemed reluctant to elaborate.

'Go on,' urged Brook.

'Well, he'd undressed the deceased and removed the padding from the abdominal cavity.'

'Padding? To keep the natural body shape?'

'In the absence of internal organs, yes. Well, he was trying to force something else into the cavity.'

'What was it?' demanded Brook.

Fifteen

TWENTY MINUTES BEFORE BRIEFING, BROOK was arranging photographs of the four missing students on a display board, having managed to obtain a photograph of Russell Thomson from the college. DS Gadd was writing up a report on the interviews at Duxbury & Duxbury. Noble walked into the Incident Room carrying two teas. He gave one to Brook, smiling an apology at Gadd then pulled out a sheaf of papers from his jacket. 'One search-warrant for the Watson house. And the Chief's on his way back. You were right – he was out of the door as soon as I mentioned the press conference.'

PC Patel knocked and walked into the Incident Room. She handed Brook an HMV bag and a two-pound coin and headed for the entrance.

Brook extracted two DVDs of *Picnic at Hanging Rock*, an Edgar Allan Poe anthology and a packet of cigarettes from the bag and stared at her. 'I gave you fifty pounds.'

'The receipts are in there, sir,' she said in mock disbelief. 'The DVDs were eighteen quid each.' She shook her head and rolled her eyes as she left.

Noble picked up one of the DVDs. 'Any joy at the funeral parlour?'

'Our man worked there briefly a year ago,' said Brook, pocketing his change.

'So he'd know about the tramps in the squat.'

'All over it, apparently.'

'So what are we waiting for? Let's go get him.'

'He was off the books, John. We didn't get an address though Duxbury thinks he might have lived near Shardlow.'

'Convenient for both dump sites,' said Noble.

'Very. Our suspect's name is Oz or Ozzy Reece. Very much the lone wolf. Nobody got to know him and he didn't give out any personal details, formal or informal. We've got an artist working up a composite.'

'Ozzy Reece. That's a name to get noticed,' observed Noble. 'Sounds phony.'

'It is,' said Gadd. 'No hits.'

'Odd to choose something so unusual.'

Gadd smiled slyly at Brook. 'It wasn't his name that got him noticed at the funeral parlour, John. There was a particular fetish which caught the attention.'

'I'm all ears,' said Noble.

'He got caught stuffing a loaf of bread into a corpse's body cavity. That's why they let him go.'

Noble chuckled briefly but stopped when neither of his colleagues joined in. He looked from one to the other. 'White or brown?' he finally said.

Brook shrugged.

'You're kidding, right.'

'Strange, but true, John,' said Brook. 'But when someone's already interfering with corpses, nothing surprises.'

'Any hits on the databases?'

'Not one. Nothing on the PNC or HOLMES,' said Gadd.

'Hardly surprising,' said Noble. 'That's one unique signature. Do we know if he did that to McTiernan and Kirk?'

'The lab's checking McTiernan again,' said Gadd. 'Kirk was in the water too long.' She shrugged. 'At least it's a lead. I'm nowhere on the booze. Nobody seems to stock barley wine any more and, of course, everyone stocks whisky. I'll have to plough through all the bulk sales. Unless . . .' She looked over at Brook.

'Unless what?'

'Unless I look for some empties outside the house.' And as Brook prepared to voice an objection, 'I'll be careful, sir. It's our only chance of getting a batch number to follow back to point of sale. And even then . . .'

Brook nodded. 'Be careful.'

'I will.' Gadd headed for the door. 'I'm off to canvass all the local bakeries.' Brook and Noble turned. 'Joke,' she grinned as she left.

Noble yawned.

'You okay?' asked Brook.

'As long as I don't pull another duty tonight.' Noble stared at Brook, waiting for a reassurance that didn't arrive. 'Right.'

'The house is our best lead, John. I know it's tough so we're switching to solo two-hour shifts tonight. Jane's on first. You relieve her at midnight.'

Noble blew out his cheeks and nodded. 'Who's after me?'

'Rob Morton's on two to four,' said Brook. 'Then it's me. I'll talk to the Chief about extra bodies when he gets back. We can't work both cases. They're too labour intensive.'

Noble took a sullen sip of tea and eyed the photo array. 'That our new student?'

'Russell Thomson, Rusty to friends. Last seen the day before Kyle's party.'

'Bedroom tidy . . .'

'. . . and phone and leaflet on the bed. No SIM card. The technicians are picking up his laptop.'

'And the mother only notices her son missing when you call to tell her. Unbelievable.'

'Well, she works nights, John. When *you* start a family . . .'

'Me? No chance. I like my independence too much.'

Brook smiled thinly at him. 'It's overrated.'

'Want me to add his mother to the parental background check?'

Brook nodded thoughtfully. 'I do. Yvette Thomson – single parent. You've got the address. She's a bit over-familiar and seems nice enough, but I want to know about a mother who can't produce a single photograph of her son.' Brook broke into a sudden grin. 'Speaking of single parents, my daughter has come to stay for a couple of weeks.'

'You have a daughter?' Noble enjoyed Brook's discomfort. 'I'm kidding. I knew that much. I've forgotten her name.'

'Theresa – Terri. She's over from Manchester University.'

'How long since you've seen her?'

Brook hesitated over the information without knowing why. 'A while.'

'I'd love to meet her. We can compare notes.' Brook was thin-lipped in the face of Noble's grin. Brook's mobile phone vibrated.

'And that explains why you've got your phone turned on.' Noble smirked in mock amazement. 'Now that *is* news.'

Brook smiled back sarcastically.

'Dad, it's me.'

'Terri.'

'Are you near a computer?'

'Yes, why?'

'Get the internet up and type in deity.com.'

Brook looked across at Noble. 'Terri. How do you know about Deity?'

'It's on that leaflet you brought home.'

He shook his head. 'I left it there? That was careless. You didn't take it out of the plastic, did you?'

'Dad, course not. But I had a look at the site, out of interest, see if it was anything to do with your case.'

'It is.'

'There's an interesting bit of film on it. I checked and the same thing is also on YouTube and getting a lot of hits. You should take a look.'

'I will.'

'What time will you be—?'

But Brook had rung off and was already typing the web address into his computer. The Deity home page loaded. It was no longer under refurbishment. The background was in grey and black. *Live Forever* and the other slogans were there in large red lettering, just like the leaflet, but there were another couple of features. In one corner of the screen, a countdown was taking place. According to the clock there were another twenty-three hours and twenty minutes to go.

In the centre of the screen was a large black box with a *Play* button in the middle.

Brook looked at the interactive whiteboard on one wall of the Incident Room. 'How do you get that screen working, John?'

Noble took a remote control from a slot at the side of the

whiteboard and flicked at a button. He nodded at Brook who clicked on the website's *Play* button. Morton and Cooper entered and turned to look at the brightening screen, unbidden.

A disembodied female voice spoke over the black background.

> *'What we see and what we seem
> Is but a dream, a dream within a dream.'*

Gradually the picture became clearer. It was night. The date on the display was 19 May – the night before the party. The person filming was elevated and a little distance away, but zoomed in almost immediately to show four burly young men surrounding another young man of slighter build.

Brook glanced at the photographs on the boards. Despite the distance, despite the less than ideal lighting, Brook was convinced that the slender young man being surrounded was Kyle Kennedy. For the next few minutes, the four stocky lads cajoled, pushed and slapped Kyle from one to the other. The sound quality wasn't the best but Brook and his team could clearly hear the laughing and jeering. One young man in particular seemed to be leading the assault. He was chunky to the point of being overweight with cropped hair and a malicious laugh.

'We're not going to witness a murder, I hope,' said Morton. Chief Superintendent Charlton entered with a cup and was about to speak when Brook held up a hand and pointed to the screen.

At that moment, another teenager, taller than the others with an athletic frame, walked into shot. The assault stopped.

'That's Jake McKenzie,' said Brook, without taking his eyes from the action. 'He was at the college today.'

Kyle walked towards Jake. An exchange took place but a minute later, Kyle walked back to his tormentors. The ringleader swung a heavy punch and Kyle fell. The aggressors left, giving Jake a wide berth. Then McKenzie ran to minister to the prostrate figure and, shortly after, Kyle seemed to revive but then ran off, screaming.

The film ended and the screen blackened.

'What was that?' asked Charlton.

'A serious assault on one of our missing students, sir,' said Brook. 'Broadcast on *deity.com*, which is a website address on a leaflet.' He gestured to a copy beneath the photographs on the display. 'We have four copies of that leaflet; one each found in the bedrooms of the four missing Derby College students.'

'Four?'

'Yes, sir. I think the lad getting beaten up is Kyle Kennedy, the first one to be reported missing. From the date on the film, it's clear this was the night before he disappeared. His mother told us she saw him go out at nine that night, but he came back late and ran straight to his room without her seeing him. Now we can understand why.'

'And after this party she found a small bloodstain on a plaster,' said Noble. 'The lab's working up the DNA.'

'From this film it likely belongs to this . . .' Charlton gestured towards the whiteboard.

'Kyle Kennedy,' obliged Brook.

'Right. Let me see it from the start. And make a recording for the boffins to enhance.'

Brook clicked the *Play* button again and raised a

surreptitious eyebrow to Noble, who forced himself not to smile. *Make a copy? We'd never have thought of that.*

When the film finished for the second time, Charlton rubbed his chin to signal he was in detection mode. '*A dream within a dream.* What's that from – *The Tempest?*'

Brook was impressed. 'That's not a bad guess, sir. But in fact it's from a poem by Edgar Allan Poe.'

Charlton nodded as though recognising it. 'What do we make of the film? Genuine?'

'It's very well acted, if not.'

Charlton was suddenly animated. 'You won't be showing that at the press conference, will you?'

'No. We've only just seen it ourselves. That doesn't mean the public won't have seen it – my daughter says it's on YouTube as well, so no telling how quickly it's spreading. But you're right; we'll need more background before we can pass it on officially.'

'Agreed.' Charlton looked at his watch. 'I've obviously arrived back just in time.' Book and Noble resisted glancing at each other this time. 'Can we get that off YouTube?' he asked, looking at the screen.

'I would think so,' said Cooper, 'but there's no telling how many people have linked it and spread it around. It could still go viral as an email attachment or a Screencast on Twitter.'

Charlton nodded sagely as if he knew what Cooper was talking about. 'Press briefing at six o'clock, you said, Sergeant. I'll take the lead.' He smiled pointedly at Brook. 'If that's okay with you, Inspector.'

'It's fine,' answered Brook. Charlton wasn't about to start trusting him in front of the press again, in spite of the conciliatory tone of their last conversation.

'You'd better bring me up to speed,' said Charlton.

Brook looked over at Noble, who moved to the photo display. 'We have four Derby College students – Kyle Kennedy, Becky Blake, Adele Watson and now Russell Thomson – missing after attending a party for Kennedy's eighteenth birthday last Friday night. It was apparently a small gathering, not your usual loud music and screaming mini-dramas. Kennedy's mother, Alice, and her friend, Len Poole, had gone to Chester for the weekend. When they returned on Sunday morning, they found this leaflet on Kyle's bed.' Noble held up the Deity leaflet. 'This is a copy. The originals are being fingerprinted. On top of the leaflet was Kyle's mobile phone. The SIM card had been removed. His room was tidy and the bed hadn't been slept in. Similar sights greeted the parents of the other three students at whatever time they eventually became concerned about their child's whereabouts. Russell Thomson was the last to be reported missing this morning, so we haven't processed his laptop yet but the SIM card was also missing from his mobile.'

'Six days. Long time,' observed Morton.

'It is,' said Brook. 'But Miss Thomson works nights so it's easy to see how Russell wasn't missed. Besides, all four teenagers are bright, apparently responsible and self-sufficient. They had their own house key to come and go as they pleased.'

'We've checked the laptops of Kyle Kennedy and Becky Blake,' said DC Cooper. 'They've been completely wiped.'

'They deleted all their files?' said Morton.

'If they'd just done that, Rob, we could've recovered everything from the hard drive, but the hard drives have been professionally emptied of everything but the software.'

'Would the students possess that knowledge?' asked Charlton.

'It's not so hard,' answered Cooper. 'Kids grow up at a keyboard these days. They know how to do everything.'

'The other two had laptops, you say?' asked Morton.

'The technicians are picking up Thomson's today but there's no reason to think it would be different. However, Adele Watson's laptop is missing,' said Brook. 'She is said to be a talented writer and poet but her writing books are missing as well.'

'So she took them with her?'

'It's possible. We also think it's possible Adele's father may have hidden her laptop as well as her writing,' added Noble.

'Why?' asked Charlton.

'We're not sure,' said Brook. 'We've been told she was scared of him and we think maybe she's been writing about her relationship with her father.'

'Relationship?' asked Morton. 'You mean sexual?'

'Not definitely. It was just a vibe we picked up,' replied Noble. 'But if there *was* something untoward, it would be natural for Watson to want to destroy any thoughts she might have committed to paper or computer – or at least hide them away until he's had a chance to sanitise. This is only speculation at this point, sir, but Watson was the only parent who gave us that feeling.'

'But why take her laptop if her hard drive has been wiped?' said Cooper.

'If he didn't wipe it, he won't know.'

'Did you check Social Services and the SO Register?' said Charlton.

'No sex offenders in the area and no social-work hits on the Watson family,' answered Noble.

'But you got a vibe off him,' repeated Charlton.

'Adele's was the only bed that was messed up and the phone moved – we think, by Watson, maybe to lie down in her room, who knows?'

'To masturbate, you think,' said Charlton.

Brook and Noble exchanged a glance and shrugged noncommittally.

'It sounds a bit thin,' continued Charlton.

'It wasn't just that,' said Brook. 'Watson tried to steer us away from Adele's boyfriend when most normal fathers would be doing the opposite.'

'Do you need a warrant?'

'We've got one,' replied Brook. 'We'll execute after the press briefing.'

Charlton nodded. 'Okay, but tread lightly. A missing daughter buys a lot of sympathy and the press may descend in numbers after they've been briefed. What about the college?'

'It's the last day before half-term tomorrow so we flood it with bodies, question everyone we can,' said Brook. 'Hopefully tonight's press conference will shake something loose. Someone must know something.'

'What about neighbours around the Kennedy house?'

'We're putting a canvass together. Not much to see or hear apparently,' answered Noble. 'We're still following up but an appeal through the media might help.'

'Other party-goers?'

'As far as we know, only the missing four and Jake, the lad in the film, were invited. He went to the Kennedy house but says he didn't go in. No idea why – yet.'

Charlton looked at his watch again – an hour to the press conference. 'So where are they? They can't just disappear into thin air, not all four of them, abducted without a struggle or a witness.'

'We agree,' said Brook. 'They left of their own accord. They each packed a small rucksack with a few clothes. They each made their bed, took apart their mobile phone, removed the SIM card and placed the phone on the Deity leaflet, on the bed. It's a statement.'

'That tells us what?' asked Charlton.

'That they've decided to leave,' said Brook.

'Why?'

'Why do teenagers do anything? Each of them, in their different way, is unhappy. Adele is having problems with her boyfriend and father, Kyle is gay and confused and Becky has had her dreams of being a model shattered.'

'And Russell Thomson?'

'Not sure,' admitted Brook. 'But there are rumours he's been bullied in the past. We're checking. Either way the artefacts send a message. They're leaving their lives behind. No computer to email them, no phone to contact them or trace their whereabouts. We've applied to their providers for a record of their email and mobile usage before they disappeared but that's still in the pipeline. DC Cooper was checking their online presence . . .'

'They don't have one,' said Cooper. 'They're not on Twitter except for Adele, and she hasn't tweeted for several weeks.'

'What's the content?' asked Brook.

'I've done a printout for the board but it's all activist nonsense about the environment, the dangers of nuclear weapons, that sort of thing.'

'Wanting to breathe clean air and avoid vaporisation,' said Brook, with a sideways glance at Cooper. 'What a weirdo.'

'Emails?' asked Noble, trying not to smile at Cooper's discomfort.

'Nothing,' answered Cooper stiffly. 'Wherever they are, they haven't sent an email using any account their parents told us about since last Friday. And any record of their emails before then, has been wiped from their computers. Not only that, they haven't even left a message on Facebook because I checked. All four of them unsubscribed on the day of the party.'

'Wow,' said Morton.

'Wow is right,' said Cooper. 'My kids would rather lose an arm than their Facebook presence. However, there's already a Facebook page dedicated to their disappearance. It was started by a Fern Stretton and I'm keeping an eye on it in case anything useful crops up. Also I'm keeping tabs on the comments on YouTube. You never know. No chat on Twitter yet.'

'Okay, I'll ask again,' said Charlton. 'Where are they?'

Brook looked him in the eye. 'At the risk of stating the obvious, we don't know. In fact, we don't know anything about their movements after the party. That's our starting-point. I rang Alice Kennedy earlier today to ask her to leave the house and touch nothing else. If the four don't come forward in the hours after the press conference, we're going to need SOCO to go over the whole place as well as each student's bedroom.'

'Are there any facts I can use at the press conference?' asked Charlton, starting to become frustrated.

'Becky and Adele both had passports from recent foreign

holidays,' said Noble. 'However, Kyle Kennedy has never left the country and according to his mum, didn't have a passport. But she was wrong. He applied for a passport three months ago. I got on to the Passport Service this morning when we found out Russell Thomson was also missing. Thomson applied for a passport at the same time as Kyle. The interesting thing is, the same person endorsed the back of their photographs . . .'

'Let me guess,' said Brook, deep in thought. 'Adam Rifkind.'

Noble smiled. 'How did you know?'

'I met Rifkind this morning. He's a lecturer at Derby College. He teaches English Literature and Media Studies to all four. He's the perfect choice to endorse a passport application. And there's one more thing. He's Adele Watson's ex-boyfriend.'

'That's not all,' said Cooper, rifling through his notebook. 'You asked me to track down the Deity website.' He found the right page in his notes. 'The domain name was registered and paid for by Adam Rifkind.'

'How did he pay for it?'

'Credit card, six months ago,' answered Cooper.

'Six months?' said Brook, mildly surprised.

'So we have a suspect,' said Charlton. 'And he's been planning this for a long time.'

'Planning what?' said Brook. 'Persuading four young adults to walk away from their unhappy lives? There's no crime in that.'

'What about the happy slapping?' insisted Charlton.

'He wasn't involved in that.'

'Somebody filmed it and it's on *his* website,' said Cooper.

'Russell Thomson filmed it. Or that's what we're meant to believe.'

'How do you know Thomson filmed it?' asked Charlton.

'I didn't say that, I said we're meant to think he filmed it because he's a film nut and because he recently acquired a camcorder from his mother. And according to Miss Thomson, the camcorder is never off his wrist,' added Brook. 'He wanders the streets filming whatever takes his fancy so the broadcast we saw could be a product of that.'

'I don't understand,' said Charlton.

'You think someone's yanking our chain?' said Noble.

Brook grimaced at the metaphor. 'I'm sure of it. But I prefer, *What we see and what we seem is but a dream*. These kids are smart, sir. They've disappeared without a trace. That takes some doing.' He looked at Charlton. 'I think we're being challenged, presented with an alternative reality. We have to question what we see, who people are.'

'You're not making sense,' said Charlton impatiently.

'The Edgar Allan Poe poem you just heard quoted on the website was also used in a film called *Picnic at Hanging Rock*.' Brook held up one of the DVDs and tossed the other to Noble. 'Adele, Becky, Kyle and Russell watched it last Thursday.'

'The day before they disappeared.'

'Right. And when we looked through Adele's bedroom, she had the anthology of Poe's poems opened at the same poem. She'd written *Miranda* in the margin.'

'Who's Miranda?'

'She's a character in the film. She disappears with her friends.' Brook looked around at all the furrowed brows. 'Exactly. Sergeant Noble and I will be watching it tonight. Anyone else who hasn't seen it should do so after us.'

'What the hell's going on?' asked Charlton. His voice had

been rising steadily. 'I can't start waffling about some old film to the press.'

'We don't know what's going on because we're not supposed to,' said Brook softly. 'They've created an enigma for us and we have to find them to understand it.'

'I don't get it. You mean this Rifkind . . .'

'Rifkind's a fall guy. He's not the brains behind this.'

'Then who is?' demanded Charlton.

Brook turned to look at the photo array. He gazed into the dark passionate eyes peering out from under a heavy fringe. 'My money would be on Adele Watson. She's the writer. She's the one with the imagination. She's also the one with access to Rifkind's wallet and credit cards while they were seeing each other.'

'Wouldn't Rifkind spot if he's paid for a website he knows nothing about?' objected Noble.

'Not necessarily,' said Brook. 'How much was it?'

'Ninety-nine pounds for the year,' replied Cooper.

'I don't go through every item on my credit-card bill,' conceded Morton. 'As long as the total looks right and no one's bought a bunch of computers in Rawalpindi.'

Brook shrugged. 'We can ask Rifkind at college tomorrow. But the thing to remember is that Adele has disappeared and the two people we're looking at are her ex-boyfriend and her father – one man who's jilted her and the other . . .' Brook held out his hands. 'Coincidence? I don't think so. Whatever's happening has been meticulously planned.'

'Think that was Adele's voice on the website?' asked Cooper.

'I do,' replied Brook.

'And she's using the website to give us clues,' said Noble,

looking at his watch, 'which means, according to the count-down, we get our next lead at three o'clock tomorrow afternoon.'

'It's an enigma, remember,' said Brook. 'I'm guessing they're going to string us along for a while, so tomorrow's broadcast will likely throw up more questions than answers.'

'This is getting us nowhere,' said Charlton. 'I need something for the briefing.'

'Just treat it as a normal "missing persons",' advised Brook. 'We're on to the legwork. First thing tomorrow we blitz the college and re-interview Rifkind and his Media Studies students – Jake McKenzie especially. He was in the Kennedy film. There's also a character called Wilson Woodrow who had a go at Kyle Kennedy in college. Maybe he took part in the assault.

'We'll be going door-to-door on Kennedy's street, see if we can find out how the four of them left the party. Did they get a lift, a cab, walk, bicycle, helicopter or what? Did they go together or separately? We check CCTV, appeal for witnesses on the Brisbane Estate between eleven p.m. Friday, and six a.m.

'That's a bit vague.'

'I'm afraid it's worse than that, sir. Alice Kennedy didn't get home on Saturday. I'm talking about six a.m. on Sunday.'

'Of course!' exclaimed Noble. 'They could have kept a low profile in her house on Saturday and left anytime before Sunday morning.'

'She got home at six a.m.?' said Cooper. 'From a weekend break?'

'No,' said Brook. 'But the sun would be up around then and if they're trying to disappear, I'm guessing they wouldn't leave in daylight.'

'So that gives them a massive window,' said Charlton. He was becoming more incredulous by the minute but he cast around for a straw to clutch. 'You mentioned passports. Are they out of the country?'

'Not officially. For now we assume they're here, even local. If they're messing with our heads, they're going to want to see us chasing around.'

'By God, if this is a hoax, we'll throw the book at them,' growled Charlton. 'This is going to cost a fortune. They'll wish they were . . .'

Brook smiled and raised an eyebrow at him.

Oz tightened the vice and picked up his file again. He adjusted his surgical headlamp and continued to work away at the brass rod held in the vice, shaping and coaxing the hook at the end. When he was satisfied, he wiped away the sharp burr and set about smoothing the blade with the file and a piece of emery cloth. Eventually he stepped away and unfastened the vice, delicately picking out the sharp instrument with two fingers. He walked across to the nearest white-tiled slab on which lay Jock's creased and slackened corpse.

His bloodless body was white and waxy from the germicides and ointments massaged into his skin. Their perfumes mingled with the bleaching agents Oz had used to try to cover the yellowed bruises dotted around the corpse. For now, Jock's myriad cuts and abrasions were barely visible under the make-up.

'You've certainly had a time of it, haven't you, my friend? Well, your own mother won't recognise you soon. You'll be back to your best.'

Oz grinned at the chalky face from under his green face

mask then knelt to examine the wound at the side of the abdominal cavity. He pressed a finger against the pale skin, nodding in satisfaction when it resisted his pressure. He giggled with pleasure. The new cavity stuffing held nicely – such a simple solution and so in keeping with the project. And, he had to admit, the sliced loaf was much easier to work with than the uncut. He wondered why he hadn't thought of it before.

He set about suturing the wound. When he'd finished his rough stitching, he re-covered the body with a surgical sheet and bent over the head with his newly fashioned tool. 'Okay, Jock. Here goes.' Adjusting the surgical light for maximum illumination, he positioned the honed end of the brass instrument up the cadaver's right nostril and pushed it up as far as it would go, then just as carefully pulled it back down. He examined the skin on the upper lip. No damage.

Now he reached under his gown to a tool belt and pulled out a ball pein hammer. He inserted the brass rod back up the nostril and, with more force this time, pushed the sharp blade through the resistance of the cartilage. After a brief check that he still wasn't breaking the skin on the face, he manoeuvred the hook into position and steadied the hammer against the base of the rod and gave it a sharp tap.

There was a sudden pop and an object flew out of the man's eye-socket and bounced across the floor with the tat-tat-tat of glass on ceramic. Oz cursed and scuttled after the glass eye which had settled under the exsanguinations tank. He retrieved it, spat on it to clean off any dirt and, after polishing it on his gown, returned to the slab and forced the eye back into the socket, accompanied by a loud sucking noise.

He took a different grip on the brass rod still protruding

from the nose and picked up the hammer again. Settling on a slightly altered angle of trajectory, he gave the base of the rod another sharp tap and this time a squelching noise like a bubble of gas in hot mud induced a satisfied nod. He withdrew the brass rod, being ultra-careful not to slice through the upper lip as he extracted it. He wiped the clear slimy liquid from the hook against his apron and placed a pair of triangular wooden props under one side of the corpse to allow the brain fluid to drain away through the now punctured membrane and out through the nose on to the slab.

Brook sat motionless on the raised stage of the briefing room while Charlton sat under the lights next to Alice Kennedy – no Len Poole – and fiddled with the prepared statement. The room was half-empty as most national media weren't interested in four young adults who had disappeared together, especially as there were no signs of foul play.

The local radio and TV stations were represented though, as well as the local newspapers. Brian Burton, Crime Correspondent of the *Derby Telegraph*, stood ready with his photographer and at one point snaked a lingering malevolent glance in Brook's direction.

Brook kept his eyes to the front. He wasn't going to be drawn into swapping insults with Burton and risk deflecting attention from the appeal. He was pleased to be sitting next to Charlton, who would politely field all questions from a journalist who had spent an inordinate amount of time trying to wreck Brook's career. Burton had long-held ties with local coppers and he shared their opinions about Brook's fallibilities. His book about The Reaper, who had slaughtered two families in the city, had been as much about criticising

Brook's failure to catch him, as profiling the activities of the serial killer.

After a heartfelt plea from Alice Kennedy, Charlton took over. 'At this stage in proceedings, it's important to stress that we are not treating this incident as abduction. It appears that all four young people willingly left their homes and their lives behind. This involved an amount of planning and pre-meditation which leads us to believe that these four young people are, very probably, safe and well.

'The fact that Adele, Becky, Kyle and Russell all have passports in their possession suggests that they may intend to leave the country. However, all the information we've received from Border Controls and the British Transport Police indicates that they have not yet done so.

'Wherever they are, we would urge them, if they are listening to these broadcasts or reading the papers, to contact a family member or the police as soon as possible. They may be unaware that their departure has created such interest and may worry about the consequences of their disappearance. Let me say now that no action will be taken against you. The only action that interests the police here in Derby is that four young people are returned to their families so that we can all get back to normality.

'Whatever problems may have prompted their decision to leave, we want them to bear in mind that there are many, many people here in Derby who cherish them and want to help them. Thank you.'

The Q&A began. Chief Superintendent Charlton fielded the first question from a Radio Derby journalist but Brook could feel Brian Burton preparing his question and knew it would be aimed in his direction.

'Inspector Brook,' began Burton a moment later. 'Given your failure to identify a single suspect in the killings of two Derby families, how confident are you that you can now find *four* missing individuals?'

Brook stared ahead without expression while Charlton glared at Burton. 'I'll answer that, Brian. First of all, those killings are not recent – the Wallis family were attacked five years ago – and that line of questioning is unproductive and an insult to Mrs Kennedy and the other parents who are worried about their children right now. Furthermore, in my service, we do not apportion blame to individual officers, working within a team, for the failure of an inquiry. Some criminals are more resourceful than others and bringing them to justice is not straightforward. That said, do not think The Reaper can rest easy. Two families were brutally murdered in our city and until The Reaper is brought to justice, those cases remain open.

'DI Brook is an experienced and talented detective and part of a highly capable *team* and I'm in no doubt that, with the help of our friends in the media, these young people will be found and returned to their families.' Charlton motioned Brook to stand, which he did. Alice Kennedy followed suit.

'Just a minute . . .' began Burton.

'No,' said Charlton firmly. 'We have work to do, and if there are no *relevant* questions about the current inquiry, it would be better for all concerned if we got on with our jobs.'

The camcorder was trained on the television screen. The uniformed Chief Superintendent was spouting his spiel but the lens rested on his face for just a moment before moving to film the Detective Inspector in charge of the search. His face was impassive and controlled. The camcorder zoomed in further when a local reporter asked a question about the hunt for a serial killer some years before. The Inspector's eyes betrayed barely a flicker of emotion. Still the camcorder stored his image, only being lowered when the press conference drew to a close.

The three police cars and Brook's BMW made their way in convoy across the city and arrived on the Brisbane Estate.

In her habitual dressing-gown, the diminutive Roz Watson opened the front door to PC Crainey and DS Noble, who explained the reason for the visit. Under Brook's instruction, the warrant was to be a last resort in case a voluntary search was refused.

'I don't understand,' she said. Her husband joined her at the door as Brook arrived.

'We can't go into details but we think Adele may have hidden her laptop somewhere in the house and we'd like your permission to search for it,' said Brook, locking eyes with Watson.

'Do we have a choice?' he asked. Noble readied the warrant.

'Not if you want to help us find your daughter,' replied Brook.

The Watsons stood aside to let Brook and his team search the premises.

Five minutes later, Jim Watson sat on the sofa next to his wife. He stared at the floor taking no interest in proceedings. PC Crainey, the Family Liaison Officer, sat on a chair opposite them both, staring at the same spot on the floor and avoiding Mrs Watson's gaze as her eyes pierced him with her swelling anger. The rest of the team swarmed over the house.

'Are we suspects?' spat Mrs Watson in PC Crainey's direction.

'It's just routine.' He looked away as he spoke which Roz Watson took as confirmation.

'Bastards,' she said to her husband's frozen face. She shook her lank grey locks at him. 'Are you just going to sit there? They think we did something to our daughter.' He glanced briefly in her direction but said nothing.

For the next few minutes the three kept silent during the scuffs and bangs of beds, chairs and other objects being inspected, emptied, moved and put back again. Occasionally they could hear the exchange of information between the searching officers.

'Bastards,' the woman said again.

Finally Watson spoke without lifting his eyes. 'Don't let them get to you, Roz. That's what they want.'

'They're just doing their jobs,' said Crainey to Roz, as though he wasn't a member of the same invading force currently rifling through the Watsons' home.

Seconds later, the steps groaned under the dual footfall of Brook and Noble and the door to the living room opened.

'Shed key?' asked Noble.

'On the hook by the back door,' said Watson.

Brook studied Watson's face to gauge stress-levels. He seemed relaxed and Brook began to worry that they were too late, or worse, that he'd misread the situation. A shout rang out from above and the stairs once again complained under the assault of descending officers.

DS Morton entered the room. 'Bathroom – under loose floorboards.' He held out two books in his latex-covered hands, both bound in shiny black. Brook took one gingerly in his gloved hands and opened it. Noble took the other.

'Adele's notebook,' said Brook, skimming through before stopping at a particular page. '"The Night Walker",' he read.

'He comes at night, The Night Walker
When the house sleeps and sighs
I feel him in my bones
I see him with my eyes.

'He comes at night, The Night Walker
When the dark is on the rise
I feel him on my bed
I feel him by my side.'

Brook looked over at Watson, who was maintaining his vacant expression.

His wife also fixed him with a gimlet eye. 'What are her poems doing under the floor, Jim?'

Watson grunted. 'Maybe she put them there. For safekeeping.'

'This is Adele's diary,' said Noble, flicking through the other tome.

'Save us some time and tell us where the laptop is, Mr Watson,' said Brook softly.

'The laptop?' shouted Mrs Watson. 'What's going on, Jim?'

Watson was about to plead ignorance when something shifted in his mood. He turned to his wife then looked over to Brook, seeking understanding. 'Behind the boiler, wrapped in towels. There's a false backboard.' Morton hurried back upstairs.

Brook nodded. 'Thank you.'

'I don't understand, Jim.'

He looked back at his wife without expression. It was over. He could be himself. 'My life is over. Time to make it official.'

'What do you mean? What have you done?'

Watson stared flatly back at her. 'I could've had my pick.'

Brook and Noble dropped the two books into evidence bags and turned to go.

'You're not leaving me here,' pleaded Watson suddenly. 'With *her*.'

'Jim?' She stood now, her head darting around searching for answers.

Brook studied him. 'Of course not. We'd like you to come to the station and assist with our enquiries.'

'Gladly – just get me out of here,' said Watson.

Brook looked over at Crainey who took out his handcuffs and bade Watson to stand. The man turned to allow Crainey to snap the cuffs into place.

'What are you doing? Jim?' said his wife, moving towards him. Brook held her away but the barrier merely increased the wiry little woman's urgency and she reached past Brook to grab at her husband.

Watson ignored her and pulled against the impassive steel without success. He smiled. 'Free at last.'

Mrs Watson seemed about to tip over into hysteria so Brook signalled Noble to move her husband outside quickly.

'PC Crainey will give you a receipt for the exhibits and talk you through what's going to happen,' said Brook, moving away.

'You're taking him? You're taking my husband?'

'Speak to PC Crainey.'

'But why have you handcuffed him? What will the neighbours say?'

'It's just a precaution. For his own safety,' said Crainey as Noble and Brook guided Watson towards the front door.

PC Crainey stood between Mrs Watson and her departing husband. 'How about a nice cup of tea?'

'Jim?' she shouted.

Outside, Watson heaved a sigh of relief as he reached the squad car. But as Noble eased Watson's head safely into the vehicle, a camera flashed and Brook found himself face to face with Brian Burton.

'Hello, Inspector. Would you care to inform our readers why you've arrested Adele Watson's father? Have you found a body? Has Jim Watson killed her?' At that moment, Morton emerged with the laptop. Burton spotted it. 'Ho ho, it doesn't take a genius to work out what Mr Watson's been up to.'

'Just as well they sent you then, Brian,' said Brook over his shoulder.

'Been browsing the kiddie sites, have you?' shouted Burton, stooping to harangue Watson, inside the squad car. 'Your daughter catch you at it and you topped her? That it?'

Brook turned back to the squad car and banged on the roof. The car sped away and Burton swung round to get in Brook's face.

'Well, Inspector.'

'It's just routine, Brian. Mr Watson is not under arrest, he's helping us with our enquiries.' Brook made for his car.

'If he's not under arrest, why is he wearing handcuffs?'

'It's just procedure.'

'Well, here's my procedure, Inspector. I've got a picture of a missing girl's father being taken away in handcuffs and that's what tomorrow's front page will show,' said Burton to his retreating back.

Brook turned round and marched up to Burton. 'I'd ask you not to print that picture, Brian, but I know that would guarantee it. Instead, I'll say this. If you indulge in wild speculation or say what you just saw as an arrest, your readers will switch off from the story thinking it's done and dusted, and the search for four young people, who may be in danger, will become that much harder.'

'What sort of danger?' asked Burton, shoving his Dictaphone in Brook's face.

Brook's face darkened and he tried to slow his breathing. 'I'm afraid I can't comment further.'

'What we see and what we seem Is but a dream, a dream within a dream.'

Brook switched off the tape.

'That's Adele,' said Watson. 'What is that?'

Brook pushed the cup of tea nearer Watson and looked across at Noble in the other chair. 'It's a message from Adele.'

'What message? Where is she?'

'We were hoping you could tell us,' said Noble.

Watson put his hands flat on the table and his head on top of them. 'I don't know,' he mumbled. 'Really I don't. I wish I did.'

'But you don't deny hiding the laptop and Adele's books.'

Watson sat up again. 'No. I did that. But that's all I did.'

'Why did you do that?'

Watson couldn't find the words to acknowledge his innermost thoughts. 'I can't tell you,' he finally said.

Brook wore latex gloves to open one of the books and began to read 'The Night Walker' again.

Watson scraped back his chair and stood. 'Please stop.' The uniformed officer on the back wall moved swiftly to reseat him. Watson sat down, defeated. 'Please. I . . . I didn't do anything.'

Brook turned to the middle of the diary and opened up the tome to show Watson. He ran a gloved finger down it. 'There are two pages missing here. They've been razored out.'

'Not by me, Inspector. I've not opened either book. I swear. I couldn't face it.'

'You don't expect us to believe that, do you?' said Noble.

'You think I'd have left "The Night Walker" in there if I'd been cutting pages out of her books?' demanded Watson.

'So that poem does refer to you?'

He hung his head. 'I've been worried about her. Maybe I . . .'

'Maybe you've what?'

Watson looked up. 'She's grown up so fast. I was losing her.' He sighed. 'I've been possessive, I realise now. You can't stop it – time. I wanted to spend time with her before it was too late, before she didn't need me. That's all.'

'Then why hide the books?' said Noble.

'I was embarrassed because Adele thought . . .' He came to a halt.

'But why didn't you destroy them? The computer too.'

Watson was silent.

Brook answered for him. 'Because they're the last link to the daughter you love.' Watson nodded his head in confirmation. 'Adele's bed was a mess and the phone and leaflet moved. You?' Watson nodded again.

'Did you masturbate?' asked Noble.

Watson stood, his eyes blazing, and fists clenched. Noble

and the uniformed Constable struggled to reseat him, Brook watching on, unmoved.

Eventually, when Watson was calm enough to hear the question again, he responded with a look of pure horror. 'How can you think that? You're sick, you are. Perverted. Worse than me. At least I'm her father – I have a right to be near her. You're strangers. You shouldn't think about other men's daughters that way.'

'We'd prefer not to,' said Brook.

'So tell us,' said Noble.

'No, I didn't masturbate. I was on the bed because I just wanted to be near her, okay, to smell her. It was in my head. Only there. Please, I promise you. I didn't do anything. Ask Ade.' His head fell to the table again and he began to sob. 'My God, what have I done? Please forgive me. I'm sorry, baby. I'm so, so sorry. I never meant to drive you away. I love you.' He sat bolt upright. 'You must believe me. I never – I wouldn't—'

'I advise you not to say another word until you've been counselled, Mr Watson.' Brook announced the time and switched off the police recorder. Noble looked across at him. 'I think you need to consult a solicitor. You're obviously distraught and that's not a good time to make a statement.'

'A solicitor?' Watson smiled crookedly and finally had a sip of his tea. 'Only God can help me now. Only God can clean these thoughts from my head.'

'Then pray to Him.' Brook rose to leave.

'There's another book.'

Brook and Noble turned back to Watson.

'Another book?' said Noble. 'Where?'

'I don't have it. It's her presentation book, leather-bound.

When she finishes a poem, when she's happy with it, she writes it in there.'

'It's not in the house?' asked Brook.

'I don't think so. She must have taken it with her. I don't have it. I swear.'

Brook nodded and opened the door to usher out Noble and the Constable.

'Inspector.' Brook turned at Watson's voice. 'Do you believe in God?'

Brook paused over the question. 'I don't have time.'

'Not a good time to make a statement?' said Noble, incredulous.

Brook dropped Adele Watson's two handwritten books back into their evidence bags. 'Get every page photocopied and on the boards after fingerprinting, then ask Don Crump to run the ESDA over the page beneath the razored pages. We might get a clue about what was on them.'

'Watson was on the verge of cracking up,' persisted Noble. 'What better time to give a statement? That's when we get the good stuff.'

'You saw him, John. He hasn't killed Adele and he hasn't had sex with her.'

'You don't know that.'

'I can't prove it, no. But I'm a father. You'll have to trust me on this.'

'Trust? If he'd carried on, we would have known for sure.'

'No, we wouldn't. He's on the edge. With the levels of guilt he's carrying, he could say anything incriminating just to make himself feel better. He needs counsel to protect him from himself.'

Noble was silent but no more convinced. Eventually he shrugged. 'So what then?'

'Get him a solicitor and give him a cell for the night.'

'I hope you know what you're doing.'

'That makes two of us.' Brook made to leave but turned back. 'And John, in case his God deserts him, make sure he's put on Suicide Watch.'

Sixteen

AT NINE O'CLOCK THAT NIGHT, Brook rapped on the front door of his cottage and marched into the steamy warmth of the kitchen. The delicious smells told him to expect a meal with bacon and onions.

'Dad. You finished early.'

'I've got an early surveillance tomorrow,' he replied. 'And I haven't finished work tonight.' He showed her the DVD. 'I've got homework.'

'*Picnic at Hanging Rock*,' she said, pulling on a large glass of wine. 'Good film – is this to do with your case?'

'It is.' Brook picked a glass from the drainer and poured out some red wine. There was only half a glass left in the bottle. He spied another open bottle of Merlot already breathing. 'You know the film?'

'*Picnic*? It's beautiful but I don't want to spoil it for you. Is this about the missing students?'

'Did it make the news?' asked Brook.

'Something on Hicksville FM. And the press conference was on local telly.'

'Good. Maybe we'll get some sightings. What are we eating?'

'Bacon and pearl barley hash,' she grinned. Brook noticed she seemed a little unsteady on her feet. 'My own recipe.'

'Sounds great,' said Brook, taking a sip of wine. He peeled some notes from his wallet and dropped them on the table. 'That should cover groceries for the next few days.'

'Da-ad. You don't have to.'

'Yes, I do. I get off easy. No shopping, no cooking, no washing up. I don't even provide the wine glasses.'

Terri laughed and began serving up.

Twenty minutes later, Brook and Terri were stretched out contentedly in front of his small TV, watching the opening titles of *Picnic at Hanging Rock*. Brook nursed his wine but Terri seemed to be throwing it down with gusto.

'How did your writing go today?'

'Okay,' she replied, declining to provide details. Brook waited in vain, before turning back to the film. As he'd found out that morning, the film opened with the lines from Edgar Allan Poe, which set the tone for the story to follow. Gradually Brook became absorbed in the story of the mysterious disappearances of three Australian schoolgirls at Hanging Rock and, the best part of two hours later, watched the end credits roll.

'What are you up to, Adele?' he said quietly. He looked over at the sleeping form of his daughter on the sofa and smiled. He mulled over the film in silence until he'd finished his wine then stood to switch off all the appliances.

On his way to the kitchen, he sat on the edge of the sofa and brushed Terri's hair. She responded by shifting her position for greater comfort but as she moved, the sleeve of her top rode up her arm.

Brook's veins turned to ice when he saw the deep scars on her wrist and he found himself catching at a breath that wasn't there. After what felt like an eternity staring at his sleeping daughter, he stood, finally able to unlock his eyes from the gnarled skin of the old wound, and crept into the kitchen.

Instead of going to bed, he sat at the table and poured himself another large glass of wine, while the questions tumbled in, one after another. *When? Why?* His mind was racing but the rest of him was numb.

'Dad.'

Brook looked up. Terri walked through the door rubbing her eyes open.

'It's late,' he said. 'You should get some sleep.'

Terri blinked herself awake and stared at his face. Her father looked as if he'd had his insides kicked out. She followed his gaze to her arm and saw the sleeve riding up her wrist. She pulled it back down over her scars.

'Dad . . .' She was unable to continue. Instead she sat down opposite her father and took a pull on his wine, her eyes searching unsuccessfully for his.

Brook sat as though in a trance, much like Jim Watson earlier, unable to say the simplest three-letter word. Finally Terri rummaged in her handbag, pulling out her cigarettes, lighting one with a shaky hand.

Brook opened his mouth to complain but nothing came out. Instead he lit a cigarette of his own and exhaled with a shuddering sigh. Eventually he managed to say: 'I have no right. I'm sorry. You don't need to tell me. Whatever prompted . . . well, at some level or another, I have to take the blame. I wasn't there when you needed me.' Self-loathing flowed from Brook's every pore.

'Dad . . .'

'In fact, I wasn't there at all, was I?'

'It's not your fault, Dad. It just happened.'

'Does your mother know?'

Terri nodded.

'What happened?' Brook felt a sudden dread overwhelm him as the answer arrived before the question was fully formed.

Terri took another sip of Brook's wine. 'It was over two years ago. I was depressed.'

Brook closed his eyes in bitter confirmation. 'You tried to commit suicide after your stepfather died.'

Terri's eyes blazed suddenly. 'His name was Tony, Dad. And he didn't die. He was murdered, remember?'

'Oh, I remember perfectly,' retorted Brook. 'There aren't many Good News days in this job. That was one of them.'

'How can you say that?' Terri began to cry. 'Whatever you think about him, he was still a human being.'

'He betrayed your mother. He betrayed you.'

'He didn't betray me!' she shouted. 'I loved him and he loved me.'

'He took advantage of you when you were fifteen years old. That makes him a rapist and a criminal in my book. How can you sit there and defend the way he preyed on you?'

'I loved him, Dad. What can I say?'

'Anything but that,' snarled Brook.

'It's the truth. After my eighteenth we were going away together. Mum would've understood.'

'Understood?' Brook laughed. He could sit no longer. He scraped back his chair and paced to the front door, opening it to let out the smoke. 'You were under-age, Terri. All she would've understood was that she'd married a pervert who'd stolen her daughter.'

'He wasn't a pervert.'

'He broke the law.'

'Love doesn't obey laws.'

'Don't hand me the same claptrap you did five years ago. The law is there to protect you from yourself because you weren't old enough to understand love!' Brook took a deep breath and wrestled for control. 'And clearly you still don't or you wouldn't sit there and justify what he did,' he added quietly. 'This is pointless.'

Terri laughed bitterly. 'My exact words as I drew the Stanley knife across my wrists.' Brook clenched a fist. He saw the sneering mask of certainty in her eyes give way to insecurity. She was too old to man the barricades of unswerving teenage conviction.

'Funny.' She smiled wistfully. 'I was okay for the first six months after he . . .' She took a quivering puff on her cigarette. 'I had Mum to look after. I had my A-levels. Then one day it all fell in on me. The life we'd planned. The way it was taken from us. So I decided to take the easy way out.'

'The easy way?' Brook scoffed. 'Young, beautiful, smart, plenty of money.' He spat out the next words. 'I mean, Christ, how much easier do you want it?'

'Easy enough so the world will know my pain without me having to express it,' she shouted back without flinching.

Brook turned away to breathe in the fresh summer air. A minute later, he turned back and found her eyes. 'Even if I say I'm sorry, even if I accept the value you placed on your relationship with that man . . .' He hesitated.

'What?'

'What do you think? Terri, you're educated, for God's sake. You must have known, no matter how bad the pain became, that one day it would pass. But to try and kill yourself . . .'

'A permanent solution to a temporary problem?' She smiled weakly at him. 'I knew. But maybe I didn't want it to pass. You see, I'd found my immortal love with Tony. No one could ever take him away from me. But if, one day, the pain stopped, then that love was lost. It *is* lost,' she added sadly. She looked up at him. 'How's *your* pain these days, Dad? Living out here on your own with your jam jars. No one to talk to. No one to share.'

Brook turned back to the breeze blowing through the door. 'We get by.'

'And no doubt your education helps you make sense of it all,' she mocked.

Brook took a final drag at his cigarette before flicking it out into the night. 'No,' he said softly. 'It's a curse. It magnifies everything until it's a hundred times worse. It disconnects me from so much, from so many people.' He sighed. 'I know what you're thinking, how it must look. Here on my own, I don't live, I exist. Is that what you want me to say? Okay, I admit it. I live out here in the back of beyond, with my jam jars and my empty fridge and my cigarettes.'

'*My* cigarettes,' said Terri, able to smile now the air was clearer.

'Your cigarettes,' he conceded. 'And yes, there's not a day goes by when I don't question . . .' He shook his head. 'I know it's the logical, educated thing to do when life becomes mere existence. But logic is cold and life is about passion.'

'And is your life about passion, Dad?'

Brook turned a baleful eye on her. 'It is tonight.'

'So we're supposed to just plod on even when we can see no point in living.'

'No point? What could be more pointless than being dead forever, without the kernel of hope that somehow there's something beyond, some afterlife? Education has robbed me of even that puerile vanity.'

'But at least you can choose your time. You're in control.'

'Believe that if you want, Terri, but you *don't* choose and you're *not* in control. On the contrary, you're a prisoner of your own weakness. Even at my age. But for a teenager it's worse. You think people would see, you think they'd take you seriously. You're wrong. All people would see is confusion and fragility, a failure of will. And your cowardice to face up to life.'

'Maybe so, but they'd also see the pain, Dad. They'd see you were hurting and that they missed it, that they should try harder next time. See, you can improve people when you go, make the world a better place.'

'By taking "the easy way out".'

'It's not easy, Dad.'

'It's easier than what I have,' he said quietly.

Terri blinked at the emptiness in her father's voice. He took a breath and turned back to the soothing void of the night.

'Then you do understand,' said Terri finally.

'Understand? Oh, sure I understand the narcissism, the sheer egotism of such an act. But I could never excuse it,' he said, swivelling round to jab a finger at her. 'Never. Don't you get it? No matter what you achieved in your life, every second that you lived would be held up against your decision to destroy yourself, every setback you faced totted up in your own personal suicide column. The manner of your death would define you. That's how you'd be judged.

'Do you think if I killed myself tonight, people would admire me for taking a logical decision? No. They'd pity me because my mental illness got the better of me. Or my divorce tipped me into depression. Or my failure to catch a criminal had driven me to despair. Every good thing about my life would be invisible set against those personal demons.'

'So what do you do?'

'I look away – look out not in, Terri. Forget who you are and go outside, take a walk tomorrow and see for yourself. Walk down the river path and listen to the water. Climb to the top of a hill and just sit down and look around. Feel part of something – something big, something wonderful and, yes, sometimes hard and sometimes cruel, but still something.'

Terri took another sip of wine. 'I know what I did was wrong, Dad. But you've forgotten what love can do to you.'

Brook lowered his eyes in defeat. She had him over a barrel. Affection, human contact – these concepts were strangers to him. 'I wonder if I ever knew,' he said to the night. 'I've been so lonely at times. All I have left is the strength to endure.' He smiled suddenly. 'And you.'

'Good job I didn't die then,' she joked. Brook allowed her a thin smile but it didn't last and Terri looked away.

'They're dead, you know,' she said softly, a moment later. 'If not now, then soon. The website is the hook. It hits all the right buttons. First the violence – perhaps sex, tomorrow. Make sure everyone's watching them, talking about them, analysing their pain. Like they probably analysed Miranda's pain and the other girls who disappeared on *Hanging Rock*.

That's where they got the idea, isn't it? That's when they realised they didn't have to continue suffering.'

Brook shrugged. 'I don't know. But you're wrong – they're not dead. It's a game. Adele, the girl who reminds me of you, she's smart, she's got things to say.'

'Maybe she's already said them.'

'I don't think so. Not yet.'

'Is she smart enough to do what I did?'

Brook looked into Terri's eyes, then down at her wrists. 'Let's hope not.'

Terri sat in silence, sipping her wine. Brook checked his watch. 'I should go to bed.'

'Tell me about The Reaper, Dad.'

Brook turned to her. The second elephant was in the room and she'd spotted it. 'What about him?'

'Who was he?'

'Haven't you heard? I never caught him. He's still at large.'

'I mean, what did he do? What was it like finding all those . . . ?'

Brook looked across at her. 'Bodies?'

Terri nodded.

Brook was silent. 'It was terrible,' he said finally – Brook's first lie to his daughter. At least, the first he could remember telling. Nineteen-ninety. Twenty-one years ago and he could remember it like yesterday. He'd felt nothing. Standing beneath the corpse of a child hanging from a rope, then the year after, a young girl tied to a chair on its side, throat cut from ear to ear. It had left him cold. No, it was worse than that. He'd felt excitement at the first one. It was just a case, another puzzle. Who and why? He'd seen too much, even as a mere thirty year old in the Met. He was dead inside, hollowed out. Looking back, that was the problem, the first step on the road to his breakdown.

'Go on.'

'It's a matter of public record, Terri. I've got a book you can read . . .'

'I want *you* to tell me.'

Brook drained his glass. 'He killed families. Cut them up in their own homes. He did it quickly and efficiently and without pleasure, like it was work, something he had to get done.'

'Why?'

'Because he'd decided that society would be better off without them. They were always petty criminal families who made other lives a misery. He figured that no one would miss them, no one would mourn their passing. Know what? He was right.'

'North London was the first, correct?'

Brook nodded imperceptibly. 'Harlesden, 1990. Sammy Elphick and his wife and boy.'

'You remember their names after all this time?'

Brook just smiled at her without showing his teeth. 'The year after, Floyd Wrigley and his girlfriend were . . . killed. Their daughter Tamara had her throat cut.'

'How old was she?'

'Ten or eleven.'

'God. Is that what started it?'

'My breakdown? It's hard to say. But it was a difficult time. You'd just been born, yet I was spending every waking hour looking for The Reaper. I became obsessed.'

'Didn't you have any suspects?'

Brook refilled his glass. 'No.' His second lie.

'And then you had your breakdown?'

Brook sighed. 'When your mum and I . . . I came to Derby to get away, to find some peace.' He managed a bitter laugh.

'But The Reaper followed you to Derby.'

'Not at first. But yes, he followed me here.'

'Why?'

'I don't know.' A hat-trick of lies. To his own daughter.

'And two more families died.'

'Yes.'

Terri appeared satisfied, but Brook knew she was preparing the ground or soon the elephant in the room would be shattering the windows. 'Tony was murdered three years ago. Just before that last family were slaughtered in Derby.'

Brook looked her in the eye. 'I know.'

Terri continued, staring off intently as though at an invisible script. 'The police interviewed me after Tony's murder. They were very interested in you. They said you had no alibi. They said you had motive – because of Tony and me. They said you came down to Brighton five years ago and assaulted him. You'd found out about our . . . affair.' She swallowed. 'Is that true?'

'Affair,' he sneered. 'Adults have affairs.'

'Is it true?' she persisted.

Brook could see his daughter was short of breath, anticipating the answer to a question long in the forging. 'Yes, it's true. I went to Tony's office. I was only going to threaten him, warn him off. Guess I lost control. Two years later, after he was murdered, they came to Derby to interview me. I was an obvious suspect.'

Terri said nothing but her mind was in turmoil, willing her on, willing her to stop.

Brook put her out of her misery. 'You can ask me.'

She took a sharp intake of breath and sought the right words. They were deceptively simple. 'Did *you* kill him, Dad?'

Brook smiled now. No more lies. He looked her straight in the eye. 'No.'

When Terri trudged back to the sofa, it was nearly two in the morning. Brook finally dragged himself up the stairs an hour before he had to set off back into Derby for his shift in Leopold Street. He didn't sleep, didn't even undress, just lay on the bed staring at the ceiling. Eventually he hauled himself back down the stairs to leave, slipping the new Poe anthology into his pocket.

On his way out, he spotted a note on the table.

Dad, you said this Adele was a poet and she bought the Edgar Allan Poe anthology the day she disappeared. But if she's anything like me she's been thinking about things for a long time. Have a look at the other books in her room. She would read poets who actually killed themselves and wrote poems to that end. They'd probably be women e.g. Anne Sexton or Sylvia Plath. Just a thought.

Glad we had a chance to talk and don't worry.

You're my immortal love now.

Love you. T x

Brook felt a childish rush of pleasure. He was loved. He glanced across at the closed door behind which his daughter slept. He wanted to sneak in and check she was safe and warm, as he'd done when she was a baby. Brook would sit for hours next to her cot just watching her, feeling the exquisite dread of the protector, the bulwark against the horrors of the outside world beyond the nursery door. He'd failed her; let her fall into the clutches of Tony Harvey-Ellis. Maybe he had another chance.

DS Morton rolled down the window. 'You're early, sir.'

'Couldn't sleep. All quiet?'

'As the grave.' Morton yawned.

'Go and get a few hours' sleep, Rob. Busy day tomorrow.' Morton raised an eyebrow. 'Today,' Brook amended with a smile.

'What time do we start at the college?'

'Nine-thirty.'

Brook manoeuvred his BMW into the tight space left by Morton. He poured a tea from his flask and texted Noble to have SOCO gather all the artefacts like books and posters from Adele Watson's bedroom. He wanted another look at her Sylvia Plath book.

He opened his anthology of Edgar Allan Poe, rereading 'A Dream Within a Dream' then skimmed through some of the other works. He alighted on Poe's most famous long poem, 'The Raven', and read it thoroughly, all eighteen verses, alighting on the lines,

> *Let my heart be still a moment and this mystery explore;*
> *'Tis the wind and nothing more!*

Brook woke with a start, strange lights dancing around in his head. When he was able to fully open his eyes, he saw the reason why. Emergency lights were flashing across the road.

He jumped from his car and ran towards the derelict house, shielding his sleep-deprived eyes from the blinding glare. He could make out a figure, walking unsteadily towards the rear of an ambulance, and quickened his pace.

'Phil,' shouted Brook. 'Is that you?'

The hunched form of Phil Ward turned. He screwed his eyes to try and focus on Brook.

'Damen?' he slurred, swaying from side to side. The uniformed ambulanceman was helping him find the bottom step of the vehicle.

Brook drew to a halt. 'What happened, Phil? Are you okay?'

'He'll be fine,' said the man in uniform, not looking at Brook. 'He's just had a bad fall.' He eased Phil carefully up the first step and on to a padded bench.

'Where are you taking him?' asked Brook.

'The Royal,' answered the man, closing the first door.

Phil gazed glassy-eyed at Brook, his head sagging, his eyes bleary with drink. 'Zat you, Damen?' He sat inside the ambulance, brought his hand to his mouth and took a long draught of barley wine.

Brook froze in realisation and he turned just in time to see a gloved hand holding something black and hard describe an arc towards the top of his head. The lights this time were multi-coloured as Brook's knees buckled and he fell to the pavement. He managed to stay upright long enough to watch the burly figure close the second door on a bewildered Phil, before plummeting to the ground with a thud.

Brook heard footsteps and tried to look up through the lights but blood had trickled into his eyes. He could just see the black shoes standing beside him and tried to store more information, but he couldn't focus. Then he felt liquid splash over him, burning into his eyes and soaking his clothes. Whisky. When the bottle was empty the man placed it in Brook's hand and the lights went out completely as he fell, spinning head first, into a bottomless black pit.

Seventeen

Friday, 27 May

BROOK'S NOSE WAS THE FIRST of his senses to return. He could smell a sickly-sweet chemical odour that told him immediately he was in a hospital. He hated hospitals. People died in them. People he knew.

'Welcome back, sir.'

Brook opened his eyes to pain and closed them at once. When the pain remained he opened them again to see Noble, grinning at him. Terri stood next to him and grabbed his hand.

'Dad, are you okay?'

'Never better,' he groaned and tried to sit up but thought better of it immediately.

'What happened?' asked Noble.

'Somebody hit me. I think.'

'One of the tramps,' began Noble.

'Well, well,' said another voice. 'How's my patient? No, I wouldn't advise moving for an hour or two, Inspector.'

Brook brought his hand to his nose and sniffed. 'Whisky.'

'Yes, we thought you were a down-and-out at first, what with the clothes and all.' Brook narrowed a beady eye at the young doctor, who continued to study Brook's chart, oblivious to the implication. 'Probably why people left you lying in the street so long.' Terri and Noble stood by, trying not to smile. 'But your blood alcohol was low so we had to rethink. It's lucky no one took your mobile phone or we wouldn't have been able to ring your daughter and your colleague.'

'They probably looked at him and thought he couldn't afford one.' Terri laughed.

Brook ignored her. 'Doctor . . .'

' . . . Roberts,' smiled the young physician. 'No need to worry. You've had four stitches in a head wound and you're going to have headaches for a day or two, but that will pass. You may have a slight concussion but I don't think we need to admit you. Don't drive for a couple of days, drink lots of hot sweet tea and see your GP in a week for a check-up. Peace and quiet should do the trick – shouldn't be a problem for someone with only two contact numbers on speed dial.' He joked, 'I envy you, Inspector. My phone rings so often I can't hear myself think.'

'Lucky you,' observed Brook drily.

The doctor moved to the privacy screen. 'Back in a moment.'

'What time is it?' asked Brook, after Roberts had left.

'Four o'clock,' said Noble.

'In the afternoon!' exclaimed Brook. 'We've missed the Deity broadcast.'

'No, we haven't,' said Terri, indicating a laptop case under her arm.

'You've seen it?' he asked. And when Terri and Noble nodded, tight-lipped, 'Well?'

'Best you see it for yourself when you're better, Dad.'

'When's the next one?'

'Three o'clock tomorrow.'

'And college?'

'It wasn't a complete waste of time,' answered Noble. 'We're still collating.'

'Oh, you're collating, are you?' Brook said tiredly. 'When are you briefing?'

'Sir, we can handle things without you for a couple of days,' said Noble, looking at Terri for support.

'You need to rest, Dad. I'll take you home.'

'I'm fine.' He looked around for his jacket and began to sit up.

'Dad, you heard the doctor.'

'When are you briefing?' Brook insisted.

'In an hour.'

Brook nodded. 'Good. Where's my car?'

'Outside,' said Noble. 'Terri gave me a lift so I could drive it back to St Mary's. The ambulance —'

'Ambulance,' Brook remembered, staring at Noble. 'It was an ambulance driver that hit me.'

Noble looked quizzically at Brook. 'Sir, I . . .'

'Not a real one, John. I mean, it was a real ambulance, or had been at one time, but the driver must have been Ozzy Reece. He was taking Phil from the house to the ambulance.'

'Phil?'

'Phil Ward. He was one of the tramps.'

'You got a name?' asked Noble.

Brook hesitated. 'I knew him once – at university. I ran against him.' He decided not to mention the lap and a half. 'He was there in the squat when I was undercover. And now thanks to me, he's the next victim.'

'Funny he's abducted this Phil when he hasn't dumped Jock's body yet.'

'We don't know he hasn't dumped him, just that we haven't found it.' Brook flicked his eyes in Terri's direction to tell Noble they shouldn't be discussing corpses in front of her. She caught it.

'Dad, I'm a big girl now.'

'How the hell does a university graduate end up sleeping rough?' said Noble.

Brook looked into Terri's eyes as he spoke. 'Weakness.'

'An ambulance,' said Noble. 'That does make sense. People are rarely suspicious of ambulances and it would be much easier for one person to manhandle a body off a bridge from a trolley. Did you get a look at him?'

'Only briefly. Middle-aged. Well built. And a slight northern accent.'

'Is that all?'

Brook remembered with a flush of guilt that he'd fallen asleep and was barely awake when he'd approached the ambulance. 'The lights were very bright.' He swung his legs gingerly to the floor.

Dr Roberts returned. 'Where are *you* going?'

'Don't want to take up a valuable Casualty bed, Doctor. I'm fine.'

'You're not fine, you need rest.'

Brook thrust his hand into the doctor's and shook it. 'Thanks, Doctor, I know.' Then he marched out a little unsteadily, flanked by Terri and Noble.

Brook examined the artist's composite of Ozzy Reece.

'Ring any bells, sir?' asked Gadd.

Brook stared at the face, trying to place it. He had the feeling it was a face he'd seen before. 'It could be the ambulance driver. It's pretty nondescript.' Brook glanced at Gadd – she was holding her head away from him. Brook sniffed his arm. He still stank of whisky but had no clean clothes in his locker. 'How many people contributed?'

'Two of the hearse drivers at Duxbury and Duxbury. They're adamant it's a good likeness.'

'Okay. Put it out there. On the ambulance angle, assuming it's a rogue . . .' began Brook.

'. . . we nail down the whereabouts of the bona fide fleet between four and five this morning and maybe we can match up some CCTV to The Embalmer's vehicle,' said Gadd. 'On it. Also I've set DC Read and DC Smee on to the private companies who sell secondhand ambulances. There are more than you'd think.'

Brook raised an eyebrow. 'Read and Smee?'

'The Chief assigned them to me to take over surveillance but I assume we're scrapping that.'

'We are. Reece won't go back to Leopold Street now he knows we're on to him. Clear it out and get a SOCO team in to go over the place.'

'Already in motion, though SOCO are getting pretty stretched,' said Gadd. 'On the plus side, I got a batch number from some of the bottles of barley wine and whisky I picked up last night. We've traced them to a Cash and Carry in Nottingham that took a bulk order from an Oz Reece.'

'Any details? Credit card? Address?'

Gadd shook her head. 'The clue's in the name. We got a mobile number but it's a dud.'

'Cameras?'

Steven Dunne

'Too long ago for film.'

Brook nodded and went to sit on a desk at the back of the darkened Incident Room, trying to tune out the pounding in his head. Charlton came to sit next to him. He looked over at Brook's bandaged head and grimaced when the odour of whisky hit his nostrils but he didn't offer comment.

Terri had gone for a walk around the centre of Derby. Brook had tried to persuade Charlton that Terri should stay and offer valuable insights into the teenage psyche but Charlton wasn't to be swayed and Brook didn't have the strength to argue.

The whiteboard screen came to life at Noble's bidding and the Deity film started. For four minutes the officers in the room watched spellbound, despite this being the second viewing for some. Brook immediately recognised Becky Blake from her photo. She was sitting in her bedroom. The picture was a little jumpy at first and it was hard to see what she was doing. Fortunately the picture improved and the bright lighting around her make-up table clearly showed Becky's reflection in the mirror. She was sitting on her bed working on her laptop.

Brook was unsure if she was aware that she was being filmed but, a moment later, something changed in her manner, and as a result she put the laptop aside and moved to stand in front of the mirror. He could see Becky was scantily clad and a second later she began to sway, gently at first, then with more rhythm and purpose. The dance ended with Becky allowing her slip to fall to the floor and she turned to stand naked, gazing directly out of the window at the camera. Luckily Charlton's presence ensured the absence of ribaldry that might otherwise have accompanied this finale.

The film ended abruptly and Rob Morton switched on the lights.

Terri was right. First violence, then sex.

'That's Becky Blake,' said Noble. 'And that's definitely her bedroom.' Even Charlton's presence couldn't stop the few sly grins at the implication. 'The film was shot from outside the house from the branch of a tree, and I've sent a Scientific Support van to do a quick sweep of the exterior but we're not hopeful.'

'The same film has also been uploaded on to YouTube and is getting hundreds of hits. It's being recirculated on Twitter and probably linked in emails and texts,' announced DC Cooper.

'The switchboard says press and TV are clamouring for information,' said Charlton. 'If it's viral, we can't sit on this even if we wanted to, so for once, we get the media to help us.'

'Agreed,' said Brook.

'This second broadcast,' said Charlton. 'Is this supposed to be Russell Thomson filming again?'

'It's an assumption,' said Brook. 'But a fair one.'

'Any sightings yet?' asked Charlton.

'Not one,' replied Noble.

'These kids are still in the country, presumably.'

'Far as we know, sir,' replied Noble. 'But as yet we know nothing about their whereabouts once the party started. We got nothing from door-to-door around the Kennedy house. No cabs picked them up. There's no relevant CCTV on the estate. No reports of suspicious vehicles or vans.'

'We're sure the students were at the party?' said Charlton.

'Adele and Becky were both seen walking up to the house. We assume Kyle was there because he lives there. No sighting of Russell but it doesn't mean he wasn't there.'

'What about the house? Has SOCO found anything?' Charlton again.

'The blood and tissue on the plaster is still our best lead,' said Noble. 'The lab is doing DNA comparisons as we speak.'

'Against what?'

'We've got Kyle, Becky and Adele's toothbrushes.'

'But not Russell Thomson's?' queried Charlton.

'No. One other thing,' added Noble. 'They found a few traces of white powder on the carpet.'

'Drugs?'

'Talcum powder.'

'Talcum powder?' echoed Brook.

Noble shrugged. 'No telling how long it's been there.'

'What would they use that for?' Charlton asked.

'Maybe one of them had nappy rash,' offered a grinning Cooper. His mirth subsided quickly under Charlton's glare.

'Or maybe Len had damp feet six months ago,' said Brook. 'It's meaningless without context.' He looked at the screen. 'Any chance of tracing these . . .' he waved a hand in the air looking for the technical jargon.

'Uploads?' suggested Cooper. 'Yes and no.'

'What does that mean?'

'It means they can identify the profile of a computer accessing a website via its Internet Protocol address,' said Noble.

'And trace any uploads to an actual physical address,' continued Cooper.

Brook narrowed his eyes. 'I'm not sure what you just said but I'm sensing bad news.'

'While you were in hospital we traced the first upload,' said Charlton.

'Elsie Shaw. An eighty-year-old widow who lives in Robincroft Road, Allestree,' announced Cooper, gesturing at a blue pin in the map of Derby. 'She had Broadband fitted so she could Skype her grandchildren in Canada. Unfortunately she didn't secure her router.'

'In English, please,' said Brook.

'With wireless technology, anybody with a modern laptop and a little knowledge can piggyback somebody else's system,' explained Noble.

'Especially if they don't need a password,' added Cooper.

'So the first Deity broadcast was uploaded to Deity from her address,' said Brook slowly.

'Right,' said Noble.

'But being wireless it could have been done from a house in the next street or even a car parked outside,' added Cooper.

'You went round there?'

'In numbers,' smiled Noble. 'Poor old girl got quite a shock seeing six of our finest banging on her door.'

'And how many of these unsecured routers are there?'

'In Derby?' said Cooper. 'Hundreds, I would think. People don't take internet security seriously enough.'

'So Deity can pick and choose where to access the site,' nodded Brook.

'I thought we had all their laptops anyway?' said Morton.

'Doesn't mean they don't have another,' said Noble.

'Did we look at Thomson's laptop yet?' asked Brook.

Cooper nodded. 'Same as the others. Professionally wiped.'

'On the plus side we do have the fruits of the Watson house,' said Noble, indicating the photocopies of Adele's diary and notebook on the array. 'Her computer was wiped like the others but there's some pretty strong stuff about Adam Rifkind and her father in the diary, as well as other things she wants to get off her chest. No direct clue to her whereabouts, but as to her intentions, there's this on the last page of her diary.' Noble held up the copy of the page containing just three words. *TIME TO DIE*.

'That's a line from *Blade Runner*,' said Gadd.

'It is,' said Noble. 'And there's a poster of the film on Russell Thomson's bedroom wall. Another connection between Adele and Russell.'

'It doesn't mean they're intent on suicide,' said Brook.

'All part of messing with our heads,' Charlton said heavily. 'Let's hope. Any prints?'

'Her father's, obviously. And another set that match all the other prints taken from Adele's bedroom. Without her here for a match, we're assuming they're hers. We're also ESDA testing the surface below the missing pages. See if we can read what was on them from the indentations.'

'What about this website?' said Charlton, pointing at the screen. 'Can we close it down?'

'The host server's in this country, so yes, we can start the ball rolling,' said Cooper.

'The question is, do we want to?' said Brook. 'Like it or not, this site is our direct line to Adele Watson and the other students. It's their mouthpiece. Ordinarily I would want to cut off their supply of publicity and maybe drive them into the open. However, she – they – have been very clever unloading the broadcasts to YouTube . . .'

'So they can continue reaching their audience even if we close their site,' Charlton finished. 'You're right, keep it open. What was this boyfriend's reaction to the site?'

'Rifkind? He didn't even know it existed until we told him,' said Cooper.

'And do we believe him?'

'I think so,' said Brook. 'He can't be so stupid as to set up a website with his own credit card knowing it was going to be used like this. He's getting nothing out of this except our scrutiny of his dubious sexual behaviour. Adele Watson played it beautifully. She gave him to us on a plate.'

'You seem very sure this girl's the ringleader, Inspector,' said Charlton.

'That's because she's the smartest, sir. She's thoughtful and reflective, she's a writer and a poet so she's used to making things up. But she had two things wrong with her life – a boyfriend who used then dumped her, and a father, if you believe her diary, who lusted after her. And what happens after she vanishes? Her father's been cautioned for obstruction and Rifkind is a suspect in her disappearance. He's paid for the Deity website with a credit card to which she probably had access, and endorsed passport applications for two of the missing students.'

'So as a suspect, he's a bit obvious,' Charlton commented.

'I'm sure Adele knows that,' said Brook. 'She just wants to embarrass him.'

'But the website was created months before they broke up,' Cooper objected.

Brook smiled at him. 'That tells us how long this has been planned and that actually Adele was using Rifkind, not the other way round.'

'Couldn't somebody else have borrowed his credit card and set this up?' muttered Charlton.

Brook shrugged. 'Who?'

'Is Rifkind married?'

'He is,' said Noble. 'His wife is Carly, a twenty-three-year-old former student – of Rifkind's, I mean. She's seven months' pregnant with their first child.'

'He likes 'em young,' chipped in Cooper.

'Sounds unlikely she'd be up for wrecking her husband's life,' said Charlton. 'Unless she found out about the affair. Hell hath no fury and all that. Somebody should speak to her.'

'Can't hurt,' said Brook unenthusiastically.

'Did Rifkind deny endorsing the passport photographs?' continued Morton.

'No, why would he?' said Noble. 'He didn't do anything wrong.'

'Tell me we got something useful from the college today,' said Charlton. 'That was a lot of expensive manpower.'

Noble smiled weakly at DS Morton who flicked open his notebook. 'Fern Stretton, Becky Blake's best friend, got a text from her before she disappeared. *The next time you hear my name you're going to be sooooooooooo jealous.*' Morton grinned. 'That's ten Os, incidentally.'

'Jealous of what?' asked Charlton. 'Becky's sudden fame? Is that what this is about?'

Brook smiled his agreement. 'We can't discount it.'

'To kids now, in a world of instant celebrity, fame is everything,' said Noble. 'You've only got to watch some of the drooling vegetables auditioning for *X Factor*.'

'And even the completely talentless can be king for a day if they get slagged off badly enough and it goes viral,' agreed Cooper.

Brook bowed to superior knowledge, if not vocabulary. He was lost when it came to young people and their tastes.

'For the record, Fern texted back but got no reply,' said

Morton. 'That was the day of the party. Fern says she hasn't heard from her since and insists to anybody who'll listen that she's abroad somewhere. According to Becky's mobile phone records, that was the last text or phone call she ever made. Kyle Kennedy also used his mobile for the last time on the night of the party. He made a call to Jake McKenzie the night before and sent a text to his mum in Chester on Friday to say he was fine. Then nothing.

'Interestingly, Adele and Russell were even more extreme,' continued Morton. 'There was no record of any activity on their phones the day *before* the party – or since, obviously.'

'They shut up shop on the Thursday?' said Brook.

'Right. We're also checking all recent texts and calls for the four of them, against the list of known contacts – but so far we've seen nothing untoward.'

'No common number texting or phoning all four?' asked Cooper.

'No.'

'Strict radio silence,' said Brook. 'Clever. Maybe Russell Thomson's her second-in-command. It would make sense. He had the DVD and he's the one with the camcorder.'

'And he arrived in Derby just before the website was set up,' added Noble.

'Good point. So what next?' asked Charlton.

'We've done all the heavy lifting for now,' said Noble. 'A blank on bins and grates around the house. We've interviewed most of the students and college staff. We can take a longer look at the parents and maybe re-interview.'

'What about the fields?' said Brook.

'Fields?' echoed Charlton.

'If these kids left on foot, which looks likely, they would

have taken the path at the back of the house.' He indicated the large map on the wall. 'There's a large area to cover but they could have walked along the path round the back of the college.'

'Or even gone across the fields through the woods,' said Morton, pointing. 'The A38 runs past. They could have been picked up from there.'

Charlton nodded reluctantly. 'That's a lot of manpower. Check the A38 cameras first.'

'Maybe they're hiding in the woods,' suggested Cooper. 'Or even dead.'

'Unlikely, Dave,' said Noble. 'Kids mess about in there. They would've been found by now.'

'Maybe.'

'Okay,' said Charlton testily. 'Get uniform on it.'

'Fingertip?' asked Noble.

Charlton glanced at Brook for help in protecting the budget.

'Not without evidence of foul play,' said Brook. 'They're not going to be there, dead or alive, but we need to have looked.'

Charlton tried to hide his relief. 'Anything else?'

'What about Jake McKenzie and Wilson Woodrow?' asked Brook.

'Remind me,' said Charlton.

'McKenzie was one of the lads in the happy-slapping film,' replied Noble. 'He wasn't in college today. Neither was Wilson Woodrow. We showed the first film to Rifkind. Woodrow was the boy who laid out Kyle Kennedy in the assault. Rifkind confirmed there was some kind of bust-up between all three of them in his lesson the day before the party. Woodrow made some homophobic comments and went for Kennedy, and Jake stepped in. We've got addresses.'

'Okay,' said Charlton. 'I think we've got all we need for the press briefing.' He eyed Brook's bandaged head. 'How are you feeling, Inspector?'

'Actually, not so good.' Brook groped for a chair and lowered himself gingerly into it.

Charlton narrowed his eyes. 'You took a heavy blow. Maybe it's concussion.'

'I'll be okay.'

'You'd better sit this one out. That bandage would be a distraction. Get some rest. DS Noble, fancy a bit of the lime-light?' Noble's ashen face told its own story but he managed to smile weakly. 'Good.' Charlton made to leave.

'Sir?' said Brook. 'Can I have a word?'

'I'm listening.'

'In private.'

Charlton looked at his watch. 'My office in half an hour,' he said as he left.

'Are you well enough to hear about Yvette Thomson, sir?' said Noble sarcastically, brandishing a wad of papers.

Brook smiled. 'I'll try to stay conscious.'

'Bad news, sir. She's Welsh.' Brook raised a disapproving eyebrow at Noble. 'Born 1978 so she's thirty-three years old, originally from St Asaph in North Wales. It's near Rhyl, if that helps at all. She was an orphan from the age of nine, when her mother died of an overdose of painkillers in 1987.'

Brook nodded. 'An orphan. Of course.' Noble looked be-mused. 'She seems . . . needy,' Brook explained. 'How long did she spend there?'

'The next seven years – St Asaph's School for Boys and Girls – an orphanage in all but name. In 1993 Yvette had a baby – Russell. Her only child. No record of the father.

Mother and child stayed at the orphanage until she left in 1994 to move to Chester.'

'She was only fifteen when she gave birth?'

'Older than many,' said Noble.

'And they didn't take the baby from her?'

'And do what?' asked Noble. 'Put it in an orphanage?'

Brook conceded with a shrug. 'It's still odd. Social Services would normally intervene; maybe put the child up for adoption. Ever married?'

'No. And she seems to have survived on benefits for most of her life. There's no record of any employment until she's twenty when she moves and becomes a teaching assistant at a primary school in Whitchurch, in 1998, just over the border in Shropshire. The following year, she moves to Uttoxeter. She's jobless and again surviving on benefits. In 2003, when Russell was ten, she returned to North Wales where she moved around at regular intervals – hardly a settled life. Six months ago, she and Russell turn up in Derby where Russell was enrolled at Derby College.'

'What about the rumours of bullying?'

'I'm still waiting to hear from some of the schools, but two that responded say Russell wasn't with them long but he was very impressionable and he was bullied. They stopped short of saying that's why Russell was taken out of their schools. But reading between the lines . . .'

Brook nodded. 'No wonder it was hard to hold down a job. Any other employment?'

'Nothing. But she might have done casual work,' said Noble.

'She mentioned bar work.'

'I spoke to Rifkind. He didn't know the details about the

last move but he'd heard there'd been some kind of cyber-bullying.'

'Cyber-bullying?'

'It's using social network—'

'I know what it is, John. But didn't Cooper say Russell and the others unsubscribed from Facebook on the day of the party?'

'So?'

'So why would Russell even have a Facebook account if he'd been bullied online?'

Noble shrugged. 'I don't know.'

Brook sighed. 'Okay. I'm meeting Terri in the car park in forty minutes. Text me Jake McKenzie's address, John. I'll meet you there at eight tomorrow morning. He and this Wilson Woodrow are overdue a visit.'

Noble picked up a clear plastic bag from the floor. 'You said you wanted these books of Adele's. They've been processed.'

'Anything?'

'A few handwritten notes in the texts. Nothing jumped out.'

'Okay. What's that?' asked Brook, nodding at a second bag.

'Russell Thomson's computer. We're so stretched we haven't assigned a FLO to return it to Miss Thomson yet.'

Brook picked up the bag. 'It's on my way. I'll take it. Speaking of liaison, you'd better get someone round to Fred Blake's house in case they don't know about Becky's striptease yet. They ought to hear about it from us before they see it on the news.'

Brook's mobile vibrated. It was Dr Petty. Noble pointed towards the door and left the office.

'Inspector, I hope you don't mind me ringing, but you didn't reply to my email.'

'Your email?' Brook set down the various bags on a desk and quickly logged on to his internal email account. 'I've not had a lot of time to reply,' he said, trying to stall. When the screen filled with unopened emails, Brook scanned down the list. He found a day-old reply from Dr Petty to his enquiry about Egypt and opened it.

Dear Damen,

Egypt does indeed come under ancient anatomy. And they were one of the first civilisations to embalm their dead. I was on a similar wavelength so I'd already done some digging – no pun intended. There was a tradition of removing the brain through the nostrils when preparing the dead for the afterlife. I can't find a name for the tool though.

AnnP

Her mobile phone number was prominent. 'Ye-es,' he said. 'I've read it. Very helpful.'

'It gets better. I've looked through three or four websites. Egyptian burial rites changed many times over the centuries but they all agree that to aid preservation of the bodies, all the organs were removed and placed in a large earthenware jar with a lid, called a canopic jar, and placed at the foot of the embalmed body. The interesting thing is the organs were removed via an incision in the left side, just like McTiernan and Kirk. But here's the best part. The priests in charge of the procedure would then put the heart back because they believed it contained the soul, which the deceased would need for the afterlife.'

'That *is* interesting,' said Brook. 'Anything else?'

'That's it for now.'

Brook put down his pencil, not sure how to end the conversation. 'I owe you one.'

'Really? I hear Darley's does good food.'

'I'd like to be put back in charge of The Embalmer case, sir. DS Noble can handle the missing students.'

'Think DS Gadd's out of her depth?'

'Not at all.'

'Then why?'

'I should've thought that was obvious, sir. We've got two mutilated bodies and two more missing, probably facing the same fate.'

'Two vagrants who died of alcohol poisoning, Inspector. Occupational hazard.'

'Sir, Phil Ward was taken last night. I saw it happen. He's the first definite abduction and it's likely the other three were the same. It's unlikely these men are just dying around The Embalmer and it's not a huge stretch to assume he's hastening their deaths before he cuts them open.'

'There's still no evidence of that,' retorted Charlton.

'I'm also worried about escalation. Leopold Street is compromised. If he thinks his supply is being cut off . . .'

'You mean he might turn his attention to real people,' nodded Charlton. 'It did occur to me.' His expression softened. 'You're right. Assault and abduction is a step up from stealing cadavers.'

'So I'm back on the case?'

'Absolutely not.'

'Sir, these missing students . . .'

'. . . are no longer just an internet sensation.' Charlton picked up a pile of newspapers and dropped them on Brook's lap. '*The Times*, the *Telegraph*, the *Guardian* and, needless to say, all the tabloids have picked up the story. I've had BBC and ITN reporters ringing the Press Office about this afternoon's Deity broadcast and likely they'll be running with it tonight. So you see, it doesn't matter if these kids are sunbathing in Wembley Stadium, Inspector. Until we find them and put this to bed, this is your priority.'

'So Ozzy Reece . . .'

'. . . is being sought by a very able detective.' Charlton rubbed his chin. 'Look, you've got my permission to offer advice at every stage. Gadd's got extra people. If there's anything else you think we need to do, tell me.'

'We need to go public. We need people to be on the lookout for the ambulance, get the facial composite of Ozzy Reece into the local press and TV and put his name out there.'

'Isn't it an alias?' said Charlton.

'Doesn't mean he hasn't used it in front of others.'

'Okay. And for good measure get Noble to prepare a statement for the end of our media briefing this afternoon,' said Charlton. 'Would that suit?'

'It would,' replied Brook. 'And after that, maybe we could go door-to-door in Shardlow.'

'Shardlow?'

'There's a chance that's where he lives.'

Charlton's expression became pained but he knew not to mention budgets again to Brook. 'Let's see what the media can throw up for us first.'

*

Brook stood next to Terri's VW in the station car park, bringing Noble up to speed on the phone.

'Should I mention any of this in the briefing?' asked Noble.

'Yes, but keep it broad. The suspect is English but may have a keen interest in Egypt, may have visited or even lived there. Something like that. I printed off Petty's email for Jane so she can chase up the Interpol inquiry. She's also putting in calls to the Foreign Office and the British Council, see if that shakes anything out. If Reece ever lived in Egypt he may have done something similar and hopefully there's a record.'

'You know we're going to get nothing, the state the country's in.'

Brook rang off and waved to Terri, who was walking towards him beside a tall young man with short, bleach-blond hair, deep blue eyes and a neat beard. He wore a back-to-front baseball cap on his head and casual but smart clothing. Brook was faintly pleased to see his trousers weren't held up by his knees. He carried several boxes and bags, only one of which appeared to be his. Terri was smiling and flirting all the way and only looked towards her father when she was in earshot.

'Hi, Dad.' She grinned.

Brook nodded. 'If you're busy, I can drive myself home, Terri.'

She blushed and looked at her companion. 'Dad, this is Ray. He's studying Law at Derby University. He helped carry my shopping.'

'Hello, Ray,' said Brook. 'Another lawyer – great.'

'Hello, sir.' Ray beamed. 'Where shall I put these, Terri?'

She opened the boot and the obliging Ray packed the bags and boxes in the small space, while Brook ran his eye over the young man, looking for tattoos. What he could see of his hands and arms were blemish-free so Brook stopped playing protector and ambled a few yards away to give them some space.

'I don't know how to thank you,' Terri gushed.

'I thought we already covered that,' he teased.

'I know,' she said, a little embarrassed. 'But I'm doing a dissertation and I'm staying with my dad.'

'Don't put me in the middle of this,' Brook shouted over, pleased to be able to embarrass her.

'There you are, Terri. Your dad knows work isn't everything.'

Terri looked at her father. 'I wouldn't be so sure.' She laughed her submission. 'I've got your number, okay.'

'Fair enough,' replied Ray. 'Nice meeting you, sir,' he said to Brook, waving a farewell to Terri and wiggling his hand in the internationally accepted sign for 'Call me'.

'You didn't waste much time,' said Brook, restraining a smile.

Terri glanced at him. 'I'm twenty already, Dad. There isn't much time to waste.'

Eighteen

BROOK AND TERRI ROLLED ALONG in silence, punctuated by his directions through the Brisbane Estate. They pulled on to Yvette Thomson's road and Brook spotted Len Poole cycling arthritically along the pavement in front of them. He held a large envelope tightly against one handlebar.

'A pensioner in a tracksuit,' said Terri. 'Could anything be more wrong?'

To Brook's surprise, Poole turned on to Yvette Thomson's driveway, dismounted and rapped aggressively on the glass door.

'Pull over, Terri.'

Terri looked at him and followed his eyes back to the squat figure of Poole. Without asking for explanation she pulled to the kerb and turned off the engine.

Brook kept his eyes trained on the house as Poole looked around at neighbouring houses while he waited, flicking the envelope against his thigh. When the door didn't open he rapped on the glass more vigorously, then walked to the large bay window and peered inside.

'What's wrong, Dad? Why have we stopped?'

Brook reached into the back seat without breaking his surveillance. 'I've got to drop off this laptop.'

'This piece of junk,' said Terri, examining it through the plastic. 'I wouldn't bother. Just stick it in the dustbin.' She reached for the other plastic bag on the back seat. 'Are these Adele's?'

Brook nodded without taking his eyes from Poole, still banging impatiently at the door. Terri isolated a book through the plastic and held it up for Brook. 'Sylvia Path, Dad. See?'

'I know. You were right.' Brook watched as Yvette Thomson finally opened the door. Unfortunately she moved back almost at once so he couldn't see her reaction as Poole stepped purposefully over the threshold. But the way she had ushered Poole into her home told its own story. The two of them knew each other.

Brook wondered whether to sit tight or gamble. A second later, he took the computer from Terri. 'Won't be a minute.'

'Can't I come with you?' asked Terri.

'What?'

'This is where one of the students lived, isn't it?'

'Russell Thomson.'

'Then get me in there, Dad. You want to find these kids, don't you? I can have a look at his room. Let you know what I think.'

Brook considered the ethics of involving civilians, let alone family, in police business. Talking things through with her was one thing, it helped him think. Giving her free rein in a missing person's room was quite another. He gestured her out with a flick of the head, still not sure he was doing the right thing. 'Don't touch anything. Don't speak.'

Brook hesitated at the door. He could hear Poole shouting. He thought he heard, *'All these years . . .'* but he couldn't be sure.

Terri shuffled uneasily next to him and kicked over an empty plant pot near the step. It rolled noisily along the concrete of the drive. The shouting from within stopped while Terri stared apologetically at her father. Brook resisted the temptation to roll his eyes and knocked firmly on the door instead.

'Hello.' Yvette smiled hesitantly, failing to invite him in. 'Oh my God, what happened to your head?'

Brook smiled back to confirm his well-being. 'I had a bit of a fall. Nothing serious.'

'You want to be more careful at your age,' she teased. Her smile disappeared as quickly as it arrived. 'Are there developments?'

He decided against getting drawn into the Deity broadcasts. If she didn't already know about them from the news, she soon would. 'Nothing concrete.'

'I saw that film,' she said. 'Poor Kyle. You think Rusty shot it, don't you?'

She hadn't yet seen the Becky Blake film and Brook wasn't about to enlighten her. 'We can't rule it out. It was shot before the party so . . .' He held out Russell's laptop which she took from him without enthusiasm, before looking across at Terri. 'This is Detective Constable Terry. I wonder if we could come in for a moment. We need to check a detail in Russell's room.'

Yvette wavered but before she could refuse to invite them in, Len Poole appeared behind her in his bright blue tracksuit.

'Inspector. I thought that was your voice. Goodness, you've been in the wars. Any news?' He looked across at Terri and gave her a lingering up and down. Brook hoped it was the unconscious habit of the ex-pathologist.

'There's a press conference shortly and my guess is it will make the TV news.'

Len nodded. 'Better get back and watch it then.' He scratched his head in consternation. 'It's a difficult time. I just came round to meet Yvette. Let her know we're there for her if she needs support,' he added, answering a question that hadn't been asked. 'We need to pull together when something like this happens.'

Brook just smiled.

'Well, I'd best be off. Nice to meet you, Yvette,' said Len, turning to leave.

'You too, Len.' Yvette smiled. 'Thank Alice for thinking of me. I'll be in touch.'

'What do you need to check, Inspector?' she said when Len had gone.

'Just something one of my underlings needs to verify. Upstairs, Constable. Chop, chop,' said Brook to his daughter. 'First on the left.'

'Right away, sir,' replied Terri, making a show of pulling on the latex gloves Brook had given her, before heading up the stairs.

Yvette followed her progress. 'She's very young,' she said when Terri was out of sight. 'I suppose that's a sign of my age.'

'Start worrying when you're as old as I am,' answered Brook. He looked beyond her to the interior. 'Any danger of a cup of coffee while I'm waiting?'

Yvette handed Brook a cup and darted her eyes anxiously round the room. She gestured him to a seat.

'Inspector Brook, you've been so kind.' She laughed

nervously. 'I can't keep calling you that.' She cocked her head at Brook.

'Damen,' he answered reluctantly.

'Damen. Interesting name.'

'It's German for Ladies,' he said. 'Don't ask.'

She smiled fulsomely at him. 'I didn't know men like you existed any more. You know, all the men I've ever met, even the boys like Wilson – they look at me in a certain way, but not you. You look at me and see a person, not a MILF.'

Brook smiled and took a sip of coffee.

'You know what I'm trying to say.'

The conversation was heading where Brook hoped it wouldn't. 'Yvette – *Eve*,' he corrected himself when she prepared to protest. 'I can't begin to imagine what you're going through.'

'Can't you? I think you can. I can see it in your eyes.'

Brook took another sip of coffee. Perhaps he was expected to give clarification, something he'd rather avoid. He kept silent, but when Yvette said nothing and wouldn't drop her gaze, he realised she wouldn't be denied.

'You're not married, are you?' she said.

'Not any more.'

'How do you cope with the loneliness?' Brook stared back without expression. 'I'm a very lonely woman, Damen. I have been all my life. I never knew my father, and my mother died when I was young. I was put in care until I was old enough to live my own life.'

'I'm sorry, I had no idea,' Brook lied.

She smiled sadly. 'I can't be alone, Damen. I won't be. Since Rusty—'

A door closed on the floor above and Terri descended to

the hall. 'All done, sir.' She pulled off her gloves with a satisfying snap.

Yvette and Brook followed Terri to the front door.

'Thanks for the coffee,' said Brook.

'My pleasure, Damen.'

As Brook followed Terri outside, Yvette allowed her hand to brush softly against his.

'See you soon,' she said.

'I reckon those two know each other, Dad – before today, I mean,' said Terri, when they were on the A52.

Brook smiled across at her. 'Chester.'

'Chester?'

'Yvette Thomson's only lived in Derby for six months – she's from North Wales and once lived in Chester. Len went to Chester with Mrs Kennedy for the weekend, the night of the party. It could be a coincidence. Len said he didn't know her.'

'He's lying,' said Terri. 'But why pretend they don't know each other when they do?'

'Why does anybody lie?' said Brook, avoiding her eye. 'Something to hide from the past.'

Terri nodded. 'Maybe it's something to do with that envelope.'

Brook squirrelled an admiring glance her way. 'You're good at this, aren't you?'

She grinned with pleasure. 'Must be genetic. What do you think was in it?'

'I don't know but I don't think he had it when he left so he must have taken great pains to hide it.'

'How do you know?'

'Because I couldn't find it when Yvette was making coffee.'

Terri narrowed her eyes at her father. 'Isn't it illegal to search a house without a warrant?'

'Absolutely. It's on a par with impersonating a police officer.'

Terri laughed. '*Yvette* didn't seem to catch on, *Damen*.'

'Let's hope she doesn't remember you,' said Brook, ignoring his daughter's insinuating tone.

But Terri wasn't to be deflected. 'Are you and her . . . ?' She tilted her head suggestively.

'Certainly not,' replied Brook. 'She's part of an investigation. Her son is missing and she's very vulnerable. That would be opportunism of the worst kind.'

'But if she wasn't involved in a case?' Brook concentrated on the road. 'Taking the fifth on that one, *Damen*? Well, she's certainly pretty.' Brook wasn't to be tempted into an answer. 'And far too attractive for that dirty old Len. Did you see the way he looked me over?'

'I did. But he may just be Slab Happy.'

'Pardon?'

'He used to be a pathologist. It's a habit in people who work with the dead. They assess people's height and weight. Just in case. They don't know they're doing it.'

Terri pulled a face. 'Gruesome.'

'What about Russell? Did you get a feel for him?'

'Sort of. There's a poster missing. Do you know what it was?'

'No. Miss Thomson couldn't remember.'

'Pity. And without books he's a tough read but, no books,' she raised an eyebrow, 'that's significant in itself.'

'How?'

'He's more of a plotter than a thinker.'

'Plotter?'

'Director would be a better word. Probably where he gets his love of films.'

'Go on.'

'Look, this may be completely offbeam. He may just be a film buff and his tastes may be completely random . . .'

'But?'

'But if you were to assume his character from the posters in his room, there are one or two pointers. *The Blair Witch Project*, for instance. Did you know the makers built its reputation by using the internet? They created a website that treated the disappearance of three students investigating reports of a supernatural entity, as a real event.' Brook looked at her. 'I know. Spooky, eh?'

'And people got hooked on the mystery like they are with Deity?'

'Exactly.'

'What happened to the students in the end?'

'It was a bit vague but I think they died.'

Brook nodded. 'Similar to *Picnic at Hanging Rock*. Anything else?'

'Have you seen *Badlands*?'

'Actually I have. I saw it with your mother a long time ago. I can't remember much about it.'

'It's about a mindless teenage killer played by Martin Sheen. He's on the run and heading for the Canadian border and safety.'

'Go on,' said Brook, trying to remember.

'He's getting away – just a few miles from the border – but suddenly he stops and shoots out his tyres.'

'Why?'

'Because he'd rather die on the electric chair and be famous than live in obscurity for the rest of his life. Think that's what Russell and the others were planning?'

'Well, they're more famous than they were a week ago.'

The press conference was now featured on the national news channels, as were parts of the two internet films from the Deity broadcasts. They didn't carry the appeal for information about the suspect in The Embalmer case although it went out after the main news on the local East Midlands bulletins.

'They've found their audience,' said Terri, looking up from the Sylvia Plath book. 'Are you feeling okay, Dad?'

He snapped out of his reverie and switched off the TV. 'Bit of a headache.'

'I'm not surprised.'

Brook padded into the kitchen for some tablets and returned to sink into a chair with the photocopies from Adele's diary. He swallowed two aspirins with a gulp of Aberlour to wash them down. 'I can't help thinking I've seen The Embalmer's face before last night – except it's wrong.'

'Wrong? What's wrong?'

'The face.'

'Looked pretty regulation to me,' said Terri. Then: 'Listen to this, Dad.' She read 'Suicide Off Egg Rock' from the Plath anthology. When she finished the line *I am, I am, I am*, she said, 'Need I say more?'

Brook nodded thoughtfully. 'Adele wrote the same line in the front of her diary.'

'You still won't let me read it?'

Brook grimaced. 'There's a big difference between giving

your impressions on her collection of books or Russell's taste in films and actually looking through their thoughts.'

'I don't see it.'

'But I do. I've been doing this a long time and, believe me, putting yourself in someone's head is not healthy. Doubly so if that person's a victim. Or a killer. I'll let you know if I need advice on something. That reminds me. What does,' he checked a detail in Adele's diary, 'WGAF mean to you?'

'Who gives a fuck?' she answered.

'I do.'

'No, I mean . . .' Terri pushed back her chair at first sight of her father's grin. 'Very funny. I'm tired. If I'm driving you in early tomorrow, I'd better get some sleep.'

Brook got out of the chair. 'Good idea. Night, darling.' He turned at the door. 'And Terri, you've already helped me a lot.'

She smiled at him. 'Night, Dad.'

Brook closed the living-room door and sat at the kitchen table to read more of Adele's diary. When he picked it up, he noticed the word Diary had been split by a hyphen added in the middle of the word. Di-ary. Why? Brook held it away from him. Di – could she be a female friend? Was Adele personalising her memoirs to make the diary an imaginary comrade?

He opened it at the first passage again. The entry was for 1 January 2011 but Adele had crossed out every date of every entry and replaced it with *Some number, some month. WGAF?*

Believe nothing. It's not real. None of it. It pours out of the screen. And the idiots suck it up. Mums and dads, neighbours too. Look at their faces, all aglow, deformed by defeat.

'Hallelujah. We believe.'

Here is the news. Drive to work, drive back, sit for hours

plugged into the stream of stuff flowing from the tube. The surrender of life, the move from first hand to second. A headshake here, a tut there, a 'serves them bloody well right' somewhere else. There's a Japanese earthquake but it's not real. How can it be? We're not there. There's no tsunami. Those poor people. Look at them run. Now that's entertainment.

A girl's body is found. They put up the maps. It's real. It happened here. It could happen to you. I wish it would. I'd be a star. Mum's mouth sags in awe. 'I've driven on that road. Who would've thought?' No one, why start now?

Bedtime. Turn it off. The Machine Stops. Time to wake up. Time to dream. No time for reality, a better world beckons from the pillow. Even waking is a dream. A dream that today will be better, kinder, full of love and hope.

The real wake-up beckons. 'Have a nice day, dear.' 'You too.' And the hours start to die, killing the day. It's over. File it with the others. U for Unmemorable, Unreal. Unrepeatable? If only.

Same old world. Not waking is the answer. Dream forever. Like the Lady of Shallot, I am half sick of shadows.

My hand is real. I examine it as I write. My body is real. My vagina is real. My breasts are real. I can still feel AR's weight on top of me, inside me. My whole being throbbing. Lungs filling. Such exquisite pain. I am, I am, I am.

Brook turned the page to a fresh entry.

Dad's face when I told Mum I was going out with someone (AR). I could almost hear the blood rushing to his head. He was in the next room but I didn't have to shout. He listens to everything I say with bated breath. Words are so powerful. To think the word 'boyfriend' can deliver such a kick in the teeth. It was all I could do not to march in there and laugh in his spluttering face. And Mother? Stupid bitch. She doesn't even know what her man is thinking, wanting. I could've kept AR secret and let Dad keep hoping, but I need to crush his heart now. I can't go on. I can't stand being around him. My own father. He comes to stand next to me just to smell me, like I'm prey. I've ignored his sly looks at my body too long, his enthusiastic hugs. Think I don't know you lie on my bed when I'm not home, Dad? Give it up. I don't want to dress like a nun around you. I don't want to cover my tits. Cover your eyes, old man. Cover your eyes.

Brook read the last entry again. Jim Watson was telling the truth. Surely he would have removed that last section, had he been censoring his daughter's thoughts. The missing pages must have been cut by someone else. Adele? It seemed likely.

Brook picked up the ESDA copy of the page below the absent pages. The technicians had not picked up all the text with the Electrostatic Detection Apparatus but there was enough to show that Adele had created the script for the leaflet. *Live Forever. Immortal. Beautiful.* She'd written the same words several times in a variety of ways, presumably as a design exercise.

Brook turned back to the diary and read other entries.

A strange boy joined our literature group. Russell Thomson. He hardly speaks and he can't bear to look people in the eye. He has a camcorder on his wrist and doesn't take it off. He looks like he has Special Needs and even Wilson thinks he's smarter than him but he's wrong. There's something about him. I don't know. It's like he knows something that the rest of us can never know and he's just working out a way to explain it to us. I saw him with his mum the other day. She's beautiful and it's hard to imagine the two are related. Wilson saw her too and was all over her like a ten year old with a toffee apple. He says he's going to pop her if it's the last thing he does. Bad boy. Dirty boy.

Then it was back to her relationship with Rifkind and the passion spilled off the page again.

Adam Fucking Rifkind. No more secrecy. No more sneaking around. No more AR code, Adam Fucking Rifkind. I should Facebook the shit out of your guilty secret, then where would you be? You think you're a god to women. Is that why you don't want me and say you don't love me? You only love yourself. You want your slag of a wife and the brand new screaming receptacle of piss and shit she's carrying. Fuck you, Adam Rifkind. (Good title for a poem.) Fuck everything about you. And another thing. Your novel is shit. You think you're God's gift to literature. You're not. No more suggestions from me. Or is that the point? I've cured your infantile story, put a line through the puerile, and you don't need me now.

Brook smiled. Rifkind in a nutshell. Adele was very astute. Was? He hoped she was alive, hoped she was too clever to give her life for fleeting fame and the momentary regret of loved ones.

He turned to her notebook of poems and read the piece that she'd composed on the blotter of her desk before transferring it to her notebook.

Live Forever. Question Mark

Life is not a rehearsal, They say
Life is not an audition, They say
Life is something that happens while
You're making plans. They say

Live Forever? Make your mark

Be someone. Face on the telly.
Or embrace mediocrity, scuttle around,
Do stuff, buy stuff, fuck stuff,
Sand through the fingers, draining away.

Does this make a living? They don't say.

He looked at the clock. Gone midnight. He took a final sip of whisky. Why was he devoting so much time to this girl and her friends? They'd run away and didn't want to be found. They weren't dead, he was sure of it – almost sure. Not like Phil Ward. Phil was out there, facing death. In his mind, Brook had already signed the death certificate.

Concentrate on the hope. Terri had come through, survived her crisis without him. She didn't need him any more. Perhaps she never did. Concentrate on Adele. Adele was alive. Adele was his daughter now. He could still save her. He could be a proper father to her. He could pore over her life in the reasonable knowledge that he'd never have to stand over her alabaster corpse. He could read her deepest darkest thoughts, and take comfort from the notion that one day they might actually meet, while deep in his subconscious Brook knew that the next time he saw Phil Ward, he would be on a mortuary slab. What good was his lap and a half now?

With a feeling of dread, Brook picked up Adele's diary and turned to the copy of the final page again. He reread the three words and tried to put a positive spin on them. She was referring to the end of her life as it had been lived to this point – looking forward to the new, to her rebirth as an internet celebrity. That had to be it. That had to be the meaning. *TIME TO DIE*.

Nineteen

Saturday, 28 May

AFTER THREE HOURS' SLEEP, BROOK tiptoed down the stairs early next morning and made tea. He caught sight of his head in the kitchen window. He'd removed the bandage and replaced it with a plaster over the stitches. The area was still swollen and the bruising was beginning to colour.

He took his tea into the tiny office at the back of the cottage, turned on his computer, typed in the Deity address and loaded the page. For no particular reason he watched the archived footage of both Deity broadcasts again but gleaned no fresh inspiration. The countdown to the next broadcast had dipped under eleven hours.

He decided to search sites with information on Ancient Egyptian burial rites and clicked on a few, confirming some of Dr Petty's conclusions about The Embalmer's treatment of the vagrants' bodies. He read up on the procedures. Petty was right. The Ancient Egyptians believed the heart, rather than the brain, was the seat of emotions and was necessary for the dead to proceed safely to the afterlife. After the organs were removed, including the brain through the nostrils, the heart was put back into the cavity as it had been with McTiernan and Kirk.

He read more information on embalming and made a list of some of the chemicals required. Maybe they could find Ozzy that way. Brook sniffed the air and then his arm. He could still smell whisky despite a shower and change of clothes. He looked around and spied the whisky glass he'd used the previous night. It still had a few dregs in it. Brook picked it up and padded into the kitchen to make more tea.

He was about to rinse out the leaded tumbler when he stopped and looked at the pale golden liquid. He stared for a few seconds then washed out the glass and opened a cupboard to put it away. There was a loaf of sliced bread in there. Terri had bought it for her breakfasts. Brook gazed at it in confusion while he thought things through. A moment later he broke into a grin and returned to the computer.

'And people worry about my mental health,' he said, typing another topic into the search engine.

Half an hour later, Brook was sitting contentedly on the garden bench sucking in the cool damp air and smoking a cigarette stolen from his daughter's handbag. It was just after five and he had the world to himself. The telephone destroyed his reverie and Brook launched himself barefoot back into the house to answer it before Terri could wake.

'You're up.'

'John. What is it?' said Brook, breathless.

'Another body.'

'Jock or Phil?' asked Brook.

'You'd better come see for yourself.'

*

Terri pulled the VW on to Meadow Road and as close to the crime-scene tape as she could manage. Brook opened the door before the car had stopped and stepped out. The noise of the river was more apparent here over the quiet buzz of Derby's city centre.

'You're sure you can find your way back?' he said to his daughter.

Terri was yawning again but managed an affirmative grunt with a nod for back-up. 'I'll be fine,' she said once her jaw was back under control.

Brook closed the passenger door and watched her reverse the car and speed away. He turned to see Noble heading over to him. They exchanged nods then Noble led Brook across the small triangular green space towards the concrete wall at the river's edge. The increasing noise of the weir was competing with the occasional car roaring over the St Alkmund's Way flyover nearby.

The river bank had clearly been a hive of activity but now the body was recovered, men and machinery stood idle, as Scene of Crime Officers walked to and from the screens hiding the corpse from potential onlookers. As he approached, Brook nodded to Keith Pullin and a knot of other emergency workers sharing a joke and a cigarette.

'Who is it?' he said to Noble.

'It's hard to tell. But it's not Jock or Phil Ward. It looks like one of our students.'

Brook shot him a glance. 'Male or female?' he asked quickly.

'Male. He's been in the water several days and the blows to the head are probably from being smacked around at the bottom of the weir.'

Without knowing why, Brook's heart began to beat a little

easier. He arrived at the body laid out on a plastic sheet. It was a well-built young male, fully dressed. The face and neck were discoloured and the body was severely bloated from the gases of decomposition. The eyes were gone, devoured by fish and microbes.

'Several days?' said Brook, walking around the corpse.

'Probably more than a week, with that much bloating,' observed Noble.

'Then why didn't he surface sooner?'

Noble nodded towards a pile of wet stones. 'The body was partially weighted down or it would have popped up sooner.'

'No ID?'

'Nothing in his pockets except this.' Noble pulled out an evidence bag. It contained a smaller, sealable plastic bag. Inside were the mushy remains of a few tablets.

'Ecstasy?'

'Or PCP. That's cheap at the moment.'

Brook got down on his haunches. The clothes were intact along the body's left flank but from the bloating and the youthful clothing and haircut, Brook already knew this wasn't the work of The Embalmer. 'You're right. It's not one of our vagrants,' he muttered. 'Messing with our heads, all right.'

'Sir?'

Brook looked up at Noble. 'How could I be so wrong?'

'I don't see . . .'

'I didn't take it seriously, John. Four young people are missing and I didn't take it seriously.'

'Nobody did.'

'Well, it's serious now.' Brook looked at the recently bagged hands, clenched into a fist, bright green weeds protruding from between the knuckles. 'Where's Higginbottom?'

'Been and gone. He said from the teeth he's confident it's a teenager. Definite drowning and no obvious signs of foul play.'

'Suicide?'

'Well, the stones rule out an accident.'

'Maybe some of this head trauma will turn out to be pre-mortem,' said Brook.

'Higginbottom says not. He also said rigor's dissipated so the deceased has been in the water at least five days, but to float with stones in his pocket is more likely a week or more.'

'So around the night of the party would be about right.' Brook stood back from the body. 'Russell or Kyle? Can you tell?'

'No.'

Brook ran his eye over the Nike trainers, the green combat trousers, Derby County football shirt and green flak jacket. The jacket had large open pockets from which the stones had been removed.

'Last seen wearing?' prompted Brook.

'I'll need to check the paperwork,' answered Noble. 'I'm pretty sure Kyle was jeans and a blue hoodie.'

'You're right.'

'What about Russell?'

'His mum wasn't sure,' answered Brook. He turned away and stepped from behind the screen leaving SOCO to photograph, scrape, bag and tag the remains before removal to the mortuary.

He walked with Noble to the edge of the river. 'Speaking of Yvette Thomson, do you remember Len Poole saying he didn't know her?'

'At Alice Kennedy's, yes.'

'I think he lied. I dropped off Russell's computer last night and Len was there and they didn't behave like strangers.'

'Maybe they're not. Len's originally from North Wales, same as her. Don Crump told me last night when I dropped into the lab. And don't forget he's moving back there with Mrs Kennedy.'

'Chester's not in Wales, John. And why would Len Poole's name come up?'

'I didn't mention him but Don's put in nearly thirty years. He knew Len before he retired. He heard he was back.'

Brook nodded. 'I suppose Poole must know a lot of the old guard.'

'I would think. I can run a background on Poole if you want?'

'I do want,' said Brook. 'There's a connection with Yvette Thomson and I'd like to know what. What news from the lab?'

'Don was whingeing about SOCO. He said they're slipping. He's trying to match the blood from the plaster.'

'And?'

'It isn't Kyle's, Becky's or Adele's.'

'What about Russell?'

'That's just it. SOCO did a number on Russell Thomson's bedroom and didn't come up with any useable DNA.'

'Nothing? No hair?' Brook looked at Noble. 'They've lived there six months – is that even possible?'

'Unusual not impossible,' said Noble. 'Russell can't have spent much time there.'

'It might explain the missing toothbrush.'

'Toothbrush?'

'There was only one at the house. It was Yvette's.'

'Or maybe SOCO *are* slipping.'

'They've got a lot on, John, but if that is Russell we just pulled out of the river, they need to get back over there and try again.'

'What about dental?' asked Noble.

'Get on it. Yvette and Russell have moved around a lot but there must be records.'

They turned and walked towards the group of emergency rescue workers chatting by the river wall. Pullin nodded at Brook.

'Keith,' Brook said, after a pause to double-check his memory.

'That's correct, Inspector,' answered Pullin with a grin. His colleagues joined in. They obviously knew the background to his reply.

Brook pressed on. 'How deep is it down there?' he said, looking down at the water.

'Deep enough.'

'We're missing four students,' continued Brook. 'This looks like one of them. Could there be more bodies down there?'

Pullin narrowed his eyes. 'If they're weighed down – it's possible.' There was a long pause. 'Would you like us to have a look?'

Brook smiled his reply and Pullin turned away disconsolately to brief his divers.

Brook sauntered along the river wall, looking across the Derwent to Riverside Gardens, with its steps leading down to the water. Swans and ducks were gliding around on the deceptively still surface. Beyond stood the City Council House and further round to the right an inquisitive crowd was gathering on Exeter Bridge even at such an early hour.

'Tell me we've got some film to look at, John.'

'Cooper's already at the Control Room.'

A commotion from Meadow Road turned both their heads. A yellow taxicab was pulling away and its passenger made a bee-line for the boundary tape.

'Let me through,' shouted a female voice. She tried to duck under the tape but a Constable grabbed her and held her fast. 'Let me go. I want to see my son.'

Brook and Noble ran up to reinforce the human barrier.

'Is it true you've found a body?' panted Yvette Thomson, still wriggling to be free. Their faces confirmed it. 'Is it Rusty?'

'We don't know yet,' said Brook, putting a hand on her arm.

'I want to see him.'

'I'm sorry, you can't,' said Noble.

'How did you know we'd found a body?' asked Brook.

She hesitated. 'Someone phoned me.'

Brook glanced over at Noble. He shook his head.

'Is it Rusty?' she demanded.

Brook didn't reply. In most of these situations, he could usually walk away from distressed relatives, safe in the knowledge that someone far more sympathetic would be available to offer comfort and soothing platitudes. Eventually he decided to put his faith in the facts. 'It's a young man but it's hard to identify him. He's been in the water a while.'

Yvette stopped struggling and steepled her hands over her nose and mouth. 'Oh my God.'

'Who phoned you about the body?' asked Noble.

She seemed not to have heard him. 'Let me see him.'

'We can't allow that,' said Noble. 'They're still pro-cessing . . .'

Yvette Thomson broke free and ran towards the screens,

Brook and Noble in pursuit but she was too fast for them. She reached the screens and stopped dead in her tracks.

'Oh God. Oh God. Oh God.' Her eyes, like small moons, were fixed on the bloated remains. Brook reached her and tried to turn her away but she shook him off and continued to stare. Eventually she turned away and ran to a nearby bench. She sat down and put her head between her knees and threw up.

Brook and Noble gave her some room. Eventually Brook approached her with a tissue. She accepted it without a glance at him, instead gazing straight ahead. 'How can you . . . ?' She looked at the ground, the sentence unfinished.

'I'm sorry you had to see him like that,' said Brook quietly.

She shook her head, still looking at the ground. Then her head snapped up, searching for Brook's eye. 'It's not Rusty.'

'You're sure?'

'Certain. It's the hair. The zigzag – I think it's Wilson Woodrow.'

Brook walked with Noble back to his car. 'Playtime's over, John. Pick up Jake McKenzie.'

'Arrest him? On what charge?'

'He was there at Kyle's assault. Use that.'

'There's no evidence he took part.'

'Then he's got nothing to worry about, but if we arrest him we can get DNA. Maybe it's his blood on the plaster in Kyle's house. And get a warrant for his computer and phone and do the same for Fern Stretton and Adam Rifkind. I want all the text messages and emails and Facebook messages they've ever sent to, or received from, Adele, Russell, Kyle and Becky. If one of them sent a carrier-pigeon ten years ago, I want to know about it.'

'You want me to sort out next-of-kin for Wilson?'

'Set it up.' Noble turned away. 'Oh, and John. Better get PC Patel over to Alice Kennedy's to let her know we've found a body before she hears it from someone else.'

'Someone else?' said Noble.

'The *someone else* who tipped off Yvette Thomson.'

Noble nodded, tight-lipped. 'Want Patel to tell her it's not Kyle?'

'As long as she makes it clear that nothing's definite until ID.'

Noble took out his cigarettes and offered one to Brook. He declined with a faint shake of the head.

'I missed it, John. I completely missed it.'

Noble's brow furrowed. 'Missed what?'

Brook looked him in the eye. 'The evil. There's a fox in the henhouse and these kids are in danger.'

'Where's Dad?' panted Jake, coming to a halt and opening the gate for his mother.

'Gone fishing,' she replied.

'Why the—' Jake stopped himself. It was pointless. He'd tried before. His mother worked all hours serving in a bakery for a pittance and his dad wouldn't give her a lift into town even on his Saturday off. 'Bye, Mum. Love you.'

Jake's mother smiled back in that way she had. *That makes it all worthwhile*, the smile told him. He knew she'd be wearing it all day. She blew him a kiss and he watched her turn the corner to catch the bus. He was relieved. He loved his mum to bits, and he didn't know why, but when he was alone, everything seemed less intense.

He finished a couple of warm-down exercises in the front yard and pulled off his sweat-stained top, closing his eyes to the piercing early morning sun. It was going to be a beautiful day and so far he had it to himself. He sat bare-chested on the front step revelling in the steam rising from his torso then fished out his iPhone to check his messages. His mouth fell open – he had a text from Kyle.

Jake read the message, dismayed. He closed his eyes again, this time squeezing a drop of moisture on to his cheek. He wiped his face brusquely and roused himself. It wasn't too late. He reread the message then dialled 999 but rang off before the first ring had ended. He tried to think. He returned to Kyle's message and sent off a reply. *Where r u? Feds looking everywhere*.

He leaned on the gate awaiting his reply, trying to forget the accusation in Kyle's message, trying to ignore its truth.

A couple of teenage girls rounded the corner, each sucking urgently on a cigarette. They both wore far too much make-up, tight, low-cut tops and short skirts. They walked arm-in-arm towards him, giggling as they drew near enough to give his smooth torso a serious examination.

Jake knew one of them and smiled faintly in their direction.

'Hey, Jakey,' said Trina. The two fifteen year olds stopped at his gate and made no pretence of looking anywhere but his body. 'We've seen you on the internet.'

'And on the news,' said Trina's friend. ''Bout that slappin'.'

Jake smiled again, wishing they'd keep walking. 'You're up early, Trina. Wassup?'

The girl from three doors down leered at him, her head

doddering on its axis like a nodding dog. 'Just jamming, beautiful. We ain't been bed yet,' she slurred. Jake could see she was drunk as she swayed against her equally drunk friend. She winked at him. 'Not to sleep anyway, eh, Shazz?' She roared with laughter and both started squealing incomprehensibly at each other.

'Whoa. Too much information, girlfriend.' Jake smiled.

'That's not a surprise,' said Trina with a conspiratorial wink at Shazz. The two smirked at each other, finishing with a synchronised, 'Mmmmmm.'

Jake continued smiling, willing them to move on.

'You got any vodka?' asked Shazz.

'We drink vodka,' confirmed Trina. 'We take drugs too, don't we, Shazz?'

'All the time. But our best drug is vodka. You got any, Jakey?'

'Shazz'll blow you for a bottle.' Trina cackled.

'Fuck off, Trin,' screamed Shazz and they both fell into a fit of the laughter, shouting and squealing as they jostled each other.

'Go on,' Trina urged Jake. 'You know you want to. She's got all the shag bands, the dirty ho.'

'She must be very proud.'

'I have too,' said Shazz, her head to one side, as though he didn't believe her. 'You got any vodka then, Jakey?'

'It's seven o'clock in the morning.'

'Don't mean we can't have a party,' replied Shazz, pouting her most alluring slut-face.

'I'll pass,' said Jake.

Shazz turned to Trina and rolled her eyes. 'Told you.'

'Told her what?' snapped Jake.

'We *heard* you was a bumder,' explained Trina. 'Wilson's mate told us. You're in love with Kyle Kennedy.'

'Piss off, you sket.'

'It's true innit?' Shazz nodded. 'Only a faggot wouldn't wanna jizz on my tonsils.'

'She swallows an' all.' Trina leered, and they started laughing and screeching again.

'You love Kyle,' they chanted. 'You love Kyle.'

Jake's breathing quickened and he grabbed Shazz by the shoulder and marched her into the house. 'Want some vodka, bitch? Wanna see how much I hate faggots?' Shazz turned round with a grin on her face and winked at Trina as Jake pushed her up the stairs.

'Wait for me, Trin,' she shouted over her shoulder. 'Shouldn't be long. Here, your mum's not home, is she?'

'Course she is. She wants to watch.' He opened his bedroom door, pushed her in and slammed the door behind him. When Shazz turned round, Jake had already dropped his tracksuit trousers. 'Come on then, ho. Get to work.'

Shazz grinned at him and took out her gum to stick on Jake's bedroom mirror. 'Nice package. But shouldn't your fuckstick be pointing north instead of south?' She giggled.

Jake grinned maliciously at her. 'That's your job, slut.'

Shazz smiled and dropped to her knees, cupping his penis in her hands. 'Shouldn't take long. Bobby P reckons I'm the best ever.'

Jake closed his eyes as she went to work and tried to concentrate, but all he could see was an image of Shazz and Trina laughing at him through their slack mouths. He strained to see her head bobbing up and down and felt any hardness waning. Then he pictured Kyle looking on and the tears began to well.

He opened his eyes and stared at the poster of Morrissey, a gift from his friend, and he began to harden again. But over and over his thoughts turned to Kyle. His smile, that little curl of hair on his puny sideburns, those beautiful eyes with their too-long lashes. He's with me, he's doing this. He loves me. He wants me.

With an almighty grind of his teeth Jake climaxed and he fell backwards against the door. Shazz was already on her feet, popping her chewing gum back in, a triumphant gleam in her eye. 'Whaddaya think? Better than a Dyson, yeah?'

Jake wrenched his tracksuit back up to his waist and closed his eyes again. *What have I done? What a bastard I am. Wanna see how much I hate faggots?* Kyle was right. 'Get out, you slut,' he whispered softly.

'Fuck off. Where's my vodka?'

'You're a whore as well as a slut. Now get out!' he rasped, his eyes bulging in his sudden rush of anger.

Shazz put her hands on her hips and planted herself. 'Not until I get my vodka, bumder.'

Jake grabbed her by the hair and hauled her down the stairs, the pair of them screaming at each other. He wrestled open the front door and threw her on the ground. 'Get. Out.'

'You fucking poof,' she bellowed as Trina came to her aid. 'You're a fucking faggot,' she snarled at him, rubbing her knee. 'He couldn't get it up, could he?' she told Trina. 'He's got fag mags all over his bedroom, and paedo porn, you wanna see it, Trin, it's dread.' Turning back to Jake, she screeched, 'You better not ha' gi'n me AIDS when you touched me, you fucking arse-loving boner bandit.'

Screaming and hurling abuse they stormed away, regaling every curtained house with news of the pervert in their midst and pointing back at Jake panting and sobbing on the front gate.

At that moment, Jake's dad pulled up in his window-cleaning van and got out. He noticed the two girls creating a racket and aiming V-signs at Jake, and nodded approvingly. Perhaps his lad wasn't such a mummy's boy. 'Nice one, son. Treat 'em mean, to keep 'em keen.'

'Fuck off, Dad.'

'Oh. A bit of spirit have we now, son? That's what I like to see,' he said, and he began to shadow-box with Jake, throwing in the occasional slap on the face.

'Fuck off, Dad!' Jake roared, on the brink of hysteria and clenching his fists.

Mr McKenzie pulled up as though slapped. He balled his fists and took a step towards Jake, then thought better of busting his son's mouth in front of the house. That'd mean a week or two's earache from Her Majesty, if not a visit from the police. 'Okay, son. That's a freebie – for now. I only popped home for more bait. And I don't mean jail bait,' he sniggered.

Jake watched his dad go inside, still chuckling and repeating his joke. Jake slumped on to the gate for support. He glanced down the road at Trina and Shazz, just disappearing around the corner. He was only three years older than them but already her age group were like beings from another planet. They were laughing and joking again, arm-in-arm, oblivious to the damage they'd done. Correction. The damage *he'd* done – Judas McKenzie. He took a deep breath. No more lies. He pulled out his mobile and texted Kyle. *Soz Kyle miss you xx*.

Still no reply. Jake opened the front door and sprinted upstairs to his room.

*

DS Morton held his warrant card to the crack in the door. The door closed and the chain was removed. The heavily pregnant Mrs Rifkind looked about sixteen to Morton. She opened the door with one hand, using the other to support her unborn baby. She looked nervously beyond Morton.

'Sorry, Officer, I thought you were a reporter.'

'Reporter?'

'Somebody found out that Watson bitch stole Adam's credit card to set up that website. They've been hanging round, trying to get an interview.'

'Is your husband here?'

'It's half-term. He's up at the cottage working on his novel and getting away from all this shit.'

'Where is that?' asked Morton.

'In the Peaks. Alstonefield.'

Morton ran his eye over her huge belly and wondered what sort of man left his pregnant wife alone to face the press while he worked on a novel. 'Does he have his computer and mobile phone with him?'

'Yes, of course.' Her eyes narrowed. 'What's this about? He's told you all he knows.'

'We'll need the address.'

Morton closed his notebook and walked back to his car, not noticing the curtain pulled aside briefly in an upstairs window.

He jumped into the driver's seat and threw his notebook on top of Fern Stretton's laptop and mobile phone, both shrouded in plastic.

Morton smiled, remembering her reaction – first excitement then consternation. She was important now. She was involved in the investigation. Police had 'raided' her home.

What a lot she'd have to tell her friends. She'd be the centre of attention. It was only when she realised she'd have no means of communicating with them that her excitement had turned to despair.

DC Cooper peered over the shoulder of the technician sat at the computer. Brook, Noble and Morton waited patiently in the darkened Incident Room, staring up at the grey square on the whiteboard. Eventually Cooper gave the thumbs up.

'Okay. We're going to see a piece of film. It's digital quality, and as you can see from the display, it was taken on the nineteenth of May at a quarter to midnight.'

'That's the night before the party,' said Morton.

'And just a couple of hours after the assault on Kyle Kennedy,' added Brook.

The film began with a view from the Council House across the weir to the river wall of the Derwent. A figure emerged from the darkness of the small triangular public garden wedged between Meadow Road and Exeter Place.

'It's the guy from the first Deity film,' said Cooper. 'The one who laid out Kyle.'

'Wilson Woodrow,' said Brook. 'Yvette Thomson was right.'

'He looks the worse for wear,' said Cooper. 'Was he on something?'

'It's likely but we don't know yet,' replied Noble.

The burly figure strolled unsteadily to the river wall and placed something on it. Then he returned to the gloom of the gardens and reappeared a few seconds later to repeat the process.

'What's he doing?'

'Can we zoom in?'

Before the technician could obey, Brook said, 'He's fetching the stones.'

'Jesus,' said Morton. 'He jumped.'

The team of experienced officers continued to watch in horrified fascination. There was no other sound, no movement, not even the gulp of an Adam's apple. After the second delivery of stones, Wilson clambered on to the river wall and began to fill his pockets with them. A second later he stepped off and disappeared under the water. The detectives watched a little longer but gradually movement and conversation returned.

'Why didn't the controllers pick up on this before . . . ?' asked Brook, clicking his fingers as if a name was on the tip of his tongue.

'Rhys,' answered the technician. 'Well, there are a hundred and seventy cameras, sir, so it's not simple to police. At that time of night, most operatives will be watching the city-centre monitors for anti-social behaviour but, if something happens, we do respond to requests for time and place. Like now.'

Brook nodded, looking at his watch as he yawned. It felt like mid-afternoon but was only ten o'clock. 'Run it again.'

Noble's phone began to croak. He answered and listened intently. 'Which hospital?' He rang off. 'The squad car that went to pick up McKenzie found him unconscious. They think he took an overdose.'

'Alive?'

Noble nodded. 'They've taken him to the Royal.'

'Another suicide,' muttered Brook.

'Two from the same peer group,' said Noble. 'Bit of a coincidence.'

Rhys restarted the film and they sat through it again, this time a little less mesmerised.

'Can we enhance Wilson, standing on the wall?' asked Brook.

A couple of clicks later and Wilson's face loomed large and the film resumed.

'He's talking,' said Cooper.

'Who to?' muttered Morton.

'He could be talking to himself, keeping his focus. Drugs can do that,' said Noble.

'Maybe.' Brook nodded. 'Do we have a lipreader on the books?' He lifted the last of his cold tea to his lips but his hand froze in mid-air. 'What's that?' he said, pointing at the screen. 'Go back.'

The technician rewound and replayed the film.

'There.' Brook leaped up to show him. 'Next to that tree.'

The film was rewound and paused. Brook pointed to a tiny red dot emanating from the darkness of the gardens.

'I see it,' said Cooper.

'What is it?' asked Morton.

'Somebody's filming it,' said Noble.

'And maybe egging him on,' added Morton. 'Of all the cold-blooded . . .'

Before Brook could ask, Rhys the technician enhanced the picture around the red dot. Behind the red dot the officers could make out the silhouette of an arm. A hood was over the face but a few large letters were visible on the chest.

'G-something-A-R.'

'Pity it's not in colour,' began Cooper.

'Blue,' said Brook. 'It's blue. That's Kyle Kennedy's G-Star hoodie. He was wearing it when he disappeared.'

*

Noble entered the Incident Room and raised a thumb. 'Okay. Two o'clock. Full briefing ahead of the next Deity broadcast. Charlton, Jane and her two DCs will be there too.'

'Any news from Pullin?'

'Yeah, no more bodies at the weir.'

'Are you sure they were thorough, John?'

Noble raised an eyebrow. 'I didn't ask that question. But if you feel you must . . .'

Brook hesitated. 'Maybe I should just take his word.'

Noble smiled patronisingly. 'You're making so much progress.'

Brook emitted a one-note laugh. 'What about Exeter Bridge?'

'Rhys is sending it over now.'

'Mine or yours?'

'Yours.'

Brook's features betrayed a tic of annoyance – another stranger with his email address. He logged on to his internal account and clicked Play on the attachment while Noble turned on the ceiling-mounted projector with the remote. That morning's CCTV footage of Exeter Bridge appeared at once.

'How good are these pictures?' said Brook.

'The cameras were upgraded three years ago,' said Noble. 'What's our time slot?'

'What time did I get to the river?'

'Just after six.'

'Okay. Yvette arrived ten minutes after me so, assuming she phoned a cab immediately someone tipped her off, it would take half an hour at the most between phoning and getting into town at that time of day. Say five-fifteen to be sure.'

Noble teed up the film to that time and set it running. The bridge, the best vantage-point to watch the recovery of Wilson's body, was deserted. But as time wore on, more people began to cross into the city centre, and the crowd watching the emergency services grew.

'Who alerted us to the body?'

'A security guard at the Council House saw the head bobbing and phoned it in.'

'Time?'

Noble checked his notebook. 'Dispatch took the call just after three.' Brook continued to watch the film at normal speed. 'Whoever tipped off Yvette didn't need to be on the bridge.'

Brook nodded. 'I know. It's just a hunch. Wilson's death has been staged and a good director would want to—'

'There!' Noble interrupted. Brook followed his digit. 'Jeans, blue hoodie, sunglasses, scarf around the face. Caucasian male?'

'Hard to be sure,' replied Brook. 'Walks like a man.' He peered at the screen. 'But unless my eyes are failing me, that does say G-STAR on his chest, doesn't it?'

Noble froze the film and zoomed in. The brand was clearly visible across a white slash on the chest. 'That's Kyle's hoodie, all right.'

'Or we're meant to think it is,' said Brook.

'Messing with our heads.' Noble nodded.

'What's that in his hand?'

The film played on. The figure in the hoodie turned away from the CCTV camera mounted high on the Council building, to lean on the bridge wall. He watched the opposite bank where, off camera, Wilson Woodrow's body was being recovered. A moment later he stood erect and lifted a camcorder to his right eye.

'You were right. He filmed us. Cheeky sod.'

'Did we see what direction he came in from?' Brook asked.

Noble reviewed the images until they could make out the figure strolling past the Brewery Tap at the north end of the bridge, towards the city centre and the CCTV camera perched on the Council House. He kept his head bowed all the way, as though he expected to be filmed.

The film continued and the two detectives watched closely, hoping to glimpse a face under the hood but the figure never removed it, or the scarf and sunglasses, and the camcorder was rarely lowered from the face. Just after six thirty, the figure stopped filming, pulled out a mobile phone and thumbed at it for a few moments.

'He's texting,' said Brook.

'Yvette Thomson said someone phoned her.'

'Text or call, it wasn't him, John. Look at the time.'

'Six thirty.' Noble nodded. 'She was already at the river.'

'Check with the mobile operators. Maybe that phone belonged to one of our students. Start with Kyle's.'

A second later, the hooded figure sauntered back up Derwent Street and out of sight.

'Whoever that was, he didn't tip off Yvette Thomson,' said Noble.

'Not in our time-frame at least,' agreed Brook.

'Then who did?'

Brook narrowed his eyes. 'Somebody who knows her and has contacts in the Force. There's no other explanation.'

'A journalist?'

'I wouldn't put it past Brian Burton to be greasing the wheels, but if he did get a whisper from an inside contact, he wouldn't be phoning Yvette Thomson.'

'And he'd have been at the scene before us, being a pain in the backside,' conceded Noble. 'Who then?'

Brook smiled faintly. 'How about somebody with a stake in our investigation, somebody with money who can be trusted to reward a heads-up, who used to be in the business and keeps in touch with some of the old guard.'

Noble nodded now. 'Len Poole.'

'There's no one else. And if we make the connection, it proves they knew each other before they came to Derby.'

Twenty

BROOK STARED AT THE MAP of Derby on the wall. Cooper had added a second pin, this time south of the city in Pear Tree, nowhere near the first location in Allestree. The uploads to the Deity website were being carried out in seemingly random areas using wireless technology. No connection between the homeowners. The fact the addresses were both in residential areas also put paid to their chances of CCTV.

Noble walked in and handed Brook a sheaf of papers.

'What am I looking at?'

'School assessment reports for Russell Thomson. "Ysgols" in Welsh.'

Brook counted the pages. 'He certainly went to a lot of ysgols.'

'And that's not all of them.'

Brook read quickly. The first school was Ysgol Emrys Williams near Rhyl in North Wales. Russell stayed there for only six weeks when he was twelve.

Russell is a timid boy with an unfortunate manner. He is easily led and even more easily provoked. He becomes distressed at even the mildest teasing and has become an easy target for those bullies seeking quick gratification. He doesn't fight back and is quick to cry and has threatened self-harm. Suggest Russell works in smaller groups where he will have to deal with fewer students and can be monitored properly.

The next school was Ysgol Bryn Towyn near Holywell. It said much the same as the first school. Russell was there for three months when he was thirteen and taken out when the bullying became too much.

'He and Yvette really moved around,' observed Brook. He skimmed through the rest of the reports.

'Now skip forward to 2008 when he was fifteen.'

Brook found the assessment from Ruthin Road High School near Chester.

22 February 2008
Subject – Russell Thomson

Following various unpleasant incidents as well as complaints by several upset parents, we have carried out a full investigation into the allegations against Russell Thomson. Although he denies sending the emails or taking the pictures, we are satisfied that he is indeed the culprit and that to discourage this form of cyber-bullying, we recommend a fixed exclusion of four weeks.

The police have been informed and Russell's mother has agreed to our course of action.

Brook looked up at Noble. 'Russell was the cyber-bully, not the other way round.'

'I know,' said Noble.

'It's like he's two different people.'

'And now we know why Russell felt able to have a Facebook account.'

Brook knocked softly on the glass panel and entered. Donald Crump turned his unshaven, heavily jowled face towards Brook, a length of sticky tape held in his hands.

'Inspector Brook,' he said without enthusiasm. 'What brings you down to the vault?' He turned back to the piece of clothing and continued dabbing it with the sticky side of the tape.

'Don. Just thought I'd come and see how you were getting on,' replied Brook, aware that his sickly grin wasn't his best effort. 'We've given you quite a workload, the last week or so.'

Donald Crump turned to Brook, his mouth opening to say something but he evidently thought better of it. He turned back to his work. 'Aye, well, things generally pick up this time of year – all that summer drinking. If the twats aren't driving into trees, they're glassing each other over a funny look. Keeps us in a job, mind.'

'That reminds me,' said Brook, panting with the effort of pleasantry. *What reminds me? What am I talking about?* 'I ran into an old friend of yours. Len Poole.'

Crump turned a sagging, red-rimmed eye to Brook. 'Yeah, he's back, I know. And I think you'll find his full name is Len Fucking Poole and he's no friend of mine so keep him out of my way if you know what's good for him.'

Brook was taken aback. 'DS Noble mentioned you'd spoken to him.'

'I didn't have a lot of choice. I've not seen the twat for years and he waltzes in here like he's still in charge. I didn't even know he was back in Derby until Gordon Grey mentioned it.'

'So you two aren't friends.'

Crump turned in open-mouthed horror. 'I wouldn't give that Welsh windbag the steam off my shit and you can tell him that from me.'

Brook grimaced. 'I don't think I will.'

Crump curled his lip at Brook. 'Did you want something, Inspector, 'cos I've got a lot on?'

'No, Don. I think I've got what I came for.' Brook turned to leave, the fake smile still distorting his face.

'I'm so pleased. And Inspector, the next time you run into Poole, use your car. Maybe that'll stop him sniffing around me for favours he should know I can't do.'

Brook turned back at this, his smile gone. 'Favours?'

'Damen.' Yvette Thomson looked searchingly at Brook. His face was grim.

'Miss Thomson. This is Detective Sergeant Noble.'

She smiled at Noble, holding her gaze on him.

'Come in, Sergeant. Would you like coffee?'

'No, he wouldn't,' replied Brook. 'We don't have time.' They sat down in the spare, unkempt living room. A large TV that Brook hadn't noticed before was on but the sound was turned down. Yvette picked up the remote, searching for the right button to turn it off.

'I was waiting for the local news,' said Yvette, as though her viewing habits needed justification. She alternated her gaze between the floor and Noble.

'How are you feeling after this morning?' asked Brook.

Yvette managed to find Brook's eyes now but lowered hers straight away. 'Not bad. Better knowing it wasn't Rusty . . .'

Her knuckles tightened around her knees. 'But I keep seeing that poor boy. Was it Wilson?'

'His grandmother identified him half an hour ago,' said Brook. 'They're double-checking his dental records to be certain.'

'His own grandmother didn't know him?'

'She knew him,' said Noble. 'But death changes things so we like to double-check. Even the recently deceased don't look right to relatives.'

'Poor Wilson – I wonder how long he was in the water.'

'I can tell you exactly, if you'd like.' Yvette stared at Brook, uncomprehending. 'CCTV cameras filmed him jumping in,' he explained. 'And they have the time and date.'

She shot a hand to her mouth. 'Oh, how horrible.'

'It was. But you can watch it on tonight's news if you want to be sure.'

'He was only eighteen,' said Yvette, not picking up Brook's tone.

'And he always will be,' replied Brook. 'He's immortalised on film forever but he's far from beautiful now.'

She shook her head in confusion. 'I don't understand.'

'Neither do I,' replied Brook. He nodded to Noble who handed Yvette a photograph of the youth on the bridge.

'This individual was watching us recover the body this morning. Could that be Russell?'

She stared down at it. 'You're kidding. He's wearing a hoodie. He's got sunglasses and a scarf over his face. How am I supposed to know if it's Rusty at that distance?'

'Okay. What about his build and body shape?'

She shrugged. 'It's possible. But kids wear such baggy clothing these days.'

'Did Russell wear those clothes?'

She looked up at Brook. 'I'm not sure.' She peered at the picture again. 'Why do you think it might be him?'

'Because this person used a camcorder to film us recovering Wilson's body,' said Noble.

'I see.' She looked at the picture again. 'I can't tell. I'm sorry.'

Noble pulled his laptop from a case and loaded the CCTV film of the bridge. They watched in silence, Noble pointing to the unknown figure strolling into shot, Brook watching Yvette.

'What about his mannerisms, his way of walking?' asked Noble. Yvette didn't reply.

Brook fancied there was the merest flicker of recognition but he couldn't be certain.

'I don't know', she said. 'Maybe. I can't be sure.'

Noble placed another picture in front of her. This time it was a grainier close-up of the camcorder. 'Could that be your son's camcorder?'

She stared, then nodded very slowly. 'It's possible. This morning, you say? Where is he now?'

'We know from other CCTV that he had a bicycle. After leaving the bridge, he cycled east through the city, then along the bike path following the river, through Pride Park towards Borrowash. After that . . .' Brook shrugged.

'Does your son know anyone in Borrowash?' asked Noble.

She shook her head. 'I don't know Derby, Damen. I've never heard of Borrowash and I'm sure Rusty hasn't either.'

'And does your son own a bicycle?' Brook went on.

'He did. It was stolen.'

'When?'

'Six months ago – shortly after we moved here. Rusty went out on it and when he came back he didn't have it. He said he lost it, but his T-shirt was torn. I guessed someone stole it from him.'

'Did you report this?'

Her answer was a short sour laugh.

Noble placed another photograph in Yvette's hands. 'This is the best shot we've got. Is this your son's bicycle?'

Yvette looked at the hooded cyclist riding his bike. 'I can't tell. Who remembers bicycles?'

'Have you a record of the insurance claim?' asked Brook patiently. 'Maybe there's a description of it from when you *did* remember his bicycle.'

Brook's tone was unmistakable now and Yvette was taken aback. 'We'd just arrived in Derby. We didn't have insurance – I couldn't afford it.' She looked coldly at Brook. 'I still can't.' The anger in her eyes was stark. 'I thought you were my friend, Damen. Rusty is missing. He might be dead and you come in here asking about bicycles.' She put her hands over her eyes.

'I'm sorry,' said Brook evenly. 'We have a job to do.'

'Then do it and get him back to me.' She looked angrily at Brook, then across at Noble with a timorous smile. 'I miss him so much.'

Brook said nothing for a while. Noble knew there were more questions to come – hard questions – but Brook knew this attractive woman better than he did, so Noble waited too.

'Are we finished?' asked Yvette, beginning to feel uncomfortable.

'We've done some digging into your background – yours and Russell's.' Brook paused for a reaction.

'I suppose that's to be expected,' she replied quietly.

'Russell had a tough time of it, didn't he?' ventured Brook. 'All those different schools, all those bullies . . .'

Yvette smiled sadly, tears welling up in her eyes. 'He did. He was so vulnerable. He just didn't know how to talk to people.'

'The other kids called him names?' asked Noble.

'Yes. They called him a bastard and they told him I was a whore. They said he was an orphan because his dad didn't want him.' The tears rolled down her cheeks.

'What happened when he was fifteen?' asked Brook softly.

Yvette wiped her eyes and took a deep breath. 'What do you mean?'

'I mean something happened to him. He changed.'

Yvette's mouth dropped open. 'I don't know what you mean.'

'Yes, you do. He stopped being a victim, Yvette.'

'And started becoming the aggressor,' chipped in Noble, pulling out the relevant documents. 'Ruthin Road High School, Connor's Quay College, Holywell College . . .'

'Russell was excluded from all these schools and colleges for cyber-bullying. You came here for a clean break before Russell could exhaust all his chances. The move to Derby College was a last chance for Russell, wasn't it?' Eventually Yvette nodded. 'So what happened?'

The tears welled again, accompanied by a bitter smile. 'You're right. He changed.'

'How?'

'Rusty just wouldn't take it any more so he took a stand, he lashed out. It's not his fault. He's a good person. Why are you asking me all these questions? Why aren't you finding my Rusty?'

'Because maybe he's tried to bully someone else, the wrong person, and they've taken matters into their own hands,' said Noble. 'Could that be possible?'

'No. He stopped all that. I bought him the camcorder. He's got a hobby now. He loves his films. He can spend a whole day filming and playing it back on his laptop. He doesn't need to lash out any more.'

'Do you think he might have filmed the wrong person, seen something he wasn't supposed to see and got himself in trouble?'

'I don't know. He loved filming. And sometimes people would get angry when he stuck the camcorder in their faces,'

'Anyone in particular?'

'No. It was never anything serious. Just annoying.'

'Until he filmed Becky Blake in her bedroom,' said Brook. 'I assume you watched the news.'

Yvette's head dropped. 'You don't know that was him.'

'Have you seen the film?'

'Yes.'

'Someone filmed Wilson jumping into the river as well,' said Brook. 'Someone with a camcorder.'

Yvette's head shot up and a hand went to her mouth. 'Was that shown on the website?'

'Not yet. But you can see why we'd wonder how you knew we'd found a body.'

'I told you,' she mumbled. 'Someone phoned me.'

'Who?'

'I don't know.'

Brook smiled. It unnerved even Noble. 'Yes, you do.'

'I don't,' she insisted.

'What's Len done to deserve this kind of loyalty?' said

Brook. Her eyes widened and her breathing shortened. 'So it *was* Len who rang you.'

'No, he didn't ring me,' she said defiantly. 'Feel free to check my phone records.' Then her face hardened. 'And now I think you'd better leave.'

Brook pulled the BMW into the St Mary's Wharf car park.

'Shouldn't we be going to talk to Len Poole?' said Noble.

'Not until we have some idea what's between the two of them.'

'You were right about Yvette Thomson,' said Noble as they stepped out of the car. 'She's very attractive.'

'Did I say that?'

'Actually, it may have been Alice Kennedy,' said Noble. 'But you're not denying it.'

'No. She's very pretty,' said Brook. They walked to the entrance and pressed their smartcards against the terminal. 'Did you notice she seemed attracted to you?'

'She's got eyes, hasn't she?' Noble grinned.

Brook smiled but rolled his eyes. 'Sorry to cast doubt on your many virtues, John, but I suspect she gives that impression to every man she meets.'

'What do you mean?' asked Noble.

'She was the same when I first met her. I think it's to do with being an orphan. It's about survival. You use what you have to get by.'

'And she uses her looks.' Noble shrugged, not totally convinced by the downgrading of his pin-up status. 'You didn't ask her about Wilson.'

'It'll keep. If Wilson called to see her after the assault on Kyle, we'll find out about it soon enough.'

'What makes you think Wilson went to see her?'

'Because, like most of the species, he was attracted to her too. Yvette told me he was always calling round.'

'You don't think she had anything to do with his death?'

'Not from the footage we saw or her reaction at the river,' said Brook. 'That's why it'll keep.'

Sergeant Hendrickson was at the duty desk. But for once, instead of marching hurriedly to the lifts, to Noble's surprise, Brook ambled over to the counter.

'Sergeant. Who was on duty this morning when the call came in about the body in the Derwent?'

Hendrickson didn't answer or approach the counter to speak to Brook. Instead he turned, thin-lipped, towards Noble, who stood behind his DI. Noble made no attempt to fill the awkward silence and, absurdly, the three officers stood motionless, locked into their mute triangle for nearly a minute.

When Brook showed no signs of moving off, Hendrickson managed to croak out a hate-filled, 'Sir?'

'You heard me,' snapped Brook. 'Chop-chop.'

Hendrickson's mouth fell open and he again sought Noble's now amused eyes, this time with an expression that hovered between pain and incredulity.

'We haven't got all day, Sergeant,' chipped in Noble.

In shock, Hendrickson approached the counter with the roster, opened it and moved a finger down the page. 'Sergeant Grey.'

Brook smiled. 'There. That wasn't too hard, was it?'

Noble fought back the grin until they reached the Incident Room where Brook finally gave him the briefest glance of acknowledgement. DS Morton handed Noble a manila folder.

'Leonard Poole was the Chief Pathologist for Derby Hospitals NHS Trust from 1999 to 2003,' read Noble. 'He retired and moved away the same year you moved to Derby.'

'So he was in Derby for only four years.'

'He may have worked in Derby for four years but he and his wife actually lived in Uttoxeter. When Len retired they sold up and moved back to Chester.'

Brook raised an eyebrow. 'That date, 2003 – sound familiar, John?'

Noble glanced up at Brook. A second later he rummaged around on his desk and located a piece of paper, holding it next to the report on Len Poole. 'Yvette Thomson lived in Uttoxeter from 1999 to 2003.'

'She did,' said Brook, without surprise. 'And I think I know where this is going.'

Noble's voice picked up speed and volume. 'He lived in Chester and was a pathologist for the old North Wales NHS Trust until 1998. He left Chester to work for the Shropshire County Primary Care Trust for a year...' he looked up at Brook '...moving to Whitchurch. Yvette Thomson left Chester that same year and also moved to Whitchurch. A year later she moved to Uttoxeter – when Len moved there to take the job in Derby.'

'And when Len retired and moved back to North Wales...'

'She moved back there as well.' Noble smiled with satisfaction. 'You were right. They've known each other for years.'

'Anything else?'

Noble read some more. 'The bastard,' he said on a reflex. 'Sorry.'

'What?'

'He was Chairman of the Board of Trustees for St Asaph's School for Boys and Girls from 1992 until he moved to Shropshire in 1998.'

'He knew Yvette at the orphanage,' said Brook softly.

'Christ,' said Noble. 'She got pregnant at the orphanage, while Poole was on the Board. She was only fifteen.'

'Older than many,' said Brook, trying not to think of Terri, falling into the clutches of her stepfather, at the same age.

'You think Russell Thomson could be Poole's kid.'

'It's possible. Or at least it's possible Poole thinks he is.' Brook nodded at the folder. 'Presumably Len and Yvette didn't move to a new area on the same day.'

Noble scanned the documents. 'Len moved first. Yvette Thomson followed a month or so later.' He looked up at Brook. 'So he sets himself up and sends for her. That explains the telly in her house.'

'Telly?'

'She had a brand new 3D-ready TV – thirty-two inches, by the look of it. Must be a thousand pounds' worth of kit right there – and she reckoned she couldn't afford insurance.'

'A lot of money for a mature student who works as a barmaid,' agreed Brook.

'So Poole's set her up in that house,' said Noble. 'He moves. She follows after Poole's sorted out a place to live. No wonder she's hardly worked a day in her life.'

'Let's not jump to conclusions, John. When I saw them together there was a degree of hostility that didn't feel right.'

Noble tapped a finger against his chin. 'There would be hostility if she was blackmailing him. If Russell is Poole's son, conceived when Yvette was a fourteen- or fifteen-year-old orphan and while he was in a position of trust . . .'

'. . . he pays up for maintenance or she goes to the authorities.' Brook narrowed his eyes. 'It makes sense except for one thing. He's engaged to be married and Alice Kennedy lives round the corner from Yvette. If Yvette was his mistress, would Len really move her that close? Would he even be getting married? If Poole and Yvette are lovers, why not just move in with her? Apart from the age difference, no one would raise an eyebrow.'

'So what do you think?'

'I think Yvette's dogging Len's every move to make sure he keeps paying for his mistake.'

'So she's got her hooks into him and she's not letting go,' said Noble.

'It would explain the envelope that Poole was carrying that night I saw him call round – and why he didn't have it when he left.'

'It was full of money,' concluded Noble. 'Which explains the new TV.'

'But if Russell's eighteen years old, presumably Len's been giving her money on a regular basis for most of that time,' said Brook.

'Seems reasonable.'

'Then why all the drama?'

'What drama?'

'You weren't there, John. It didn't feel like a routine visit. The way he banged on the door, Poole had an agenda. He was shouting at her for some reason.' Brook thought for a moment before a look of enlightenment filled his face. '*All these years* . . .' he said softly. He turned to Noble. 'That wasn't money in that envelope.'

'How do you know?'

'Because I had a word with Donald Crump this morning.'

Noble's curiosity was piqued. 'Really? You're getting very brave all of a sudden, running around talking to colleagues on your own.'

Brook shrugged to accept the mocking. 'Before I realised it must be Grey who tipped off Poole, I thought it might be Crump – he is one of the old guard.'

Noble raised an eyebrow. 'Don can't stand him.'

'I know that now,' conceded Brook. 'But here's the thing – Poole went to see him to ask him a favour.'

'What favour?'

'Crump told me Len wanted someone to run a DNA comparison for him. He wouldn't give details until he'd agreed to do it.'

'Don agreed to do it?'

'No. He told Len to— go elsewhere.'

Noble laughed. 'I'll bet. But surely Len would've expected that reaction, so why not get the test done elsewhere to start with?'

'I suspect he didn't want the results stored anywhere so he took a chance.'

'Why would he worry?' said Noble. 'Those private firms are hysterical about client confidentiality. He must know that.'

'Perhaps, but suspecting he's the father of an illegitimate child born of an underage girl in his care might induce a little paranoia.'

'I suppose. Do we know which firm he used?'

'No idea. *All these years* . . . that's what I heard Len shouting at Yvette.'

'Meaning what?'

'Meaning he got the results which told him Russell wasn't his son.'

'*All these years . . . shelling out for a son who isn't mine,*' finished Noble. 'Makes some kind of sense. One thing doesn't though.'

'What?'

'Scene of Crime went through Russell's room with a fine-tooth comb and they didn't find any DNA. Where did Poole get it?'

'Well, Poole and Yvette have been living in close proximity for nineteen years. Maybe Len already had something of Russell's with his DNA or . . .' Brook smiled suddenly. 'Toothbrush.'

'Toothbrush?' repeated Noble.

'When I searched Yvette's bathroom, there was one brand new toothbrush which belonged to her. Russell's was missing.'

'So Len stole it to get a sample.'

'Why not? He was in the business. A toothbrush is the first thing a professional would go for.'

'There's another possibility,' said Noble. 'Maybe Poole's got Russell locked up somewhere.'

Brook pulled a face. 'Abduct him just to avoid a paternity?'

'He'd go to prison if it came out,' answered Noble.

'And Adele and the others walk in so he takes them too? I don't think so.'

'Okay, it's a stretch, but we should at least bring him in and ask him.'

Brook considered for a moment. 'You're right but we may have lost the element of surprise.'

'Why?'

Brook looked at his watch. 'We left Yvette's house an hour

ago. What's the betting she rang him the moment we were out the door?'

'Honestly, Inspector Brook, I can't be sure.' Alice Kennedy watched the CCTV images come to an end then peered back at the still photograph of the boy on the bridge. She looked haggard and had large bags under her eyes. 'That's definitely Kyle's hooded top, but I can't tell if it's Kyle. This boy looks too tall and he doesn't walk like Kyle.'

'Okay,' said Brook, looking at his watch. 'There may be further footage in this afternoon's broadcast. We may need you to look at it, at some point.'

'Okay – I've nothing better to do. You say this person was watching Wilson's body being recovered.'

'On Exeter Bridge this morning.'

'Poor Wilson. I didn't know him. Kyle never mentioned him. Terrible. I didn't even know he was missing.'

'No one did,' said Noble. 'He wasn't reported because he moved between his mum's, his dad's and his grandmother's houses.'

'So he fell between the cracks.' Alice sighed. 'It's terrible, I know, but I just thank God it wasn't Kyle.'

'When did you find out we'd recovered a body?' asked Brook.

'PC Patel came round first thing, she was very comforting. Where are my manners? Would you like some tea, Inspector?'

'We have to get back,' said Brook. 'Is Len not here? I didn't see his car.'

'No.' She hesitated, unable to look at Brook. 'I've moved back in now your people have left. I need to be on my own for a while. It's not fair to Len,' she added unconvincingly.

'I see.'

'You know he's renting a house on Station Road. Have you tried there?'

'We will. Sergeant Noble is going to give you his mobile number. If Len shows up here, could you ask him to phone?'

'What about?'

'We wanted to ask him something about DNA.' Noble smiled.

Brook looked across at the laptop on the kitchen counter. The screensaver was on. He nudged the mouse on his way past. The countdown on *deity.com* was down to an hour and a half. 'You're watching the broadcasts?'

'Isn't everybody?' said Alice Kennedy. She began to cry. 'It's my only link with Kyle . . .'

Twenty-One

A T TWO O'CLOCK, THE INCIDENT Room was packed with two teams of detectives. Brook's team, investigating the death of Wilson Woodrow and the disappearance of the four students, relaxed in chairs, minus Noble who had gone to pick up Len Poole. DS Gadd and her small team, DCs Read and Smee, were preparing to brief Charlton on developments in the search for The Embalmer. Brook sat at the back with Charlton.

'Noble said DS Gadd and her team have developed an interesting theory about The Embalmer,' Charlton muttered to Brook.

'I wouldn't know anything about it, sir,' replied Brook. 'It's all Jane's work.'

'You rate her highly.'

'Very. She and John should've been promoted two years ago when DI Greatorix retired.'

Charlton turned to Brook, wondering if there was any point mentioning the budget again. Instead a better idea came to him. 'As soon as there's a vacancy,' he said, keeping his head steadfastly to the front.

Gadd stood and the room fell silent. 'I won't bore everyone with a recap of The Embalmer's activities but our research has thrown up some interesting facts about his method.' She threw a brief glance at Brook, a little embarrassed to be taking the credit for Brook's efforts.

'Have the missing vagrants washed up yet?' asked Charlton.

'No, sir. And if we're right they may not surface for some time. No pun intended,' she added with a hesitant smile. She indicated the portable photo array brought in from The Embalmer Incident Room. There was a fifteen-year-old photograph of Phil Ward dug up from the DVLA. Already the ravages of drug and alcohol abuse were visible around the eyes and on his skin. Jock didn't even merit a picture, just a hastily put-together artist's impression. He might as well never have existed.

'We're not sure why, but we think The Embalmer, Ozzy Reece, may be getting to the end of his process.' Gadd waved a hand at the images of the two bodies dumped in the water. 'We're certain Reece is working to a blueprint of Ancient Egyptian burial rites and we now think Barry Kirk and Tommy McTiernan were rehearsals. Whether he abducted them or simply offered them room and board for a few nights, once under Ozzy's control these men conveniently died of alcohol poisoning and shortly after, Ozzy started practising on their corpses.'

She moved over to a picture of Barry Kirk's bloated, barely recognisable head. 'As you know, both men had their blood drained and their internal organs removed. Both men had significant scarring below the nostrils and both had experienced physical damage to the brain, despite the skull being intact.

'Pathology concluded that each victim had had a sharp tool with a small hook attached, forced up into the nostril, piercing the brain. The tool was then used to hack at the brain matter and the hook was used to pull the pieces out through the nostrils.'

'And now we know why?' ventured Morton.

'It's a procedure used by the Ancient Egyptians to slow decomposition and to prepare the dead for the afterlife. The Egyptians would take bodies to the place of purification, sometimes called the Ibu. There, the brain was removed through the nose, and the other organs and viscera were removed through an incision in the left side. Just like Kirk and McTiernan. All the organs would then be packed in large jars, called canopic jars, and treated with natron, a kind of salt, to dry and preserve them. Here's the interesting bit – the heart was left in the body cavity because the Egyptians thought it was needed for the afterlife.'

'Fascinating,' said Charlton.

'Yes, sir. But there's something else. As we know, Ozzy Reece picked up his vagrants at a squat on Leopold Street. To keep them there he provided regular supplies of barley wine and whisky bought from a cash and carry in Nottingham. We also know he worked briefly across the road at a funeral parlour – Duxbury and Duxbury – presumably where he first became aware of the squat and got the idea that it could provide a steady stream of available subjects.

'One day the proprietor of the funeral parlour caught Ozzy interfering with one of the corpses. He'd removed the packing placed inside the body cavity to maintain normal body shape and was trying to replace it with a loaf of bread.'

'A loaf of bread?' said Charlton, trying not to laugh. Others who hadn't heard the story were less successful. 'Why?'

'Barley, sir. The Ancient Egyptians cultivated it. It was

central to their existence. They ate it, baked bread with it, used it for medicine, brewing beer and at one time they even used it to stuff the bodies of the dead, it was so revered.'

'That's why he gave them barley wine,' observed Cooper.

'Whisky too,' said Gadd. 'It's also made from grain. He was feeding it to them because he didn't want his subjects to be tainting their bodies with anything else.'

Charlton looked at his watch. 'But you said he was just practising.'

'Look at the scarring under the nostrils, sir. Kirk was the first victim. He was the first body dumped. His upper lip is nearly sliced through. McTiernan was the second victim. The cuts under his nostrils are less obvious. The Embalmer's getting better at what he does. He's trying to prepare these bodies for the next stage and to leave them as perfect as he can. Removing the brain was his weak spot. My guess is that once he's perfected this technique, the victims will start showing up fully embalmed, maybe even mummified.'

'But not for a while,' said Brook.

'No, sir, the embalming takes much longer. That's why we think Jock and Phil Ward's bodies haven't been dumped yet.'

'As far as we know,' said Morton.

'That's true.'

'And that's why you think he's coming to the end of his process.' Charlton nodded. 'Anything from the appeal?'

'We've got people manning the phones and taking names. We're checking them against what we know – description, history.'

'History?'

'Well, given the level of skill, we think The Embalmer may have worked with the dead. And given that the bodies we've found were in the initial stages of preservation, he has a working knowledge of how to embalm as well.'

'He could just be getting it all from the internet,' said Cooper.

Gadd shrugged. 'Possible. But the key question now is where he's doing all this. He needs space for the bodies and equipment and, of course, absolute privacy. The two dump sites we know about suggest somewhere in the countryside east of Derby.'

'What about the ambulance? You think he worked in a hospital?' asked Morton.

'It's possible,' replied Gadd. 'But you'd be amazed how many secondhand ambulances can be picked up for a few thousand pounds.' She looked across at DC Read.

'We've been looking at CCTV footage for the night you were attacked,' said Read to Brook. 'We've found an ambulance that doesn't belong to either city hospital or any private medical facility that we've contacted. It's a 2002 Mercedes Sprinter – licence-plate BA52 SWT. We know you were attacked around four that morning, sir.'

Brook blanched, remembering his unscheduled nap. 'Around then.'

'It has to be, because a half-hour later, the rogue ambulance was caught on film turning off the southern ring road on to the Shardlow Road towards the A6 and the M1.'

'Shardlow,' said Brook. 'And from there?'

'No idea,' answered Gadd, walking over to the large map of Derby. 'But if we assume the cameras on the A6 would have picked up the suspect vehicle, the fact they didn't must mean the ambulance either turned off into the housing estate around Boulton Moor or, more likely, the B5010 towards Shardlow.

Taking that route, our suspect can head for Borrowash, where Tommy McTiernan was found in the river, or on towards Shardlow and the gravel pit where Kirk was found.'

'He could also have turned off to Weston-on-Trent or Aston-on-Trent,' offered Morton.

'Also possible,' agreed Read. 'Either way, he has good transport links to a vast uninhabited area east of Derby in which to conceal himself.'

'You've traced the ambulance?' asked Brook.

DC Smee took over. 'It was licensed in Birmingham and released from service at Birmingham General in 2007. It was bought at an auction in Lincolnshire, two years ago,' Smee paused dramatically, 'by a man called Ozzy Reece. Unfortunately, this being the motor trade, it was a cash deal and the vehicle has been untaxed since that time, so no lead there.'

'Ozzy Reece,' repeated Brook for no apparent reason. Everyone turned to watch him shake his head. 'Ozzy Reece,' he said again.

'You've logged the number-plate into the Automatic Recognition database,' said Charlton, looking sideways at Brook.

'Yes, sir,' answered Smee. 'If that ambulance is on the streets with those plates and one of our ANPR cars spots it, the computer will cough out an instant alert and we've got him. We're just waiting for him to show his face.'

'Excellent,' said Charlton. He stole another glance at Brook. This time the DI had a huge grin on his face. 'Something to add, Inspector?'

'Ozzy Reece,' he said for the third time. 'It didn't strike you as odd?'

'Odd?' asked Charlton.

'Why someone trying to escape detection should choose such a memorable alias – seemed a bit perverse to me.' Brook walked across to the artist's impression. 'Ozzy Reece. May I present Osiris, Ancient Egyptian God of the Afterlife.'

With the Incident Room in darkness DC Cooper prepared to show the two pieces of CCTV film again for the benefit of those who hadn't seen them. Brook stood at the back with Charlton but was distracted by Noble gesturing to him from the door and slipped out while Charlton, Gadd and DCs Read and Smee watched Wilson Woodrow preparing to jump to his death.

'Poole wasn't at his house and his Jag was gone,' said Noble. 'But Alice Kennedy rang me. Len arrived ten minutes after we left. She said he got a call on his mobile just as he arrived and he left straight away.'

'Did Len say where he was going?'

'No, but I'm guessing Yvette spooked him because Alice said he was coming here to speak to you.'

'Did she say why?'

Noble shook his head. 'Maybe he's going to make a clean breast of things.'

'That sound like him?' answered Brook.

'Not really.'

'More likely he's going to try and get ahead of the game, find out what we know about his relationship with Yvette. And if he's found out he's not Russell's father, he's got a much stronger hand.'

'Maybe he'll do a runner.'

'I don't think so, John. He's got a lot to lose. And the way he's kept Yvette secret all these years, I don't see him panicking. And if he thinks we know how far they go back, he might even start cutting her loose.'

'What do you mean?'

'He might try and turn the tables, John. After all, Yvette's the one who's followed Len from place to place. It wouldn't be hard to characterise her as some kind of stalker, would it?'

'It would if we started pulling his financials.'

'He may have been careful,' suggested Brook. 'If his late wife was the one with the money, it would have been easier to hide any payments.'

Noble shrugged. 'Not that easy.'

Brook looked back into the Incident Room. The first film had been shown twice with Cooper pointing out the mystery figure with a camcorder, in the bushes. 'Let's not pin our hopes on Len. I know we don't have a lot to go on, but their relationship is academic at the moment. We don't even know if it has anything to do with our missing teenagers.'

Cooper started the second piece of film. He froze the image to show the young man on Exeter Bridge walking towards the camera. Here, Brook took up the reins.

'Early this morning we were called out to the recovery of Wilson Woodrow's body following the events you've just witnessed. Wilson was a Derby College student and a participant in the first Deity website broadcast.' Brook pointed at the screen. 'As we recovered Wilson's body from the river, this unidentified young man was on Exeter Bridge watching and filming us. He's wearing a G-STAR hoodie, identical to the garment Kyle Kennedy, one of our four missing students, was last seen wearing on the evening of May nineteenth – that's according to Mrs Kennedy.'

'So we think that's Kyle Kennedy,' said DS Morton, nodding at the screen.

'We don't know for sure,' replied Noble. 'We showed Alice Kennedy the film and some stills but she didn't think it was Kyle – too tall. She couldn't be sure for obvious reasons – his face and eyes are covered, the clothing is very baggy. She could only identify his hoodie. Same story with Russell Thomson's mother.'

Brook picked up again. 'The first film you saw shows that Wilson jumped into the Derwent at a quarter to midnight some two hours after he'd assaulted Kyle Kennedy. The figure behind the red dot in the trees is filming Wilson's last moments and close examination leads us to believe that he appears to be wearing the same hoodie as our young man on the bridge.'

'So the kid who got gay-bashed is getting his revenge,' said DC Read. 'Good motive, Guv.'

Brook was pleased to see Charlton frowning at the back of Read's head. He'd obviously not been brought up to speed on how to conduct himself. Brook glanced casually across at Noble who acknowledged this with an amused nod.

'When I restart the second film,' continued Brook, 'you'll see the boy on the bridge using a camcorder to record the retrieval of Wilson's body.'

'Wasn't Russell Thomson the kid with the camcorder?' asked Gadd.

'Yes.'

'So that could also be Russell Thomson, wearing Kyle's hoodie,' concluded Gadd.

'Yes. Or even a third person who's holding Kyle and Russell hostage and has access to their clothes and possessions,' replied Brook. 'Including Russell's camcorder and Kyle's mobile phone which was used to text a message to Jake McKenzie at six thirty this morning.'

'Who's Jake McKenzie?' asked DC Smee.

'A friend of Kyle's,' said Noble. 'He stepped in to stop the assault.'

'I'm confused,' said Charlton.

'I'm not surprised,' said Brook. Charlton wondered briefly whether to take offence. 'Messing with our heads,' explained Brook with a smile.

'Did we get a trace on the phone?' asked Charlton.

'We did though we didn't need one. The phone was on Exeter Bridge with the unknown male.'

'How do we know?'

'Because the operator told us that Kyle's mobile number was being used at the exact same time and place as the bridge footage.' Noble looked over at DC Cooper, who moved the film to six twenty-nine that morning. When he restarted the footage, the young man on Exeter Bridge had lowered his camcorder and extracted a mobile phone from a pocket. He began to tap out a text.

'Hang on. If that's Kyle, he's got hold of another phone but put his own SIM card in it,' said Morton. 'That doesn't make any sense. Why not just get a new Pay As You Go? Then we wouldn't know who's doing the texting.'

'Actually we don't know who's doing the texting, Rob,' said Noble. 'But that's a valid point unless we assume they want us to know it was Kyle's phone and that it was on Exeter Bridge this morning.'

'They?' queried Charlton.

Brook shrugged. 'He. She. Whoever.'

'All part of messing with our heads,' nodded Charlton.

'Exactly.'

'And since the text?'

'The phone was turned off as soon as the text was sent.'

'So we can't triangulate his present location,' said Charlton, for once on sure ground.

'No.'

'And the phone didn't have GPS?'

Brook looked over at Cooper for help. Cooper shook his head. 'No. But we have a few CCTV images which put the suspect on the bike path travelling along the Derwent, past Pride Park, towards Borrowash.'

'On a bike?'

'Yes, sir.'

'Great,' said Charlton with a sigh. 'So our students are hiding out somewhere to the east of Derby. That narrows it down to about a hundred square miles.'

'Maybe they're kipping down with The Embalmer.' Cooper grinned.

Charlton's glare prevented further jocularity. 'Do we know what the text message was?'

'*I hate you, Jake. I hope you're ashamed of yourself. You betrayed me when I needed you most,*' Brook recited from memory.

'Funny thing to say to someone who tries to save you from a beating,' muttered Charlton.

'It's complicated,' answered Brook, deciding not to elaborate further. 'But after receiving it, Jake McKenzie tried to kill himself. He's recovering in the Royal.'

'So it *was* Kyle on the bridge?'

'The text message seems to point that way, sir,' agreed Brook.

'Any forensics from the crime scene?' asked Charlton.

'Crime scene?' said DC Cooper, before he could stop himself.

'Even if that boy jumped of his own accord, whoever's filming from the trees is assisting a suicide,' said Charlton in his direction. 'That's a crime – last time I looked.'

'The Chief Superintendent's right,' announced Brook. 'Until we get the PM results, all bets are on. We found tablets on the body which the lab should identify by tomorrow.'

'So there's a possibility Wilson was drugged to soften him up.' Morton nodded. 'He looked a bit shaky.'

'At last – an old-fashioned murder,' smiled Noble.

'He could have self-administered,' pointed out Gadd.

Charlton held up his hands. 'Well?' he said, to restate his question. 'Were there any forensics?'

'SOCO did take a look in the bushes, but it's a public space, sir,' said Noble.

'And it was over a week ago,' said Charlton. 'Fair enough. What about the bridge?' He glanced briefly at Brook before answering his own question. 'Not even worth trying – no, I can see that. When's the post mortem on Woodrow?'

'Tomorrow morning, sir,' said Noble.

Charlton waved an arm at the screen. 'Why do you think he was filming you?'

'I strongly suspect one or both of these home movies will make up a Deity broadcast,' said Brook, looking at his watch. 'Maybe even this afternoon.'

'How long?'

'Fifteen minutes.'

'Anything else?'

Cooper stood up. 'We've made a start on Fern Stretton's computer to see if she's got any pictures or messages.'

'Fern who?' asked Charlton, with a heavy sigh.

'Best friend of Becky Blake and the girl who started the Facebook memorial site, dedicated to the disappearances,' answered Cooper. 'Lots of chit-chat with Becky, going back a year or more, but nothing of interest yet. No messages from Russell, Kyle or Adele. Various other *Friends* have tagged photos of our missing students and I've put a hard copy of them all on display. Nothing untoward that I could see, just the usual posing and gurning.'

Charlton stood up from the table. 'Weren't we searching the fields behind the Kennedy house?'

'We had fifty uniformed officers all over that area. Nothing,' said Noble, tight-lipped. 'And cameras on the A38 drew a blank. We still don't know how they left the estate.'

Charlton surveyed the room with barely concealed frustration. 'So what are we doing now?'

'We're doing what everybody else is doing,' answered Brook. 'Waiting for the next broadcast.'

'And if it shows the film of Wilson jumping into the river, we're going to have a media storm on our hands,' snapped Charlton. He began to pace about. 'We have to be seen to be doing something.'

'The next broadcast—' began Brook.

'The next broadcast, the next broadcast!' Charlton shouted now. 'So we're going through the motions waiting for four eighteen-year-old college kids to spoonfeed us clues, is that what you're saying?' He looked round at the wary faces, all trying to avoid his eye. 'If that's all we have to say at tonight's press briefing, Inspector, then you're the one who's going to be saying it.' Charlton's finger jabbed at Brook. 'No sick-notes this time.'

Brook nodded. A second later he broke the silence. 'There is one thing. It may be a bit of a tangent but we've discovered a link between Russell Thomson's mother and Len Poole, Kyle Kennedy's future stepfather. It's a bit delicate because Poole has connections to this Division.'

'The ex-pathologist.' Charlton nodded.

'Yes, sir. They're both from North Wales and we think they once had a relationship. Russell might even be Len's son.'

Charlton smiled sarcastically. 'And you want to trot off to Wales to follow it up. If you can't stand the heat—' He stopped in mid-sentence. He'd gone too far and he knew it at once. *Never in front of the troops. Never. Turning valid criticism into humiliation was a recipe for disaster.* 'I'm sorry. That was uncalled-for.'

All eyes turned to Brook. After a second he smiled. 'Forget it, sir. We're all under a lot of pressure. Let's take a break before our next spoonfeeding.' There was a ripple of nervous laughter around the room and even Charlton managed a toothless smile as he hurried from the Incident Room.

Noble pulled out his cigarettes and sidled up to Brook. 'Coming outside for a quick one while Charlton changes his underpants?'

Brook shook his head. 'Go easy on him, John. It took a lot of guts to apologise to a serial failure like me.'

'You're mellowing in your old age.'

Brook raised an eyebrow.

'Late middle,' conceded Noble from the door.

Brook watched his nicotine dealer leave and resisted the

urge to follow. The countdown stood at nine minutes. He strolled over to the new photo array and examined the pictures from Fern's Facebook site. Naturally enough most of the pictures were of Becky – she was Fern's best friend and an aspiring model, after all. Some of the pictures he recognised from the glossy pile torn from her wall and hidden under her bed. All of them showed the blond-haired student striking the regulation poses to be seen in every Sunday supplement.

Kyle and Adele were less well represented, being mainly tagged in group shots. Kyle seemed naturally shy in most of the pictures but what few there were of Adele showed her confident and staring defiantly at the camera. The dearth of pictures of Adele showed she didn't thirst for attention like most aimless young people.

There was only one shot of Russell Thomson, though it was hard to tell it was him; one half of his face was covered by his camcorder as he filmed himself in his bedroom mirror. Brook looked closely at what detail was visible – his lank, dark brown hair, his pallid skin and shaving rash. His hands were long and artistic and the one eye not covered by the camcorder was squinting to allow the other eye to see through the lens.

Brook glanced across at the only other recent photograph of Russell they'd tracked down – a headshot, the one taken for his Derby College entry pass and the same one he'd also used for his passport application three months earlier. His bland features were partially covered by his unkempt hair as though Russell wanted to hide as much of his face as he could, despite the use to which the image would be put.

Something about the Facebook picture struck Brook as interesting but he couldn't put his finger on it. Then he looked again at the hands. They hung out of a long-sleeved sweatshirt, only the fingers visible. He thought of Terri and her scars. Could Russell be hiding similar scars from a suicide attempt? He'd certainly had a troubled life, by all accounts. But he was eighteen now, on the cusp of leaving fulltime education, the trauma of school bullying behind him. Surely if he was going to enter into some kind of suicide pact, it would have happened before now. Then again, he could say the same for the others.

He looked either side of the squinting Russell's head and narrowed his own eyes to see clearly. There was something in the background. DC Cooper returned to the Incident Room with three cups of tea.

'Can we get this photograph enlarged? Here and here,' added Brook, circling two areas with a pen.

'No problem,' said Cooper.

The room began to fill up again for the broadcast. Noble approached, reeking of the sweet perfume of tobacco.

'Don't you get bored being right all the time?' said Noble. Brook raised an eyebrow. 'Poole was waiting downstairs to have a word with you. I put him in Interview Two.'

Charlton returned with a coffee and took his usual table at the back without looking up at Brook. He dangled his legs a foot above the floor and sipped quietly on his cup to wash down the humble pie.

Noble extinguished the lights. A few seconds later the Deity homepage appeared. The countdown was at fifteen seconds.

At zero, a soft and melodic piece of choral music began to play, all weeping violins and lamenting voices. It sounded like some sort of Requiem to Brook but he knew it wasn't Mozart – that particular piece of music was seared on his memory from his struggles with The Reaper. However, the churchgoing

Charlton nodded in recognition. Brook heard him mutter, 'Verdi.'

Meanwhile the small video screen opened with the front page of a newspaper. Cooper maximised the screen. The *South Wales Argus*, dated December 2007, sported the headline: *17th TEENAGER TAKES LIFE*. Beside the headline was a grainy picture of the doomed teenager, perhaps a few years younger, smiling happily for the camera next to a birthday cake – a poignant image never intended for use outside the family album.

Before the assembled officers could read the story, the picture changed. Another newspaper, another young person ending her suffering – *BULLIED GIRL TAKES OVERDOSE*. This time the local paper was in London. And so it continued. *GIRL JUMPS TO HER DEATH AFTER LOVER'S TIFF* in Surrey. *JOBLESS TEENAGER FALLS UNDER TRAIN* in Yorkshire. *UNKNOWN BOY HANGS HIMSELF* in Denbighshire. This last was accompanied by a picture of a youngster hanging, neck snapped, from the end of a rope.

The sequence and the music ended and the film began. Brook had been right. It was the footage of Wilson Woodrow's suicide, taken by the mysterious figure in the bushes. The doomed Wilson was framed against the river wall with the Council House building in the background. He grunted and turned away from the river, puffing towards the camera. A murmur of surprise ran through the Incident Room. They had sound.

Wilson approached the bushes, walking unsteadily, the camera following his movement as he looked furtively on the ground for large stones. He bent down to pick one up and tottered back with it towards the river wall and returned for more. Then they heard it. The words were slurred and scattered between Wilson's grunts of effort but the rhyme was unmistakable. 'She loves me, she loves me not. She loves me, she loves me not.' The film ended with Wilson clambering on to the river wall, sobbing and chanting, 'She loves me not,' and stepping off into the river.

The screen went blank and a male voice poured softly from the speakers. 'Bye, bye, Wilson.'

There was silence for several minutes as they waited for more.

'Cancel the lipreader,' said Brook, still staring at the screen, waiting for the countdown to start again.

Instead the funereal music began again and the pale face of Becky Blake filled the screen. Her eyes were closed, her lips slightly parted and her skin was deathly white. Her hands were crossed, the tips of her fingers just visible under her chin. They were also deathly white. A second later the picture changed to Kyle Kennedy in the same pose. Like Becky, his face was ashen, but peaceful and still. There was a pronounced swelling on his jaw, presumably a souvenir of Wilson's punch.

Finally Adele's face appeared and Brook's breathing quickened. She had the skin of an angel. Not a blemish, not a hair out of place. Her mouth and eyes were closed, her head slightly to one side. Brook saw carpet encroaching on the shot in the top right-hand corner.

The image faded and with it the music. Brook smiled. 'They're alive.'

Twenty-Two

'TRUST ME, SIR,' INSISTED BROOK to a disbelieving Charlton. 'Those last three pictures were faked.'

'Why would they fake them?' asked Noble.

'They want people to think they're dead to increase media attention,' explained Brook. 'That tells us they're alive. You're forgetting . . .'

'. . . what we see is but a dream? No, Inspector, we're not,' said Charlton. 'But I want more than inverted logic to tell me they're still alive.'

'Look at the carpet next to Adele's head.' Brook pointed to the frozen image on the screen.

'What about it?'

'It's on the floor in Alice Kennedy's living room.' Brook looked at Noble. 'John?'

Noble narrowed his eyes at the screen. 'You're right.'

'So what?' argued Charlton. 'So they were killed there.'

'And their bodies spirited away in a van that loaded them up without a single witness noticing,' replied Brook. 'No, sir, these shots are faked. They must have done it before they left the house. Remember the talcum powder SOCO found on the living-room carpet?'

'Yes,' replied Charlton doubtfully.

'They rubbed it on their face and hands and tried to play dead.' Noble smiled.

'Exactly,' said Brook.

'That only means they were alive at the Kennedy house,' argued Noble. 'They could still be dead.'

'True, but then why show us fake pictures? If they're dead, why not show us the real thing? Deity has had no qualms so far about broadcasting violence and death.'

'You got me there.' Noble nodded.

'So what do we tell the press and TV?' asked Charlton. 'Do we denounce these pictures as fakes?'

'No. That might provoke a reaction,' retorted Brook.

'You talk as though Deity is an entity, a being with power over these kids.'

'Somebody's got a hold over them,' said Brook. 'Look how Wilson was manipulated – Jake McKenzie too. If we denounce these pictures as fakes, whoever's behind this might feel compelled to come up with the real thing.'

'We have to say something, if only to the parents,' said Charlton.

'We tell them that we're accepting nothing at face value and they shouldn't either. That goes for our investigation and how we respond to the media.'

'I hope you know what you're doing, Brook,' said Charlton.

Noble rang off. 'Alice Kennedy.'

'She recognised Kyle's voice in the broadcast?' ventured Brook.

Noble nodded. 'Bye bye Wilson.'

'It doesn't mean Kyle was shooting the film or spoke to

Wilson as he drowned. It could've been recorded at any time in a completely different context and added later.'

'I told her. The technicians are on it.'

'How's she holding up?'

'Okay. Patel's with her.'

'What can I do for you, Len?'

Poole looked up from the hard chair. He held Brook's eye for a moment before breaking into a grin and looking round the room. 'I can see why people crack up in these places,' he said. 'They're not exactly welcoming.'

'That's the idea.' Brook moved from the door to sit at the table opposite Poole. 'DS Noble's bringing us tea, if that'll help.'

'A cigarette would help more. If you've got one.'

Brook smiled faintly. The guilty smoked like laboratory beagles in the Interview Rooms. 'I will have when DS Noble gets here. I didn't know you smoked.'

'Just the occasional one when I'm on my own. When you've spent a lifetime dealing in death . . .'

'At least I won't need to explain the health risks to you,' observed Brook.

Poole laughed. 'No. I've seen a few Grow Bags in my time. That's what we used to call heavily tarred lungs in my day,' he explained. 'Though tumours were the only things that grew there.'

'You sound like you miss it, Len.'

'Sometimes I do, but only because it was a part of me when I was younger. That's what nostalgia is really.'

'A desire to be young again?'

'Young, innocent, carefree.'

'It's a myth, Len. Kyle's predicament should tell you that much.'

Poole lowered his head. 'I suppose.'

Noble entered carrying a tray of plastic cups and set them down. 'No sugar, sorry.'

'I'm sweet enough.' Poole grinned. Neither officer cracked a smile.

'So what's a life of indolence like?' asked Brook.

'Can't complain,' answered Poole. 'I've got a decent pension and Eileen left me well looked after, God rest her soul.'

'Good to be back in Derby?' asked Brook innocently. 'Seeing old friends.'

Poole paused and took a sip of tea. 'It's okay. I'm only here until Kyle finishes college and Alice sells the house. Then it's back to Chester.'

'Back to your voluntary work,' said Noble.

Poole stiffened. 'Voluntary work?'

'Oh, I'm sorry,' said Noble without a trace of apology in his voice. 'I thought I read somewhere that you worked with orphans.' He smiled politely to drive up the temperature. Just wait, Brook had always taught him. The guilty abhorred silence – they always talked through it, not about their guilt, not at first, but about anything that came into their heads. Eventually, if you were prepared to wait long enough, the drivel ran out and the only thing left to talk about was their confession.

'Yvette,' said Poole, nodding, as though the link were self-evident. Then he hardened his features. He wasn't here to defend himself when attack would be the better foot forward. After all, he was a professional, a well-respected man, a man with qualifications and expertise, a man with a certain standing in the community and, best of all, though he prided himself on never being blasé about it, he had money. 'I don't know what she's been telling you, Inspector, but there's something I think you need to know about that woman.'

'Yvette?' asked Brook.

'She's delusional, Inspector – a complete fantasist. It's tragic really, but not atypical for an orphan to develop these fantasies.'

'And what sort of fantasy would Miss Thomson want to tell us?' asked Noble.

'I don't know why I'm even mentioning this,' said Poole, looking at the older detective for understanding.

'Sure you do,' replied Brook.

Poole briefly put his head in his hands then sat straight and stared defiantly back at his inquisitors. 'Yvette thinks that she and I have a relationship – a sexual relationship.'

Brook and Noble's expressions didn't change. They gazed evenly at Poole, declining to give him a hint of their reaction.

'And do you?' asked Brook finally.

Poole did his best to look Brook in the eye. 'No.'

'And have you ever had such a relationship?' asked Brook.

'How dare you ask me that!' shouted Poole.

'How dare I?' Brook shouted back, standing up and knocking over his chair. 'I didn't ask to see you. You came to us, and if you want to sit there playing games and looking coy, you can leave now. I'm not here to whitewash your version of history. I've got four young people to find and I don't want my time wasted.' Brook made to leave and beckoned Noble to join him with a flick of his head.

'Inspector,' said Poole. 'I'm sorry. You're right.' Brook and Noble stood frozen by the door. 'Please sit down.'

Brook, apparently reluctantly, moved back to pick up his chair. Noble followed suit, trying to hide his amusement behind a hand. Brook's 'Bad Cop' was a rare sight and all the more convincing for it.

'We're listening.'

'I'm worried. Yvette – she's unstable. I'm afraid she might do something to hurt me or even Alice.'

Brook hid his surprise well. He wished he could turn on the tape recorder but Poole was not under arrest or caution. 'Why would you think that?'

'Because you were right. I did have a sexual relationship with her once.'

'When?'

'A long time ago.'

'When?'

Poole knew better than to answer the question. 'You should've seen her, Inspector. You think she's pretty now.' He shook his head. 'Boy, she was something back then. She knew all the tricks. I was putty in her hands.'

'Where did you first meet her?'

Poole laughed. 'I knew as soon as Kyle disappeared that it would come to this.'

'What?'

'That you'd do background checks, that you'd discover Yvette and I knew each other. And from where.'

'I'd still prefer you tell us.'

'St Asaph's School for Boys and Girls. It was an orphanage a few miles from Chester. I joined the Board of Trustees.'

'How old was she when you met her?'

'She was fourteen. Her mother had died. But I deny anything untoward took place at the orphanage.'

'So would I, in your shoes. Nevertheless, while Yvette was in care, she got pregnant and gave birth to Russell at the age of fifteen.'

Poole's tone became almost haughty. 'Well, I'm not the father, Inspector. Like I said, nothing improper happened between us.'

'Was it your decision to let Yvette keep the baby at the orphanage?'

Poole hesitated. 'Partly.'

'How would that work?'

'We had suitable family quarters away from the rest of the residents. It seemed . . . unnecessary to separate mother and child.'

'Especially if you were over a barrel and had to do as you were told,' sneered Noble.

'I'm not the father,' insisted Poole. 'How many times?'

'You can prove that?' asked Noble.

'I don't need proof. You can't tie me to unlawful sexual intercourse because it never happened. It would be the word of a deranged young girl against mine.'

Brook's eyes narrowed. His show of temper had thrown Poole off-balance and loosened his tongue but the ex-pathologist was smart enough to avoid crowing about DNA tests.

'So you don't have proof,' persisted Brook.

Poole looked away. 'I told you. I don't need it.'

'If we find out which company you used to test your DNA against Russell Thomson's, all the denials in the world won't wash,' said Brook quietly. 'Even if there wasn't a match, the fact that you sought a professional judgement is damning enough.'

Poole looked puzzled for a second then broke into a wide grin. 'Good luck making that case, Inspector,' he said, almost laughing now. Brook was wrong-footed for the first time.

'If you're not the father, who is?' asked Noble.

'Take your pick,' said Poole. 'Yvette did. She could string anyone along. All the boys lusted after her at St Asaph's. You've seen her. She must have given you two the treatment. She always does.' Brook stared back at Poole while Noble shuffled uncomfortably on his seat. Poole grinned again. It was an unpleasant sight. 'I see she did, Sergeant. Did she come over all vulnerable? Did she make you feel strong and masterful?' Noble made to stand but was halted by Brook's voice.

'Then there's the money.'

'Money?'

'The money you used to set her up.'

Poole shrugged. 'I could deny it, but why would I? I felt sorry for the girl. I helped her out when she left the orphanage. I could afford it.'

'And that's when the sexual relationship started?'

'Yes.'

'Did your wife know?'

'No, thank God.'

'And Alice?'

Poole just shook his head.

'And now?' asked Brook.

Poole sighed. 'Now I'm getting married again, I've decided to turn off the tap. She can make her own way in the world. She won't have any trouble finding another benefactor.'

'But she doesn't see it that way.'

'She thinks I owe her. I move and she follows. Then she asks for money.'

'Which you gave her willingly for eighteen years.'

'I told you, I felt sorry for her. And I could afford it.'

'What changed?'

Poole became evasive. 'I just said. I'm getting married. I decided – enough is enough.'

'And you're worried she might take it badly and come after you, spouting her lies.'

'Hell hath no fury . . .' Poole shrugged.

'Did she threaten you?'

'Not exactly. But with this lad drowning . . .'

'Wilson Woodrow!' exclaimed Brook. 'You think she had something to do with that?'

'It was a suicide,' added Noble. 'We have it on film.' Noble knew he'd said the wrong thing almost at once. Brook's imperceptible glance in his direction spoke volumes.

'Maybe not then,' admitted Poole. 'But this Wilson – the lad who drowned – he was always pestering her, trying to get into her bed. He may even have succeeded, for all I know.'

'Yet you still rang her this morning after Sergeant Grey tipped you off?'

Poole hesitated. 'I didn't ring her,' he said firmly.

'But Grey rang you.'

Poole picked his words carefully. 'He's a friend. He thought it might be Kyle's body. He thought I ought to know.'

'But you didn't think Alice ought to know.'

'Pardon?'

'You rang Yvette in the early morning to tell her we'd found a young man's body, maybe Russell's body, maybe Kyle's body, you had no way of knowing . . .'

'I told you—'

'. . . but you didn't see fit to tell Kyle's mother,' pressed Brook.

'It wasn't Kyle.'

'You didn't know that.'

Poole took a deep breath. 'I didn't want to alarm Alice. She's sensitive.'

'And Yvette isn't.'

'Only to her own needs.'

'You think she didn't care that her own son might have drowned?' said Noble. 'She was there in a shot.'

Poole stared back, mute.

Brook drained his tea. 'When we check the call you made to Yvette . . .'

'I told you,' answered Poole confidently. 'I didn't ring her. Go ahead and check. I've got nothing to hide.'

Brook smiled his understanding. 'No, you didn't need to ring her, did you? When Grey rang you, you were already there, at her house. In her bed.'

Poole stared straight ahead. When Brook and Noble wouldn't break their gaze, he sighed. 'I felt sorry for her.'

Noble bristled and his fists clenched. 'You snivelling—'

'*John.*'

'She can't be alone, Sergeant,' said Poole. 'Believe me. It kills her. Since the orphanage, she's always . . .' He hung his head. Noble's breathing slowed. A moment later, Poole looked up. 'About that cigarette.'

Noble reluctantly pulled out his pack and offered it round. There was silence as each lit up, appreciating the temporary kinship of tobacco.

'Does Alice have to know?' said Poole finally.

'Oh, I think Alice already knows what she's getting into without our input,' replied Brook.

'What does that mean?'

'It means, like Yvette, she knows the basis of your relationship and what it makes her.'

Poole's face betrayed his fury. 'I don't think there's any need for that!'

'Did money change hands?' asked Brook, ignoring Poole's indignation.

'Money?'

'Grey. Did you pay for the heads-up?'

'Not . . .' Poole tightened his lips around the rest of the sentence.

'Not yet.' Brook took a long pull on his cigarette. 'Let me speak plainly, Len. Sergeant Grey is no friend of mine. He's a time-serving dinosaur and has no place in a modern Force. However, this job does something to people and he may once have been a decent officer. So, if he's a friend of yours, can I suggest, for the sake of his pension, that you never mention even the promise of money changing hands again?'

Poole nodded and stood to leave.

'Where are you going?'

'I've said my piece.'

'Then it's our turn. Tell me about Russell.'

Poole reluctantly sat back down. 'I hardly know him and that's the truth, Inspector. When he was two or three I saw him quite often when Yvette moved to Chester. He was a cheerful little chap if a bit shy. When he got to five or six and started school, I barely ever saw him.'

'Because that's the time you met your wife.'

'I'd already moved to Uttoxeter, met Eileen and we got married.'

'But Yvette still followed.'

'Yes. But I hardly ever saw her unless I ran into her in the town by accident. I was working in Derby, see. In 2003 we moved back to North Wales. Yvette followed and I'd give her help getting set up, but they couldn't settle in one place because of Russell's problems.'

'The bullying?'

'That's right.'

'And when you moved back here six months ago, you set Yvette up again.'

'I didn't even know she was here, believe me. Do you think I would have put her in a house so close to Alice, and let Russell attend the same college as my future stepson? I had no idea, until three months ago when she turned up on my doorstep asking for money – that's the truth.'

'Which doorstep?'

'Not Alice's, thank God. The house I'm renting in Station Road.'

'So she found you and started blackmailing you again.'

Poole stiffened. 'I told you. I'm not Russell's father. It wasn't blackmail, I –'

'– felt sorry for her,' finished Brook sarcastically. 'Tell me, did you get Russell's DNA from his toothbrush? It was missing when we processed Yvette's house.'

Poole smiled. His smugness had returned. 'I didn't steal Russell's toothbrush. The lad must have taken it with him.'

Brook gazed at Poole, choosing his words. 'What have you got on Yvette?'

Poole sneered at Brook. 'I don't know what you mean.'

'Yes, you do. Your relationship with Yvette is tawdry and exploitative. And whether Russell is your son or not, Yvette has every reason to shout about you from the rooftops, especially if you've stopped paying for her silence. But has she done that? No. Has she spoken to Alice? No. She didn't even admit to us that you'd told her about the body in the river. But that's not the worst of it. The fact she's prepared to sleep with you without being paid . . .'

'How dare you!'

'Don't bother. You say she's unstable but I say she knows exactly what she has to do to survive. That's why you're worried, isn't it? You know something about her that's keeping her in line but that knowledge also makes you a target. What is it?'

'Inspector, you're barking up the wrong tree,' Poole told him.

'Is it something to do with Yvette having no photographs of her son?'

Poole bristled, unable to look at Brook. 'I wouldn't know about that. She said they got lost in the move.'

'So you asked her about that as well?'

Poole glared back at Brook and stood to leave. 'Goodbye, Inspector.'

'What do you think?' asked Noble, back in the Incident Room.

'I think Len is a very easy read,' replied Brook, firing up his computer.

'Think he's lying about when he started having sex with Yvette?'

'Wouldn't you, if you exploited a fourteen- or fifteen-year-old girl in your care?'

'If only we could get a DNA comparison between Len and Russell.'

'That's what worries me, John. He was too confident on that score. I think he was telling the truth.'

'About not being Russell's father?'

'About *believing* he's not Russell's father.'

'Then why support Yvette financially all these years?'

Brook shrugged. 'I don't know. Guilt maybe. Can you cue up the last broadcast for me? There's something I want to see.'

DC Cooper came in at that moment and dropped a large envelope on Brook's desk. 'One enlarged photograph of Russell Thomson in his bedroom.'

Brook thanked him and absentmindedly pulled it from the envelope. It showed Russell's face in close-up but in no greater detail, but Brook wasn't interested in that. He took out a magnifying glass and looked again, holding the lens against the background by Russell's left ear.

'What is it?'

'This picture. Behind Russell's head there's a piece of a film poster. I think it's the missing one. Can you read that?'

'A-N-D something, something R-A-O-H-S,' read Noble.

Brook wrote it out. 'I need one of those crossword solvers.'

'What about Google? Type the first word and see what it suggests.'

'But what if AND is also the end of a word?'

'Then guess. Hand, sand, land, band.'

Brook tried HAND and various permutations of smaller words like 'in the' and 'of the' but was offered nothing that created a match with the end word. He tried again with SAND but came up blank again.

Noble started the recording of that afternoon's Deity broadcast. 'Sir.'

Brook closed his laptop and looked up at the screen as the first newspaper flashed up its sombre headline – BULLIED GIRL TAKES OVERDOSE. A moment later, Brook pointed at the screen. 'There. Pause it.'

'UNKNOWN BOY HANGS HIMSELF,' read Noble.

'Right. The *Denbigh Examiner*,' said Brook, making a note. He skimmed what he could read of the story but it was just an expanded version of the headline.

'Unknown,' said Noble. 'That's pretty unusual in this day and age.'

'For a teenager anyway,' added Cooper. 'No parents? No dental?'

'Obviously not.'

'An orphan then,' said Noble. He looked up excitedly at Brook. 'St Asaph's.'

Brook smiled. 'Just a few miles away. Okay, move it on. Stop.'

Noble halted the film at the picture of the youngster hanging, neck snapped.

'Pretty gruesome for a local paper,' said Cooper.

Brook nodded. 'That's what struck me. They normally show them alive and well.'

Noble chewed the inside of his lip. 'To be fair, it's not actually in the local rag. It's just a random photograph on its own. I don't see a caption, or any text.'

'Good spot,' said Brook. 'It's not from the *Denbigh Examiner*. But it's been placed next to it so we unconsciously accept it as part of the package. It doesn't belong.'

'You think someone from Deity has shuffled this picture into the pack,' said Cooper.

'I do.'

'Why?'

'To tell us this boy's death means something, maybe,' said Noble.

'I think so,' said Brook. 'I think we need to speak to the local police in Denbigh. This looks like a Scene of Crime photograph to me.'

'The local paper wouldn't have access to SOCO pictures,' said Noble.

'And they wouldn't print them if they did,' said Cooper.

'Agreed. I only said it looked like a SOCO picture,' said Brook. 'But if it isn't, somebody else has taken this at the scene.'

'Meaning?'

'Meaning Wilson Woodrow may be the latest in a long line.'

'What do you want? I've done nothing wrong.'

Brook smiled at Jake and sat down at the side of his bed, Noble on the other. *I've not done nothing* was the default response. Jake looked pale and washed-out; he scratched at the tube feeding saline solution into his arm.

'How are you feeling?'

Jake looked sullenly at the crisp white cotton of his top sheet. 'Where's my mum?'

'She's taking a break. You gave her quite a shock.'

'I suppose. Do they know what happened?' Jake was unable to meet their eyes.

Brook and Noble exchanged a glance. 'You took an over-dose of your mum's sleeping pills, Jake. They had to pump your stomach.'

Jake made a pathetic attempt to fly his version of events, shaking his head in mock disbelief. 'I thought they were aspirins.' He looked up at Brook. 'I had a headache.'

'Must have been some headache to take twenty tablets,' he answered.

'It's a good job the squad car called or we wouldn't be talking,' chipped in Noble. Jake said nothing.

'Why would you try to kill yourself, Jake?'

'Kill myself? Are you tripping?'

'Don't waste our time,' said Noble. 'We can put you under arrest right here.'

'I want my mum. Fetch my mum.'

'You're eighteen, Jake,' said Noble. 'We can speak to you without her permission.'

'Actually, Sergeant, I don't mind if Mrs McKenzie sits in while we talk to Jake about his relationship with Kyle.' Brook rose to fetch her.

'No!' retorted Jake sharply, raising his unattached hand. 'Don't. It's okay. I want to help.'

'Good.' Brook smiled and read from his notes. '*I hate you, Jake. I hope you're ashamed of yourself. You betrayed me when I needed you most.*' Jake looked steadfastly at the sheet. Brook placed the printout from T-mobile in his hands. 'You received that text this morning. It's from Kyle Kennedy's mobile number.'

'You've got my phone?'

'Your computer too. We have a warrant.'

Jake was silent.

'This is the first direct contact from one of our missing students since they disappeared eight days ago. And of all the people Kyle could have contacted, he contacted you, Jake. Why?'

'Can I have a drink of water?'

Brook poured him a cupful from a nearby jug. 'According to my information, Kyle Kennedy also rang you on his mobile, the night before his eighteenth-birthday party – the night before he disappeared.'

Jake took a sip of water. 'Sounds right.'

'What time was it?'

Jake became exasperated. 'You've got my phone. Why don't you tell me?'

'Because we need you to get your memory of that night working,' said Noble.

Jake cast around, thinking. 'About nine o'clock, I think.'

Brook nodded. 'Close enough.'

'Well, then.'

'Why did he ring you?'

Jake was silent for a moment. 'He wanted to invite me to his party and to thank me.'

'Thank you for what?'

'Somebody at college went for him. I stepped in.'

'You're referring to Wilson Woodrow,' said Brook.

'Yes. He started picking on Kyle in Media Studies. That smarmy git Rifkind wasn't going to do anything so I got in between them and broke it up.'

'That was good of you.'

Jake shrugged. 'I don't like bullies.'

'Really. So you don't like Wilson Woodrow.'

'No. He's a sherm.'

Present tense. Brook and Noble exchanged a glance. 'Sherm?'

'A knobhead to you.'

'So what did Kyle say exactly?' asked Brook softly.

Jake smiled. 'Thank you,' he replied, as though talking to an idiot.

'And that was it? He thanked you and then less than an hour later – half a mile from your home – you just happened to wander past at the exact time Kyle was being assaulted by Wilson.' Jake became tight-lipped. 'You have seen the assault on the internet, I take it?'

'Who hasn't?'

Brook waited. Silence was the heaviest pressure. 'According to Mrs Kennedy, Kyle left her house before nine that night. He was carrying a poster and a CD. He told his mum they were for a friend.' Still Jake was silent. 'When we searched Kyle's room after he disappeared, we discovered what a huge fan of The Smiths he is – posters all over his walls, every CD they ever released.' Brook paused to look up from his notes. 'If we searched your room . . .'

'He came round.'

'To your house?'

'Yes. In fact, when he phoned me, he was already outside.'

'Why didn't he just knock on the door?'

Jake shrugged. 'Guess he knew my dad hates faggots.'

Brook nodded and looked into Jake's eyes. The teenager turned away.

'What was he wearing?' asked Noble.

'Jeans – and he had his G-STAR hoodie on. He never took it off.'

'What colour?'

'Blue.'

'So you went out to speak to him?'

'Yes, and he gave me the poster and a CD he'd burned as a thank you.'

'What was it?'

'The Smiths. Like you said – Kyle was nuts about them.'

'Was?' queried Noble. 'You think he's dead?'

Jake looked up. 'I don't know.'

'And the poster?'

'It was the lead singer – Morrissey.'

'You know Morrissey is a gay icon?'

'I guess,' answered Jake.

'Did you know Kyle was gay?' asked Noble.

Jake started laughing. It subsided quickly. 'Yes.'

'Is that why Wilson bullied him?'

'That sh— knobhead doesn't need a reason.'

Brook and Noble exchanged another glance. Jake was either being very clever or he honestly didn't yet know Wilson's body had been discovered that morning.

'These gifts,' said Brook. 'Do you still have them?'

Jake nodded.

'How long were you talking outside your house?'

'About five minutes. No more.'

'And did Kyle say anything other than to thank you and invite you to his party?'

'No.' Jake decided against mentioning the ten-ton truck.

'Then what?'

'Then I went back in.'

'You went back in? But forty minutes later . . .'

'I listened to the CD and decided I didn't like it so I went looking for him to give it back. I was on the way to his house . . .' He shrugged as though the rest was obvious.

'And when you found him, Wilson and his friends were beating him up.'

'Yes.'

'This time you didn't step in.'

'There was no need. Wilson stopped when he saw me.'

'And Kyle came over to you.'

'Yes.'

'Then what?'

When Jake spoke his voice was barely audible. 'I threw it on the ground.'

'What?'

'The CD.'

'What did Kyle say to that?' No reply but Jake's lip began to quiver. 'Was he upset?'

'Yes.'

Brook nodded. '*You betrayed me when I needed you most.* Is that what the text was referring to?'

Jake looked at Brook. There were tears in his eyes. 'Looks like it.'

'Then he walked back over to Wilson.'

'You've seen the film.'

'Then Wilson knocked him out.'

'Yes.'

'Did he say anything?'

'Who?'

'Wilson.'

Jake laughed bitterly, through the tears. 'After he hit Kyle, he got all self-righteous. He said Kyle liked the violence and that disgusted him, like the fat fucker and his thick crew were offended by having to smack him around, like Kyle was a pervert and they'd been forced to hit him.' Jake let out a quivering sigh. 'Then Wilson left. Said he was going to get laid to get the gayness out of his head.'

'Wilson said that?' Brook looked up at Noble. 'Did he say where?'

'No. It was just talk anyway. That fat sherm couldn't get laid if he was a carpet.'

'Then what?' said Brook.

'Then I tried to help Kyle. I went to get water from the stream.'

'But he ran off into the fields.'

'Yes.'

'Did he say anything?'

'He said he hated me.'

Brook studied Jake. 'But you know that wasn't true, don't you?'

'What do you mean?'

'A gay young man giving you presents. That tells me quite a lot.'

'Like what?'

'His mum told us Kyle was in love,' chipped in Noble.

There was silence for several minutes.

'Kyle isn't an active homosexual, according to Mrs Kennedy. He has crushes on people from afar. Do you think he could have been in love with you?' asked Brook finally.

Jake looked up in confusion then returned his eyes to the bed. He opened his mouth to speak but thought better of it.

'Okay. Was that the last time you saw Kyle?' asked Brook.

Jake didn't answer.

'Well, was it?'

'To speak to, yes.'

'What does that mean?'

'I saw him the next night.'

'Did you!' exclaimed Brook. 'What about Wilson? Was that the last time you saw *him*?'

Jake's brow furrowed in confusion. 'Actually, yes.'

'You didn't follow Kyle into the fields?'

'No.'

'And you didn't go after Wilson?'

'No, why would I?'

'To exact revenge for the attack on your friend,' offered Noble.

'I picked up the CD and went home. End of.' Jake finished his water and wiped his mouth.

Brook gazed at Jake. 'So you did go.'

'Go where?'

'To the party.'

Jake looked away. 'I told you before, no.'

'But if you saw Kyle, that wasn't true, was it?' No reply. 'You stood at the same lamp-post, the one I first saw you under when we searched Kyle's room. You were seen.'

Jake looked glassy-eyed into the distance. 'I went to the house. I stood under the streetlight – that's true. I wasn't sure whether to go in. After I'd thrown his gift back in his face . . .'

'Then why go at all?'

'I'd bought him a present. To say sorry.'

'*Picnic at Hanging Rock*?'

'Yes. We'd seen some of it in Media Studies that day. He watched it all with the others. It blew Kyle away. He wrote a review of it the same day and gave that to me as well.'

'Where is it?'

'On my computer.'

'And the DVD?'

'I've still got it. We were watching it the day you came into Media Studies. Rusty brought it the previous week but he hadn't turned up.'

'So what happened? Did Kyle throw your gift back in your face?'

'No, nothing like that.'

'What then?'

'I couldn't go in so I left,' shouted Jake. There was an edge of hysteria in his voice.

'You didn't go in the house?'

'No.'

'But you'd bought Kyle a present. You went all the way to his house. Why couldn't you go in?'

Jake clenched a fist. 'I tried to go in. I tried but I couldn't hear anything – no music, no talking – so I went round the side of the house to see what was going on. There was a crack in the curtain, I could see into the living room.'

'What did you see?'

'They were playing some weird game.'

Brook looked up at Noble. 'Game? What game?'

'Becky and Adele were on the floor. Their faces were white and they were just lying there. They looked like they were dead and Kyle was filming them with Rusty's camcorder.'

'Kyle was doing the filming? What about Russell?'

'I didn't see Rusty.'

Twenty-Three

BROOK READ THE SCRIPT OF Kyle Kennedy's film review in grim silence. The entire essay was devoted to the notion that *Picnic at Hanging Rock* was a rallying call for suicide. The weak, impressionable, unhappy Kyle saw only the attraction and drama of self-destruction. The hunger for that brief inferno of interest in his pathetic life dripped from every word.

They're dead, you know . . .

Brook turned to the photograph of Kyle on the display board. For the first time he was prepared to accept that Terri might be right. He gazed at the picture of Adele Watson, her dark eyes burning into him. Could she destroy herself?

No. Brook wouldn't accept it. Kyle, yes. Becky too. The discovery of their bodies would give them their dearest wish – their names on the lips of the country. But Adele . . . what was in it for her? The sources of her pain, if pain she felt – her father, Rifkind – had already been exposed. What more could be achieved by going to her grave? There had to be something, some reason for her to embrace death. Surely she wanted more. Surely the brief hand-wringing at her funeral couldn't compensate her for oblivion.

*

As the press conference drew to a close, Brook took the opportunity to look around the packed media room. Their first briefing had been sparsely populated but then the Deity broadcasts had become an internet sensation and now, with the film of Wilson Woodrow's suicide to pick over, every national TV, radio and newspaper was represented and hungry for a story for the early evening news or next day's newspapers.

Brook was next to Charlton as question after question rained down about the death of Wilson Woodrow. Was he on drugs? Was he in love? Was he obsessed with death? Who was filming his suicide? Brook marvelled at how long it took Charlton to answer questions that required only a simple, 'We don't know.'

The speculation surrounding the three photographs purporting to show three of the missing students dead, had been batted away by Charlton. Although Brook had convinced him the shots were fake, Charlton stopped short of saying so, merely dismissing them as 'unsubstantiated and potentially misleading'. The FLOs dispatched to the worried families carried the same message.

Then questions switched to how the suicide of Wilson Woodrow could have been recorded, yet go undetected for over a week. Fortunately Charlton could deflect all such questions in the direction of Derby City Council.

Then a BBC journalist asked why the website hadn't been closed down.

'This is a question that is under constant review,' said Charlton. 'But we felt that with the plethora of social-networking sites available to carry such material, even for a short time, to close down one particular avenue for Deity broadcasts would .not only be pointless but would put our investigation at a disadvantage. We're sure the individual or group producing these films is aware of this.'

'Do you know where these uploads are being made?'

'I can't comment on that.'

'But is it true that you've interviewed a lecturer at Derby College responsible for setting up the Deity website?'

'I can confirm that financial details were fraudulently obtained and used to set up *Deity.com*. The individual to whom you refer is not – I repeat *not* – a suspect at this time. More than that, I'm not prepared to say.'

'So he was an unwilling dupe?'

'No comment.'

Brook tried not to smile imagining Rifkind's dismay at being so described.

'We saw a bewildering array of reports of teenage suicides in today's broadcast,' said a female journalist. 'Do you think whoever filmed Wilson's death was involved in those other suicides?'

Charlton looked across to Brook.

'It's extremely doubtful,' said Brook. 'Those deaths took place over several years and in different parts of the country. Obviously we can't rule it out, but I'd be more inclined to think that Deity is trying to claim credit for deaths that were way beyond its influence.'

'So you won't be adding those deaths to your inquiry?'

'Other forces are welcome to reopen those investigations, and if they uncover anything relevant to the death of Wilson Woodrow, we'd be happy to listen. We will only be looking at why some of those cases were selected for broadcast, not looking into the actual deaths, no.'

The questioning moved on and Brook was relieved and a

little surprised, that no one else had noticed the rogue picture of the unknown hanged boy.

'Still think we should let that website keep broadcasting?' asked Charlton when they'd reached the sanctuary of the Incident Room. Noble and Cooper were still there despite their early start that morning. 'Their output is starting to seriously impact on our ability to get things done.'

'It's your call, sir,' said Brook. 'But I'd say we've only got one or two more broadcasts at the most.'

Charlton looked at his watch. 'Let's hope so. Eight o'clock – nineteen hours until the next one. So what the hell are we going to see tomorrow?'

'You want me to answer that?'

'If you can.'

Brook considered for a moment. 'Best guess – more deaths.'

Charlton closed his eyes briefly. 'Go on.'

'Every broadcast has been an escalation of the last. Violence, sex and now death – the human experience right there. There's nowhere to go except more death.'

'Who?'

'Maybe Russell. Maybe all of them.'

'Why Russell?' said Charlton.

'He's the only one we haven't seen, who hasn't had his moment in the sun.'

Charlton nodded. 'Fake deaths?'

'I would hope so. And we may get a parting message. But it's important to Deity that nothing is resolved. Like *Picnic at Hanging Rock*, they want us to be talking about them years from now.'

'Fame at last,' said Noble.

'But if they follow the film to the letter it's going to end in death,' put in Cooper.

'That's what I'm afraid of,' said Brook.

'Or they pack it in and come home to soak up the attention,' said Charlton.

'I hope you're right,' replied Brook. 'But enduring fame without talent sometimes requires extreme measures. Some commit murder like Lee Harvey Oswald or Mark Chapman. Others die young or commit suicide.'

'And a nobody becomes a somebody,' muttered Cooper.

'Adele Watson's got talent,' pointed out Noble.

'Then let's hope she's in charge,' said Charlton.

'So much for just messing with our heads,' said Cooper absently.

Brook looked across at him. 'Unfortunately Wilson's death changes everything. Someone's realised that to make it stick you have to make the sacrifice. Sometimes to live forever, you have to die – for my generation Marilyn Monroe, James Dean, JFK. For these kids, it's . . . well, you know better than me.'

'And this isn't off the cuff,' said Noble.

'No.'

'Because the website was set up six months ago.' Charlton nodded.

'It's longer than that,' said Brook.

'What do you mean?'

'The newspaper reports of the suicides we saw in today's broadcast. They go back years,' said Brook.

'You told the press conference there was no connection,' said Charlton.

'There is and there isn't,' said Brook. 'But we think there's a suicide in Denbigh three years ago that may be linked to Wilson's. We're waiting for a call back.'

'To tell us what?' asked Charlton.

'Sir, someone's got a hold on these vulnerable kids, someone who doesn't belong, who's twisting what they want to his or her ends, someone who enjoys manipulating people to kill themselves, but not by bullying, by being a friend, by telling them they're doing the right thing. Telling them they'll be famous, that they'll live forever, telling them they're giants because they're taking control. That's what the website's for – to reach as many vulnerable people as possible and encourage them to do the same. It's a project, sir. A game, almost.'

'And the night of Kyle's party was D-Day,' said Noble.

'I think so. That's when it started. Jake McKenzie saw them that night. Kyle was filming. Adele and Becky were on the floor, their faces white, playing dead, practising their death masks.'

'I thought they were faking it for the broadcasts.'

'They were, John. And maybe they also thought it was a game and don't know what Deity's got in store for them.' Brook looked at the dark-eyed Adele Watson glaring at him from the display board. 'At least, some of them don't.'

DS Gadd burst into the room and hurried over to Charlton. 'Sir, we've got a lead on The Embalmer.'

'You've found the ambulance?'

'No, but we've got the same name three times in response to our facial composite. One of the sources works in the chandler's shop on site at Shardlow Marina. Lee Smethwick,' she read. 'Forty-four years old. He lives on a canal boat at the Marina. He works in catering for Derby Education, was formerly in the Merchant Marine and spent three years in

Egypt in the nineties working as an engineer – model employee apparently. Nothing flagged up from Interpol and there's no criminal record here. We're trying to rouse someone at the council to get a photo.'

'Sounds promising,' said Charlton. 'Let's go and get him. God knows, we need a result.'

'Derby Education?' echoed Brook. He spun round to look at the artist's impression of The Embalmer, picked up a sheet of A4 paper from the printer and held it across the forehead of the portrait. He smiled. 'A chef. That's why his face was wrong – his forehead was under a chef's hat.'

'You've seen him?' said Charlton.

'He works at Derby College – in the refectory. I was there with Yvette Thomson.'

'Small world,' said Charlton.

'We were all over that place yesterday morning.' Cooper sighed. 'He was right under our noses.'

'He wasn't there,' said Noble. 'The refectory was closed, remember.'

'Let's go get him,' said Charlton.

'Good hunting,' said Brook.

Charlton eyed him suspiciously. 'You're not coming?'

Brook glanced at the picture of Adele Watson and back at Charlton. 'It's not my case any more.'

'You've changed your tune.'

'My team have had a very long day, sir, and we're not finished yet. DS Gadd's in charge. If Smethwick's there, she'll bring him in.'

Charlton paused for a second longer. He'd never understand Brook. He walked out ahead of Gadd, who lingered briefly to nod her appreciation.

*

Brook slumped on to a chair and put his head in his hands to rub his eyes. Noble sat down and began to look over some papers. He yawned.

'Go home, John. Get some rest,' Brook told him. 'You too, Dave.'

The two detectives left and for something to do, Brook turned on his laptop to play around with more combinations for Russell's film poster.

The phone rang. It was a DI Gareth Edwards from North Wales Police.

'Is DS Noble there?'

'I'm DI Brook, his superior.' Brook quickly typed Denbigh into Google maps.

'Your Sergeant put in a call to ask about a suicide three years ago.'

'The unknown boy in Denbigh. You worked the case?'

'I did. I was only a DS at the time but it certainly made an impression. He was just a kid.'

'Well, his picture popped up on a website we've been monitoring.'

'Deity. You don't need to tell us. I think the whole country's picked up on it. We were going to call you anyway as soon as we saw it. Your Sergeant was right. The local paper didn't carry a photograph because we couldn't find any of him alive. We figured releasing a picture of his corpse was a step too far.'

'Especially at the end of a rope.'

'That's just it. The picture from the website couldn't have been circulated to the public because we didn't take it.'

'It wasn't one of your crime-scene shots?'

'Definitely not.'

'Why so sure?'

'Because the guy who found the body got him down and tried to revive him.'

'Who was that?'

'A local builder, walking his dog.'

'And he was never a suspect?'

'A suspect in what? The kid hanged himself. He tied a rope round his neck and jumped. Broke his neck instantly.'

'He couldn't have been pushed?'

'There was no bruising anywhere except his neck – I'll email you the autopsy. And two people couldn't have stood on the same branch of that tree . . .'

'So that picture was taken by someone who was actually there when he jumped.'

'That was our conclusion. The file's still open and we're taking another look but we're not hopeful because we never found out who the kid was.'

'Did you—?'

'We tried everything. No schools reported missing pupils. No parents reported missing kids. It's like he was a ghost. Fingerprints and DNA were a bust. And there didn't seem to be any dentalwork.'

'Did you try anyway? There would still be records even if his teeth were in mint condition.'

'Of course we tried. If he'd actually ever seen a dentist even to have his teeth X-rayed we might have found him. He had teeth missing but no fillings or any visible work. We came to the conclusion that he hadn't seen a dentist, certainly not in Britain.'

'So you thought he was foreign.'

'We didn't think anything. We had no facts. It was just another angle.'

'Were drugs involved?'

'No. The lad had a small amount of vodka in his system but not enough to get him drunk.'

'No sign of coercion?'

'None. He just climbed the tree, put the noose around his neck and jumped, as far as we could make out.'

'What time of day?'

'Mid-morning. On the bend of the River Elwy. It's a local beauty spot but it was cold and likely deserted. We never rustled up any witnesses who saw him alive.'

Brook stared at the map of North Wales. 'There's an orphanage in St Asaph's. Did you check there?'

'No.'

'But it's only about five miles from Denbigh.'

'The lad hanged himself three years ago. The orphanage was closed in 2003 – five years before.'

'I see,' Brook said. 'Can we get access to the boy's DNA?'

'I don't see why not.'

Brook expressed his thanks and rang off. He turned off the laptop and looked at his watch. Ten o'clock. He'd been up for nearly nineteen hours with only biscuits to sustain him. He walked to the door of the Incident Room but didn't leave. After a moment's thought, he returned to his desk and packed his laptop into its case and left the building.

Len Poole pulled his car to the kerb and parked under the shadow of a tree. He didn't know this quiet cul-de-sac on the Brisbane Estate, only that it was out of the way and Alice was unlikely to walk past and see his Jag in the dark. He took a deep breath and stared into the rearview mirror then straightened his comb-over with a pudgy hand.

'No more, Len. This is the last time. She's not nicotine.

You can kick the habit. You must kick the habit.' His yellow grin glinted in reflection. 'But not before I move back to Wales, you blackmailing bitch.'

He nodded to his reflection. All these years paying out like a fruit machine for a mistake any man could make – a temporary weakness that she'd exploited to the full. No more. Now he was in the clear he was going to fill his boots. He took a swallow from a bottle of mouthwash and stepped from the car, hitching his tracksuit on to his bulging waist to rearrange his genitals.

'Question is, can she kick the habit with me?' he chuckled to himself.

The fleet of cars were on silent approach after they turned off the London Road, past the village of Shardlow. DC Read parked his car to block the only road in or out of the marina complex, and got out to follow the other three cars moving quietly past a plot of static holiday cabins on the left. A hundred yards later, the plot gave way to a large basin which opened out into an expansive site with a car park, bar, shop and caravan park round to the left. The darkened marina lay dead ahead.

DS Gadd pulled to a halt when she saw a man signalling her with a torch. The other cars followed her lead and the uniformed officers, including Charlton, poured silently from the cars, easing the doors closed behind them.

'DS Gadd. Are you Henry Huff?'

'I am.'

'Any sign of Lee Smethwick?'

'Not seen him for a couple of weeks to be honest but then he never makes a song and dance. The lights are out but that don't mean he's not in there.'

'Lead on.' They turned to walk quietly towards the shadowy outlines of the canal boats. There were well over a hundred, a few showing lights, but most in darkness.

'Are all these occupied?' she asked.

'Oh no. It's Saturday night. There's not a whole lot to do round here. Most of these are part-timers – you know, Sunday boaters, holidays maybe.'

'Are all the boats...' Gadd searched for the right words '... seaworthy?' She heard the expulsion of amused breath from Huff and smiled. 'None of them are seaworthy, right?'

'No. But most can get out on the river if they're in a good state of repair.'

'And Smethwick?'

'Never seen him go out once and he's been here ten year.' Huff put a finger over his mouth and pointed to the dim hulk of wood and metal looming out of the darkness. Gadd turned and held out an arm to her colleagues. There was a locked gate across the walkway and Huff pulled out a set of keys and unlocked it. It opened without noise.

Gadd pointed at DC Smee who took three uniformed officers to the far side of the boat. She and the rest fanned out around the walkway. Charlton hung back to observe.

Gadd rapped on the door. 'Mr Smethwick – police. Open the door, please.' She listened before issuing a second summons. When that failed she backed away and nodded to the two officers carrying the Enforcer Ram.

Brook pulled to the kerb across from Yvette Thomson's house and killed the engine. Downstairs was in darkness but there was a light on in the bedroom. He reached over for his laptop and was about to open the driver's door when his mobile buzzed.

'DS Gadd, sir. We found Smethwick's boat. He's not been seen for a couple of weeks and it doesn't look like he's been on the boat in a while.'

'Anything to show he's The Embalmer?'

'Plenty. There's a lot of stuff about Egypt, books on embalming and something interesting you should see – except we're thinking we should stake the place out and wait for Smethwick to show.'

'You mean Charlton's thinking that.'

'Yes, sir.'

'What do you think?'

'That we should go through the place with a fine-tooth comb.'

'Did you find any surgical instruments?' asked Brook.

'No, sir.'

'What about the ambulance?'

'No one we spoke to has ever seen it.'

'Your instincts are right, Jane. He's gone and he's not coming back!'

'Gone where?'

'If he's taken his instruments, he's gone to wherever he takes his victims.'

Poole lay on his back, panting. Yvette climbed off him and put her head on his densely thatched chest. He nodded with satisfaction. 'Still got it.'

'You're a superman, Len,' said Yvette, trying to drum up some sincerity.

'You think?'

'I do.' She twirled his chest hair with a manicured finger. 'Len . . .'

'What?'

'Why don't we get married?'

Poole sat up. 'What?'

She pouted alluringly at him. 'It's not too late. We'd be perfect together,' she said in her most vulnerable voice.

'Marry you?' repeated Poole, this time with a hint of disbelief.

'It's the ideal solution, Len. Rusty's gone and I don't know if he's ever coming back, even if he's dead or alive. I'm lonely. I don't want to be on my own.' Poole declined to comment so Yvette lifted her head from his chest again. 'Can Alice do what I do for you?' She grinned at him and nuzzled at the wiry hair on his flabby breast. 'Well, can she?'

Poole pushed her away. 'No. That's why I'm here now.'

'Then why don't you marry me?'

'Because you're a mental bitch.'

Her face soured and she prepared a fist but was halted by a rap on the front door. She turned off her bedside lamp and tiptoed to a crack in the curtain.

'Who is it?' whispered Poole.

'It's Alice,' said Yvette with a sneer.

'You lying cow,' hissed Len Poole, pulling his underpants and tracksuit trousers on. 'Who is it?'

'It's Inspector Brook, if you must know,' she whispered from the window.

'At this time? What does he want?'

'How should I know? Probably the same as you,' she spat. 'A two-minute quickie.'

Poole looked daggers at her as he zipped his shiny tracksuit top to the neck. 'That was at least five, you cow. I looked at the clock. Is it really Inspector Brook?'

'See for yourself. That's his BMW.'

Poole crawled to the window. The knocking on the door sounded again. 'Shit. I'd better go.'

'Should I ring Alice and tell her you're on your way?'

Poole darted back from the bedroom door and grabbed her by the throat. 'Listen, you fucking whore, you go near my Alice and the game's up for you – and then there'll be a lot more coppers than Inspector Brook out there. Understand? *Understand?*' insisted Poole.

She nodded as best she could and Poole loosened his grip. Yvette massaged her neck and got her breath back as Poole darted out of the bedroom and down the stairs to the back door. He slipped out quietly and hopped over the fence at the back and scuttled away into the night.

Ten minutes later, Len arrived back at his car. The cul-de-sac was in darkness and he flicked at his key fob to unlock his car. The light in the cab of his Jaguar came on and Poole jumped on to the cracked leather of the driver's seat, enjoying the tackiness of recent conquest along his inner thigh. Mental or not, that bitch certainly knew all the buttons to push. He grinned at his reflection in the rearview mirror but, as he glanced back towards the ignition, he caught a movement out of the corner of his eye and looked back to the mirror to see a yellow-toothed grin flashing at him from the back seat.

Brook watched the light go out in Yvette's bedroom. He knocked one more time then returned to his car with his laptop. Maybe it was for the best. It had kept this long; it could keep for another night. He sent a text to Noble to prepare the ground for the next morning and set off through the estate towards the A52 for the drive to Alstonefield, the picturesque village about ten minutes from Brook's home in Hartington.

Thirty-five minutes later, Brook banged on the door of a small stone barn on the outskirts of the village. He hadn't needed the address given him by DS Morton, because Rifkind's sleek black Porsche, sitting on the flagged drive, had been visible from the main road. Brook inspected it as he waited. No answer. He knocked again and stepped back to look for a light. The place was in darkness – no sign of life.

'Mr Rifkind, I'm not a reporter, it's DI Brook. I know you're in there. I have a warrant for your computer and mobile phone.' Still no answer. 'If I have to come back we'll be breaking down the door.'

He traipsed back to his car, defeated. Rifkind's wife had obviously called him to expect a visit and he wasn't about to surrender his precious computer without a struggle.

Ten minutes later, near exhaustion, Brook dragged himself from his car and almost sleepwalked his way into his own dark cottage.

'Terri!'

No answer. No Terri. When he flicked on the kitchen light he saw the note.

Been out walking with Ray today.
You were right. Peaks beautiful.
We're in the Duke rehydrating (kind of).

T

Brook sighed and looked at his watch. It was past eleven o'clock. He was starving and his evening meal wasn't on the table. 'It's just not good enough,' he said, and smiled.

He left the cottage to walk down the hill to the village but caught sight of the pair staggering, arm-in-arm, back up the hill. He returned to the cottage and poured himself a glass of red from an open bottle then looked in the fridge. There was a bowl of cooked pasta from a few nights before. Brook gratefully swallowed three spoonfuls before the front door opened and Terri, singing badly out of tune, fell in.

'Mr Brook, you're here,' said Ray, helping Terri to a chair. He stood awkwardly, the baseball cap still glued back to front over his bleach-blond head.

'Actually it's Detective Inspector,' Brook replied tersely.

Terri squinted up in his direction 'Dad. You're here. Just in time for a drink.'

'You've had enough,' said Brook and Ray in unison.

Terri's head swayed between the pair of them, trying to focus. 'Don't be so mean,' she said. 'It's a celebration,' she smirked before hiccuping. 'Oops.'

'She needs to get to bed, sir – Detective Inspector, I mean.' 'Give me a hand, will you?'

Ray helped Brook hoist the mumbling Terri towards the sofa in the living room and place her down as gently as they could. She lost consciousness before they laid her out and Brook took off her shoes before ushering Ray back to the kitchen. Brook picked up Terri's handbag and helped himself to a much-needed cigarette.

'Is this your idea of a good time, Ray?' he said, opening the front door to exhale. 'Taking my daughter out and getting her drunk.'

'Sir, honestly, we've had a great day out on the hills and I'm whipped. I tried to leave three hours ago but Terri wasn't budging and . . . I couldn't just leave her there.'

After a moment, Brook nodded. 'I'm sorry. Thanks for staying with her.'

'No problem, sir. Where did your daughter learn to drink like that?'

Brook stopped raising the glass of wine to his lips and returned it guiltily to the kitchen table. 'She didn't get it from me.'

Ray smiled. 'It's okay. I've . . . er, had the full version at the Duke. And so has half the village, I'm afraid.'

'That bad?'

'That bad,' echoed Ray. 'And don't get me started on her swearing.' He shook his head. 'Terri's a great girl, sir, but she's certainly got . . . issues.'

'Issues,' repeated Brook, risking a Methodist's sip at his wine. He scraped back a chair and sat down. 'Take a seat, Ray.'

Ray sat, rather reluctantly.

'Drink?'

'No thanks, I'm driving.' He looked hesitantly at Brook. 'Who's Tony?'

Brook looked up from his glass, wondering if this was ground he wanted to cover. He decided to keep it simple. 'Someone Terri got close to,' he said after a moment. 'He died.'

'So I gather. Tel took it hard, didn't she? It can't have been easy.'

Brook declined to comment but took a larger gulp of wine.

'She's lucky to have you though, sir. You're her hero.'

'Hero!' exclaimed Brook. He looked into his wine glass. 'I don't think so. I haven't seen her for five years.'

Ray shrugged. 'You're her father, sir. You'll always be her hero. That's how it works.' He scraped his chair back against the slate floor. 'I must be off. Work tomorrow.'

'I thought it was half-term.'

'It is, but essays don't write themselves.'

Brook stood to see him out. 'Got any tattoos, Ray?'

'Tattoos? Not really my thing, I'm afraid. In my opinion, they're for people who don't have any personality. They get a tattoo so they'll have something to talk about. Why?'

Brook smiled and held out his hand to shake Ray's. 'No reason.'

Twenty-Four

Sunday, 29 May

BROOK FIDDLED WITH THE STRAP of his laptop case as he looked up at Yvette's bedroom window. The curtains were drawn. He checked his watch and knocked loudly on the glass door. After five minutes of rhythmic knocking, Brook heard footfalls and the door finally opened.

Yvette tried to focus on her visitor in the piercing light. Her black hair was tousled and her eyes sleepy as she tied the belt of a silk robe tightly round her waist. The curve of her breasts and her shapely legs were, as usual, available for inspection. 'Damen. It's Sunday morning. Do you know what time it is?'

'It's six o'clock,' said Brook helpfully. He removed his laptop from his shoulder.

'What the hell do you want?' She kept the door open enough to converse but no more. 'Have you found Rusty?' she said with sudden hope.

'No.'

'Then . . .' She looked annoyed but in a trice her manner

became flirtatious. 'You should ring next time, Damen. I might have had company.'

'Len!' shouted Brook at the top of his voice. 'You still in there?'

'Stop that,' she spat, looking round at neighbouring houses. 'What do you think you're doing?'

'Just checking,' explained Brook. 'I think he's gone now. He wouldn't risk a sleepover with Alice three streets away.'

She narrowed her eyes at him. 'What makes you think it would be Len Poole? I might have your Sergeant upstairs in my bed.'

'I don't think so.'

'Then you don't know men like I do, Damen. The Sergeant was very taken with me, don't you think?'

Brook was sombre. He couldn't lose sight of the fact that maybe Yvette was herself a kind of victim. 'He'll get over it.'

Her lip curled. 'So what do you want?' she said, cocking her head.

'I need to ask you about yesterday's Deity broadcast. It's important.'

Yvette's face hardened as she sought the excuse she needed but it wouldn't come. Instead she walked away from the door and Brook, uninvited, followed her into the sun-dappled sitting room.

'I haven't seen it,' she said, sitting demurely on the sofa.

'What do you mean, you haven't seen it?'

'Just that.'

'It was on the Deity website, it was on the news in the evening. Are you telling me that you haven't seen a piece of film that might have a bearing on your son's disappearance?'

She didn't reply. Instead she went to the kitchen. 'I'm making coffee,' she explained. 'Want one?'

'You're making coffee?'

She smiled sweetly at him. 'Got to start the day with a cup of hot coffee.'

'Is that what you did when you found your mother's body?'

Her eagerness to please vanished for a split second but resumed almost at once. 'I was only nine. And it was a can of Lilt back then.' Her eyes lowered in sadness. 'She left me on my own.'

'I'm sorry,' said Brook.

Yvette found her smile a second later. 'No use crying over spilled milk.' She breezed back to the kitchen.

'I brought Russell's computer back yesterday,' shouted Brook, looking around the living room. He spotted the laptop on a side-table still in the plastic bag he'd returned it in. He picked it up. 'Why didn't you watch the broadcast, Yvette? I want an answer.'

She appeared at the doorway. 'No sugar, right?'

'You're a mother. Your missing son could be on that film,' insisted Brook. 'The son you begged us to find.'

She looked right at him now, her lips quivering. 'Russell's not coming back. He's dead.'

'Russell!' exclaimed Brook. 'Did you say Russell?'

She hesitated. 'My son, yes.'

Brook smiled sadly. 'Your son is dead? How do you know?'

There were tears in her eyes. 'A mother always knows.'

'Of course she does.' Brook pulled Russell's laptop from the plastic and turned it on.

'Why are you turning that on? There's nothing on there. You said yourself.'

'The files on here were wiped but the software wasn't touched,' answered Brook.

Yvette looked at him, processing the information. 'I don't understand.' Her eyes suggested otherwise.

'Don't you?' The software loaded and Brook flicked his eyes around the desktop. 'Word, Recycle Bin, Help – and an old web browser. Is that all that's on here?' Yvette didn't reply. Brook clicked on the browser icon.

'It takes ages to load,' she said with a faint smile. 'It's really old.'

Brook nodded. 'I know,' he said softly. He turned to face her. 'But only yesterday you told us Russell was a film buff, that he spent hours filming and watching his films on a laptop.'

'I . . . er, that's right.'

'On this?'

No reply.

'I don't think he watched films on this piece of junk, did he?' Yvette didn't answer. 'He had another laptop.' Still no reply. 'An expensive one capable of uploading and watching films.'

Yvette stood up and smoothed down her robe. 'No, he used that one,' she said airily.

'Then show me the software,' said Brook.

'I don't know about that stuff.'

'I think you do. Where's the other laptop?' said Brook. 'And more importantly, where is Russell?'

She glared at him briefly before returning to the kitchen to pour two coffees. She placed one next to Brook with a coquettish smile. 'You did say no sugar.'

Brook's face was like stone. He swung his own laptop case from his shoulder and turned on his machine. He cued up the last Deity broadcast as Noble had shown him and swung the screen round to face her.

She glanced at the screen but didn't react. A moment later, Brook paused the broadcast on the picture of the hanged boy. Yvette's eyes widened. 'No, no, no!' she screamed and threw her coffee cup at Brook, who just managed to duck in time, though hot coffee scalded his hand. 'Leave us alone!' she wept, and leaped towards the front door. Brook had anticipated her and blocked her way so she turned and headed for the back door. Brook declined to follow, instead pulling out a handkerchief to cover his burning hand.

A few seconds later he heard more screaming, and a struggling Yvette was being restrained with some difficulty by Noble and PC Patel.

'Yvette Thomson. You're under arrest for the murder of Russell Thomson.'

Brook plucked the nearly new toothbrush from the cup and dropped it in the evidence bag. He jogged back down the stairs where Don Crump was waxing lyrical about his antipathy to early mornings.

'It's Sunday, for Christ's sake – middle of the night too, I mean, fuck me . . .' He stopped when his colleagues' eyes were drawn first to Brook on the stairs and then to their tasks. Crump turned to Brook, who handed him the evidence bag. 'What's this?'

'Yvette Thomson. DNA profile, please.'

'Is that all?'

'No. You can clear Russell's room of all the artefacts. I want them bagged and tagged,' said Brook, over his shoulder.

'What about his DNA? SOCO already looked, remember.'

Brook turned at the front door. 'You may have to separate it from other samples,' he said, 'but I'd try Mrs Thomson's bedroom.'

Crump rolled a lascivious eye to colleagues and in his best Kenneth Williams accent, said, 'Ooh, Matron!'

Cooper scrolled through all the texts on Yvette Thomson's phone as Brook and Noble looked on.

'Since the students went missing, Yvette's sent him fifteen texts. All asking where he is and when he's coming back and all increasingly desperate. All unanswered as were the thirty calls she placed to his mobile number. If she's faking it, it's pretty impressive.'

'Anything else?'

'You want to see her snapshots?'

'Why not?' said Brook. 'We might get a better likeness of Rusty.'

Brook placed the evidence bags and photographs on the table and turned on the recorder to announce the time, date, his own name and those of Noble, PC Patel and the duty solicitor, Roger Sands. Yvette Thomson sat perfectly still and stared into space. She seemed to be in a state of shock. 'State your name for the record, please.' No reply. 'Yvette.'

The solicitor touched her arm and Yvette looked up. She roused herself to think. 'Yvette Gail Thomson.'

'Have the charges been properly explained to you?' said Brook.

A pained expression infected her features. 'I did not kill my son,' she answered.

'But you accept that he is dead,' said Brook.

'Don't answer that,' said Sands.

Brook shot him a malevolent glance and picked up a picture of the hanged boy taken from the Deity broadcast and pushed it towards her. 'Is that your son?'

'You don't have to say anything, Miss Thomson,' said Sands. 'They have no evidence.'

'Is that your son, Yvette?' persisted Brook. 'Look at it.'

She darted a glance at the photograph then closed her eyes, forcing tears on to her cheeks. After several minutes of silence she finally answered. 'Yes. That's Russell.'

'Not Rusty.'

'Pardon?'

'Every time you referred to your missing son before this morning, you called him Rusty.'

'Well, I could hardly call him Russell, could I? Out of respect.'

'So Rusty is not your son.'

'Miss Thomson, I advise you . . .' began Sands.

'No.'

'He's your lover.'

'Miss Thomson . . .'

She hesitated but then said proudly. 'Yes.'

'Miss—'

'Keep quiet,' spat Yvette at Sands. 'I'll shout about our love from the rooftops if I want.'

Brook smiled at Sands. 'How long has Rusty been your lover?'

'Four years.'

'And Russell died three years ago, is that right?'

'When we – I – lived in Wales, yes.'

'Near Denbigh?'

'Briefly.'

'So you met Rusty the year before your son died.'

'Yes.'

'Where?'

Yvette smiled with remembrance. 'On the beach at Rhyl. Me and Russell were having a day out in the holidays. Rusty, this beautiful young man, just walked up to me with a strange smile on his face and sat in the sand next to me. I'll never forget what he said to me. He said, "I've found my soulmate." And he had.'

'Where was Russell when this was happening?'

'He was having a ride on a donkey.'

'This would be in 2007.'

'If you say so.'

'When Russell died the year after, how old was he?'

The tears started again. 'Fifteen.'

'And how old is Rusty?'

Yvette shook her head. 'I'm not sure.'

'You don't know?' said Brook, surprised.

'Older.'

'Well, how old was he when you met him?'

'Four years younger than he is now,' she sneered.

'You're telling me you don't know how old your lover of four years is?'

'Twenty? Twenty-five? Maybe older.'

Brook took a sip of water. 'I find it incredible that you don't know.'

Yvette shrugged. 'It never came up. We were in love. It wasn't important.'

'Never came up,' Brook repeated. Then: 'You're an orphan, Yvette. It must've been tough so I'll try not to judge.'

'What does that mean?' she growled at him.

'It means that everything that happens is all about you, isn't it? What you want. What you need.'

Yvette looked down at the floor, searching for a rebuttal. 'I . . .' She shook her head.

'What about Rusty's real name? Did that come up?'

Yvette took offence at Brook's tone and replied icily, 'He said it was Ian.'

'Surname?'

She shook her head, shamefaced. 'I don't know.'

'Did you ever see any ID – passport, birth certificate, driving licence?'

'Nothing.'

'How about credit cards?'

'Rusty has no use for money. He says it imprisons those who have it.'

'Does he? So you have no idea if his name is really Ian.'

'No.' She smiled suddenly. 'Rusty said he didn't exist before he met me. He really loves me, you see.'

'Why did you kill Russell?' asked Brook.

'I didn't kill him,' replied Yvette firmly. 'He killed himself.'

'But he was your son and you didn't report him missing. Why?'

'He wasn't missing. He was dead.'

'Then why didn't you contact the police to identify his body?'

'Because . . .'

'. . . they would've asked why you didn't report him missing,' said Brook before Yvette could answer. 'Your son has not had a decent burial. He has no grave to mark his passing. How do you feel about that?'

'Terrible,' she replied. 'What mother wouldn't?'

'Then why allow that to happen?'

'I didn't see the point of it,' she snarled at Brook.

'No use crying over spilled milk?' suggested Brook. No reply. 'Why did Rusty kill him?'

'Russell committed suicide. He did it of his own accord. Ian – Rusty – told me.' She began to cry. 'Russell was depressed. He was being bullied. Rusty just . . .' She closed her eyes, forcing more tears down her cheeks.

'What? Encouraged him?'

She nodded. 'I didn't know, I swear. Rusty told me later. He said it was for the best, that Russell would always be unhappy. He said he realised as soon as he met him that Russell was a soul in torment. Rusty – Ian – was just waiting for the right time to . . .'

'. . . help your son end his life,' said Brook.

She hung her head. 'Rusty's very persuasive. He could charm the birds out of the trees. He was Russell's friend, he supported him. He said it was for the best, best for Russell too. He was too sensitive to live; he'd always be in pain. That's how he put it. He said I shouldn't say anything. If the police got involved or found out who Russell was, then they'd make him a scapegoat and put him away, and . . .'

'. . . you'd be alone again.'

'Yes.'

'Why couldn't they identify his body? There wasn't even a dental record.'

'I took him to the dentist when he was small. The first time, he screamed the place down, wouldn't let the dentist near him. Nothing worked. I told you – he was sensitive, see?' She shrugged. 'I looked after his teeth best I could from then.'

'But why did nobody else know who Russell was or report him missing?'

'We'd just moved into the cottage two days before. Nobody knew us.'

'And that made it the right time for Rusty to carry out his plan,' observed Brook.

Yvette looked down at the table. 'We'd had to leave Prestatyn because Russell was being bullied. We hadn't even started the new school. Only the landlord knew I was in Denbigh and he never saw Russell. They'd gone out for a walk together. My two lovely boys.' She smiled wistfully, then her face hardened as she looked at the picture of the hanging. 'We left at the end of the month. Me and Rusty. The school weren't going to fret over a boy they'd never seen. Besides, if anyone asked, Rusty had become my son.'

'So your son, Russell, just ceased to exist,' concluded Brook. 'Why not just send Rusty to the new school instead of Russell?'

'I couldn't live there after what had happened. What sort of person do you think I am?'

Brook glanced up at Noble's expression of disgust. PC Patel was trying to keep a poker face. 'So you moved away again.'

'Yes.'

'And got rid of all the pictures of your son.'

'Rusty said I had to, if he was going to take Russell's place properly. He had to become him in every way. He was very good at it. He dressed like him, talked like him, picked up all Russell's mannerisms, pretended he was shy and nervous . . .'

'. . . but he was far from that,' said Brook. 'He changed your son from victim into bully. He couldn't help himself, could he? How ironic. He became just as much trouble to schools as Russell had been; only this time others were on the receiving end of *his* viciousness. And instead of verbal taunts and threats he used the computer.'

'There were some issues, yes.'

'Issues with your new son's behaviour that meant you had to keep moving around as much as before.'

'We didn't mind as long as we could be together, don't you see?' pleaded Yvette.

'Perfectly. You were so desperate and needy that you allowed your lover to kill your son.'

'You're making me sound like a monster.'

Noble snorted from his position at the back wall.

'Am I?' said Brook, flashing Noble an admonishing glance.

'You know you are. You're twisting everything. And I'm not stupid. I know that's how it looks but I'm really not. I was a good mother but Russell was dead,' explained Yvette. 'Don't you get it? I didn't know it was going to happen, but it did. There was nothing I could do to bring Russell back.'

'If there had been, would you have done it?'

Yvette fiddled with the hem of her skirt and absorbed the question. 'Of course.'

'Even if it meant standing up to your lover?'

'I'm a mother,' insisted Yvette. 'I would have done anything to protect my son.'

Brook was silent for a moment. 'Let's move on to your relationship with Len Poole.'

'What relationship?'

'You tell me,' said Brook. 'There's no reason to hide things now, is there?'

Yvette stared at him for a few minutes before coming to a decision. 'I suppose not.'

'Start by telling us when you first met him.'

'I was fourteen. He was at the orphanage.'

'St Asaph's School for Boys and Girls?'

Yvette smiled. 'Girls? I was never a girl. I was a woman. Everyone could see that. Len noticed me as soon as he arrived. He appreciated me, bought me little gifts and gave me money for clothes.'

'In return for sex.'

'Don't be disgusting,' she yelled, standing up. 'Do you think I'm a whore?'

'Sit down, please,' ordered PC Patel, placing her hands on Yvette's shoulders and pushing her firmly back into her chair.

'No,' said Brook steadily, when she'd calmed down. 'Far from it. You were under age. Len was an adult. He had a duty of care. Anything you felt pressured to do with him, no matter how severe or gentle that pressure, was the result of his criminal behaviour.'

Yvette's breathing returned to normal. 'He said he loved me.'

'Len?'

'Yes.'

'You had sex with him while you were at the orphanage,' said Brook quietly.

A pause. 'Not actually at the orphanage,' she replied. Brook looked at her, waiting. 'Yes,' she said almost inaudibly.

'Louder, please.'

'Yes,' she repeated, her face like thunder.

Brook glanced across at Noble, who left the room, his face set hard, concealing the merest hint of anticipation. *I'm going to enjoy ruining that Welsh pervert's life.*

'Detective Sergeant Noble has left the room,' announced Brook for the tape. He looked back at Yvette. 'You became pregnant at the orphanage?' She nodded.

'Please answer yes or no for the tape.'

'Yes.'

'Was Len Poole the father?' She lifted her head as though trying to remember. Brook assumed she was calculating if the knowledge still possessed monetary value. When she'd decided that it didn't, she was able to answer.

'Yes. Len was Russell's father.'

'And so you were able to persuade him that he should provide for you and Russell, in exchange for your silence.'

She was amused by Brook's diplomacy. 'Persuade, yes. I *persuaded* him that he owed me a comfortable living.'

'And he provided that living because if his paternity ever came to light, he would be ruined,' said Brook. Yvette shrugged as if only just realising. 'So wherever he moved, he would send for you and set you up in a place nearby.'

She smiled. 'Something like that.'

'And give you money.'

'Yes.'

'Cash?'

'Always.'

'Even after he married his late wife?'

'Len was aware of his responsibilities,' said Yvette carefully.

Brook paused before the next question. 'Did the sexual relationship continue after Russell's birth?'

'I'm not a whore,' repeated Yvette. 'I don't have sex for money.'

'Is that a no?'

'That's a no.'

'Because once you left the orphanage carrying his child, you had the upper hand in your relationship.'

She shrugged again. 'You could say.'

'But something changed recently, didn't it?' Yvette opened her mouth to speak but thought better of it. 'When I called last night, Len was at your house, wasn't he?'

She looked up, startled. 'How did you know?'

'I didn't. But I knew you had somebody with you and I suspected it was either Adam Rifkind or Len.'

She narrowed her eyes. 'You know about Adam?'

'Not for certain, but he called you Eve when we dropped in on his lecture. That automatically makes him a *special friend*.'

'It was only that one time at his holiday cottage,' she mumbled.

'So last night it was Len.'

'Yes.'

'You had sex with him?'

Yvette grinned at Brook. 'For what it's worth.'

'What does that mean?'

'It means that two minutes is all the old bastard can manage these days.'

'You don't sound very fond of him.'

'I hate him,' spat Yvette.

'Then why did you have sex with him?' No answer. 'He demanded sex, didn't he?'

Yvette looked down at the floor. 'Yes.'

'Why?'

'Because he's a dirty old man,' she replied sourly, looking at Brook with contempt. 'Like all men. Like you. Wherever I go you look at my body as if it belongs to you. Lusting after me. You, your Sergeant, Adam, that dopey kid Wilson. You only want one thing and you won't be satisfied unless you get it.'

Brook's expression was unmoved by the accusation. 'Does that mean you refused?'

The wind taken out of her sails, eventually she answered, 'No.'

'Because you didn't have the upper hand any more?'

A pause. 'No.'

'Because he knew about Russell's death.'

Yvette shook her head. 'No. He didn't know the first thing about Russell. Len wasn't interested and never had been.'

'But he knew something was wrong.'

Yvette sighed. 'Me and Russell bumped into Len from time to time as he grew up. Small towns – you couldn't help it.'

Brook nodded. 'But when you followed him to Derby six months ago, he knew Rusty wasn't his son.'

'Yes. After Russell . . . we tried very hard to make sure Len never saw Rusty and it worked fine until Len spotted him at Parents' Evening. He came to pick Alice up and Kyle introduced them. He knew straight away he wasn't Russell.'

'So what did Len do?'

'At first he threatened to stop the money, but then he seemed to change his mind. Said he was sorry, that he'd been hasty. A couple of days later he came round with the money, as usual. But instead of just dropping it off, he said he needed to use the bathroom.' She laughed. 'Well, Rusty was wise to that.'

'He was there?'

'No, Rusty was never at home, always out filming stuff in the streets. But he knew after meeting him that it wouldn't take Len long to look for proof he wasn't his father. And then . . .'

'No more money,' finished Brook.

'Right. So we were careful. Rusty's bedroom was a fake – his idea. His books, his posters – simple. *His* room but he never went in there, not once, so he couldn't leave DNA, hairs, that sort of thing.'

'So you set the room up to make it look like his.' Brook nodded.

'And when Len called we knew he'd be straight in there looking for DNA. Well, it used to be his job, didn't it?'

'And when he went to the bathroom he stole Rusty's toothbrush,' said Brook.

'No. Rusty wasn't stupid. He hid his toothbrush in the bottom of my knickers drawer.'

Brook picked up an evidence bag and placed it down in front of Yvette. 'This toothbrush?'

Yvette stared at it. 'Where did you find that?'

'Where you said. In your underwear drawer, in your bedroom.'

'In my bedroom,' she echoed.

'Is that Rusty's toothbrush?'

Yvette stared some more.

'Yvette.'

She looked up at Brook and nodded faintly.

'Please answer yes or no.'

'Yes,' she said.

'Thank you. Now this is where I get confused. If Rusty hid his toothbrush in your bedroom, how did Len get proof Rusty wasn't his son?'

'He didn't. But he did the next best thing.'

Brook stared at her for a moment, processing the information. 'Of course. He took your toothbrush instead. That's why you had to buy a new one.'

'Yes,' said Yvette.

'Len didn't need to prove that he wasn't Rusty's father, just that you weren't his real mother. And if you weren't Rusty's real mother then he *couldn't* be the father.'

'Sly old bastard. We didn't think of that.'

'But that still begs the question: if Rusty's bedroom was clean, how did Len get a sample of Rusty's DNA?'

Yvette shrugged. 'That I don't know.'

'Where is Rusty?'

'I don't know,' she repeated with more force. 'Everything I've told you about his disappearance is true. I haven't seen him since the day before Kyle's party. I don't know where he is. I wish I did. You've got my phone. You must know how many times I've tried to get in touch with him.'

Brook took the phone from the evidence bag and handed it to her. 'Show me a recent picture of Rusty.'

'I told you. We had to be careful. There aren't any pictures of him.'

Brook took the phone from her and, following Cooper's instructions, scrolled down several photographs until he had the one he wanted. 'Then who's that?' He turned the phone round to show Yvette the picture of the dark-haired boy with a small goatee beard. It had been taken three weeks previously.

Yvette gazed at the picture and smiled faintly. Her expression returned to neutral and she pushed the phone back to Brook. 'That's Philippe.'

'Philippe?'

'I called him Phil. He was an exchange student from Paris.'

'Was?'

'He went back to France two weeks ago. I met him at the college.' She smiled fondly. 'He's an orphan like me.'

'Is he a friend of Rusty's?'

'Rusty doesn't know him. He's a student, that's all. Rusty

435

was spending more and more time . . .' Yvette pursed her lips around the rest of the sentence.

'And did you sleep with Philippe?'

This time there was no tantrum. She sighed. 'He was nice to me.' She looked at her solicitor who picked up the baton.

'Is this relevant?' said Roger Sands. 'Is my client being charged with being friendly to her fellow students?'

Brook smiled. 'Sorry. Just trying to be thorough. Let's talk again about the boy filming on Exeter Bridge. You said you weren't sure if it was Rusty. Was that a lie?'

She nodded. 'I think it's him. He looked like Rusty, moved like Rusty.'

Brook sat back in the chair. 'Tell me about him.'

'I love him.'

'Don't tell me about you. Tell me about *him*,' insisted Brook.

'Don't you think we ought to take a break there, Inspector?' interjected Sands, the solicitor. 'My client has cooperated fully.'

Brook didn't take his eyes from Yvette as he raised his hand to halt the interruption. 'What about the other students? What do you think he's up to?' continued Brook.

'I honestly don't know,' said Yvette. 'But as soon as he arrived he latched on to that Adele Watson. She felt sorry for him at first but she's smart. She knew he had . . .' she paused, looking for the right words '. . . hidden depths.'

'So he became her friend.'

'Sort of.'

'Like he became Russell's friend?'

'What do you mean?'

'Do you think Rusty saw Adele as another soul in torment?

Do you think he's encouraging her to end her suffering? And Kyle? And Becky?'

'You think he enjoys it!' exclaimed Yvette.

'I do.'

'Rusty could be dead, for all you know. *He* could be the victim. Somebody could be hurting him as we speak.'

'You still protect him even though he's not coming back.'

'What do you mean?' she flared. 'He loves me. Of course he's coming back.'

'He doesn't love you any more, Yvette. That's why he gave you to us.'

'What are you talking about?'

'Three years ago he helped Russell kill himself then took photographs of his dead body. And when he decided the time was right, he included the picture of your dead son in the Deity broadcast for the whole world to see. He's moving on, Yvette.'

'No.'

'Was it jealousy? Couldn't he stand sharing you with Len? Or Wilson? Or Rifkind?' Brook studied her as she processed the information.

'It must have been a mistake,' protested Yvette. 'He wouldn't betray me.'

'He already has. How long do you think it took us to make the link? He knew we'd be doing background checks on all the parents. He knew we'd find the link with Len. He knew we'd spot the picture and work out that you were living in the area at the time of the hanging. He knew we'd get a sample of Russell's DNA to compare with yours. He's given you to us on a plate, Yvette, because he's done with you. Now, why don't you tell us where he is?'

Her eyes blazed. 'I don't know, I don't know, I don't know,' she screamed, sobbing furiously now.

Brook looked at his watch and then at Sands for the first time. 'Now we can take a break.'

'Do we believe her?' asked Charlton, staring at the monitor showing Yvette Thomson, head in her hands, in the Interview Room.

'I think so,' said Brook, draining his tea. 'Don't forget she rushed down to the river when Len told her we'd found a body. She wouldn't have done that unless she thought it might be Rusty. And if she'd had anything to do with Wilson's death she wouldn't have set foot near the place.'

'So what are you thinking? This fake Russell Thomson is responsible for all this?'

'He's the fox in the henhouse, sir. He doesn't belong. He's not a teenager and he's not vulnerable. But everyone he meets who is disposed to suicide is at risk from him.'

'And Wilson?'

'My guess is he went to pester Yvette for sex after the assault on Kyle. Rusty was filming the assault and must've followed him. Somewhere along the line, Rusty got hold of him and got into his head. And then he killed himself.'

'Softened up with drugs?' asked Charlton.

'We get the autopsy results today. But I'm betting he was. By all accounts Wilson was too stupid to be vulnerable otherwise.'

Charlton blew out his cheeks. 'Why's he doing this, besides messing with our heads?'

'Rusty?' Brook thought about it for a second. 'The short answer – fun.'

'And the long one?'

'It's about control,' said Brook. 'Taking power from others gives him a control he needed in his early life but never had. Persuading people to kill themselves puts him in charge of his destiny – and others'. Maybe Yvette's son *was* the first. But after that he got a taste for it.'

Charlton sighed and looked at his watch. 'Four hours to the next broadcast. What are we charging Yvette with?'

'We're holding her under the murder warrant at the moment until the DNA checks are done.'

'But you don't think that will stick.'

'Do we really want it to?' said Brook. 'I mean, she's almost as much a victim as her son.'

'I know, but *Assisting a Suicide* or *Allowing the Death of a Child* hardly seems sufficient,' replied Charlton.

'No charge does. Reserve your anger for Leonard Poole, sir. Noble's picking him up now.'

'No Sergeant Noble today?' asked Dr Petty.

'We're a bit stretched at the moment,' said Brook with a smile. 'Don't worry. He's working.'

'That's no comfort for my loss of a Sunday lie-in.'

'No. We appreciate it, believe me,' replied Brook, deep in thought.

'Glad to hear it.' She held his gaze a moment, waiting for more concrete evidence of his appreciation but Brook was oblivious. 'So, Osiris, eh? Some people are never happy in their own skin. And making sure he has a few helpers in the afterlife – seems logical when you think of it like that. Any news?'

'He won't get far. Not that he wants to. He's digging in somewhere.'

'Here we are. Phencyclidine,' she read. 'PCP or angel dust on the streets. Wilson had high levels in his bloodstream and would've been prone to hallucination and in a severe dissociative state.'

'So – easily handled or manipulated.'

'Very suggestible,' agreed Petty. 'But even without someone egging him on, anything is possible. There have been numerous cases of suicides, self-mutilations . . .'

'Anything else of note?'

'Yes. I skipped breakfast this morning and I'm starving.'

At that moment Brook's mobile began to vibrate. 'John.' He listened for a moment. 'I'll be right there.'

'Rain check?' ventured Petty.

Instead of staying to ask if she was American, Brook raised a hand in acknowledgement and headed for the door.

Brook stood staring at the Jaguar. 'Len's precious Jag, not even locked.'

'The keys are in the ignition.'

'You've tried his house and Alice's.'

'No sign. She hasn't seen him.'

Brook moved round to the driver's door and peered inside. He took out a handkerchief and opened the door and examined the cracked leather seat. 'You're right. It's blood. You checked the boot?' Noble answered with a mocking eyebrow. 'Sorry.'

'You thinking what I'm thinking?' asked Noble.

'That maybe someone was waiting here for him and took him.'

'But who? Yvette?'

'She had motive and plenty of opportunity,' said Brook.

'But if she was going to abduct or attack him she could have done that at her house and she wouldn't have had to sleep with him first.'

'Who then?'

'Only one other candidate,' answered Brook. 'Rusty.'

'Why?'

'Because he does have feelings for Yvette and he wants to even the score for her. Wilson's been dealt with . . .'

'. . . and now Len's stopped paying the bills, he's expendable,' finished Noble.

'Get a team over here. Have you canvassed?'

'Not yet.'

'Get Cooper to help you.'

'Not your skill set?' teased Noble.

'I promised Gadd I'd run my eye over Lee Smethwick's boat.'

Twenty-Five

BROOK PARKED NEXT TO THE Scientific Support van and stepped from the car. The sun was shining and the Trent sparkled invitingly. He checked his watch – two hours until the next broadcast, maybe the final one – then stepped under the police tape. A watching elderly couple billed and cooed their excitement at living so close to a potential crime scene and gaped at Brook in wonder, as though he were the star of a film première.

'Sir.' DS Gadd beckoned Brook on to the narrow boat.

'Jane. Found anything?'

'A treasure trove of evidence – he's got books about Egyptian funeral rites, Ancient Egyptian gods, embalming, mummification . . .'

'All circumstantial – anything linking him to the vagrants?'

Gadd shook her head. 'Not yet. He knew we were coming. There's no paperwork and no hint of where he might have gone. Maybe Forensics can turn something up.'

'You've worked up his background?'

'Yes, sir. Lee Smethwick. Forty-four years old. Originally from Bradford. No wife, no children, no living relatives. He's widely travelled with the Merchant Marine but that was nearly twenty years ago. One thing – Smethwick has lung cancer and he found out six months ago that it was terminal.'

'Sounds like a trigger.'

'He's got a year at most.'

'The same as most of his victims,' said Brook. 'No criminal record, you said.'

'No.'

'Work record?'

'Varied. He doesn't seem to stay in jobs longterm. He's worked as a chef at Derby College for the past year and before that, cooking at various pubs. He did a turn at Rolls-Royce ten years ago. Not in the kitchens though. He's a qualified engineer, which may explain something we found on the boat.'

'Show me.'

She ushered Brook through the only door. The boat was sparsely furnished befitting the single male – a shelf of books, a sofa which doubled as a bed, a small television, a stove and a tiny galley. Dominating the middle of the cabin was a table with a scale-model of some kind of building on it. Gadd walked over to it.

'A model of a building,' said Brook.

'Yes, sir, but here's the interesting part.' She pointed at a doorway on the model which had a small rectangular piece of stone balanced on its end in front of it. The stone was held up by an intricate web of string which was trapped under another small block of stone, itself balanced over a hole. 'Watch.' Gadd removed a pin from a small hessian pouch, containing sand. The sand began to trickle out into the hole beneath the second stone. As the hole filled, the pressure of the rising sand increased on the second stone until it was lifted sufficiently to allow the string to be freed, thus lowering the first stone across the doorway. 'Wherever he is, we think Smethwick may be intending to seal his victims inside the building.'

'As well as himself.'

'Sir?'

'The Ancient Egyptians sealed burial chambers from the inside,' said Brook. 'To thwart grave robbers. Usually a priest would sacrifice himself along with hundreds of slaves, who would then accompany the Pharaoh to the afterlife to do his bidding.'

'Ah. That explains the film poster,' she said, nodding behind Brook's head. 'I Googled it and it's about precisely that.'

Brook turned. His eyes swept around the room until they alighted on the poster for a film starring a young Joan Collins. Brook's mouth fell open. *Land of the Pharaohs*. He checked the spellings in his head. There was no mistake.

Len Poole woke with a bad back and a splitting headache. He raised his head gingerly to look over at his bedside clock. It wasn't there. Then he remembered. The clock was at his bedside but he wasn't.

He moved his left arm but knew without looking that his watch was gone and he dropped his head back with the thud of a ripe melon. Shockwaves of pain surged through his skull and he reached delicately back to feel the bruising and what felt like dried blood matted in his hair.

Day or night, he couldn't tell – just that it was black as pitch wherever he was. He moved his hands around his head and massaged his neck where most of the pain was centred. Then he felt around his immediate surroundings – his bed was hard and unforgiving. He sat up and felt around some more. He was lying on cold tiles on some kind of raised plinth. He could hang his leg off the side and just touch the floor.

Poole lifted his head again, this time ignoring the pain. He swung his legs down over the edge of the slab and held out his arms like a blind man to feel his way through the blackness. A few yards away he stubbed his toe against a hard object and felt the cold tiles of a similar plinth to his own. He groped his hands warily around the slab. Something covered in cloth lay on it. He shrank back – his muscle memory told him it was a body.

He took a breath and felt again. He found the hands crossed on the chest. He felt for the face and rubbed his fingers together after touching it. Some kind of waxy substance had transferred itself from the skin. There was a hint of perfume. Poole guessed it was some form of mortician's preservative or cream mixed with cosmetics for use in embalming bodies. He was in some kind of mortuary, a house of the dead. He knew about those. What worried him most was that he had his own slab.

He realised with a feeling of dread that he must be in the lair of The Embalmer, the sicko he'd read about in the papers, fighting in vain for space with the Deity case. There'd been an appeal at the end of a Deity press conference and they'd shown an artist's impression. The man who'd attacked him must be The Embalmer and this was where he did his grisly work.

Poole damped down the rising panic – he had to find a light. Groping his way around the cadaver, Poole's left foot and knee hit something heavy. It fell with a smash and a splash and Poole fell with it, landing in a foul-smelling unction of soft spongy matter which covered his hands and knees.

A second later the smell of rancid meat and pungent salts hit his nostrils, followed by something far worse – the knowledge of what he'd fallen in.

In his fever to get away, his hands slipped on soft, slimy objects which he realised were organs. He cast them away as he scrabbled backwards from the stench – kidneys, lungs maybe, and the shape and texture of the intestine was unmistakable. Worse, as he scrambled for distance between himself and the viscera, the intestine wrapped itself around his feet until he could wriggle his way no further without unravelling the offending gristle from his ankles.

He tried to hold back the rising dread but now he screamed long and loud – to no avail. And when he fumbled his way, hands and knees across the slimy floor, broken shards of pottery lacerated his leathery palms.

Finally he sat motionless amongst the stinking wreckage of a former human being, trying to protect his damaged hands and sobbing as the vile moisture began to soak through his tracksuit to his buttocks.

Brook fumbled for his phone on the narrow deck. As he plucked it from his pocket, it began to vibrate.

'John.'

'Sir, we've found a witness who saw what happened to Len last night. We were right. He was abducted.' Brook received the information without answering. *'Are you there, sir?'*

'I'm here, John.'

'And you'll never guess what the abductor was driving.'

Brook emitted a short, noiseless laugh. 'Was it an ambulance, by any chance?'

There was a pause at the other end before Noble rejoined, *'How do you do that?'*

'It's one case, John. Smethwick and Rusty. They're working together.' Brook closed his eyes and shook his head. 'Live

Forever. They're going to embalm those kids and then they're going to mummify them. Like Tutankhamun. The tramps were just practice so they could do a good job on their perfect young bodies.'

'*And Len?*'

'Not sure, but Poole's a pathologist. Maybe they need him for some reason.'

'*He might still be alive then. How did you find out?*'

'I found the missing poster from Rusty's bedroom. *Land of the Pharaohs*. It's about sealing a dead Pharaoh safely in his tomb. Rusty knew it would tip us off so he took it down and gave it to Smethwick to keep. It's hung on the wall of his canal boat.'

'*Jesus. What do we do?*'

'We find them before it's too late.' Brook rang off. *They're dead, you know*. Gadd was suddenly beside him. 'Did you catch that?' She nodded. 'Find out everything there is to know about Smethwick. Everything. I don't care how far back you go. He's near and we've got to know where he's gone because that's where Adele and the others are.'

Poole sat with his head bowed, trying to block out the stench of human remains with the bloody handkerchief tied around his face. It wasn't that he hadn't experienced such smells before, just that he'd always done so in the relative comfort of his air-conditioned, temperature-controlled Pathology lab.

Here, in the darkness, he tried to shut down all the senses he didn't need, keeping his eyes closed and relying on his ears for sensory input. Unfortunately they registered every squelch as he shifted his position. But then his ears told him that he might have a bigger problem than the odour of human remains. Rats.

He heard them first. Only one, then another and then another darting around to investigate the smorgasbord of offal that Poole's clumsiness had provided. His hearing became supercharged, picking up every scurry, every squeal as the rodents went about their foul business gnawing on the bloody banquet. There were other sounds that kept him alert, gave him hope. He'd heard a distant rhythmic thud from time to time that seemed to come from the bowels of the earth. It suggested some kind of building work in progress though it never lasted more than half an hour.

He also fancied he could hear someone groaning, but not out of pain or fear but the effort of some unknown hard labour. This was always followed by a hacking cough. At least someone was near, and this gave him hope.

Training his ears on his immediate situation, however, didn't bring comfort. The increasing volume of curious rodents confirmed his worst fears and he pressed himself nervously against the cold wall. First contact was when he felt a nuzzling against his trousers and kicked out, giving rise to an intense screech that only served to amplify the sense of urgency amongst the other bustling rodents, dashing this way and that. Something ran across his hand and he pulled them both across his chest for protection, but still they kept coming. Another ran up his leg and showed no disinclination to get off until Poole flung a hand in its direction, receiving a nip on the knuckle for his trouble.

'Please God. Not like this. I don't deserve it. Please.'

To his horror a rat then dropped down on to his head and squealed loudly when Poole battled to disentangle it from his wiry thatch. Enduring the bites, he grappled with its slick furry body and quick tail, trying to get a grip before extricating its talons from his tonsure. Finally his grip locked and he flung the beast against the far wall with a piercing shriek. The rat's colleagues, however, were not discouraged and Poole became increasingly frantic as four, five, six of them mounted their challenge for fresh meat.

'Please God.'

At that moment a large vertical bar of dazzling white light opened on to Poole, widening rapidly to illuminate the stark and bloodied vault in which he sat. The rats scampered back to the sanctuary of dark corners and Poole felt emboldened to scramble to his viscera-flecked feet, gazing all the while at the radiance beyond. The intensity of the light dipped as a figure with an elongated head stepped in front of the beam. For a split second, Poole wondered if he were encountering an alien.

'God is listening, Anubis,' said a man's gravelly voice. Poole saw a hand held out towards him holding a shepherd's crook. 'Fear not, mortal. I wear the Atef Crown of Osiris. Come.'

'Do we know if it's the same ambulance?' asked Charlton back in the Incident Room.

'Not for sure,' said Brook. 'But it is.'

'But if they changed the number-plates, it's not going to get picked up, is it?' snapped Charlton. He looked at his watch. 'Five minutes to broadcast. You think Rusty met Smethwick at college?'

'Where else?' said Brook.

Cooper and Noble walked through the door and marched over. 'Mrs Mansell, three doors down,' said Noble. 'We don't have a photograph yet but we showed her the composite. She got a good look at the guy and she's certain it's Smethwick.'

'What happened?'

'Not sure. She noticed the top of the ambulance driving into the cul-de-sac. It was dark so she went upstairs for a better view and saw Smethwick closing the back doors. A couple of minutes later he drove away and this morning she noticed Len's Jaguar parked in the street. She didn't see Len.'

'Did she get a number-plate?' said Charlton. Noble shook his head. 'What about CCTV?'

'None,' said DS Morton.

'But once we knew The Embalmer might be involved with the students, we looked at roads surrounding the Brisbane Estate for the night of the party and found an ambulance parked at the bus stop on Western Road near the new housing development. There's a CCTV camera. It's some way off but you can definitely see people getting into the cabin around four a.m. on Saturday morning. The techs are trying to enhance it, but . . .'

'At least we know we were right,' said Brook. 'They must have walked to Western Road through the fields at the back of Kyle's house.'

'And then where?' said Charlton.

'When we know that, we find our students,' said Brook.

'We're rechecking all CCTV for the night of the party,' said Morton. 'Assuming the ambulance had the same plates as when Inspector Brook was attacked, if there's any sighting we get an approximate location.'

'Keep on it.'

'DS Gadd and her team are digging into Smethwick's past,' said Brook. 'Assuming Rusty Thomson's not local,

Smethwick's background gives us our best chance to find them.'

Without waiting for a second invitation, Poole skidded towards the light with only the briefest wary glance at the gore on the floor around him. As he drew near he was able to see the shadowy outline more clearly. The figure didn't have an elongated head but wore some kind of white headdress with feathers on the side. His legs were tightly bound and encased in a slim-fitting white robe, held in place by a long trailing sash wrapped around his waist.

As the figure turned and shuffled back to the light, Poole caught a glimpse of the man's hands and face. They were dark green. He wore green knitted gloves on his hands and what appeared to be thick make-up on his face and neck.

Poole hesitated. 'What the fuck is going on?' The scratch of a rodent's talons on the concrete floor induced a nervous glance behind him and he hastily skipped after his saviour.

'Let me out of here,' he demanded. He looked around for a weapon but saw nothing suitable. He considered rushing him, but his bizarrely dressed captor looked tall and powerful. Poole hoped there'd be a better opportunity.

Through two more large white-tiled rooms they travelled, the stranger not looking back once. At the entrance to a brightly lit third room, Poole could hear the whine of a generator. His green guide turned and ushered him into a large dome-like space at the centre of which was a sunken white-tiled dry pool, surrounded by a wooden rail. Too small for swimming, Poole guessed it was some kind of treatment pool. High windows at the top of the dome allowed Poole's first glimpse of natural light – the sun was shining.

In the middle of the dry pool lay a large empty sarcophagus. It looked extremely sturdy. At the base stood a large jar with a heavy stoneware lid, much like the one Poole had kicked over in the darkness a few rooms away. It was empty. To one side stood a hefty wooden table. Next to it was a large copper tank with two tubes attached. With a sinking heart, Poole realised it was for draining and storing the blood from a corpse. Next to the large table was a smaller table on which sat a loaf of bread and two wine glasses. There was also a variety of surgical instruments, most of which he recognised. He picked up a bone cutter and brandished it.

'Ra smiles on us, Anubis,' said Osiris.

'Let me out of here,' snarled Poole.

His captor stood, arms folded, before him – in one hand the crook and in the other some kind of whip or flail. His eyes were closed as though in prayer and when he opened them, the bloodshot whites of his eyes were picked out in stark contrast to the dark make-up covering every inch of his face and neck. Poole fancied he recognised the man in his rearview mirror.

'Think you're going to cut me up and dump me in the river, sicko?' growled Poole, mustering some aggression. *Over my dead body*, went unsaid. 'Let me out of here.'

'Fear not, my subject. I mean you no harm.' Osiris raised his face to the heavens to intone with great solemnity: 'Geb, Nut, Father of the Earth and Mother of the Sky, I prepare to join you in the Underworld. Horus, my son, I call on you to continue my work in this world as I . . .' At that moment, the man fell into a violent coughing fit which ended with him covering his mouth with a white-robed sleeve. When he pulled the sleeve away, Poole saw blood there.

'What the hell's going on?' demanded Poole, advancing on the man. 'You abduct me in the middle of the night and bring me here. How dare you? Let me go.'

The green face returned to the horizontal and the man glared at Poole. 'I am Osiris, insect, and I dare to bring you to this holy place.'

'What place? Where are we?'

'We are at the Ibu, Anubis.'

'Ibu? Anubis?'

'The place of purification where I must prepare for my journey. Come, Anubis, eat.' Given his almost bound legs, the man walked as best he could over to the table bearing the food. Poole readied the bone cutter.

Osiris waved a hand at the loaf and the bottle. 'Sacred barley for your sustenance. Wine for your thirst.'

Poole screwed up his face in disbelief. 'You don't expect me to touch that, do you, you fucking fruitcake? Now let me out.'

'Unless you join me in a sacred meal, Anubis, you will never look upon Ra, the Sun God, again.' Poole hesitated, tight-lipped, gripping his weapon. 'Fear not. The food is blessed.' Still Poole stared until Osiris could be patient no longer and snarled at his guest in the broadest Yorkshire accent: 'Fucking eat summat or you'll get my khopesh up your arse.' He reached under his garments, drew out a large sickle-shaped sword and brandished it above his head. It glinted in the muted sunlight and Poole shrank back. 'Eat, I command you.' Osiris regained his composure and smiled beatifically, a better argument occurring to him. 'Or would you prefer to return to the first chamber and the shelter of Apep's black cloak?'

Poole slowly approached the table. He picked up the loaf,

all the while watching the bizarre figure before him. He tore off a corner of bread without breaking his gaze and chewed half-heartedly. Osiris smiled his approval. After the first wary mouthful Poole realised how hungry he was and tore off some more. Osiris picked up the bottle and made to pour it into two glasses. Poole's eye was drawn by a colourless crystal substance resembling sugar in the bottom of one of the glasses. He stiffened and raised the bone cutter.

'No wine for me.'

Osiris smiled and poured wine into the clean glass and placed it next to Poole who didn't pick up the glass until Osiris showed him the sword again. Poole took a wary sip. Osiris then poured wine into the other glass and stirred the liquid with a hooked brass rod from the array of surgical tools. When the crystals had dissolved, the man raised the glass to make a toast.

'Anubis, God of Embalming, you bestowed your gifts upon me and now I return them with thanks. Use your skills, Jackal-headed One . . .' He coughed heavily for a few moments then grinned through bloody teeth. 'And prepare me for immortality.' He declined to drink and instead laid the large sword on the floor and clambered on to the wooden table. He took off his domed crown and lay on his back then rummaged under a sleeve and exposed Poole's wristwatch.

'It is time.' Propping himself on an elbow, Osiris swirled the dark red liquid around his glass and drained the contents in one gulp. 'I shall await you on the other side, Anubis.'

He lay back down but sat up almost immediately, his broad Yorkshire accent to the fore again. 'Oh, and don't go kicking *my* guts around t'floor, you clumsy bastard,' he snapped. 'I'm already a servant down, thanks to you.' A second later he was overcome with serenity once more and lay back.

Poole stepped nearer the green-faced man then made a grab for the misshapen sword. 'You fucking weirdo. What's going on? How do I get out of here?' But already the man's eyes were rolling back in his head and his breathing had begun to grate. The empty glass threatened to break from his green-fingered grip and Poole rescued it and raised it to his nose. 'Potassium cyanide? Jesus.'

Poole felt for a pulse around the neck but couldn't find one. He grabbed Osiris by the shoulders and shook him violently. 'How do I get out of here?' he screamed. His voice was flung around the tiled walls. 'Tell me.' A moment later, he lowered the man's shoulders on to the table. He was dead.

Len ran back through the other chambers, looking all the while for doors or windows. The only doors led to other rooms and the only windows were too high and filled in with bricks, or boarded up. Next to the chamber with the rats, Len found another door but although it wasn't locked he couldn't budge it. It was blocked on the other side. He banged on it and hacked at it with the sword, screaming for help but heard no answering cry save his own, echoing through the building.

Reluctantly he returned to the dry pool. At least there was light here. He decided to finish the loaf to keep his strength up and began to chew while he considered his options.

A sudden noise spun him round and he trained his eyes on a darkened corridor which led away from the pool chamber. Although it was dark, Poole could just make out the doorways of other rooms opening off the unlit passage. He turned and took a pace towards the blackness. 'Who's there?'

'Len,' whispered a voice from the shadows. 'Is that you?'

*

'Sir' shouted Cooper, nodding to the large screen. The Deity broadcast was about to begin. Someone switched off the lights and the room fell silent. The countdown reached zero.

Becky Blake sat on a wooden chair in a bare white-tiled room. There were no windows visible and the light appeared to be artificial. The time and date display showed the film had been shot on the Sunday after the party at five o'clock in the evening. Becky wore a long white robe with a V-neck. She held a piece of A4 paper in her hands but didn't look at it. Brook could make out a couple of paragraphs of handwritten text on the sheet.

Becky grinned enthusiastically at the camera but then made an effort to get her excitement under control. 'I'm Becky Blake. I'm eighteen years old. I want to say goodbye to my mother and father and to my best friend Fern.' She hesitated then glanced down at the paper. 'The world is a terrible place and I don't want to see any more of it. I'm looking forward to a different reality. You won't see me again but please don't mourn. Time to die.' The shot ended with Becky gazing earnestly into the camera, trying to suppress a smile. Then she reached off-screen for a glass and, after a quick swirl, downed it in one.

A few seconds later, Kyle sat in the same chair in the same room and seemed to be wearing a similar robe to Becky. The display showed the same date but ten minutes later than Becky's monologue.

Kyle was nervous. He licked his lips and flexed his swollen jaw, looking hesitantly at whoever was holding the camera. At an unseen signal he nodded and began. 'My name is Kyle Kennedy. I'm eighteen years old and come from Derby. I want to say goodbye . . .' For a moment, emotion paralysed his vocal cords. He cleared his throat and looked back up into the lens. 'I want to tell my mum goodbye and that I love her. Dad, I'm sorry I wasn't the son you wanted. I didn't choose this path. If I had, I would have chosen to be gay in a more understanding place.'

He gathered himself before continuing. 'I'd like to say goodbye to Jake.' Again he paused and looked away. 'The ten-ton truck is here, Jake, and I'm standing in the middle of the road. Goodbye, Morrissey. I love you.' He prepared to stand up but relaxed back on to the chair and, almost as an after-thought, added, 'Time to die.' He reached for his own glass . . . then downed the contents.

Brook's heart began to beat faster as Adele Watson appeared on the screen. The scene was shot in the same format as the others, fifteen minutes later than Kyle. Adele Watson sat confidently on the chair and gazed mockingly into the camera. Her dark eyes reached across cyberspace and burned into Brook's. He could see from her manner that she meant business, her thin smile almost scornful in its superiority. She wasn't to be cowed and wouldn't shrink from the path she'd chosen – Adele was totally in control.

'Hello, faceless voyeurs. I hope you're all enjoying the show. I'm Adele Watson and I've existed for eighteen excruci-ating years in a little backwater of Hades called Derby. Don't worry, it's not long to the money shot – what you've all been waiting for. But first I need to ask a favour. I need all you good people to take a moment after you've witnessed our humble sacrifice and think about what we're about to do because it's not selfish. We do this for you. We go willingly for the chance to speak to you, to show you that the world is fucked and we want no part of it.

'Look around, citizens. What do you see? Does it make you happy? Everywhere your eye falls, man is gorging himself on the planet. The animals, the oceans, the soil, the weak, the poor, the downtrodden – shit, even the air particles we breathe are being fucked over so a few members of a sad and lonely and unhappy elite can feed on what's left of our ailing world. If this elite were aliens, we'd organise, we'd resist and we'd fight with our dying breaths. But whilst our world is being raped, we do nothing. We scuttle around doing their bidding, making their lives richer and the planet poorer. And do we protest? No. Do we rise up? No. Instead, we struggle blindly on and hope they'll leave us alone or if we're really good boys and girls, let us join their club.

'And the membership card? Money. You remember that stuff. Course you do. You've all had some, you've all wanted more, so you can buy stuff you don't need and which won't make you happy. But that doesn't stop you. Obviously you haven't bought enough stuff. Must try harder. That nagging doubt where your soul used to be has to be driven out. Work more, eat more, buy more. The pursuit of happiness depends on it.'

Adele smiled into the camera. 'Our gluttony knows no bounds. But will it mean we can live forever? No. Our corporeal existence will end and our memory will be held in the minds of those who come after us. How do you want to be remembered, friend? As a heartless rich bastard who climbed over others to reach the sunlight – or as a doer of good works? Be forgotten in hate or revered in love? Decide now. Make a stand before it's too late. You have the power. Goodbye parents, goodbye world. Remember me as one who cared. Time to die.' She threw the contents of her glass into her mouth without breaking her gaze to camera.

The screen blackened and Brook blew out his cheeks. There was silence in the crowded room.

'No Rusty,' muttered Brook.

'Rusty?' said Charlton. 'But he's the fox in the henhouse. You said so yourself.'

'He is,' replied Brook. 'But he can't be certain we know that. Why isn't he keeping up the pretence that he's a victim too?'

Cooper went to hit the lights but before he reached the switch another piece of footage began.

It was night. Becky Blake was framed in the light of her bedroom window, naked. The camera was lowered to point towards the ground. There were branches of tree in the frame. A second later the ground hurtled towards the camera and the assembled officers heard a muffled expulsion of air. The camera helpfully panned back up to the tree from which the cameraman had just jumped.

'That must be the tree outside Becky Blake's house,' said Noble.

Brook looked at the time display. 'It's the night of Becky's naked dance – the night before the party.'

An excited voice boomed from the speakers. 'Body Double – *directed by Brian de Palma. Result or what?*' In case they were in any doubt about the origin of the voice, the camera turned towards its owner and the grinning face of Rusty Thomson leered into the lens. Then the screen went blank.

A few seconds later, another piece of film and the screen erupted into noisy life; the detectives covered their ears to the cacophony. The picture seemed to be rolling at speed between a hard pavement and the night sky as though the camera was being bounced along the ground. For a split second Brook fancied he also saw a bike-wheel in shot. He winced as the soundtrack gave way to a mixture of screaming and loud banging as the camera came to a halt. The time display showed ten minutes had elapsed since Rusty had filmed himself jumping from the tree.

'What the devil?' muttered Charlton. 'What is this?'

The camera was on the ground. A few yards away, Rusty Thomson lay face down on the pavement, a hand clutching at his neck. A moment later Rusty looked up and reached his bloodstained hand to the lens before his breath gave out and he sank back to the ground. He lay still as the camcorder continued to record.

Brook stared at Rusty, his eyes narrowing. 'I know it's dark, but . . .'

'What?' asked Charlton.

Brook stared a moment longer then looked back at Charlton and shook his head. 'Nothing.'

The screen changed to black until the caption DEITY – THE END flashed up. No countdown followed. It was over. Cooper turned on the lights. Again there was silence until broken by Charlton.

'Did we just see our prime suspect murdered?' he asked. Nobody answered for a moment. Charlton turned, as usual, towards Brook for an injection of expertise. 'Inspector?'

Brook roused himself to answer. 'If so, he died the night before the party.'

'That would explain why he didn't have a monologue,' said Cooper.

'And why Jake didn't see Rusty at the party,' added Noble.

'Then who the hell filmed the other three students? And who the hell was at the river with Wilson Woodrow?'

'It must have been Kyle,' said Morton.

'Jake saw Kyle doing the filming at the party.' Noble nodded.

'What about Rifkind?' ventured Charlton.

'That wasn't Rifkind at the river or on the bridge,' said Brook.

'But you can't be sure,' argued Charlton. 'It's impossible to tell.'

Brook didn't answer but remained deep in thought. 'Yvette identified Rusty from the bridge.'

'Then maybe that last piece was a fake,' said Cooper. 'Make us think Rusty's dead and take the heat off him.'

'Did that look faked to you?' asked Morton, nodding at the screen.

Cooper shrugged. 'Not really.'

'Which means Rusty was killed on Thursday night,' began Noble.

'Are we sure he died?' said Charlton.

'What we see and what we seem is but a dream,' intoned Brook to no one in particular. Everyone turned to him. 'Dave, play that last bit back again – in slow motion.'

Cooper moved his hand back over the mouse and restarted the film in slow motion. The lights went off and detectives could clearly see the blurred film of night sky and ground, either side of indeterminate shots of vegetation and distant streetlights.

'Stop,' commanded Brook. He stood and walked towards the screen. The bicycle-wheel he'd seen before was clearer now. Next to it was a leg dressed in a bright blue tracksuit with red and yellow chevrons and bright white chunky training shoes.

'Len Poole,' said Noble. 'He killed Rusty.'

Brook nodded without taking his eyes from the leg. 'When we asked Mrs Kennedy if Kyle had a bicycle, Poole said he'd been out on it, remember?'

'So Poole killed Rusty Thomson,' said Charlton uncertainly.

'We don't know that,' said Brook.

'He looked dead to me,' said Charlton. 'I know, I know,' he added, before Brook could make his objection. 'We could be having our heads messed with. But we need to find Poole.'

'He's been abducted.'

'How do we know that wasn't faked?' asked Charlton, waving his hand at the screen.

'We don't, said Brook. 'But we know Lee Smethwick and Rusty are connected. We know Smethwick is terminally ill and hung up on Egyptian burial rites. We know Poole is a pathologist.'

'We also know Poole's connected to the students,' interrupted Charlton. 'He's connected to the house where they were last seen and now we have film of him attacking Rusty Thomson.'

'Poole's not behind Deity.'

'You sound very sure of that.'

'Why would Poole upload footage to implicate himself in a murder?' said Brook. 'If anything, Deity has shone a searchlight on his past indiscretions. Why would he want that? Besides, Poole's not smart enough to run rings round us like Deity has for the past week.'

'Those are opinions,' answered Charlton. 'Fact – Rusty Thomson left Poole's illegitimate son at the end of a rope. That's motive where I come from. Fact – we have film of him attacking Rusty Thomson.'

'Motive?'

'Revenge for his son's death.'

'Yvette Thomson said Poole didn't give a damn about their son,' pointed out Noble.

'Exactly,' agreed Brook. 'Poole didn't even know his son was dead. That's why he continued supporting Yvette long after Rusty had taken Russell's place.'

'You saw what I saw,' said Charlton, waving a hand at the screen. 'If Poole didn't give a damn about his son, why did he attack Rusty?'

'I don't know,' confessed Brook. 'But I know Poole didn't abduct Kyle, Becky and Adele. He wasn't even in Derby.'

'How do we know Kyle, Becky and Adele weren't still at the Kennedy house when Poole and Alice got back from Chester?'

'So now Alice is involved in kidnapping her son?' Brook smiled at Charlton's discomfort. 'Sorry, but it just won't hold up, sir. The only interest Poole had in Rusty was finding out—' Brook stopped in mid-sentence and raised his face to the heavens. 'The plaster,' he said with a sigh.

'What?' said Charlton.

Brook looked into space with a hand on his forehead. 'Rusty *was* at the party.'

'But the night before —' objected Charlton.

'— the night before, Poole was following Rusty on Kyle's bike,' continued Brook. 'And when he got the chance, he pounced. He cut Rusty on the neck to get a sample of his DNA. That's how he got his proof. He didn't kill Rusty, he surprised him and Rusty dropped the camera. By sheer fluke, it captured shots of him bleeding on the pavement so he acts out his own death scene.

'It's perfect,' said Brook, warming to his theme. 'By now

Rusty must know we've got Yvette because he gave her to us. He must know he's our prime suspect. But he's got this amazing piece of film that shows him being attacked. Not faked but real. So what does he do? He broadcasts it so it throws all our theories up in the air. We'll think he died before any of the abductions happened. That's why he doesn't appear in any broadcasts until now.'

'But what about the party?'

'When Jake looked through the curtains for a second he didn't see Rusty. It doesn't mean he wasn't there. The plaster puts him there – the blood didn't belong to Kyle, Becky or Adele. That much we know. That's Rusty's blood from the cut on his neck. I guarantee it.'

There was silence for a moment, as everyone searched for a flaw. Finally Charlton nodded. 'Okay. At least he got sloppy and left us his DNA.'

'I don't think this man does sloppy,' replied Brook softly. 'More likely he didn't care because he's not on the database. But that's good for us.'

'Why?'

'Because he thinks he's invulnerable and that's a weakness.'

'And what about Kyle, Adele and Becky?' asked Noble. 'If those monologues are to be believed, they were dead before we even interviewed the parents.'

Twenty-Six

'LEN. I KNOW YOU'RE IN there.'

The back of Poole's neck tingled. The disembodied voice floated out of the darkness. Poole had had a bellyful of groping around in the murk but he knew he'd have to summon the courage if it meant the chance of a way out. He looked longingly back to the shaft of sunlight above the empty pool. With a deep breath, he turned and stepped into the shadows, inching his way towards the disembodied voice. 'Who's there?' he shouted. His voice echoed around the vaulted ceiling of the pool room.

'Len?'

'Where are you?'

'I'm here – at the end of the passage.

'I don't see you.'

'Follow my voice.'

Poole reached the first room leading off the corridor. He could barely see through the shadows but he was sure there was another sarcophagus by the room's far wall.

'Hurry up, Len. I haven't got all day and you certainly haven't.'

Poole continued to inch blindly down the corridor,

passing another open room. Again he fancied it contained a sarcophagus of some sort but it was too dark to see. As he approached the third room, he could make out a dim light from beyond the bend of the corridor. Again he hesitated. Again he glanced into yet another darkened room to his right and again he could discern the shape of a coffin. This time he leaned into the room and ran a hand along the wall. He found the light switch but it didn't work.

'Hurry up, Len. Or you can stay there and rot.'

Poole took another deep breath. The heat in this part of the building was oppressive and Poole unzipped and discarded his tracksuit top. His bottoms stank worse but he couldn't remove them and retain the dignity he so cherished.

He crept onwards. The light became brighter with each watchful step. He passed a fourth room, which was lighter than the others. No coffin. No sarcophagus. But there was a chair. A chair that sat beneath a rope which dangled from an iron cross-girder above.

'Last chance, Len.'

With improved visibility, Poole quickened his step towards the light, turned another corner and stopped in dismay. Instead of a way out, the dim light that drew him on belonged to a laptop open on a small folding table. A grinning face greeted him from the monitor.

'Hi, Len.' The young man beamed happily from the screen.

Poole tried to place the face. 'Who are you?'

The talking head spoke, fake emotion distorting his voice. 'Dad, don't you know me?'

Puzzled, Poole squinted at the screen. 'Rusty?'

'Give the man a cigar.'

'Jesus. You look different. What have you done to your face?'

'I've had a makeover, Dad.'

'Just who the hell are you?'

Rusty grinned again. 'Who was I last week or who am I next week?'

'I don't understand.'

'That's the idea, Dad.'

'Don't call me that. I'm not your father.'

'One reason I don't have your cowardly genes.'

'What?'

'I'm not a victim, Len. Not like your progeny – not like little baby Russell. You didn't work it out yet?'

'What have you done with him?'

Rusty shook his head mournfully. 'He didn't make it, Pop.'

'What do you mean? He's dead?'

'As a dodo.'

Poole nodded. 'I did wonder. Did you kill my son?'

'Your son,' sneered Rusty. 'Like you gave a shit.'

Poole pulled in a huge tired breath. 'It doesn't mean I'm happy he's dead. Did you kill him?'

'Don't be so melodramatic, Len. I didn't touch him. Russell killed himself. Despite sucking on the teat of your generous patronage, your *son* just didn't have the stones for modern life.'

'And Kyle and the others? Did you kill them too?'

Rusty just smiled. Poole watched as he leaned forward and reappeared with a pint of beer in his hand, taking a couple of gulps before putting it back down. The sun was shining in the background. Poole guessed he was in a beer garden.

'Wouldn't you like to know?' said Rusty, wiping a sleeve over his top lip. 'You're not having a lot of luck with your offspring, are you, Len?'

'What do you mean?'

'Well, your real son killed himself and your future stepson was a whining, self-absorbed faggot . . .'

'Was?'

'I'm all the family you have left.'

'What have you done to Kyle?'

'I'd worry about you, Len. Your death will be much slower if you don't pull your finger out. You seen the size of those rats? Scared the living shit out of me, they did.'

'So you're going to kill me too.'

'Again with the melodrama. I don't kill, Len. I just help people realise how worthless they are, and then let them make their own decisions.' He raised the pint to his lips again and looked behind him. 'It's a beautiful day. Makes you feel glad to be alive. I'll miss Derbyshire, it's really . . . elemental.' He raised a hand in mock apology. 'Sorry. I'm here catching a beer and some rays and you're stuck in there with a dead lunatic. I assume he's safely on his way.'

'You mean the green-faced nut job? He's dead, all right.'

'Man, he actually went with that make-up?' Rusty shook his head and laughed. 'Gotta hand it to Lee – the guy didn't do things by halves.'

'He was ill, wasn't he?'

'Lung cancer, he told me.'

'So he topped himself to avoid a slow and painful death,' said Poole. 'He can't have been that crazy.'

Rusty gazed back at Poole from the monitor. 'Indeed.'

'So what now?'

'It's time to get to work, Len.'

'Work?'

'Well, Lee rather hoped, in his befuddled way, that he'd become immortal.' Rusty grinned. 'You could say he'd set his heart on it – and several others too,' he added with a chuckle. 'That's why you're there, Len. To make him live forever.'

'What do you mean?'

'You've got all the knowledge, Len. The tools are there. Work it out.'

'You want me to embalm him?'

'There you go. Anubis – God of Embalming,' he said with great solemnity, before breaking into laughter. 'There should be cloth and bandages as well. He wants full mummi-fication.'

'I don't have those skills.'

'Really? Well, you better develop them because if he's not processed in twenty-four hours you'll die there. In case you hadn't noticed, the whole building has been specially rigged. As soon as Lee put his Egyptian costume on, he would have sealed you both in – just like they used to do in the pyramids. There is an escape route, but that also seals twenty-four hours after his death. Something to do with sand trickling out of a tank. It's very dramatic, Len. Well, you can't be too careful with all the tomb raiders roaming the badlands of Erewash Borough.'

'Twenty-four hours?'

Rusty looked at his watch. 'Actually less now, as you kept me waiting. Lee said the whole embalming should take about three days but I'm on a bit of a schedule, so chop chop.' He laughed at his own joke. 'See what I did there.'

'You're crazier than he is.'

'Name-calling won't help you, Len. So get to work.'

'How will you know if I've done it or not?'

'The Eye of Horus sees all,' he bellowed grandly, before lapsing into mirth again.

'Horus?'

'Son of Osiris.' Rusty shrugged. 'Lee liked it when I played along.'

'And what if I don't finish in time?'

'You will. Then tomorrow I'll be here to tell you the way out. Now don't hang about, out with the blood, the guts and the brain.'

'The brain? I didn't see a cranial saw.'

'Well, that's not how the ancients did it, Len. Don't you know anything? There should be a long brass hook which you push up the nose to chop up the brain. He made it himself – quite brilliant. Then you pull the bits out with the hook. I shouldn't be telling you all this – just soft-hearted, I guess. Which reminds me – leave the heart in. He needs it for the journey.' Rusty chortled again. 'I ask you.'

'What a fucking headcase.'

'Headcase,' sniggered Rusty. 'See? You're getting the idea.' He held up a hand in apology.

'Why are you going to all this trouble for him?'

'It's not like me, as you know. Or rather don't. Lee's been a big help and I promised him. I couldn't have got Project Deity off the ground without him.' Rusty's face hardened. 'Besides, I couldn't let you get away without paying for the way you treated Yvette, not to mention the attack on me.'

'Serves you right,' sneered Poole, managing to resurrect a little righteous indignation. 'I hope it hurt.'

'More shock than pain,' said Rusty, rubbing his neck and finding his grin again. 'But you know what? It worked out perfectly. Bit of a fluke really. The camera caught the whole thing and with a bit of judicial editing, it actually looks like I'd been killed. Inspector Brook will be scratching his head for weeks.'

'Brook scratching his head? You don't know him, son.' Poole smiled. 'He's a lot smarter than you think.'

'Yeah, right, Dad. Well, better get on.' He leaned forward to break the connection.

'Wait!' shouted Poole. 'What's the rope for?'

Rusty smiled coldly at Poole. 'The sands of time are running out, Len. Finish the job and tomorrow you get your escape route.'

Brook sat down next to Charlton. Noble was the other side. The Press Briefing Room was jammed. Cameras flashed for several minutes despite the absence of quivering parents who were certain to be watching from home with the Family Liaison Officers despatched to comfort them. Finally Charlton took up his script.

'Thank you for attending tonight. By now the whole country will be aware of what appears to be the final broadcast from the Deity website. Monologues by Kyle Kennedy, Rebecca Blake and Adele Watson, filmed the day after their abduction, confirm what we concluded at the start of the investigation. The four students who disappeared on Friday May twentieth, during or after a birthday party for Kyle Kennedy, did so of their own volition. That much is clear from their statements on *Deity.com* this afternoon.

'What has become clear to us is the fact that three of the

students who vanished had reason to be unhappy with their lives and a clear motive for leaving behind the homes that had nurtured them.

'However, their intention – beyond disappearing – is still not certain. The Deity website has offered tantalising hints about their fate but as yet no clear conclusion.

'We believe the young people had become obsessed with fame and, as you saw this afternoon, were willing participants in the kind of output from *Deity.com* that has served to spread their celebrity.

'We also believe that any impression they left concerning a suicide pact is, as yet, unproven – and we believe it is still possible these youngsters may be found alive.'

There was a murmur from the assembled journalists and Charlton looked up from his statement to let it subside. Brook stared unblinking to the back of the room.

'Having said that, we are now looking for three other individuals as a matter of urgency, and what pictures we have are in your packs. We would urge you to give maximum publicity to these photographs because the individuals concerned are of extreme interest in our investigation.

'One of the four students who disappeared – Russell "Rusty" Thomson – is an imposter. He is not an eighteen-year-old student and his identity is unknown. We believe this man is the person who filmed the suicide of Wilson Woodrow on Thursday May nineteenth as well as the assault on Kyle Kennedy and the film of Rebecca Blake in her bedroom earlier that same night. Suffice to say that we consider this individual to be highly organised and dangerous, and he should not be approached if recognised.

'Today's Deity broadcast shows Thomson being attacked

and apparently killed by an unknown assailant. We believe this film to be a misdirection which was included on the site to throw us off Thomson's scent.

'On a related note, we are pleased to report that we have an identity for the so-called Embalmer, who we linked to the discovery of two dead bodies in the rivers and ponds around Derby. His name is Lee Smethwick and we believe he is also involved in the disappearance of Kyle Kennedy, Rebecca Blake and Adele Watson.'

The press erupted and Charlton was forced to give way to questions which he directed to Brook.

'What's the connection between Thomson and The Embalmer?' asked a TV reporter.

'We believe Smethwick and Thomson are working together to keep Kyle, Becky and Adele incarcerated . . .' began Brook but he was swamped by noise again.

'Is Smethwick going to cut them up like he did the tramps?' shouted Brian Burton from the back.

'Brian, that language is totally inappropriate. The parents of these young people will be watching this briefing,' Charlton said angrily.

'We hope not,' said Brook, jumping in. He paused to compose himself. For once Burton's salacious eye for detail might just get the public interested enough to respond. He decided to risk Charlton's ire. 'But I'm afraid we can't discount the possibility. The bodies of the missing men found in the river had been gutted and the brains had been removed through the nose in preparation for embalming and possibly even mummification.' There was stunned silence. Charlton hung his head.

'Smethwick is a highly disturbed individual who likes to

play with corpses,' continued Brook. 'He has disappeared and it is vital that the public help us find him. Smethwick has lived locally for many years and has a boat at Shardlow Marina. He was a chef at Derby College until recently, where we believe he made contact with Thomson and the other students.

'We know Thomson to be a cold and calculating individual, extremely organised, manipulative and charming.' Brook raised a finger for emphasis. 'However, we are convinced he is not local, so it's highly likely that Kyle, Becky and Adele are being held in a place that connects to Lee Smethwick's past. Any information we receive, maybe going back years, could be vital in locating them.'

Brook looked back at Charlton who held his gaze for a second longer than polite. After the Chief Superintendent had introduced the pictures of Smethwick, Thomson and Len Poole, the three officers wound up the briefing and left through a side door. Charlton rounded on Brook as soon as it was closed.

'My God, Brook. Do you realise what you just did?'

Brook nodded sombrely. 'Yes, sir. I woke people up.'

'Woke them up?' Charlton shouted and began to wave a finger in Brook's face. 'You handed out sensitive information!'

'I don't care about the trial,' Brook retorted calmly. 'At this rate there's not going to be one.'

'But if the DPP—'

'I don't care about that either,' repeated Brook slowly. 'All that matters is finding Adele and the others. It was time to remind everybody out there, all those *faceless voyeurs*, tucking into their TV dinners, that Deity is not entertainment. It's not a show, there is no acting. Three young lives are at stake. They need our help and we need the public's.' Brook motioned Noble to leave.

'And what do I say to hysterical parents when they ring up?'

'I don't give a damn what you say to them as long as you keep them away from my team so we can do our jobs.'

'And I suppose that goes for me too.' Charlton laughed bitterly.

Brook paused, ready to speak, but a touch on his arm from Noble prevented him. He turned away. 'I'll be in the Incident Room.'

'You know, I've tried with you, Brook, I really have,' scowled Charlton. 'So let me lay it on the line for you. If you don't find those kids by this time tomorrow, I'm taking you off the case.'

Brook turned from the doorway. 'I understand,' he said coldly.

'That went well,' said Noble. Brook gave him a lopsided smile. 'Think Charlton's cracking up?'

'He's not used to the pressure at our end,' said Brook, logging on to his computer. 'He should stick to budgets. Anything from the techs on our latest broadcast?'

'Nothing. Want me to chase it up?'

Brook shook his head. 'But load it up for me, please. I want to take another look.'

Noble smiled. 'You know, we run courses for IT dunces,' he said, putting his hand over the mouse and clicking the appropriate icons.

'That's *Inspector* Dunce to you.'

Noble laughed. He switched on the large screen and Becky Blake grinned excitedly at them from cyberspace.

Noble pulled out his cigarettes and padded to the door, turning to look at Brook gazing saucer-eyed at the film. He sighed and closed the door, pulling up a chair next to Brook. They watched together in silence.

When Becky finished her monologue, Noble paused the film on her barely concealed smirk. 'Did her speech bother you at all?'

Brook turned to him. 'Becky?' He thought for a minute. 'She went through the motions of claiming she was unhappy, but actually she seemed excited.'

'Agreed,' said Noble. 'And if she's preparing to take her own life, where's the fear? Fear of pain. Fear of the unknown. She wasn't afraid.'

Brook looked at Noble. 'Like maybe she's unaware that she's supposed to be committing suicide.'

'Exactly. She's smiling almost as if she knows she's famous enough now to walk into the modelling contract of her choice. Charlton was right – now she's famous, she can come home and milk the attention.' He started the broadcast again. 'Contrast with Kyle.'

They watched Kyle's statement. He was edgy, his delivery halting and fretful.

'Now that is someone who thinks he's about to die.'

Brook nodded. 'That friend of Becky's?'

'Fern Stretton.'

'She's always believed Becky was in no danger. Maybe there's a reason for that. Let's take another run at her. After tonight's press briefing she might finally realise Becky is in trouble.'

DS Gadd and DC Smee walked into the room. Gadd's face betrayed her mounting frustration.

'Nothing?' asked Brook.

'No. Read and a couple of others are manning the phones. We're working through any tips but nothing stands out as a viable location. Smethwick is a real loner. He has no relatives and no friends we can find. We're hunting up his old employers but it's slow going.'

'You mentioned pubs before.'

'Right. He worked in five altogether, mainly as a grill chef or barman. The problem is pubs change hands, even breweries.'

'They're all local?'

'Yes, sir.' Gadd turned to the large map. 'Three in the city centre. The Brunswick . . .'

'Forget the city, he's isolated. Where else?'

She consulted her list, pointing at the map. 'The Crewe and Harpur in Chellaston. Then he seems to be off the radar for a while. A year later he started at the Malt Shovel in Aston-on-Trent. That was seven years ago.'

'Aston-on-Trent – that's only a mile from Shardlow Marina,' said Brook. 'Get over there and have a word.'

Gadd looked at her watch. 'It'll be after closing when we get there.'

'Jane, right now I don't care if you have to burn the landlord out to speak to him, we need a break.' He sighed, suddenly aware of how tired he was. 'Just get them to speak to you,' he said kindly.

Noble watched Gadd and Smee leave and pulled out a cigarette. Brook took his jacket from the back of the chair. His eye was held by the image of Adele Watson, frozen in time on the monitor, wearing her white dress and smiling confidently into the camera at the start of her manifesto.

'Adele looks like an angel,' said Noble.

'That's what I'm afraid of.'

'You were right about her,' continued Noble. 'She was impressive. She does have a lot to say.'

Brook nodded. 'Let's hope there's more to come.'

Noble lit up on the steps of the station as Brook's phone began to vibrate. It was Terri.

Dad. When are you coming home?

'Terri, I know it's late but I may not make it back tonight – things are hotting up here. Don't wait up, okay?'

There was a pause. *Dad, I need you to come home.*

'Terri, I—'

I need you to come home now.

Brook paused. 'What's wrong?'

Another pause. *I've been depressed, Dad. About Tony. I've taken something. Pills.*

Brook pushed his face closer to the phone as if to be better heard. 'Terri, listen to me. What have you taken?'

Again a pause. *I don't know, but I had a lot of them. I don't feel so good.*

By this time Noble had cottoned on to a problem and was also listening intently. 'Terri, listen carefully. I want you to hang up and dial 999.'

Another pause. *I've called the ambulance, Dad, but I need you to come home.*

'Okay, darling. I'm on my way.' He covered his phone for a moment. 'John. Can you see Fern on your own?'

'She'll keep,' said Noble firmly. 'I can drive you home.'

'John, I'm fine. I'll be quicker, I know the roads. Talk to Fern and let me know.'

Brook sprinted to his car and jumped in. He screeched away from the car park, speaking into his phone. 'Darling, I'm here. Terri, I want you to stand up. If you can, walk around until the ambulance gets there. Make coffee. Whatever you do, don't lie on your back.'

'Why?'

Brook shook off an image of his daughter choking on her own vomit. 'Just do it and stay awake. If you can, make yourself throw up. I'll be there in half an hour.' He threw the open phone on the passenger seat and slammed the BMW into a lower gear to make the lights next to the Radio Derby building. The black car hurtled along St Alkmund's Way then Brook flung it sharp right on to Ashbourne Road, heading for home.

Gadd and Smee pulled on to the green in Aston-on-Trent and parked by the Malt Shovel. Once inside they strode to the near-empty bar, pulling out their warrant cards. The young barmaid eyed them uneasily.

'We've stopped serving,' she said before she saw their ID.

'Is the landlord in?'

'He's on holiday. I'm the relief manager.'

Gadd and Smee exchanged a resigned glance. 'Never mind.' Gadd turned away but hesitated. 'How long has the current landlord been in the pub?'

The barmaid smiled blankly. 'No idea.'

'Ten years,' said a tarry voice from the far end of the bar belonging to an overweight, grey-whiskered old man, who wore a flat cap and straining woollen cardigan despite the warmth of the evening. 'What's Austin been up to? Watering the beer again?'

'And you are, sir?'

'Who wants to know?' he demanded. Gadd thrust her ID in his face. 'Name's Sam,' he muttered resentfully.

'We're trying to locate an ex-employee. Lee Smethwick.'

'Lee Smethwick.' Sam snorted. 'I remember that weirdo, all right.'

'You knew him?' said Smee.

Sam blew out his cheeks. 'Not so much to talk to, thank God. He was a few sandwiches short of a picnic. You'd finish your pint and you might be the only soul in the bar but he'd just stand there like some stuffed dummy, staring into space. When you finally got his attention, you'd think you'd disturbed a sleepwalker.'

'He lived on a boat in Shardlow Marina but he's missing,' said Gadd. 'Did he have any haunts that he mentioned, any special places he liked to go? Somewhere big and private, say.'

Sam glanced down at his nearly drained pint then meaningfully back up at Gadd.

'It's past closing,' began Smee.

'Can we get another pint over here?' Gadd called to the relief manager. She hesitated over her glass-drying. 'It's okay. He's a local,' said Gadd, as though it were some new by-law.

'Thanks,' said Sam, taking a large pull on the freshly drawn pint, a minute later.

'Well?'

Sam just sat there, smiling inscrutably.

'What can you tell us?' said Smee.

'Feel a bit of a fraud, accepting your pint,' he said chuckling. 'See, he did voluntary work at the Village.'

'The Village?'

'Aston Hall Mental Hospital – but they called it the Village. Make it sound welcoming, I suppose. You can see it from the end of the road. Just a lot of empty buildings and broken windows now. They closed it six, seven year ago after the fire. Lee volunteered there then did the odd shift in here. You ask me, he should've been a patient.'

Brook skidded to a halt behind the bright green VW. No ambulance. No lights on. Maybe it had been and gone or worse, hadn't arrived yet. As Brook hurried towards the cottage he heard the sound of an engine block cooling down. He put his hand on the VW. The engine was still warm. He tried the driver's door but it was locked so he sprinted up to the darkened cottage and burst into the kitchen.

Peeping Tom. *Directed in 1960 by Michael Powell, starring Carl Boehm as a serial killer who films people as they die. Cool.*

Brook saw the red dot in the shadows and around that a sinister figure sitting at the kitchen table. In spite of the darkness, Brook saw the light.

'What have you done with my daughter, Ray?'

Brook heard a low chuckle. He leaned back towards the door to snap on the light.

'Or are you still Rusty?'

Ray grinned back at him, the camcorder covering one eye, a pose Brook recognised from the Facebook picture of Rusty. But where Rusty's skin had been pale and spotty, Ray looked tanned and healthy and, with the baseball cap still back to front on his head, the blond hair and the beard, Brook could plot Rusty's transformation into Ray.

'It's amazing what you can do with facial hair, a bottle of

dye and tinted contact lenses,' said Ray, his visible eye still squinting as he filmed. 'And – cut,' he called, lowering the camcorder and fixing Brook with his blue eyes.

'Where is she?' said Brook, moving towards him.

'Stay where you are or the girl gets it,' he roared. He had an open laptop on the table in front of him and a finger hovered over the Enter button. A moment later, the grin returned. 'Film?'

'Where is she?' repeated Brook.

'You're right,' beamed Ray. 'It could be any one of a dozen movies, and not very good ones either. Our dénouement promises to be a much classier affair.'

'Where is she, Ray?' Brook advanced menacingly.

'She's safe,' said Ray, turning the laptop screen to face Brook. Terri's image glared back at him. Her eyes were closed and she wore an oxygen mask.

'Where?'

'She's alive and will stay that way if you sit down.'

Brook looked at the screen, where Terri's chest was rising and falling. There were a couple of tubes leading into the mask and Brook could see small red and green lights flashing next to two small tanks.

'See those tubes? One is feeding her oxygen as we speak.' He dangled a finger theatrically. 'If I press Enter, the tank of cyanide gas will cut in and your daughter will be dead in seconds. Now sit down, we've got a lot to get through.'

Brook stared at the monitor. He recognised his bedroom and glanced towards the stairs.

Ray followed Brook's eyes. 'By the time you get there, she'll be dead. Now please sit down.' He indicated the chair opposite.

Brook gazed at him for a few seconds more, then scraped back the chair and sat.

'Thank you,' said Ray.

'Terri didn't take any pills.'

'That was just a ruse,' smiled Ray. 'There's a script in front of you if you want to see it.'

Brook pulled a sheet of A4 paper towards him. *Tell him you're depressed and have taken some pills.* v. IMPORTANT – tell him you've called an ambulance already.

He pushed it away. 'Very clever – she says she's called the ambulance so I don't do it.' Brook's eyes burned into his uninvited guest. 'Ray, Rusty, what should I call you?'

'Take your pick, Inspector. I have many names. I'm Moriarty. I'm the Star Child. I'm Horus. I'm Keyser Soze. I'm the Fifth Element. I'm Hanging Rock. I'm Deity. I'm everything and nothing, the unknown, always behind you, always beyond your field of vision.'

'My daughter . . .'

'Your daughter's fine. For now.'

Brook glared at him. 'What do you want, Ray?'

Ray rummaged in a khaki-coloured laptop bag at his feet. 'You can autograph my book for a start.' He pulled out a copy of *In Search of The Reaper* by Brian Burton and slid it across the table. Brook snorted in bitter amusement. When it became clear he was serious, Brook opened the book and wrote a few words in the front before sliding it back across the table.

'You know, for a star detective, you don't seem to catch many killers,' said Ray.

'You haven't got away, yet.'

Ray laughed. 'Killer? Me?'

'You killed Yvette's son.'

'I never laid a finger on that little pansy and I've got the photographs to prove it – the same with the others.'

'Others?'

Ray raised a digit. 'Getting me talking. Very good.' He flipped open the book to read the dedication. *'You're sick and need help. Let me help you.* Signed *Damen Brook.'* Ray looked up and laughed. 'Maybe Len was right, Damen. Maybe I have underestimated you.'

'You took Len. Is he with the others?' Ray nodded. 'Dead?'

'I'm not sure. I just finished recording my final message to him before you got here. Then we'll see. Or rather you will. I'll be long gone.'

'And Adele?'

Ray looked at Brook with a mixture of appreciation and curiosity. 'You single her out?' He nodded. 'You feel the same as me. Mesmeric, isn't she? She's going to be a great example.'

'Is? You mean she's alive?'

'I mean she will provide ongoing inspiration to all those unhappy souls seeking a solution.'

'And Kyle and Becky?'

He shrugged. 'Who cares? Window-dressing. Adele is the key. Adele was my Miranda.' He looked wistful for a moment. 'You know, I'll miss her. She was a good friend.'

They're dead, you know. 'So you have killed her.'

For once Ray's restrained amusement gave way to consternation. 'Don't be vulgar, Damen. I've told you, I'm not a killer. I help people – help them to see their true value so they can clear their minds and do what has to be done.'

'You mean you prey on the vulnerable and manoeuvre them towards their deaths. Like Wilson.'

Deity

'Wilson was a bonus. I did him a favour. He threw himself at Yvette so I made him throw himself at the river.' Ray laughed at his own joke. 'Will he be missed? I don't think so. The fat fuck is more famous now than he could ever have dreamed. He should be grateful. He was a bully and a sex-pest. But now the worldwide web has made him a star.'

'What happened?'

'After I filmed Kyle's slapping I followed Wilson back to Yvette's. He made it so easy for me. Did I kill him? No. Did I offer him mind-altering drugs? Absolutely. But *he* chose to take them. After that, a few choice words and his own papered-over inadequacies did the rest. He made quite a splash, don't you think?'

Brook shook his head. 'Why?'

'Why what?'

'Why are you doing this? Preying on teenagers on the verge of starting their lives? Is it because they have a future that you can only imagine?'

'Where's the fun in emptying out the old people's homes? That's no challenge, it's a public service,' Ray said. 'But those with their whole lives in front of them . . . getting them to step off is very rewarding.'

'Because they have prospects that you were denied,' snarled Brook. 'You're another orphan, aren't you? Only you got bitter and twisted because people didn't worship the ground you walked on. They couldn't see how special you were. Is that how you hooked up with Yvette – two needy, grasping narcissists against the world?'

Ray's face hardened. 'And so the cheap psychoanalysis begins.' In a whining voice he said, '*It all started when I got a taste for pulling the legs off insects, Doctor. Pretty soon I moved on to drowning cats . . .'* He couldn't continue for laughing. 'I wouldn't expect a stupid policeman to understand.'

'Try me.'

'Try you? Okay. Start with this. What do you see when you look at a teenager?'

'I don't know what you mean.'

'Don't you? Tell me you don't look at teenagers with hatred and envy – envy because you wish you could be their age so you could show them how to live, and hatred because you know they're going to ignore you and waste all that precious youth.'

'Youth is wasted on the young – that it? Well, like you, I already had my go round.'

'And did you piss it all away?'

'Of course. Everyone does,' said Brook. 'One way or another. That's how it is. That's why we can never look back without regret. How did I miss that opportunity? Why did I let myself get blown off-course? It's called drift. That's what teenagers do because they have all the time in world. And sure, they're wrong about that, but so what? We all were. And as a result, we don't waste time later in our lives because now we know we have less of it.'

'Drift? All that potential, all that energy lost in an orgy of sex and booze and drugs. Too stupid to see how to grab life by the hand.'

'That's experience talking,' said Brook. 'Experience of wasting your best years. That doesn't mean you should take somebody else's as recompense. I know the young have it all. And they're too weak to know it won't last. That's how it has to be – so they can waste it, like every generation before them and then spend the rest of their lives wondering how it happened.'

Ray smiled. 'You do understand.'

'About weakness?' Brook hesitated. 'I've encountered it.'

'Weakness? The young aren't weak, Damen. They're sinners. They offend God. They've taken the deadliest of the Seven Deadly Sins and used it as their personal mantra.'

'Vanity.' Brook nodded.

Ray pointed an emphatic finger. 'Exactly. These idiots think the universe revolves around them, but they lack the experience and confidence to cope when they finally realise it doesn't. That's the flaw, their Achilles heel. And that's the moment, the exact second, when I have to be there. It's a drug to me. That delicious instant when it dawns on them that the world no longer cares about them, that nobody is going to bail them out. "Boo hoo – I'm not going to be famous. Boo hoo – I'm going to be one of the nobodies I used to sneer at". Broken heart – tough. Fallen out with your friends, lost your job, can't afford the latest phone – life's a bitch.'

'So they have to die?'

Ray grinned. 'Yes, they do – and they deserve it for being so unprepared. And it's so wonderful to be there to help them escape that first setback, that thunderbolt that tells them how ordinary they are. And know what? They're even grateful. When the knowledge hits, I can give them what's beyond their grasp.'

'Fame,' said Brook softly.

Ray nodded. 'It's a trade-off. I give them the attention, the validation they want; they give me what *I* want. It's a small price to pay to rise above the anonymity of the masses.'

'And that's what Adele wanted?'

'Above all things, Damen. So bad she could taste it. She couldn't take the chance she might go through life unheard.

You heard her manifesto. Magnificent, wasn't it? What a talent. Just watch the clamour for her thoughts now.'

They're dead, you know. 'It's not their fault, Ray. Adele, Kyle, Becky. They're not to blame for expecting their lives to run to their own agenda.'

'I know that,' chuckled Ray. 'You think I don't? That's what makes it all the more delicious. See – they're the innocent. That's the drug – I'm not interested in punishing the guilty.'

'The guilty?'

'You, Damen. Mr and Mrs Watson. Alice Kennedy. The Blakes. You're the guilty ones – all the parents. They're the ones in the dock. They're the ones who perpetrate this appalling fraud on their kids. *Look at me, Mummy. Listen to my drivel.* Yes, darling, of course I will. Everything you say is fascinating. Everything you do is interesting. *Make it better, Mummy. Make it better, Daddy, Grandma, Grandad, primary-school teacher.* Course I will, darling, and even if I can't, the effort I make will still make you think the sun orbits around you.'

'Is that how your parents treated you?' asked Brook. 'Smothering you with their love and concern – what an ordeal for you.' Ray didn't appreciate the sarcasm but declined to reply. Instead, Brook went on: 'Wait – no. Those were the parents of your friends. Those were the parents you wished you'd had so that for a brief glorious moment as a child, you might feel special. I bet those kids weren't friends for long.'

From below the table Ray produced a gun and turned it in his hand. 'Recognise this, Damen? I found it in the attic. What's a British policeman doing with a gun in his attic?'

'What are you going to do with Terri?'

'I was asking about the gun.'

'It's a souvenir.'

'Of what?'

'A case. An opponent.'

'A souvenir?' Ray looked at the M9 automatic in wonder. 'Remember that bit in *Badlands* when Martin Sheen allows himself to be caught on the Canadian border – when he gives one of the pursuing officers his lighter?'

Brook glanced again at the image of his daughter on the monitor.

'Remember the contentment on Sheen's face,' continued Ray. 'The peace. "Here, son, have my lighter. I'm famous. Share in my glory. Tell people about the day you caught a legendary killer and how he gave you his lighter."' Ray frantically rummaged in his pockets and peered into the small shoulder bag lying on the table. 'Now you've got me going. What can I give you to remember me by? It needs to be something personal. I know.' He rummaged in a pocket and pulled out a set of keys. 'Adele's house keys.' He slid them across to Brook. 'Put 'em in your pocket, Damen. I insist.' Brook made no move to pick them up.

'I said put them in your pocket.' Ray's hand hovered over the laptop keyboard until Brook pocketed the set of three keys. 'You'll thank me sooner than you think. Know what you can do with them? When her mum goes out, you can nip round there and lie on Adele's bed. That's what her dad used to do. Just to smell her, she said. Fucking pervert didn't even pull himself off. How wrong is that?'

'If you're giving out souvenirs, I'd prefer a lock of your hair,' said Brook. 'Or that used plaster on your neck to match against the one you left at Kyle's. I'd treasure that.'

'You're good.' Ray grinned.

'How is your neck, by the way?'

'Better, thanks.' Ray removed the cap and touched the skin-coloured plaster now visible on the back of his neck. 'Old Len certainly took a gouge out of me, the sly old fucker. Who'd have thought he had it in him?'

'So Len's attack wasn't faked.'

'Far from it. I was walking along, innocently plotting the suicides of my classmates when I felt this searing pain in my neck. Next thing I knew, I was on the ground but when I looked up at the camera, not only was it fine, it was actually filming. Then it came to me. My hand was covered in blood and I nearly had a *Soylent Green* moment. You know, Charlton Heston, reaching out with his dying breath. "*Soylent Green is made out of people.*" ' He laughed. 'What a fucking ham. But I managed to stop myself and it turned out perfectly.'

'What we see and what we seem is but a dream,' said Brook quietly.

Ray looked at him, an appreciative smile curling his lips. 'I'm glad I prepared properly. That didn't fool you for a minute, did it?'

'Maybe just a minute,' replied Brook. 'I see you've got over your aversion to swearing. Don't need to play suitable boyfriend any more, Ray?'

'Don't forget the tattoos.'

'That was a nice touch.' Brook nodded.

Ray shrugged. 'I can't take the credit – Terri mentioned it. See, fathers of daughters always have the easiest buttons to push. Like Adele's father, for instance.' He took out a mobile phone and read from the screen. '*I'm happy now, Dad. I'd rather die than live a minute longer under your roof. Goodbye. Adele.*'

'You've got Adele's SIM card,' said Brook.

'Kyle and Becky's too. They've helped me reach out to the vulnerable.'

'First Jake McKenzie. Now Jim Watson.'

Ray smiled. 'I sent him that an hour ago. The phone company will probably be contacting you about it. Now, how do you suppose he'll react to that a few hours after seeing his daughter say goodbye to the world?' Brook didn't reply. 'You're right, Damen. It's a cheap shot and I wouldn't normally bother with people that age – their failure is endemic. And for a grieving father of a beautiful daughter into the bargain, well, self-destruction is almost inevitable.'

'Then why send it?'

Ray pushed the gun across to Brook. 'To show you how easy it is to put people out of their misery. Pick it up.'

Brook looked at the gun. 'You're going to kill Terri, aren't you?'

Ray laughed. 'Again with the drama. How many times? I don't kill people.'

'Then why all this?' asked Brook, gesturing at the laptop.

'To get control,' insisted Ray. 'So we can talk like civilised men. I'm the director. I have to have control. I wouldn't kill Terri unless I had to – a great girl like that. Besides, she's too old. She had her chance to make a statement but she blew it and now she's got a lifetime of despair and decay ahead.'

'Just like me,' said Brook.

'On the contrary,' said Ray, looking first at the gun and then at Brook. 'We haven't . . . you know, if that's what you're wondering. Not that I couldn't have. I could tell she wanted to but it didn't seem right. Fucking the grieving daughter is a bit grubby.'

'She stopped grieving for Tony a long time ago.'

Ray laughed. 'She's not grieving for Tony, she's grieving for you – or will be. You're the big prize. Why do you think I'm here?' Ray stretched his arms wide, reading the imaginary headline. '*SUICIDE DETECTIVE TAKES OWN LIFE*. What better advert for all those lost souls out there? What bigger boost for Deity? Forget Tony, Damen. I've come for you.'

Twenty-Seven

D S GADD FLICKED THE TORCH up and down the metal barrier that separated the derelict hospital site from the road.

'How do we get in?' asked Smee. 'There's no gap.'

'We climb,' replied Gadd.

A minute later the two detectives dropped down on to the weed-encrusted drive on the other side and began walking slowly towards the dark buildings which were surprisingly modern and spaced out across the site in small units. Inspecting the buildings in turn, they observed that most of the damage was superficial – windows and doors smashed, weeds and shrubs running amok – but two of the units had been severely damaged by fire. At one of them, the sign beside the overgrown parking bay informed them that this was the administration block.

Gadd shone her torch across piles of blackened wood and the twinkling display of shattered glass on the floor. On they walked, occasionally kicking through the detritus of old cans, sometimes spooked by darting animals and the urgent diving of bats.

At the far end of the site a final building loomed, which didn't seem to have come under the same level of attack as the rest. All its windows were securely boarded or bricked up, and doors seemed to be securely fastened. Gadd turned the handle of one entrance. Although the door seemed to be unlocked, it wouldn't open even under the shoulder of the burly Smee. The same was true of the other doors they could see. One had the sign, *Hydrotherapy Pool*, hanging off but it was just as uncooperative as the others.

'The whole building seems to be sealed off.'

'*Land of the Pharaohs*,' said Gadd.

'Hear that humming?'

Gadd cocked an ear. 'I hear it.'

'Sounds like a generator.'

On the other side of the building they came upon a low outhouse that might once have been a multi-bay garage. All the doors were gone and large holes had been sledgehammered into the walls. Gadd stepped into one of the bays. It smelled of human waste. The scurry of a rat turned her head and she resisted squealing with a male officer present. She was about to leave when she spotted another hole in the wall where an entire breeze block had been hammered out. There was something on the other side of the wall. She stepped closer to be sure she was right.

'So you want my life in exchange for my daughter's,' said Brook. He spotted Terri's handbag on the next chair and picked out her cigarettes and lighter. He lit up with a sigh. 'I accept.'

'Come on, Damen – that would be too easy. What parent wouldn't die to save their child?'

'I've met plenty in my line of work.'

Ray smiled. 'You're just like Adele. You think about things.'

Brook glanced at the monitor and took another pull on his cigarette. 'Tell me about Adele.'

'I dreamed up Deity for her. The others were just to make up the numbers. She was such a strong character, such a challenge. But gradually I was able to get under her skin. She was already disillusioned with life and the world around her. That's when she showed me her poems. Can you believe it? She actually handed me her innermost thoughts for me to use against her. How naive, I thought at first.' He shook his head. 'And yet I was the naive one. She knew. She was nice to me but she wasn't dumb. She knew I wasn't what I appeared.'

'The fox in the henhouse,' said Brook.

'The fox in the henhouse – I'm so liking that. Yes, that's what I was – and Adele was the prize chicken. Once I had her, the others would be easy. So I made her a promise – to make her famous, to make her thoughts immortal. I told her she would make more of a mark with a single gesture than a lifetime of toil and protest.'

'Is that when she gave you her boyfriend's credit card to set up the website?'

'What better way to put that sleazebag in the firing line? We knew it wouldn't hold up but it would be fun watching Rifkind squirm. Her dad too. That's when we put it to Kyle. We knew he was unhappy but he refused. He was in love with Jake. Can you imagine those two together? Forget it. Adele and me, we knew it was doomed so we waited.'

'Waited for what?'

'For the Kyle Kennedy train-wreck. And it worked out beautifully. Wilson saved us at least two weeks. The party was the next day so it was all systems go. Kyle wasn't sure at first but after he'd seen *Picnic at Hanging Rock*, Adele was even more convinced we had him. Jake's rejection just pushed him over the edge.'

'Kyle didn't apply for a passport, did he?'

'Course not. I nicked a passport photo of him from his wallet and Adele got Rifkind to endorse it. She'd already borrowed both birth certificates on a previous visit and put them back on the night of the party.'

'And Adele and Becky already had theirs.'

'Exactly. It would seem like we'd left the country.'

'And Becky?'

'You saw the film in her bedroom,' answered Ray. 'What self-loathing. She was so desperate for fame she would have done anything.'

'But suicide – that must have taken some persuasion?'

'Not really. Fern let slip to Adele that Becky's modelling career was in jeopardy and we knew we had our hook. The rest was just organisation. Adele made the leaflets. I wiped their computers so there could be no clues and made sure they brought their SIM cards, house keys and passports to the party. It had to be like we'd disappeared off the face of the earth.'

'Why didn't Jake see you at the Kennedy house?'

'I hid upstairs. I knew Jake was invited but I was pretty sure after Wilson's slapping that he wouldn't show.' Ray's brow furrowed. 'Guess I underestimated the power of love. Did Jake see them filming?' Brook nodded. 'Yeah, shame that. Those death masks would have had quite an impact if you thought they were real. I could tell you weren't impressed on the news. I assume Jake survived his final text from Kyle.'

'Only just. He took sleeping pills but we caught him in time.'

Ray shook his head. 'Pity.'

'Go on.'

'We watched a couple of films and waited until early morning then we walked across the fields to our rendezvous and disappeared into thin air.'

'Just like *Picnic at Hanging Rock*,' said Brook. 'We know about Lee Smethwick. We know about the ambulance waiting.'

Ray shrugged. 'It doesn't matter.'

'We'll find out where you took them any time now.'

'I'm counting on it. I promised Adele – Lee too. It cements the deal. Lee had his uses, but you were always going to find him because he was a whack job.'

'Was?'

'He killed himself. That was always his plan.'

'Because of the cancer.'

'Partly, yes. You'll see when you find him. It's funny, it's always the quiet ones. Lee had an aura, like an invisible shield, keeping normality at bay. And he loved Deity. He was desperate to be included. Well, he had the ambulance, he had the premises and a sackful of misappropriated drugs. And he insisted on showing me what he could do with those tramps. It wasn't a great leap from there to tie his skills into Deity. Leave a good-looking corpse that lasts forever. What wannabe isn't gonna love that reward for their misplaced vanity?

'It's interesting,' he went on. 'Lee with his Ancient Egyptian thing, wanting to live on after his body gave up on him. In their way, Adele and Kyle and Becky were just the same. Only they'll live forever rattling around in cyberspace, same as Wilson. Once you're immortalised in there, you can kiss obscurity goodbye.'

'Where are they?' said Brook.

'They're in the Village.'

'Which one?'

'I can't tell you until Len's done his work.'

Brook narrowed his eyes. 'Work?' He took a moment to figure it out, then: 'He's embalming Lee.'

'Right. In what the Egyptians called the Ibu . . .'

'The place of purification.'

Ray laughed. 'Oh, brother. You're living this case every second, aren't you? I knew it. The first time I saw you at the press conference hiding behind those lifeless eyes I could sense something in you. And then I just had to find out all I could. And when I'd done that, I had to meet you. And when I'd done that – well, my work was done but after meeting you, it wasn't enough. I saw the pain you were in. I saw you needed help.'

'I'm flattered by your concern.'

Ray clapped his hands together. 'You kill me.'

'I will if you've hurt Terri.'

Ray's grin faded and he nodded at the gun. 'Speaking of help – it's time to die.' He held his finger dramatically above the Enter button on his laptop. 'Point that at me and your daughter goes before you.'

Brook picked up the gun and flicked off the safety. 'You know about guns?'

'Internet,' replied Ray.

Brook picked up the M9 and examined it. He had never used it before, didn't even know if it would work. 'The firing pin was disabled, you know.'

Ray held Brook's gaze. 'You think I didn't try it out first? You don't know me, Damen.' He grinned. 'Shit, *I* don't know me.'

'You fixed it,' said Brook. Ray continued to smile. 'Internet, right? How do I know you'll keep your word, Ray?'

'If I can keep a promise to a dead man, I can keep a promise to a friend in his final moments.'

Brook nodded and moved his hands over the gun. He checked the magazine. It was full. 'A friend – so much more effective than a cyber-bully.'

'Isn't it!' exclaimed Ray. 'Russell made me realise and, well, Deity's results will speak for themselves.' He lifted the camcorder to his eye. The red dot appeared. 'I told you it would be classy, Damen. *The Deer Hunter* directed by Michael Cimino – Oscar winner, no less. De Niro finds Christopher Walken playing Russian Roulette in a bar in Vietnam and tries to save his friend.' Ray sniggered. 'He fails.' He held a hand ready to start the scene. 'Ready for close-up. And – *action*.'

Brook lifted the gun to his temple and took a final look round his sparse kitchen. 'One thing I need to tell you, Ray.' He glued his eyes on to his opponent's. 'I'm not your friend.'

Then Brook pulled the trigger. There was a loud click and Ray burst out laughing. Brook tossed the gun on the table.

'Your face!' Ray giggled and pointed. 'What am I like? I don't know shit about guns, Damen,' he continued, barely able to speak, 'except it didn't work when I fired it either.'

Brook stood and walked to the cupboard. Ray readied a finger over the keyboard. Brook ignored him and took out the leaded tumbler and filled it full of whisky. 'Drink?'

'I'm driving.' Ray motioned Brook back to his chair. Brook glanced up the stairs to his bedroom door then took a sip of whisky before reluctantly returning to his seat.

'Want to know something, Damen? I knew you'd pull the trigger.'

'Want to know something, Ray? I knew the gun wouldn't work.'

'How?'

'Because now I've seen your personality disorder at close quarters, I know a bullet's too quick.'

'What do you mean?'

'I mean that someone as sick as you needs to see the terror in people's eyes as they die. You need to know that last second of life is as precious to them as it is worthless to you. You need the dying to see you watching on, living the life that they cling to. And you need to make that sensation last so you can feed on that energy in an effort to revive your own dead soul, if only for a few minutes.'

Ray stared at Brook, his grin absent. The silence hummed between them like an electricity pylon. 'But Russell was quick.'

'That's when you found out you needed more. That's why Deity is so drawn out. So you can watch the suffering. The parents, the friends, even the policeman trying to catch you.'

Brook's vibrating phone broke the tension. Brook ignored it.

'Go ahead,' said Ray. 'But don't say the wrong thing.'

Brook looked at the display. 'John. She's fine – false alarm,' he said. He listened for a few minutes. 'Understood.' Then rang off.

'Progress?' teased Ray.

'Becky Blake.'

Ray narrowed his eyes. 'What about her?'

'We wondered why she was so upbeat in the last broadcast. Now we know.'

'It's because she's famous now, remember.'

'We spoke to her friend again. Fern. Guess what? Becky told her she was going away but not to tell anyone. She told her she was leaving the country to disappear like the girls in *Picnic at Hanging Rock*. She said it was going to be all over the internet and when it was over, she was going to be famous. Then, a year later, she'd turn up alive and well and ready for a life in the public eye.'

Ray searched, thin-lipped, for an answer. 'No. She couldn't have, she didn't have her phone. I checked all their texts and calls at the party. We'd unsubscribed from Facebook—'

'That's the really odd thing.' Brook smiled. 'They had a conversation face to face. The afternoon of the party, she swore Fern to secrecy, told her to say nothing. That she'd see her soon.'

Ray slammed a fist on the table. 'I told the cunt a million times. It was because of her I took all those precautions. I'm deleting all her scenes just for that.'

'Take it easy,' said Brook, worried that he'd smash his fist on the keyboard in a fit of temper.

Ray took a deep breath and gradually regained his composure. 'Okay, we misled her. I admit it. I told Adele to spin her a yarn.'

'A desert island for a year?' sneered Brook. 'And she believed it?'

'We promised to make her famous. She believed what she wanted to hear and Adele was very convincing. I'd be filming the whole time, enough for a documentary, maybe even a movie . . .'

'And that's why you all had to have passports, even though you had no intention of leaving the country.'

'To convince Becky, yes.' He chuckled. 'Actually I'm glad. I feel better knowing she betrayed me. It makes deceiving her that much sweeter.'

'Deception won't be at the top of the charge-sheet, Ray, I promise you.'

Ray shrugged. 'I had to teach her a lesson, Damen, while there was still time. See her off to her Maker with a little humility in her bones. You should've been there. The others had taken their pill and gone to prepare, but I switched Becky's to Rohypnol – enough to paralyse her but not enough that we couldn't have some fun first.

'You've heard of those tribes who pluck out the beating heart of their enemies then eat it while it's still pumping to assume their power. Well, that's the way we felt – Becky and me. When she opened her eyes and realised what was happening, man, what a rush. Deity? Fucking A – I was God to her, Damen. I put life inside her and then took it away.'

Brook's eyes bored into him.

'Don't look at me like that, she had it coming. She was a nasty, spiteful bitch and I swore that one day I'd look into her eyes as she died and fuck her. And I always keep my promises.' Ray took a deep breath and looked into the distance. 'And boy, was it something – the best I ever had – even better than Yvette, the night after Russell hanged himself. Filmed it too. You want to see it?'

'I'll save it for your trial.'

Ray's eyes widened. 'My trial? That's very tempting – almost worth giving myself up so I can be there to watch it.'

Brook stood, pushing his chair back. 'All this high-minded talk about helping people with their pain and all you are is a tawdry little rapist.'

'Careful, Damen.' Ray held a dramatic finger over the

keyboard. Brook took a step towards him but stopped, darting a glance at Terri on the monitor. 'Sit down,' commanded Ray.

Brook stood, glaring at Ray, aching to put his hands on him. Ray moved his digit closer to the keyboard.

'Did you rape Adele as well?' Brook asked.

Ray's lip curled. 'Why are you so vulgar! Adele was my friend. I gave her dignity.'

Brook looked across at the image of his unconscious daughter, thinking the unthinkable. Then a minor glitch on the picture darkened his features. *All that we see* . . . He reached for the glass of whisky and took another step towards Ray.

'What are you doing?'

'It's brilliant,' said Brook. 'I can't deny it.' He raised the glass. 'To Deity.' Then he flung the contents into Ray's eyes as he leaped for the laptop. Ray gasped as the whisky hit him but he was able to sway back towards the keyboard, crashing his hand on to the Enter button.

Brook grabbed him, his face contorted, fist drawn back to strike. 'Where is she?'

'I didn't want that, Damen,' said Ray, trying to break free. 'You killed her, not me.' He ducked out of the imagined assault but Brook had already thrown him to the floor and was bolting up the stairs.

'Terri!' he shouted. Brook grabbed the handle on his bedroom door. It was locked. He ran to the end of the corridor, catching sight of Ray through an upstairs window, laptop under his arm, jumping into the VW. Without giving it a second thought, Brook turned and hurtled towards the bedroom door, flinging himself against the frame. The door buckled but didn't give, so Brook backed up again and this time literally ran through the door.

*

Moments later, Brook regained consciousness on the floor by his bed, lying amongst shards of lacquered wood. He was aware of blood streaming down his face from several cuts as well as his stitches, which had burst open. He put up a hand to staunch the flow only that he might see better. With a sickening feeling, he saw the bed was empty. He'd been watching a recording of his daughter immobilised in his bedroom and played over and over on a loop. It could've been filmed at any time that day.

Brook scrambled to his feet and careered down the stairs in two strides, falling at the bottom. He jumped up, swept the car keys into his hand and staggered to the car, jerking the BMW's engine into life. He roared to the junction at the bottom of the hill, already debating left or right in his befuddled brain.

At the junction, he turned left and tore through the village at top speed. Within seconds he was out of Hartington and hurtling through dark country lanes. A mile away, on the other side of the valley he saw another car's lights and gave chase. A minute later, cresting the brow of a hill, two minor roads – one left, one right – sheared off into the darkness.

Brook did a quick double-take and, seeing retreating headlights at the bottom of a long dip, hung a left in pursuit. He realised where Ray was headed but it was getting harder and harder to follow because his vision was blurring and he was drifting towards unconsciousness.

He reached the bottom of the long dip and began to climb. A rabbit caught in the headlights was squashed as Brook pushed the accelerator closer to the floor. It was no use. His head began to sag and the fog in his brain closed in around his vision. He almost crashed headlong into a drystone wall but managed to wrest the wheel round in time and screech to a rubber-burning halt.

He came round moments later, woken by a loud explosion, and saw a bright flash of light in the distance. He gripped the steering-wheel harder and flung the gearstick into first, covering the 500 yards to the junction in seconds.

He staggered out of the car. The wall at the junction had been wrecked at high speed, evidenced by the black tyre- and bright green paint-marks on some of the displaced stones. Several layers of limestone had been dislodged but the VW was nowhere to be seen. When Brook clambered on to the remnants of the wall he saw the flames fifty feet below, down a steep shoulder of land that ended in a dry gulley. Sheep and new lambs were scampering for dear life away from the burning debris.

Brook, however, half-ran and half-fell towards the fireball of blackening metal. Once there, he ran to the blazing boot and, covering his hand with no more than a handkerchief, tried to pull it open.

'Terri.' He screamed with pain as his skin sizzled against the metal but still he tugged without success.

Brook removed his hand and felt his skin come with it as he lurched round to the driver's seat to look for a release mechanism. He could see the burning body behind the wheel but couldn't get within ten feet as white-hot flames surged from the car. His lasting memory as he passed out was the crackling and spitting of a human being, the acrid stench of melting rubber and the delicious aroma of roasting meat.

*

'Terri!' screamed Brook.

Noble grabbed him around the shoulders and began to push him down. 'Easy.'

'I've got to find Terri.' Brook struggled but his strength was gone and he was unable to overcome Noble. His eyes stung with smoke and he closed them to ease the fire under his eyelids. When he was able to open them again, Noble's face appeared at the end of a long dark tunnel. 'John.' His voice was muffled by a face mask which was feeding him the sweetest gas, but Brook yanked it off and tried again.

Noble pushed Brook back down on to the stretcher. 'Sir. Take it easy. We've got to get you to hospital.'

'Terri,' pleaded Brook. The sky behind Noble's head turned into the roof of the ambulance and Brook sat up despite the burst of pain behind his eyes. He saw the flashing lights of police vehicles in the blackness and realisation dawned.

'Sir, your hand is seriously—'

'Terri was in the boot of the car.'

'The VW?'

Brook levered himself off the trolley and put his right hand down on it. He felt a sickening pain. He looked down. His hand had been wrapped in a sterile bandage. At the same time he became aware of a tight wrapping around his head.

'You need to rest,' insisted Noble.

'Then the sooner you let me see the car, the sooner I rest.'

Noble turned to the paramedic behind him.

The paramedic shrugged. 'There doesn't appear to be any smoke inhalation but he may have concussion and he needs to be on fluids for those burns.'

Brook cut short the consultation by getting to his feet and hopping unsteadily from the ambulance. He fought off the nausea and stepped gingerly around the loose limestone blocks and over what was left of the wall, then climbed down the slope towards the smouldering car. Noble appeared by his side a moment later and supported him down the slope.

Keith Pullin and his team of emergency workers delicately laid the blistered and charred remains of the body on to a canvas sheet. The knees were pulled up towards the chest and the desiccated hands were held near the face. The mouth was frozen in an oval of agony.

'Male. About five ten, I'd say, though it's difficult to tell height when they get themselves into that position,' said Pullin. 'Do we have a name, Inspector?'

Brook barely shook his head, gazing intently at the yawning boot of the car that Pullin had crowbarred open at Brook's request. It was empty. He began to totter back up the slope, Noble in pursuit.

'Hell of a blaze for a VW,' said Pullin, taking out his cigarettes.

Brook turned. 'What?'

Pullin inhaled a belt of tobacco smoke and turned to Brook. 'Hell of a blaze for a VW. They don't have large tanks.'

Brook's eyes narrowed. *What we see* . . . 'Think there might have been an accelerant?'

'Very possible,' replied Pullin. 'We'll know more in the morning.'

Brook walked back to the body and got down on his haunches to run an eye over the corpse. He stood and looked into the blackened shell of the car. The remains of the laptop Ray had gathered up as he made his escape, sat in the passenger-seat well. Brook turned to climb up the slope again.

*

'. . . be on the lookout for a black Porsche Carrera, number-plate AFR 110, registered to an Adam Rifkind. Approach with caution and detain all occupants.' Noble replaced the handset and looked across at Brook in the passenger seat. 'It's done.'

'And we need to upgrade the alert at ports and airports to be on the lookout for Kyle Kennedy.'

'Care to explain?'

'It was too easy, John. That's not Rusty Thomson or Ray down there. And he's got four passports, remember. I'm guessing he won't try to leave the country as himself or either of the girls.' Brook held his good hand up to his head. His vision was blurring again.

'Sir, you should be in the ambulance. You're suffering.'

'My daughter's missing and it's my fault. Why shouldn't I suffer? Start the car and follow this road,' added Brook, able to nod sufficiently to indicate a direction. Noble eyed him, unmoving. 'Please.'

Noble started the car. 'Where are we going?'

'To find my daughter.'

'I don't understand.'

'Back at the cottage. When I got there, the VW's engine was warm. Ray had been somewhere before I got home. Somewhere close because Terri rang me from home so Ray only had half an hour to move her.'

'I thought she rang you on her mobile.'

'She did but her script for the call was in the kitchen. After she rang me, he took her somewhere then drove back to the cottage.'

'And you think . . .'

'I think it was too easy. He could have got clean away but

he didn't. He came for me, John. He wanted me to know about Deity. And he wanted me to come after him.'

'So he engineered a fake crash?' said Noble doubtfully.

'The fire was too strong. Ray used an accelerant to burn the body beyond recognition. We'd think it was him and stop looking. At least until we identified the real victim.'

'So he buys himself a few days, maybe a week.' Noble nodded slowly.

'Time enough to make a fresh start somewhere else. New face, new identity . . .'

'Okay, it's a bit of a stretch but I'll buy. So how did he get away from the crash?'

'Rusty had a bicycle, remember. I'm betting he stashed it there earlier. He's been a step ahead all the way. Until now.'

'He won't get far on a bike,' said Noble.

'He won't need it for long. He's got other transport nearby.'

'You mean Rifkind's Porsche.'

'Exactly. It was parked outside Rifkind's holiday cottage. Remember – Adele and the others had their own house keys. I'm betting Adele also had a key to Rifkind's cottage so she could let herself in to wait for him.'

'And now Ray's got it and can help himself to the Porsche keys.'

'He took the Porsche keys before, because he gave me Adele's house keys tonight. Insisted on it.' Brook pulled out the keys given to him by Ray. 'I'm guessing one of these gets us in.'

'But why give you the keys?'

Brook looked across at Noble in the dark. 'It's a reward. For playing a good game.'

'And the reward is Terri.' Noble found it hard to get his

bearings in the dark country lanes but he tried to speed up where he could. 'Okay, so who was that in the car?'

'Ray's cleaning house, John. He gave us Yvette but I think he still has a protective instinct towards her. Wilson wanted to bed her – he's dead. Len slept with her and he's missing . . .'

'The body was too tall for Len,' said Noble.

'Exactly. That leaves one other person.'

At that moment, the road sign for Alstonefield leaped out of the dark at them.

'Rifkind.' Noble nodded.

Noble shone a torch over Adam Rifkind's sturdy front door. The house was in darkness, the Porsche Carrera gone. Noble found the right key on the bunch and unlocked the door. He pushed through before Brook and shone his torch into the compact cottage. The small sparsely furnished front room was empty. Brook padded through to the tiny kitchen, also empty.

He pointed a finger to the upper storey and the two detectives noiselessly made for the stairs. Before they could set foot on the first step, however, Brook heard a muffled noise at his feet.

'Can you hear that?'

The noise seemed to vibrate through the floorboards so Noble shone the torch on the rug at their feet then fell to his knees and pulled it aside. He groped at a shiny brass handle recessed into the wood and yanked open the trapdoor. The stench of sewers hit their noses and Terri's tear-streaked face peered up from the shadows.

Noble jumped down to help her up the steps. She mumbled something through the gag in her mouth and Brook watched helplessly as Noble untied the gag and then the rope tying her wrists behind her back. Eventually she was able to fling her arms around Brook's neck, squeezing him so violently, he yelped in pain.

'Dad, thank God.'

'Are you all right?'

'I will be when I get into the fresh air. It stinks to high heaven down there.' She looked aghast at his roughly bandaged hand and head. 'What happened to you?'

Brook hugged her again. 'Forget about me. Ray didn't hurt you, did he?'

'No, Dad. Please, I need some fresh air.' They were both shaky on their feet and supported each other out into the cloudless night. Noble's phone began to croak and he moved away to answer it.

Brook walked Terri to the road and she sat on the drystone wall. 'I'm sorry,' he said.

Terri looked into his face. 'For what?'

'Everything,' said Brook, after a pause.

She opened her mouth and was about to speak when Noble hurried back to them.

'Gadd's found the ambulance.'

Twenty-Eight

Monday, 30 May

BROOK STOOD IN THE DOORWAY. His head and hand throbbed with pain and he felt as if he needed to sleep for a week. He closed his eyes for a second and stepped towards the sarcophagus. When he lifted his eyes he saw Adele Watson. Young. Beautiful. Immortal. She seemed at peace. Her face was calm, and her long slender hands were crossed beneath her smooth throat.

'Don't touch anything in the coffin,' said a white-suited SOCO.

Brook picked up her cold hand and caressed it with the thumb of his good hand.

'Didn't you hear me?' said the SOCO. 'We've not done the coffin.'

Brook turned blankly to the officer. 'Get out.'

'Pardon?' said the officer.

'Get. Out.'

Noble appeared at the doorway. 'Graham,' he called to the officer. 'Got a minute?' Reluctantly Graham hauled himself into the corridor, preparing to berate Noble in Brook's place.

Noble waited for him to pass then glanced up at Brook but he'd already turned back to Adele.

Brook picked up her hand again. 'Forgive me, Adele. I let you down.' He placed her waxy hand back down on to her chest and carefully opened the handwritten volume resting on her stomach.

The missing book. She'd left her diary behind. She'd left her rough notes behind. But when sudden fame engulfed her, she had her collection, her anthology of doom, ready for the world. Be damned and publish. Brook flicked through it with some difficulty. Every page was full of poetry. She had a lot to say.

He placed the book back on her bandaged abdomen.

Brook and Noble walked slowly through the derelict building, following in Gadd's footsteps as she explained what little she knew. The two Detective Sergeants covered their noses against the sickly-sweet smell of old blood mingling with the caustic chemical odour of embalming. But Brook was oblivious to all sensory input. Noble monitored his empty expression. He'd seen him this way before. He was back on the tightrope.

'The hospital closed in 2004,' explained Gadd. 'Smethwick used to volunteer here but we're still looking for documentary proof of that. My guess is when it closed he had the run of the place and decided it would be a perfect base of operations.'

'How come it's not as wrecked as the rest of the site?' asked Noble.

'It's the furthest building, for one thing. And I'm guessing he made a big effort to secure it from intruders. He was an engineer, remember. He boarded and barred all the windows and barricaded all the doors from the inside – except the way he came in. He seems to have rigged something up that only he can access. It took us ages to break in.'

Gadd looked sympathetically across at Brook but he was completely blank. 'We found Phil Ward and Jock – they were embalmed and partially mummified. Jock's insides are on the floor. It looks like Poole knocked over his canopic jar. From the look of his tracksuit, he must've spent some time sitting in the remains . . .' She shuddered.

Noble's phone began to croak. He listened for a few moments then rang off with a puzzled expression. 'That was Cooper. Traffic found Rifkind's Porsche. It was in the centre of Derby, just pulling into Westfield car park.'

Brook cocked his head. 'Derby?'

Noble was glad to see Brook back with them. 'That's not the weird bit,' he said. 'Rifkind and his wife were in it. They were going shopping.'

'But the cottage . . .' began Brook.

'Rifkind says he wasn't living there; he was working on his novel at home. He told his wife to lie to anyone who called.'

'But I saw the car at his cottage,' said Brook.

'Rifkind said you told him to keep it out of sight because of Adele's father, so he left it at the cottage. He fetched it yesterday.'

Brook's smile was thin. 'So Rusty escaped on a bicycle.'

'Bicycle?' said Gadd. 'We found one in the same bay as we found the ambulance. It looks like the one Rusty was riding towards Borrowash.'

Noble smiled over at Brook. 'No bicycle. No Porsche. Face it, Rusty didn't get away. He's impersonating a slice of toast at the mortuary. You got him.'

*

The mid-morning sun shone weakly through high skylights in the domed roof. On a large wooden table lay a bizarrely dressed figure wearing tight white binding around his legs and dark green face paint which matched his dark green knitted mittens. A white conical headdress with feathers was on the floor nearby.

'Lee Smethwick aka Ozzy Reece aka Osiris,' said Gadd.

'He's not been embalmed,' said Noble.

'No,' replied Gadd. 'Should he be?'

'That was why they took Len,' murmured Brook.

'Ex-pathologist,' explained Noble. 'He had the skills to embalm Smethwick's body so he could live forever in the Afterlife.'

'Well, obviously Poole didn't play ball,' said Gadd.

'Len must've realised what lay in store if he got out,' said Brook softly.

'Good riddance, I say,' snarled Noble.

A voice boomed from the shadows. *'Len. It's Rusty.'* Noble and Gadd looked at each other then ran back to the corridor which led to the rooms where Adele and the other three bodies had been discovered. The voice emanated from there.

'Sorry I can't speak to you live but I have to be somewhere. I have a confession, Len. I lied – there is no way out. You'll have to twiddle your thumbs until the police arrive unless you burn the place down. The good news? They'll be there very soon.'

DC Cooper walked out of the gloom and beckoned them to follow. He led them past the four rooms. Adele's body was in the first, Kyle's the second and Becky's the third. As they passed the fourth room, a SOCO taking photographs illuminated Poole's limp body dangling from the end of the rope.

'They're very keen to speak to you. They know about Russell and they've arrested Yvette. She told them everything. Never mind. You've plenty of work there to take your mind off things.'

They arrived at the end of the corridor. Rusty appeared on the monitor of a small laptop. He was sitting in Brook's kitchen, baseball cap on his head. Brook could see the night sky through the window.

'Sorry to be the bearer of bad tidings, Len.' He laughed. *'But look on the bright side. Treat your incarceration as good practice for prison.'*

Rusty grinned now. *'Inspector Brook. If you're hearing this you must have found the hospital. Quite a place, isn't it? And you must admit Lee did a great job on Adele and the others. Wait until those pictures hit the internet. Everyone's going to know her and her work.'*

He waved a hand behind him. *'As you can see, I'm talking to you from your kitchen, waiting for you to get home, so I can unveil myself. That's right, we haven't played out the final scene yet but I'm trying to talk to you as though we have. I know – the timeline's weird. Have you seen* Back to the Future *? It hasn't aged well.*

'Let me give you some good news if you haven't already worked it out. Terri's safe and well and under the floorboards at Rifkind's cottage. I left her there about ten minutes ago. No need to thank me. She's a great girl and I wouldn't want to deprive her of the chance to mourn you when you finally decide you've had enough.

'I've been staying at the cottage on and off. Adele had a key and I thought what better finale than to deal with Rifkind and drive into the sunset in his Porsche. Unfortunately the bastard was never there when I was around, although his car was. No keys either. Can't figure that one out but I'm going to have to settle for the VW. Well, if it was good enough for Hitler . . .

'Goodbye, Inspector. Don't forget our little talk that we haven't

had yet. I know you won't let me down. A legion of confused and unhappy people are counting on you for a lead. Know what? When you go I might pop back and do a stint in the Constabulary – all those vulnerable souls. Must be great. Ah, I think I hear you driving up. Sorry about having to drug you but you know how it is. Actually you don't because I haven't done it yet. Confusing, isn't it?' He grinned. *'Time to fly.'*

He reached for the screen and the message ended but began again at the start almost at once. Cooper silenced it with an emphatic digit.

Brook turned to walk back to his car, his face like granite. He ignored everything and everyone on his journey back to the light – the officers cutting down Len Poole's body, the remains of the three teenagers he'd hunted for so long, the bizarrely dressed chef beginning to turn green under the make-up, even the rats scuttling around in the blood-soaked room near the entrance.

When he reached the sunlight he turned like a robot and stumbled through the weeds towards his car. Charlton approached from the other direction and slowed when he neared Brook.

'Not good news, I hear, Inspector. At least the perpetrator didn't—'

Brook walked past the spluttering Charlton without a word or even a glance of acknowledgement and continued on his way like an automaton, unblinking and ignorant of the increasing urgency and volume of the Chief Superintendent's demands.

Brook got in his car and drove to the recently created gap in the perimeter fence, where a Constable on crowd control was exchanging banter with a couple of young kids. Brook wound down the window.

'Constable. Have you got a cigarette?'

'Don't smoke, sir.'

One of the kids, a gap-toothed fourteen year old, chirped, 'I've got fags. I'll sell you one.'

'How much?' asked Brook.

'A tenner,' he answered, trying not to laugh. His friend cackled and held out a fist to tap.

Brook rummaged in his pockets and produced a twenty-pound note. 'I'll take two.'

Warily the boy approached the note. After checking its authenticity he took out two cigarettes and held them out to Brook, not letting go until he had a hand on the note.

Brook put the first cigarette in his mouth and pushed in his lighter while the boy showed the note to his amazed friend. He lit up with a sigh.

'Those things'll kill you, Inspector,' said the Constable.

Brook looked at him as he pulled away. 'That's the plan.'

Twenty-Nine

Wednesday, 8 June

BROOK FINISHED POLISHING HIS SHOES and man-oeuvred them on to his feet with some difficulty. The skin on his burned hand still felt tight, but an hour after taking the painkillers he was able to tie a vague knot in his shoelaces. He stood and flexed his feet inside them. The shoes felt harsh and uncomfortable, as did every other garment on his body. His white shirt was tight and his black suit and tie were shiny with wear. He hated funerals.

It was a beautiful sunny day as he set off to drive towards Derby. In the week he'd spent recuperating from his wounds, Brook had managed to spend quality time with his daughter until her departure for Manchester earlier that morning in her hire car. Terri was none the worse for her ordeal, having been unconscious for most of it after Ray/Rusty had knocked on Brook's door. Her sunny disposition contrasted sharply with Brook's as he continued to brood over the case. At least he'd found time to organise some basic creature comforts so that fridges were filled, grazing cats were fed and large quantities of cigarettes purchased.

Brook pulled into a lay-by and cracked open a new carton

from those on his passenger seat. He lit up with something approaching pleasure. The pain would arrive soon enough.

Half an hour later, Brook reached the end of the A52 and turned off towards Markeaton Crematorium on the northern edge of the city.

After struggling to park, Brook located Noble and Gadd standing together in the crowd. The small chapel was overflowing with mourners, well-wishers and vast numbers of media, filming and recording the service. Noble and Gadd were both dressed in expensive black suits, though only Noble wore a tie. Despite his shabby attire, Brook manoeuvred his way to stand beside the two Detective Sergeants.

'How are you, sir?' asked Gadd.

'Better.'

'Hand okay?'

'Better.' Brook took out three packets of cigarettes, handed two to Noble, who pocketed them with a grin. He offered the other open packet around before lighting up himself. 'Smoking too much though.'

'Please don't give up again. I can't afford it.' Noble exhaled smoke through his grin and Brook looked sideways at him.

'Becky Blake . . .' began Brook after a suitable pause.

Noble rolled his eyes to the heavens. 'Not this again. Why can't you accept—?'

'Because it was too easy, John. The accelerant, for one thing.'

'So there were six bottles of embalming fluid in the car. We know Rusty or Ray or whatever you want to call him, was mixed up with Lee Smethwick. Maybe it was for him.'

'But why put the bottles in Terri's car? Why bring them to Hartington?'

'Who knows? Maybe he was storing them at Rifkind's cottage.'

'John . . .'

Noble shook his head. 'Sir, it's a decent result. There's nothing we could've done. The kids were dead before they'd even been reported missing, and you hunted down the person responsible. The DNA from the body in the car is a match to the semen inside Becky Blake. It also matches the tissue on the plaster found at Alice Kennedy's house and the toothbrush recovered from Yvette Thomson's bedroom. What more do you want? Even the Chief Super's happy we got a closure.'

'But remember what Habib said about Becky when we told him she'd been raped.'

Gadd leaned over to pick up the reins. 'But she'd been given Rohypnol, sir. It's a relaxant. That's why there was no sign of forced intercourse.'

'But Habib was surprised she'd had intercourse at all.'

'He didn't say it was impossible,' replied Gadd. 'There were traces of condom lubricant in her vagina as well as semen.'

'That's another thing. Why use a condom at all if he's then going to spray his semen all over her?' said Brook, making an effort to keep his voice down. 'It doesn't make sense.'

'Maybe he had an accident when he took it off,' rejoined Noble. 'Who knows?'

Brook shook his head and continued the conversation with himself. 'It's out of character. Sexual domination isn't his thing. But he wanted me to know. He flagged up to me that he had raped her – and that gave us his semen. Why?'

'Because he was a criminal,' said Noble indulgently. 'And criminals make mistakes.'

'Then there's the transport issue,' continued Brook.

'Transport?'

'How did Rusty get to my cottage? His bicycle was at the hospital.'

'What did Terri say?'

'That when he arrived he was sweaty.'

'There you are,' said Noble. 'He walked from Rifkind's cottage. It can't be more than an hour. And he'd have the VW at his disposal after he got to your place.'

'But how did he get from Derby to Rifkind's cottage? Not on a bike, it's a forty-minute drive.'

'There must be a bus service,' reasoned Noble.

'Or maybe Rusty had a car that we don't know about. Maybe he walked to my cottage from the intended crash site after leaving that car nearby.'

'A car nobody saw,' said Noble.

'With a body hidden in the boot which matched his DNA?' added Gadd with a doubting eyebrow. 'That doesn't sound very likely, sir.'

'And don't forget they found the incinerated laptop and camcorder . . .'

'Props,' said Brook. 'Like the laptop he left in his bedroom.'

At that moment the hearse pulled into the large crescent-shaped driveway followed by relatives' vehicles. Press cameras began to whirr.

Roz Watson stepped from the first vehicle in a black trouser suit. She was tiny and Brook almost didn't recognise her without her grey dressing-gown. Her husband's coffin was in the hearse and the pall-bearers gathered at the doors to carry it into the chapel.

James Henry Watson had watched the final Deity broadcast in horror, while staying at the house of his brother and his wife. His mood had worsened during the day, according to all witnesses, and later that evening after receiving a text purporting to be from his daughter, he had snuck into his brother's garage and hanged himself with an extension cord.

Roz Watson kept her eyes lowered from the flash of the cameras, but when she saw Brook, she stopped and marched defiantly over to him. 'Bastards,' she screamed as though the dialogue during the search of her house had never ended. 'This is your doing.'

The cameras flashed even more urgently at the scent of conflict, but the three detectives maintained expressions of stone in the face of such an absurd accusation. Taking their silence as admission, the shrivelled woman raised a hand towards Brook but thought better of it, instead snarling, 'When can I have my Adele back?'

Brook lowered his head. 'Her death is still the subject . . .' He choked on the official language and took a breath before looking directly into the wizened face of the grieving wife and mother. 'As soon as possible,' he mumbled.

She stared for a moment longer then went away to follow her husband to his final resting-place. Brook caught sight of Charlton in full uniform. They exchanged a nod of acknowledgement before Charlton ran a surreptitious eye over Brook's suit.

Brook arrived home late that evening, finally able to park outside his cottage. After the Watson ceremony he'd attended a simple service for Phil Ward that Brook had arranged and paid for himself. He was the sole mourner. A few hours on the phone had turned up an elderly mother in Harrogate but she had been too infirm to travel and, not having 'clapped eyes on him for thirty year', she couldn't be persuaded to accept Brook's offer of a taxi-ride down the M1.

Back at his cottage as night fell, Brook sat on the garden bench in shorts and T-shirt, a jar of whisky and a cigarette in one hand. He spent a couple of hours mulling over the Deity case, trying to form the qualms he'd expressed to Noble into a credible theory. Defeated, he trotted up to his doorless bedroom and went straight to sleep, dreaming about walking up a strange rock formation in Australia and meeting Rusty at the top.

What we see and what we seem is but a dream.

Brook woke in the night and sat bolt upright in bed.

'Sir, it's three o'clock in the morning.'

'It's Philippe, John.'

'Sir?'

'The body in the car.'

'But the DNA—'

'. . . is all his. Philippe, the exchange student from Paris. He was supposed to return to France, so who's going to miss him if someone abducts him.'

'Abduct him? Who would do that?'

'Rusty. He abducted him, drugged him but kept him alive until he needed him.'

'Why?'

'Because he's perfect. Remember Yvette said she was drawn to him because he was an orphan like her. Who better? Who's going to miss him? And if he slept with Yvette, and Rusty found out about it then . . .'

'*. . . he put himself in danger like Wilson, Len and Rifkind.*'

'Exactly.'

'*Okay, I get that – but how do you explain the DNA match?*'

'That's the best part, John. After Len attacked Rusty and cut him, Rusty does the same to Philippe, and when he goes to the party he leaves the plaster with Philippe's blood and tissue in the bin. If it's not Becky's, Kyle's or Adele's, we're bound to think it's Rusty's.'

'*But the semen?*'

'Philippe and Yvette must have had sex using a condom. Rusty waits for his chance, hoping it doesn't get flushed. They throw it in the rubbish and he recovers it, probably stores it in a freezer so it doesn't degrade, and when Becky's dying he smears it in and around the vagina. That's why Habib was surprised when we told him she'd had intercourse. She hadn't.'

'*And the toothbrush?*'

'Simple. Once Rusty had Philippe and his belongings, he switched them. Remember Yvette was confused when we showed it to her.'

'*I left to pick up Len, remember.*'

'Then check the film. She was confused because she knew it wasn't Rusty's and she didn't know why. Maybe she even knew it was Philippe's, I don't know, but right now Rusty is passing himself off as Philippe. He has his passport and papers and he's probably made himself over to look like him.'

'*But where did he keep him? The hospital?*'

'At first, maybe, but it's too far away, John. Remember the stench in Rifkind's cellar? I'm guessing Rusty drugged him and kept him there until he needed him. That's why it stank like a sewer. When he took Terri to the cellar, he switched her with Philippe.'

'Great theory – pity it's all circumstantial. How do you prove it?'

'The car. Philippe must have had a car here. Either he drove it over from France or hired one. If Rusty dumped it, we're in business. That's how he got to Rifkind's cottage. That's how he got away from the crash site.'

'And if Rusty didn't dump it but returned it to the hire company or drove it back to France as Philippe?'

Brook sighed. 'That just makes it a bit harder. If we can find out which company Len paid to test Rusty's DNA against Yvette's, we get the real thing. And Rusty's DNA will be different from the samples he left us.'

'Without Len that could take forever and even then we may not get access. What about Philippe? If he was in the cellar we could get his DNA there.'

'No good. If he didn't clean up, Rusty's DNA could be there as well and we'd have no way to tell them apart.'

'There is another possibility, sir. Maybe Rusty died in that burn-out. He lost control of the car, hit the wall and burned to death. Case closed. Are you sure you want to prove to the world that we got our butts whipped?'

'Are you American, John?'

'I mean it.'

'First thing tomorrow, get Philippe's details from the college and find that car.'

Thirty

Y VETTE THOMSON ARRIVED WITH THE female warder looking, if anything, even prettier in her washed-out grey uniform. The bright smile for her warder dimmed only briefly when she saw that Brook and Noble were her visitors.

The warder smiled back at her and gestured her towards the chair. 'I'll be right outside, Eve.'

'Still working your magic, Yvette,' said Brook, after the warder had left.

Yvette sat at the table and gazed blankly at the two detectives but declined to speak.

'You look well.' A quizzical glance from her was Brook's only answer. He pushed the evidence bag towards her. 'The last time we spoke, you identified this toothbrush as belonging to the man you knew as Rusty Thomson. Will you take another look, please?'

'You've got a nerve coming here. Unless it's to apologise.'

'Take another look, please.'

Yvette looked at him then slowly pulled the bag towards her. 'That's Rusty's toothbrush.'

'I don't think it is. I think you were shocked when you first saw it – until you recognised it. It belonged to Philippe, didn't it?'

'You killed my Rusty.'

'Impossible,' Brook told her. 'Because he's not dead. The man who died in that car was Philippe. Rusty did a switch, just like he did with the toothbrush.'

'Why?'

'So he could disappear. So he could start afresh.'

Yvette emitted a one-note laugh. 'They said you were mental.'

'Whose toothbrush is this?'

'My Rusty's.'

'You know it isn't.' Brook took a breath and tried again. 'It wasn't the only switch. After you slept with Philippe . . .'

'Who says I did?' snarled Yvette.

'After you slept with Philippe, Rusty abducted him.'

'Phil went back to Paris last month . . .'

'Rusty was probably watching your house – filming too, knowing him. He saw everything. Then he found the condom you used with Philippe and took it. He kept it . . .'

'That's disgusting.'

'. . . and when Philippe had packed his bags and was preparing to leave, Rusty was waiting. He drugged him and kept him in a safe place. Then he went to your house and made the final switch, swapping his toothbrush for Philippe's.'

'What are you talking about?'

'DNA, Yvette. Rusty wanted Philippe's DNA to pass off as his own. When we sampled the DNA from the body in the car, he knew we'd get a match against all the other samples he left us, including the toothbrush. Rusty knew we'd assume Philippe was him.'

'I told you, Phil's in Paris.'

'Shall I tell you where Philippe really was, Yvette? In a derelict hospital full of rats. After that, he was locked in a dark and cold cellar. He was pumped full of drugs and left to rot.'

'You're sick, you are,' sneered Yvette.

'Want to know what's sick?' asked Brook. 'While Philippe was still alive, Rusty took a heavy object and smashed all his teeth so we wouldn't be able to trace the dentalwork. His ordeal only ended when Rusty put him in the boot of my daughter's car and, when he was ready, stuck him behind the wheel and drove it down a hillside in flames. We'd think he'd smashed his teeth on the steering-wheel.'

'What kind of mind dreams up a fantasy like that?' said Yvette. 'I pity you.'

'Philippe Deschamps,' began Noble. 'Twenty-one years of age, drove to Dover and took the ferry to Calais *five* days ago. We have his car on film boarding the ferry.'

Yvette shrugged. 'So he did a little sightseeing before going home.'

'Deschamps has yet to appear back at his apartment in the Rue Garibaldi in Paris or attend any of his scheduled classes at the Sorbonne,' continued Noble. 'However, somebody arrived in Paris because Philippe's bank account was emptied and his credit cards were maxed out, withdrawing cash.'

'So Phil is in Paris then.'

'Since when, he's dropped off the radar,' Noble finished.

'I've got to hand it to Rusty,' said Brook. 'He doesn't do things by halves. He's got a new identity, a new passport and a new nationality. And over thirteen thousand pounds to spend, to add to the money he doubtless took from you.'

Yvette's blank expression turned sour. 'He never took a penny from me and you killed him. And now I've lost both my lovely boys.'

'Rusty destroyed your son and you let it happen, but if you help me stop him, I'll do whatever I can to help you.'

To Brook's surprise she smiled at him. 'You've already helped me more than I dared hope.'

'What do you mean?'

She twinkled at him. 'You don't know?'

'Know what?'

'I'll be out of here tomorrow – day after at the latest, thanks to you.'

Brook shook his head. 'Yvette, even with the most sympathetic judge, the best you can hope for is three years.'

Now she started laughing. 'You really haven't seen yesterday's *Telegraph*, have you?'

Brook looked at Noble. 'John?'

'Something about the Deity case,' said Noble. 'So what?'

'Didn't your daughter tell you?' smirked Yvette. 'They carried a picture of her. *DEITY DETECTIVE'S DAUGHTER SURVIVES ORDEAL*. Very moving.'

Brook's heart turned to ice and he fished out his mobile. He had seven new messages. All from Terri. He closed his eyes in realisation.

'What's the problem?' Noble shrugged. 'I know it's an invasion of privacy but I still don't see what—'

'Let me enlighten you, Sergeant. You see, DI Brook's daughter posed as a police officer to gain entry to my home and search my Rusty's bedroom.'

Noble's face fell and he stared at Brook. 'Is this true?'

'It's true all right,' answered Yvette for Brook, who remained silent.

'Did you know about this?'

Again Brook was unable to answer.

'Of course DI Brook knew about it.' Yvette chuckled. 'He was with her.' She pushed back her chair and banged on the door. 'No court in the world would prosecute me after that deception.'

Brook found his voice. 'Yvette – that changes nothing. If you don't help me, Rusty is going to kill others.'

Noble stood, ashen-faced. 'Let's go.'

'He enjoys it too much.'

'Inspector Brook,' said Noble sharply, grabbing his arm. 'We've got nothing.'

Brook glanced up at him, a look of shock and confusion on his face.

'Sir, it's over. Let's go.'

Brook left the path that skirted the banks of the River Dove and marched the last mile into Hartington across verdant, manure-rich pastures. The golden orb of the sun was dipping below the horizon but Brook could still feel the glow it had left on his tanned face.

He reached the public toilets on the edge of the village and swung his rucksack from his back. He downed the last of his water, sitting on a nearby bench, watching birds feeding on flying insects. He hadn't felt this good in years. A month after his suspension had kicked in, Brook was fit, brown and relaxed. He was eating properly and had put on a stone in weight, much of it muscle on his legs after four weeks spent walking a minimum of fifteen miles a day. Better yet, he hadn't had a cigarette in three weeks and, more importantly, hadn't wanted one.

Two days earlier, for the first time in years, Brook had started to entertain the idea of leaving the Force. He had plenty of money, even without his pension, and his lifestyle was not exactly lavish. The day after, he'd drafted his resignation letter which sat in his printer waiting for a signature and an envelope. He wouldn't hand it to Charlton yet, not without speaking to Noble first – he owed him that much.

Brook continued his hike through the village and up the steep incline to his cottage.

He saw the postcard as soon as he opened the door. He bent to pick it up, but before it was in his hand he recognised the Eiffel Tower. When he turned it over, it was blank apart from Brook's address. It had been posted in Paris four days earlier. He plucked his mobile from his shorts and thumbed at Noble's number. A second later he rang off and turned the phone off.

He opened a cupboard and reached past the wine glasses for a jam jar. He poured a generous measure of whisky into it and topped it up with water before taking a large gulp. Then he rummaged for his lighter in the drawer, managing to ignore the pack of cigarettes he'd opened three weeks earlier.

Brook spent an hour staring at the postcard and sipping at his jar on the garden bench. Finally he finished his drink and held the lighter to the edge of the postcard to ignite it. A second later he stopped and extinguished the small flame catching at one corner.

He returned to the kitchen and stuck the postcard under his sole fridge magnet, gathered up a pack of cigarettes and, after a quick detour into his tiny office, returned to his bench to light up. The smoke from his first cigarette for three weeks was harsh on his lungs.

Instead of extinguishing the lighter, Brook held his resignation letter over the flame until it caught fire then dropped the fireball and watched it burn at his feet.

The Levels

Sean Cregan

It is Newport City's dirty secret – a failed housing development left to ruin for decades. Overrun by the homeless and controlled by the untouchable Sorrow, it's the last place on the US East coast you would choose to go.

For three people though, the decision has been made.

Ghost – one of Sorrow's teenage assassins, the Furies. She has finally escaped Sorrow but can she escape the Levels itself?

Nathan Turner – ex-CIA operative. Everyone thinks he's been murdered but he's headed for the Levels in search of answers.

Kate Friedman – a suspended cop with only days to live. Infected by a serial killer, the Beast, Kate must track him down before it's too late.

Now, as their lives collide in this feral, lawless place, it's anyone's guess if they'll find what they're looking for. Or if they'll make it out alive . . .

978 0 7553 7114 3

headline

88 Killer

Oliver Stark

THREE UNCONNECTED CRIMES
The abduction of a teenage girl.
A woman, shot point-blank during a brutal robbery.
A young man tortured, his body found wrapped
in barbed wire.

ARE ABOUT TO BE LINKED
With nothing to indicate that the three crimes are connected, NYPD detective Tom Harper and psychologist
Denise Levene must look beyond the surface to find a
killer's true motivation. And they believe that they
have found a murderer conditioned to hate and
willing to go to any lengths to make his victims suffer.

IN THE MOST CHILLING WAY IMAGINABLE
The killer has nothing to lose.
Harper and Levene have one chance to catch him.
Sometimes hate is just the beginning . . .

Praise for Oliver Stark and *American Devil*:

'An exceptional new talent' *Daily Mail*

'If this is the future of crime, then bring it on' *Tangled Web*

'This is a stunning first novel' *Crimesquad*

978 0 7553 7014 6

headline